D1622893

TARA DUNCAN

AND THE SPELLBINDERS

TARA DUNCAN
AND THE SPELLBINDERS

HRH Princess Sophie Audouin-Mamikonian

TRANSLATION BY **William Rodarmor**

Sky Pony Press
New York

Sky Pony Press books may be purchased in bulk at special discounts for sales promotion, corporate gifts, fund-raising, or educational purposes. Special editions can also be created to specifications. For details, contact the Special Sales Department, Sky Pony Press, 307 West 36th Street, 11th Floor, New York, NY 10018 or info@skyhorsepublishing.com.

Sky Pony® is a registered trademark of Skyhorse Publishing, Inc.°, a Delaware corporation.

Visit our website at www.skyponypress.com.

10 9 8 7 6 5 4 3 2 1

Library of Congress Cataloging-in-Publication Data is available on file.
ISBN: 978-1-61608-733-3

Printed in the United States of America

CONTENTS

CHAPTER 1

POWERS AND LIES

She was in her nightgown, floating half a mile above the ground. It wasn't exactly what you would call a normal situation.

Tara swallowed and moved her feet a little. To her great relief, she didn't fall out of the sky.

That was something, anyway.

The dream she was having was bizarre, to say the least. She was flying above a highway. With a stab of fear, she abruptly descended and flew above a powerful black limousine, effortlessly matching the car's speed. It was night, and the peaceful sleeping towns and villages of the southwest were bathed in moonlight. Inside the car, four dark figures sat quietly, cautiously respecting the silence of the fifth, who startled them when he suddenly burst out laughing.

"At long last!" he said jubilantly. "What an honor and a pleasure to be the one to destroy the powerful Isabella Duncan! We'll reach Tagon in a couple of hours, and we attack tomorrow night. Be ready!"

Tara was shocked. Her grandmother, Isabella Duncan? She struggled to wake up, vaguely sensing the terrible danger emanating from the black car, but the dream was already fading, bearing the sleeping girl toward other shores.

As Tara stirred in her bed, the big limousine was eating up the miles, getting closer to the village of Tagon with every spin of its wheels. And the hiss of tires on the asphalt whispered *soon . . . soon . . . soon . . .*

The magpie was late. Its golden, red-rimmed eyes glinting evilly, the bird chattered in frustration. Tara had once again escaped its surveillance. The bird anxiously scrutinized the village of Tagon as it passed beneath its black-and-white wings. If it didn't find the girl soon, it risked winding up roasted on a spit, something it really preferred to avoid.

The magpie suddenly dove. Whew—saved! It had just spotted Tara's slim figure sprinting across the fields. The girl yanked a barn door open and slipped inside. The magpie cursed. Rats! What could it do now? It circled the old barn twice before catching sight of Tara's pursuer. He went into the barn too, and the bird flew in right behind him. It perched on the barn's ridge beam, where it could watch the action. Folding its wings, the magpie settled itself comfortably.

Hiding behind a big bale of hay, Tara held her breath. Her pursuer could arrive at any moment.

A creaking in the barn alerted her that he was there. He had followed her in. Tara pushed a little deeper into the hay, desperately struggling with an urge to sneeze.

A sudden deep chuckle made her jump.

"I know you're in here, Tara," said a sinister voice. "I *feel* you're in here. And I'm finally going to get you!"

High above the scene, the magpie repressed a sarcastic cackle. It had a front-row seat for the final act—great!

The person who'd spoken had yet to spot the girl, whose light-colored clothes matched the hay enough to help her pass unnoticed.

Tara was watching as he turned on his heel, about to give up, when a field mouse clambered onto her left shoe. When it realized that the mountain it was climbing was alive, the mouse gave a discreet little "Eeek!" But Tara let out an "Aaaaaaahhh!" that rang through the whole barn. She shot out of the hay like a rocket, right into the arms of the person hunting her.

Realizing she was caught, Tara's reaction was completely instinctive and sent her attacker ten feet straight into the air. There he hung upside down, arms and legs flailing.

"Tara!" he yelled in protest. "You promised!"

"It was your fault," claimed Tara disingenuously. "You scared me!"

"Well, that was sort of the idea," a voice behind her murmured, making her jump.

"Betty!" exclaimed Tara in surprise. "Are you crazy, sneaking up on me like that? I almost had a heart attack."

The chubby brunette smiled. Given her weight, Betty was amazingly light on her feet, and she moved like a cat.

"Tara!" yelled Fabrice, who was still hanging in midair. "Get me down!"

The girl snagged the strange white strand that stood out in her shock of golden hair and started furiously chewing it.

"Ummm, the problem is that I don't know how."

"What do you mean, you don't know how?" cried Fabrice in a panic. "I wanna get down! Do something!"

Tara concentrated with all her might, waved her hands, frowned fiercely, held her breath, and squinted her dark blue eyes. Nothing happened.

Stifling an imminent attack of the giggles, Betty tried to think of possible solutions.

In a complete panic, Tara turned to her.

"What are we gonna do? I can't even move him!"

Above them, the magpie was in no mood to laugh. Its eyes had practically bugged out of its head when it saw Tara levitate her opponent. By Demiderus, *the kid had the gift!* Wow, wow, wow. Things were about to get complicated. And the other two kids seemed to know all about it!

Fabrice quit struggling and let himself hover, glowering at Tara with dark eyes whose unusually long lashes drove the girls in Tagon half wild.

"Tara, try to remember," said Betty calmly. "What were you feeling when you pushed him away?"

The girl thought carefully.

"Fear, anger . . . and some irritation at the mouse who mistook me for a hay bale."

"All right," exclaimed Fabrice. "What if I said you better get me down real fast because otherwise everybody's gonna learn about your gift and you'll wind up being dissected like a frog in some laboratory? What would you say then?"

"I'd say I still don't have the slightest idea how to do it," she answered, her jaw tight.

Betty shook her brown curls and pointed to a neatly coiled rope hanging from a nail.

"What if we use that rope? We could pull Fabrice over to the hayloft. It isn't very far."

In fact, he was floating just a few inches from the loft where his father's tenant farmers stored sacks of grain.

"You're right," said Tara. "Let's try it."

They took the rope and after several attempts managed to toss it to Fabrice, who tied it around his waist. Then they very carefully towed him over to the hayloft. He had barely touched the planking when all his weight suddenly returned. Caught unprepared, he almost fell. Then he raced down the ladder and planted himself in front of an embarrassed Tara, who was energetically chewing on her white forelock.

"All right, let's take it from the beginning," he growled. "What did we agree on at the start of the game?"

"No levitation, no telekinesis, nothing," she obediently recited.

"So please clear something up for me. When I was floating ten feet off the ground, what was that?"

"Levitation, no doubt about it," said Betty with a chuckle.

"Listen, Tara," Fabrice said, trying to keep his tone reasonable. "When you discovered you were some sort of mutant and told us about it, we all swore to keep it secret. But every time you use your gift, we've had problems. Like that time you wrecked the other barn and screwed up the tractor."

"That wasn't my fault," she grumbled. "Besides, you were the one driving the tractor."

"Yeah, and I was the one who got punished. I'm happy to do experiments to try to understand what's going on with you, but not when we're just having fun."

Practically in tears, Tara slumped to the floor.

"I don't know what to do anymore!" she moaned. "I don't want to be different! I don't want this stupid gift! And I especially don't want to send people flying whenever I get scared."

Fabrice calmed her down.

"Come on now, this gift of yours is terrific. True, it's a little out of control right now, but that'll change, I'm sure of it. Listen, here's what I suggest: we'll have practice sessions every day. Vacation ends in two weeks, right? If between now and then we can't figure out what to do, we'll go see your grandmother and tell her everything."

"Never!" snapped Tara savagely. "She's the very last person I'd want to talk about it with."

"Why?" asked Fabrice, baffled by her anger.

"You know 'Brutus,' don't you?"

"Pascal Gentard, the big bully? Of course. He tried to push me around, but since I'm as big as him, he wound up leaving me alone. Why?"

"In elementary school, he got his kicks cutting off girls' hair. So you can imagine, with that braid of mine, he couldn't resist."

"So what happened?" asked Fabrice, intrigued.

"Well, as soon as I felt him grabbing my hair, I turned around and pushed him."

"You didn't! You mean like with me just now?"

"Not quite. I was only nine, and my gift wasn't that strong. But he still wound up on his butt a couple of yards away."

"Oooh, now I understand!" said Fabrice with a grin. "That's why he always looks at you as if you're going to turn into a slavering monster and eat him alive!"

"Yeah. Problem was, I got punished for 'inappropriate roughness with a classmate.'"

"Ouch," he said sympathetically. "So?"

"I went to see Grandma to have her sign my punishment slip and to explain what had happened to me."

"And of course she didn't listen," Betty broke in, who knew the whole story.

"She punished me for fighting," continued Tara sadly, "and she didn't listen to my explanation. Ever since, I've sworn she would be the last person to know about my gift."

"Then let's go see my dad," said Fabrice. "He'll know what to do. If we aren't able to help you before then, that is. Meanwhile let's go back to the castle. I don't want one of your panic attacks to wreck this barn too. If we keep demolishing his buildings, my dad's eventually going to get suspicious."

The magpie preened its feathers, thinking hard. So Tara had known about her gift since she was nine years old. *The little sneak!* Young as she was, she'd hidden her power remarkably well. All right, it was time for the bird to make its report, and it knew someone who wouldn't be too happy to get it. Chuckling at the surprise it had in store, it took off and flew unnoticed out of the barn.

Tara and Betty had a lavish afternoon snack at the castle of Fabrice's father, the Count of Besois-Giron, then slowly headed for the pink stone manor house that Tara and her grandmother Isabella had moved into after the death of Tara's parents.

"How are things with your grandmother?" asked Betty.

"Same as usual," said Tara with a sigh. "All she cares about are my grades. If they're good, she doesn't say anything; if they're bad, she complains. That's the only communication we have."

"That sucks," she said, frowning. "Have you been able to get her to talk about your parents?"

"No way!" answered Tara bitterly. "Every time I try, she clams up. 'They're dead,' she always answers. 'They caught a virus when they were doing archaeological research in the Amazon jungle, and it killed them.' That's all I can get out of her. And when I told her I wanted to become a biologist so I could track and destroy viruses, you know what she said?"

"No, what?"

"She just said I'd have to work harder in math if I wanted a career in science."

There was nothing Betty could say to that. Feeling sad for her friend, she left Tara at the gate to the manor grounds.

Surprisingly, the talk actually did Tara good. In a more hopeful mood, she decided to have another conversation with her implacable grandmother, and headed for her private part of the house.

Behind her, the magpie flew to an open window, banked neatly, and slipped inside. It made its way to a workout room where a young woman was practice-sparring with a mannequin, her bare hands a blur of movement. She raised her hazel eyes to the magpie, which started gesturing and waving its wings, as if it were explaining something. What the young woman heard must have startled her, because she put her hand to her mouth to stifle a gasp of surprise just as Tara raced past the gym. The running girl slipped on the black-and-white marble in the hallway, recovered her balance in the little yellow parlor, and burst into her grandmother's big study.

As it happened, Isabella Duncan was alone in the wood-paneled room, which was normally crowded with visitors from the four corners of the world.

When Tara burst into her sanctuary, Isabella was consulting a book. She snapped it shut, but the girl had time to see the title before her grandmother put it away: *Pandemonium Demonicus*. A tall woman with gleaming silver hair, Isabella had green cat's eyes on a face that was hardly wrinkled, in spite of her age.

"Well!" she exclaimed. "What manners, Tara'tylanhnem! I've already asked you not to run in the manor!"

Tara made a face. She hated it when her grandmother used that weird first name of hers, which she carefully kept from her friends.

"Sorry, Grandma. Can I talk to you? It's about my friend Fabrice."

"I don't have much time, child, but I'm listening. What happened? Did you have an argument?"

"No, no, I wouldn't bother you for that. Actually, we were talking about our parents. You know his mother is dead and he lives at the castle with his father, right?"

"Yes, I know that."

"Well, his dad tells him about his mom all the time, but you never talk about my parents. It hurts me not to know. I feel you're *hiding* something from me."

Her grandmother seemed to catch her breath. Tara then realized that Isabella was gripping the edge of the table so tightly her knuckles were white.

Yet her grandmother's voice was completely calm when she coldly answered, "I have nothing to hide, Tara'tylanhnem."

"So why won't you talk about it? Every time I raise the subject, you send me to my room or you find something else to distract me. It pis— . . . It's a real drag! I'm not four years old anymore!"

Isabella made an almost painful effort to let go of the table. She flexed her fingers and was thoughtfully drumming them on the beautifully inlaid tabletop. Tara noticed with surprise what looked almost like burn marks on the wood. But within seconds, they disappeared.

She turned her attention back to her grandmother.

"You're only twelve, Tara'tylanhnem," Isabella continued, "and I'm not about to discuss what I should and should not tell you."

But Tara had inherited from her grandmother a stubbornness at least as strong as hers.

"Why not? She was your daughter, but she was my mom. All I have are a few photos and no memories. Why won't you share yours with me?"

Isabella took a deep breath, the old sorrow overwhelming her. Tara'tylanhnem looked so much like her beloved daughter, Isabella thought. She had the same willful chin, the same straight nose and intelligent forehead. From her father she'd inherited the mass of golden hair marked with that characteristic white forelock, and those unusual, deep blue eyes. Isabella couldn't help herself. Each time she saw the girl she suffered, and that suffering drove away the tenderness she felt for her granddaughter, leaving only duty, responsibilities, and the pain of exile.

"I don't have to give you any explanations," she said coldly. "Go to your room."

Tara felt completely frustrated. She had so many questions on the tip of her tongue. Why did she and her grandmother have the same last name, since her parents had been married? Why didn't Isabella ever want to talk? Why didn't her parents have a tombstone? And what was the mysterious work her grandmother did?

Tara had glimpsed the briefcases full of dollars and euros. From the library window she had seen not only the local farmers and businesspeople but also big limousines and watchful bodyguards with the ill-disguised bumps of their revolvers. And her grandmother was often away, traveling to unknown places.

Two village girls came every day to do the housekeeping, and three other people lived in the manor besides Tara and her grandmother: Deria, Tachil, and Mangus. Deria was a young brunette who never let Tara out of her sight and gave the odd impression that she was there to protect her. A beautiful woman with a curious aura of wildness, Deria was like a cat, always on the alert. It was impossible to catch her unawares (and not for want of trying!) or get her off balance. Tara had watched as Deria trained, easily lifting weights that Tachil would have struggled with. Tachil was tall and skinny, and the woodcarvings he was always making threatened to take over the big house. He was in charge of the garden, which he tended with maniacal care. Mangus, the cook, was short, fat, and balding. He enjoyed life, was always laughing, and produced some amazing dishes. Betty and Fabrice thought it odd that the gardener and the cook lived at the manor house, but Tara was so used to it, that she would miss them terribly if they ever left.

She heard a rustling behind her. Pet magpie on her shoulder, Deria strode into the study to announce Isabella's next visitor. Tara was annoyed to sense that her grandmother was relieved to end their discussion.

"I'm terribly sorry, Tara'tylanhnem, I must meet with this gentleman. Go on child, I'll see you later."

There was no point in insisting, Tara knew. She shrugged and left, dragging her feet. She went up to her room and jumped onto her bed.

Tara lived in a spacious, comfortable manor house that had been restored in the nineteenth century. She was especially fond of two places in it. One was her room, in the left-hand tower. It was big and very sunny, and had a view of the lawn that sloped gently down to the nearby forest. At dawn and twilight, Tara could see deer, stags, and even wild boars roaming at the edge of the woods. The other place was the library. She had loved reading ever since she was little, especially mysteries and adventure stories.

Tara was about to get up when the ringing phone startled her. Deria had put the call through.

"Tara?" came a whisper on the phone.

"Fabrice?" Tara answered, instinctively whispering as well. "What's up?"

"You'll never believe it! You've infected me!"

"What?"

"Your gift, that thing of yours. I did it too!"

"Listen, Fabrice, if this is a joke—"

"It's no joke," he said, his voice shaking with excitement. "There was an accident. I went to the north tower to see the renovation that the workers had just finished. They hadn't bolted the scaffold properly and it came crashing down just as I was walking underneath."

"Really? Are you okay? Are you hurt?"

"That's what I'm trying to tell you. You must be contagious, because when I saw the scaffold falling on me, I did like you do: I held out my hands and sort of pushed. And it worked! The whole thing flew up. But I've got a heck of a headache now."

Tara sat up in bed, thunderstruck.

"And you think it's really me who—"

"I don't know. I don't know any more than you do. Listen, we've got to get together. Because my father saw it all."

Tara groaned. "What did he say?"

"That's where things really got weird. He took me in his arms and started to cry. Then he said this was the best day of his life and the biggest gift I could ever have given him."

Tara was speechless.

"Are you still there? What should I do? Should I tell him about you too?"

"No!" said Tara instinctively. "I'd prefer if we talk about it tomorrow. Meet me in front of my place at nine o'clock. And until then, not a word, okay?"

"Okay."

Fabrice sounded disappointed, but he didn't argue.

As soon as she hung up, Tara grabbed her forelock and started chewing on it. What if Fabrice was right and she really was contagious? Tara ruminated on this for ten full minutes, then sighed. There was no point in worrying; she would see tomorrow. There was also no point staying locked in her room. She may as well go down to the library and see if she could find something distracting to read.

Moving like a shadow, Tara made her way to the big library with its thousands of books. Opening the door, she gave a sigh of pleasure. Tara had access to almost all the works, although one section of the library had some that were under lock and key. That always tickled her. Was her grandmother afraid that the books would run away, or what?

She was glancing at the familiar titles in silence when a murmur made her stop her search. She could hear something.

To her surprise, she realized that the sound was coming from a point high above the fireplace.

The voice was her grandmother's. She was on the phone, and sounded so angry, she could probably be heard at the other end of the village. Tara couldn't quite make out what she was saying, however. She had to get closer to the source of the sound, but it was ten feet off the ground!

She quickly climbed the rolling wooden ladder used to reach the highest books. Stretching as far as she could, she leaned toward the upper part of the mantelpiece and cautiously stepped onto it. She was crouched pretty precariously, but could now hear the conversation.

"You're the guardian of the Transfer Portal, Besois-Giron!" her grandmother yelled. "You were forbidden to tell your son the truth. That's unacceptable!"

Yikes! The count was getting a royal chewing out. He must've answered something, because Isabella's voice dropped to the point where Tara had to strain to hear.

"What do you mean, he is *like us*?" hissed Isabella. "You must be joking!"

"..."

"He did *what*? He *pushed* the falling scaffold back? Emanations? What emanations?"

"..."

Her grandmother's voice became dangerously threatening.

"Let me see if I understand this, Guardian! You're telling me that you, a descendent of a long and faithful line of totally *nonspell* guardians, have produced a spellbinder, your son Fabrice, because the emanations of the Portal somehow affected your wife? That hasn't happened in nine hundred years, so why should it happen now?"

Tara caught her breath. A *what*?

Still furious, her grandmother continued: "I didn't tell Tara anything because I have to protect her! If nobody knows Tara might be a spellbinder, she'll be safe. Anyway, she hasn't shown the least sign of magic up to now."

"..."

"That's out of the question! Telling her the truth and presenting her to the High Council is completely off the table. Before her father died I swore to him that she would stay out of all that. And I'll keep my word even if I don't agree. In the meantime I want no further contact between the two children, understand? Fabrice must go to OtherWorld. Oh, and one more thing, Guardian. This is not a suggestion; it's an *order*."

Isabella slammed the phone down, ending the conversation. Tara clung to the slippery marble, her ears ringing with what she had just overheard.

Her grandmother *knew.* She was a . . . *spellbinder*! But what did that mean, being a spellbinder? And Fabrice was one too, apparently. Except that in his case it wasn't usual. The count was the guardian of a portal that gave off some sort of emanations. But a portal to where? And what was this mysterious High Council?

Her head buzzing with questions, Tara didn't know what to do. And she suddenly felt that her grandmother was a stranger to her.

Then she stood bolt upright on her perch: Betty! Her best and most faithful friend, who had never breathed a word about anything Tara ever told her. She would talk to Betty. Tara wasn't a mutant after all; she was a spellbinder. And she did magic, not telekinesis.

Tara leaned toward the ladder, very cautiously stretched her leg out, and began to shift her weight from the mantelpiece to the ladder.

But she had forgotten one small detail.

The ladder was as close as possible to her, but was free to roll the whole length of the library in the other direction. And that's exactly what happened.

With a gulp of surprise, Tara felt her support slipping away. She jerked her leg back but instinctively hung onto the ladder. So she wound up with her tiptoes on the mantelpiece and her hands desperately clutching the ladder, with her body bridging the empty space in between.

She stayed suspended like that for a couple of tense moments, unable to make a move.

The problem was that the bookcase hadn't been designed to take the weight of a girl twisting every which way in an attempt to regain her balance. A sharp, snapping sound froze Tara's blood. She looked at the top of the bookcase and turned pale. With a dull creak, the metal fasteners that held the bookcase against the wall were popping out one after another.

Tara could feel sweat running down her back. She absolutely had to climb back onto the mantelpiece before a total catastrophe happened. Eyes wide, she watched as the last fasteners gave way. With an apocalyptic rumble, the bookcase slowly began to topple. Tara was yanked off the chimney, the books tumbled out, and all was lost.

Strangely, her fall was both fast and slow. The air seemed to thicken, as if to bear her up. She could feel her white forelock crackling like electricity was running through it. Amazingly, she landed on her feet, but was horrified to see half a ton of books falling toward her.

Terrified, Tara stretched her arms out to protect herself. Books now blanketed the entire room but miraculously stopped a few inches from Tara's feet, forming a perfect circle around her.

Speechless, the only thing she could say was, "Oops!"

Then she took a deep breath and added, "I may as well go pack my bags. Grandma's gonna kill me!"

A cough near the door caught Tara's attention, and she turned around, her heart pounding. Attracted by the noise, Mangus was standing there, gaping at the catastrophe.

Tara gave him a hesitant smile.

"I'm . . . I'm terribly sorry, Mangus. I climbed the ladder but I slipped and everything fell down."

"I see," answered Mangus calmly, who could hardly ignore the disastrous spectacle of books covering the floor. "And did the young lady find what she was looking for?"

Normally, Mangus's archaic phrasing amused her, but the fat, balding young man now seemed more threatening than amusing.

"Yes, Mangus. I even found more than I expected. Listen, I have to go see Betty. I forgot I have to tell her something. And I'll come back to straighten everything up. I promise."

Mangus squinted at the mantelpiece, where the mark of Tara's sneakers could be seen clearly, at the book carnage, and finally at Tara, standing unhurt in the center of a perfect circle.

"I'm sorry to have to do this, young lady."

Waving a chubby hand upward, he said: "By Pocus you're paralyzed on the spot. You might want to move, but I'd rather you not."

Tara was immediately immobilized, as if frozen stiff. She could move her head and speak, but the rest of her body no longer obeyed her. She could breathe but not control her breathing. She was standing upright but couldn't move her legs.

"What have you done to me?" she yelped. "Help, Grandma! Help!"

Isabella, who'd thought an elephant was skipping rope overhead when the books and the bookcase crashed down, was already on her way upstairs. Within seconds she burst into the room, eyes blazing and her outstretched hands giving off a curious blue glow, ready to pulverize anyone threatening her granddaughter. When she saw Mangus, Tara, and the thousands of books on the floor, she stopped dead in astonishment, and the glow on her hands faded.

"She climbed onto the mantelpiece and overheard your conversation, my lady," Mangus calmly explained. "She was going to tell her friend Betty about it. That did not seem appropriate to me. Moreover, I think that she has unconsciously used her power, as she remains unhurt despite falling."

"Praise Demiderus!" Isabella exclaimed. "You did well. Did you cast a paralyzing Pocus?"

"That is correct, my lady. I was afraid she would escape, as she is very quick."

During this time, Tara was struggling to regain control of her body. Panicked by the realization that she couldn't, she turned on her grandmother.

"You lied to me! You've been lying ever since I was little. But I have too! I didn't use my power unconsciously. I've been using it for a long time, and I know what we are. We aren't like other people. We're different, we're—"

"Spellbinders."

Her grandmother may have been surprised to learn that her granddaughter was aware of her gifts, but Isabella's confirmation left Tara just as astonished.

Score: 0–0.

Tara swallowed hard.

"We're *spellers*?" she stammered.

"No, we're *spellbinders*. In the old language, people who can bind spells. Non-spellbinders, or *nonspells*, as we call them, must've heard about people who cast spells and called them sorcerers or wizards, instead of using the right terminology. In short . . . will you promise not to run away if I free you from the Pocus?"

"I won't run away if you swear to tell me the whole truth," answered Tara, determined to learn as much as she could.

Her grandmother stiffened.

"I can't tell you the whole truth, so I refuse to swear. But I can reveal some details that concern you. Take it or leave it. That's nonnegotiable."

Tara understood that her stiff-necked grandmother was in no mood to argue. So she wisely decided to be satisfied with what she had to tell her—at least for the time being.

"I won't run away. Please free me from this Pocus thing."

Mangus was about to obey when Isabella stopped him.

"Wait!"

The cook stopped and watched her carefully.

To her granddaughter, Isabella said: "Tara'tylanhnem, let's see what you can do. Close your eyes and visualize a net with a turquoise mesh around you."

Tara obeyed. She closed her eyes and was startled. In her mind she could see herself wrapped in a blue net that kept her from moving. She opened her eyes and was surprised when it disappeared. She closed them, and it reappeared. But suddenly she knew exactly what she had to do, as if a voice had whispered it in her ear.

She took a deep breath and imagined the net disappearing, but this time for real.

A loud *snap!* startled her, and she was once again free to move.

When Tara opened her eyes again, she noticed that Mangus was staring at her in amazement, and at her grandmother with satisfaction.

"You didn't even need to recite the spell! Your gift is extremely powerful for your age. What a waste! But a promise is a promise, and I can't break this one, even if I'm dying to."

"That's one of my questions, Grandma. We're these spellbinder things, but why and how? We have gifts, and you spoke about a portal, guardians, emanations, Fabrice and the count, and a council. And what's this promise about?"

"Oh my," said Isabella with a groan. "I didn't realize you'd heard so much! I would have to explain thousands of years of history to you, and you're only twelve. There are lots of things that you wouldn't be able to understand. Not because you aren't intelligent," she added when Tara was about to protest, "but because you're still too young. I'm very sorry. And what I'm about to do now is for your own good."

Before Tara could react, Isabella waved her hand as if she were wiping a blackboard, and said: "By Mintus your memories I now erase, and leave pleasant music in their place."

The amnesia spell hit the girl and she tottered, about to fall. Mangus caught her just in time.

Isabella leaned back against the sofa, suddenly looking very weary. Then she straightened and said, "Mangus, ask Deria to put her to bed. The amnesia spell should keep her from remembering what happened. I will straighten up the library."

"Lady, you are exhausted. You work too hard. This child is very intelligent. If you allowed her to follow her path, it would be easier both for you and for her."

Isabella gave a small, sad smile.

"I don't have any choice, Mangus. I promised her father that Tara would lead as quiet and human a life as possible. By protecting her as I do, I'm sheltering her."

"But you will not be able to hide her for very long, my lady. Her gift is extremely powerful. I know very few spellbinders who are able to free themselves that quickly from one of my Pocuses. Especially without any training. Her gift seems instinctive."

"Yes, I know. That's what I wanted to test, and I was as surprised as you were. Don't worry, everything will be fine. Give her to Deria. When she wakes up tomorrow morning, her life will go on as usual."

Isabella waved, and the bookcase fastened itself to the wall. She waved again, and the books docilely headed for their respective sections.

"No, not there!" she exclaimed irritably. "The books on botany go under B and the cookbooks under C, please. Come on, hurry!"

Seized by panic, the B and C sections collided, and a few books lost pages in the accident. Then each row returned to its proper place while the orphan pages flew around the room like white birds as each tried to find its book. A few tried to enter the locked section, but after being practically devoured by an especially aggressive encyclopedia, they realized they'd better not hang around, and they flew toward the B and C sections.

Isabella rolled her eyes, and groused: "By Demiderus! You would think these books would have at least *some* intelligence!"

Finally, every book was back in place, leaving no sign of the catastrophe.

"Go on now," she said to Mangus.

"Very well, my lady."

Mangus felt Isabella was being quite optimistic, but he chose not to argue. The cook saw how Tara had freed herself, and it was obvious that she had instinctively used her power to protect herself as she was falling. It wouldn't be possible to control her much longer.

CHAPTER 2

A MIDSUMMER NIGHT'S SCREAM

Snug and warm in her bed, Tara was asleep. Her stuffed toys stood guard near the window. A hi-fi glowed softly in the darkness. Because it was still vacation time, the desk was clear of school books and folders.

Suddenly a powerful gust shook the curtains and slammed the French doors open, and a ghostly white shape floated into the room. Very gradually, as if painfully, the apparition took on human form: a beautiful young woman with long, wavy, brown hair, looking terribly sad. The pale ghost approached the bed and leaned over Tara, seized by a powerful wave of love for the girl.

"Tara . . . Tara, darling, listen to me, hear my voice!"

The girl smiled in her sleep.

"Mom . . . Mommy? Is that you?"

"Yes, love, it's me. I've finally succeeded in sending my spirit to Earth. Listen carefully, because I don't have much time. You and your grandmother are in terrible danger!"

Her eyes still closed, Tara frowned.

"Mom? You aren't dead?"

"No, darling. I was kidnapped by Magister, the terrible master of the Bloodgraves. He made everybody think I was dead, but I'm alive and being held prisoner in the Gray Fortress on OtherWorld."

"We have to . . . we have to warn Grandma, and free you."

"No, anything but that!" the woman cried with alarm. "Magister put a deadly spell on me. You mustn't try to find me, darling. You just need to take care of yourself. Listen, when I'm gone, I want you to wake up and go see your grandmother. Tell her that you had a strange vision, that a man with a shiny mask was attacking the manor house. I doubt Magister will come himself. He'll probably send his right-hand man, Treankus. Your grandmother will know what to do to protect against him. But don't tell her about me, Tara. I forbid it, do you understand?"

Before Tara could protest, the apparition touched the girl's forehead to implant her command, but jerked her hand back.

"By my ancestors, an amnesia spell! Your grandmother put a Mintus on your mind! So you've already come into your powers! Now I understand why Magister wasn't interested in you before now. He was waiting for you to become a spellbinder. My god, Tara, the Mintus will erase what I just told you! You're going to forget it all!"

The phantom desperately tried to break the Mintus, but she was too weak and the spell too powerful. It was already erasing her presence and her words from Tara's mind. With a painful moan she quit struggling and disappeared after a final warning: "Remember! I'm begging you, daughter. *Remember!*"

But Tara remained sunk in a deep sleep induced by the Mintus, and the hours passed, heavy and cold, without her stirring.

Suddenly a scream rang out through the open window. Tara opened her eyes and sat up. She had no idea how she'd wound up in her bed, but one thing was sure: she had heard a strange noise.

Another scream rang out. Heart pounding, she jumped out of bed and ran to the window, where she witnessed a nightmarish scene. By the light of the waning moon, four dark figures were fighting with Tachil and Mangus, who were struggling desperately not to be overwhelmed.

Tara gave a frightened shriek and raced from her room. Her grandmother was already running down the stairs, and she followed her. When they emerged in front of the manor, Tachil and Mangus were lying on the ground. The four dark shapes bending over them straightened up menacingly. Tara turned pale. These things weren't human! Short fur covered bulging muscles, and their paws sported fearsome steel-colored claws. The lumpy, awkward bodies didn't look too steady on their stubby legs, but they rushed toward Tara and Isabella at incredible speed.

The old woman didn't flinch. She raised her hands high, which were glowing with blue fire, and cast a spell: "By Retrodus, I banish you to the depths of hell, to languish in anguish until your death knell."

A bluish ray leaped from her hands and hit the four monsters, who swelled and writhed, screaming in pain. Despite their efforts to get to Isabella, the spell took effect just as their claws brushed the hem of her long, white nightgown, and they vanished.

But a fifth shape was stealthily moving closer.

Isabella couldn't see the figure behind her back. He was dressed in dark gray, his face hidden behind a mirror mask. He yelled: "By Rigidifus hold the spellbinder fast, then Carbonus fire its deadly blast."

Tara screamed when the ray hit her grandmother. Unable to defend herself, Isabella crumpled as the ray changed color, turning blood red. But the shock shattered Tara's amnesia spell, and she suddenly remembered everything! She acted in a flash. In a desperate attempt to divert the red fire, she grabbed the ray and bent it back toward the attacker, hitting him full in the face.

Screaming with rage and pain, the man staggered backward, then blindly retreated to the waiting limousine. The long black car spun around in a screech of tires and roared off.

Tara rushed to her grandmother, but she felt as cold and hard as stone. It was like touching a statue. Tara moaned, not knowing what to do. Just then Deria came running, alerted by the cries.

Keeping her cool, the young woman rushed over to Isabella and carefully palpated her body, then did the same to the two servants. Looking Tara right in the eye, she said, "Tara! Stop crying and listen to me. I'm going to need your help."

"Deria, what happened? What in the world happened?"

Tara had no idea what to do, but she remembered it all: the conversation, the Pocus, her grandmother's betrayal, the amnesia spell—and the fact that her mother was alive.

"I'm such a fool," Deria answered bitterly. "I was tired and I fell asleep. I failed as a protector. I came running when I heard the screams, but was too late. You'll have to tell me what happened."

"A protector?"

"Yes, I'm a kind of bodyguard. Your grandmother had me look after you. And I've been very efficient, as you see. I've done a wonderful job protecting you from bees, mosquitoes, and snakes, but apparently that's all I'm able to do."

Deria's remorse seemed so profound that Tara affectionately patted her on the shoulder.

"That's okay," she said. "You can't be on guard 24/7. These humpy things with claws attacked Tachil and Mangus, and then Grandma came out and she zapped the monsters, but a man in gray with his face hidden, he hit her with this ray, so I grabbed it and turned it, and it hit him right in the face. And he screamed and ran away."

Deria was breathing noisily.

"You grabbed the ray and turned it on him? Good heavens, I've never heard of such a thing!"

"But what did they do to Grandma? What turned her into a statue? And what about Tachil and Mangus? Are they—?"

"Dead? No, just unconscious. Monsters usually like their prey to be alive when they . . . well, let's say that without you they would've been in for a very rough time. You saved them. The attacker didn't want to use his powers against two ordinary spellbinders. He was saving that for your grandmother. Hmm . . . let me think . . . he must've used wizard fire. Did you see what color it was? I know it's hard for an inexperienced spellbinder to tell, but it's important that you try to remember."

"White first and then red," Tara answered promptly. "The ray was red."

Deria gave her a sharp look.

"Red, eh? All right. It would be a new kind of petrifying carbonizer, of course. Makes sense. When you bent his ray aside, it had time to petrify your grandmother, which prevented her from casting a counter-spell. He would have carbonized and killed her then, but you redirected the ray back into his face. You'll have no trouble recognizing him from now on. It's a wound that never fully heals. His face will burn until the end of his days, unless you cancel the spell, or you die."

Tara said nothing, but she felt a kind of savage satisfaction.

"All right," said Deria. "Listen to me. Your grandmother isn't dead, but her condition is serious. We can't leave her here. I have to go get help. I'm going to use a levitation spell to transport the bodies. I want you to watch me very carefully, because you're going to have to do exactly the same thing."

Tara was startled.

"A spell?"

"A levitation spell, yes. It lets me lift the bodies without touching them. I'll show you on Tachil and Mangus, and you can try with your grandmother."

Tara was too shaken up to think, so she didn't argue.

Deria explained: "You make a gesture of lifting and you say, 'By Levitus, I raise you in the air. You obey and float midair.'"

Under the girl's astonished eyes, Tachil and Mangus's rigid bodies rose smoothly off the ground. Deria began to push them toward the manor, and Tara turned to her grandmother.

This whole business was completely nuts, Tara thought. She knew from experience how hard controlling her gift was, so it was without much conviction that she gestured the stiff body upward while imagining that it would obey her and begin to float. She was so skeptical that she even forgot to recite the spell.

Suddenly her grandmother took off, and not just by a couple of feet—much, much higher! Before a baffled Tara had time to stop her, she had already soared above the treetops and was rising in the sky toward the moon.

"Come down, Grandma!" yelled the panic-stricken girl. "Come down!"

For one terrifying moment, she felt that her grandmother wouldn't obey her. But then the body obediently began its descent, gracefully coming to float in front of her. Struggling to calm her pounding heart, Tara swallowed painfully, then very gingerly pushed her grandmother toward the house. The body moved effortlessly. All she had to do was to give it a push, and it moved in the desired direction. She had a little trouble turning into the main door, and going up the stairs had its anxious moments.

"Bring the lady to her bedroom, Tara!" shouted Deria. "I'll set Tachil and Mangus on their beds and come over."

"All right," answered Tara, who was concentrating on keeping her grandmother from drifting away over the railing.

When she finally got Isabella nicely floating above the embroidered quilt on her bed, Tara heaved a sigh of relief. True, Isabella's feet were at the pillow end and her head at the bottom, but she didn't want to move her any more. On entering the bedroom, she'd miscalculated her grandmother's momentum and almost sent her shooting out the open window.

Before long, Deria arrived. Despite the seriousness of the situation, she smiled when she saw that Tara had positioned her grandmother backward and was clearly reluctant to touch her for fear of doing something wrong.

The big room was cluttered with books, papers, musical instruments, stuffed animals hanging from the ceiling, crystals, vases, and piles of stuff on the sofa, both tables, and three armchairs. And that wasn't even counting Isabella's black Labrador, Manitou, who lay snoring in his basket, indifferent to all the commotion. He was the only dog Tara knew who could spend twenty-four hours asleep without so much as twitching an ear.

"Wait, I'll help you!" exclaimed Deria, startling Tara, who hadn't heard her come in.

Together, they turned Isabella's body around. Then Deria told Tara what she had to do next.

"We don't have the power to undo the spell she's under. We'll have to get Chemnashaovirodaintrachivu. I'm sure he'll be able to un-petrify your grandmother."

"Chem-who?" asked Tara.

"Chemnashaovirodaintrachivu. He's one of the wizards of the High Council. High wizards are the most powerful spellbinders. The problem is that I have to go through the Transfer Portal to contact him, and I don't dare leave you here all alone."

"But Grandma can't stay here like this! And you said that the person who attacked her was burned, so he isn't going to come back right away. If you hurry, you can call your High Wizard Chem-thingamabob and get back in a few minutes. Is the Portal in the Besois-Giron castle?"

Deria shot her a piercing glance.

"You're a very smart girl, you know that? Yes, you're right, that's where the Portal is located. You sure this is what you want to do?"

Tara took a deep breath.

"Listen, I don't understand half of what's going on. How can you expect me to make good decisions? I don't have any choice. Grandma *has* to wake up! Please go, Deria, and fast. I'm not afraid."

"Okay darling, I obey," said Deria with a bow. "It will take me five minutes to get to the castle, and about ten to go through the Portal, call Chemnashaovirodaintrachivu, and bring him back. Come downstairs with me. We're going to close all the manor's windows and shutters. I'll leave instructions for Tachil and Mangus. As soon as they wake up, they'll go to the front room and keep any visitors from getting into the house."

"How are they?" asked Tara, a little ashamed that she had forgotten the two faithful servants.

"They'll wake up with splitting headaches," said Deria, smiling, "and they won't be able to cast any spells for a few hours. Aside from that, they'll be fine."

Tara would've preferred Tachil and Mangus to be in better shape, but she couldn't do anything about that.

"All right, let's go."

Tara obediently followed Deria downstairs. The young woman went to stand in front of the front door and said: "By Lockus doors and windows close, and keep them barred against all foes."

With a dull rumble, the manor's windows and doors slammed shut and the shutters came rattling down.

"The house is secure now," said Deria, "except for the front door, which you will lock behind me. The spell will activate as soon as the bolt slides home, and nobody will be able to come in without your permission. Don't worry, I'll be quick."

Tara nodded bravely. She turned the key the moment Deria went out, then went upstairs and did the same thing in the bedroom.

Now she was alone in the big manor house—or at least the only person who was conscious—and she felt completely abandoned. She'd been showing off when she told Deria she wasn't afraid. Actually, she was scared to death.

And at night, everything seemed so . . . different. Outside, the moon cast a harsh, silvery light, illuminating the dark forest whose trees stood like silent skeletons. Tara shivered, feeling like the star of a low-budget horror movie.

Suddenly she froze, gripped by the terrifying sensation of a presence just behind her left shoulder. She felt—no, she *knew*—that something was creeping toward her. Her heart started pounding faster. She was so scared it felt like her heart might burst out of her chest. Holding her breath, Tara very, very slowly turned around. Suddenly, a black shape jumped on her, and she screamed with terror. She leaped onto the bed to get away, roughly sending her grandmother crashing onto the dresser. For a second she couldn't identify her attacker, but then she yelled: "Manitou! You stupid dog! You mangy moron! You can't go jumping on people like that! You almost gave me a heart attack! I mean, how dumb can you be? You idiot!"

Awakened by Tara's conversation with Deria, the dog barked joyfully, happy to be playing a new game. Then he went to a corner of the room and put his paw on the blue-green carpet. To Tara's great surprise, a big hole opened up in the carpet. Before she could stop him, Manitou jumped down it. The carpet closed up again, leaving no trace of the secret passage.

Tara turned to her peacefully floating grandmother and said, "Hey, Grandma, you and I are going to have to have a serious talk."

With great care, she repositioned the rigid body above the bed, and continued: "I'm getting sick and tired of all these secrets and lying. First of all, lies should be forbidden. You tell me all the time that I shouldn't lie, that I should tell the truth, yadda-yadda-yadda. So what do you do? You hide the fact that you're a spellbinder. That Deria, Tachil, and Mangus are spellbinders too. Why not Manitou, while you're at it?"

Then she caught herself.

"No—not Manitou. That dog is too dumb to be a spellbinder. In other words, you've been constantly hiding lots of things from me. And that's really lousy. There are secret passageways in your room and probably in the count's castle too. And I don't know anything about anything, as usual! But that's all over. You can try and cast some sort of forgetting spell on me, but it won't work because I'm powerful. That's right, I am! Well, I will be once I understand what's going on. And I know something that you don't know, and I'm not going to tell you, either. Mom is alive. And I'm going to find her!"

Tara, who had been very angry, now felt a lot better. And her heart sang at the memory of her mother's tenderness when she leaned over her. She remembered the conversation between the count and her grandmother, who'd been furious that he had revealed the spellbinder secret to his son. Tara also remembered that her mother had told her not to tell anyone about her "resurrection."

She continued shouting at the motionless body, delighted to be able to give her grandmother a piece of her mind without fear of retribution.

Suddenly she heard something outside. The sound of a car.

In a bound, Tara was at the window.

The shutters were closed, but by squeezing her face against the windowpane she could see through the bottom cross bars. What she saw froze her blood: a black limousine and a large man getting out of it.

There was no way to see his face because it was hidden behind a kind of shiny mask, like the first attacker. But he was much taller, and his body was wrapped in a handsome gray cape—it was so dark that it looked black in the moonlight—with a large red circle on the chest.

The man stood at the front door of the manor. In a voice like liquid velvet, softly sarcastic, he called: "I want to see the little Duncan girl. Tara! You don't need to hide. I know you're in there. If you come out, I'll give you a nice reward. Want some candy? I have lots."

Tara wrinkled her face in disdain. This guy must think she's a doofus. Candy? Not even a four-year-old would fall for that one!

She nervously grabbed her strand of white hair and started chewing on it. What was she going to do? Mangus and Tachil were out of action, and so was her grandmother. And Deria was taking much longer than the fifteen minutes she had promised.

A movement off to the side caught her eye. The carpet had started to boil. The hole reappeared and Manitou popped up into the room. Delighted to see Tara crouching by the window, he padded over and joyfully stuck his cold muzzle in her neck. Tara caught the dog and hugged him tight.

"By Trebidus, as Grandma would say, we're in a real pickle. If Deria doesn't come back very soon with her high wizard, we're in big trouble!"

She pressed her face against the window again and saw some sort of agitation behind the masked man. Two, three, and eventually four *things* climbed out of the car and started prancing all around him. They were covered with hair and had huge, toothy jaws—but were quite unlike the monstrous creatures of the previous attack.

In spite of the mask covering his face, the man seemed annoyed.

"Stop, you stupid Mud Eaters!" he thundered. "Encircle the house, right away. And don't let anyone out, understand?"

"Master, Master, nice Master, encircle the house, no one out, encircle!"

But the Mud Eaters stayed close to the man, not moving.

"What are you waiting for?" he screamed, as his mask turned an angry shade of red.

One of the Eaters shuffled up to him and asked: "Er, what mean 'encircle'?"

The man's mask now turned crimson, and Tara thought he was going to explode. The Mud Eaters felt it too. They froze, staring at him in fear.

"Encircle," he hissed, "means circling the house so no one can get out. Is that clear?"

"Very clear, luminous Master, very clear!"

"Then get going, you stupid mudders!"

The hairy, drooling beasts headed toward the manor house and vanished behind a corner.

The man took a few deep breaths and his mask gradually reverted to its shiny gray color.

"Tara, answer me!" he cried. "I don't want to hurt you. I'm a spellbinder. I'm Magister, Master of the Bloodgraves. I just want to tell you about your parents and your grandmother. Isabella has lied to you and misled you. She has denied you your inheritance, Tara! She hasn't told you anything. She claims it's to protect you, but that isn't true. It's because she knows that you will be much more powerful than she, that you will become the Imperial Spellbinder, and she doesn't want that to happen!"

Tara held the dog tighter. She had no idea what an imperial spellbinder was, but what the Bloodgrave was saying wasn't wrong. And she *was* dying to know more. Who were her parents? Where did her grandmother, Deria, Tachil, and Mangus come from? Why had Magister kidnapped her mother and held her prisoner? But if she answered the spellbinder, he might be able to locate her. And he would certainly harm her grandmother.

The Bloodgrave master seemed to realize that Tara wasn't going to move, because he walked up to the door and put his hand on the handle. A spark shot out from it. He cursed and took a few steps backward.

"I know you're in there, Tara," he snapped. "I can sense your conscious mind in the house. The confinement spell won't work against me because I have strength and power. Watch this!"

He was behaving exactly like evil wizards do in the movies, and it was so fascinating that Tara lost precious moments just watching him.

With his billowing cape making him look like a giant bat, the man raised his hands very high, shouted something, and sent a jet of light crashing into the door.

As if she were psychically linked with the house, Tara sensed that it would hold out, but not for long. Thinking fast, she came up with a plan.

She got up and grabbed her grandmother. Then, without bothering to keep her from bouncing against the walls, she unlocked the bedroom door and ran to Tachil and Mangus's rooms. They were still asleep.

She remembered what Deria had told her. It was enough to visualize the bodies rising and make the gesture. She couldn't remember the spell, but she hadn't needed it the last time and maybe she wouldn't now. She concentrated, and the two bodies floated in midair.

Okay now, how to hide everybody? The man outside had said that he could sense her conscious mind. So if he couldn't detect her mind in the house, he would leave her alone. All she had to do was to hide the three unconscious bodies—and she had already figured how to do that.

She took a pair of scissors, walked over to the curtains, and cut the cords that held them. Tying her grandmother and the two servants together, one after another, she raced upstairs to the attic, tugging the bodies behind her. The attic ceiling was very high and dark. Tara took a broom and used the handle to smash the only light bulb in the attic.

She looked at the unconscious bodies.

"Okay now," she muttered. "If I send you up there, will that do the trick?"

She raised her hand and visualized Isabella, Tachil, and Mangus stuck up against the ceiling. To her great relief, the three bodies obediently rose upward and vanished into the shadows, completely out of sight.

"Great! So far, so good! Let's hope the Bloodgrave is like most people and doesn't think to look up. Now it's my turn."

Quick as a flash, she raced back down to her grandmother's room and locked the door. She could sense that the spell protecting the house was about to give way. She ran over to the carpet and felt the place where Manitou had put his paw. Nothing happened. At that moment, the protection spell broke with a sharp *snap!*

"Ready or not, here I come, Tara!"

Tara rolled her eyes. Even though she was terrified, she thought the Bloodgrave was really, like, pathetic. A total loser. She stared at the carpet again, but it wasn't cooperating in the least: not a ripple, nothing.

"Let's see," she thought. "It doesn't want to open because I'm human, but if I were a dog . . . Manitou, come here!"

Growling at the sound of the intruder entering the house, the Labrador obediently came over from his position by the door.

"Manitou, we have to get out of here fast. You have to open the passage, do you understand?"

But the dog just whined, gave Tara's face a big lick, and went back to the door.

Downstairs, the spellbinder was searching for Tara, calling her name.

"Come here, you stupid dog," she fumed, "and open this trap door!"

Manitou looked at her and barked, and a despairing Tara heard the spellbinder react to the sound. He stopped rummaging around and headed straight for the stairs.

"I don't know exactly where you are, Tara, but I feel that you aren't far. Come on, sweetie, there's no need to be afraid."

If there was one thing Tara really hated, it was being called "sweetie." She dove at Manitou, dragged him to the carpet by the scruff of his neck, grabbed his paw, and forcibly set it on the carpet.

Nothing happened. The dog twisted away and ran off. Thinking they were playing a new game, he darted across the room, jumped on the bed, slipped under the table, then returned to the carpet where he wagged his tail like a maniac, taunting her.

Tara could hear the spellbinder climbing the stairs to the landing.

"Manitou, you've got to get us out of here," she moaned. "Good doggie. Out—*now!*"

The Lab cocked his head, seeming to listen to her carefully. He moved, and then without doing it on purpose, put his paw on the carpet. Miraculously, the hole opened just as the bedroom door lock yielded to the Bloodgrave's incantation.

Tara grabbed the dog and dove headfirst down the secret passage with him. The hole closed up behind them.

The two of them tumbled down the passage, which seemed to be shooting them outside. The passageway stone felt warm and oddly pliable. Tara decided she really didn't want to know what she suspected—that the tunnel was alive!

They burst out onto the grass behind the manor at the edge of the woods. She tensed, waiting for a Mud Eater to jump her. Given a choice, though, she preferred those hairy beasts to the Bloodgrave. So she was startled to see the Mud Eaters walking away from her, marching all altogether toward the front of the house.

At that, she laughed. The Bloodgrave master didn't tell them that they had to *stay* behind the house, only that to encircle meant to go around it, which is probably what the Mud Eaters had been doing for the last quarter of an hour.

Repressing an incipient attack of the giggles, Tara ran to hide in the woods. Even in the dark, she knew every tree and clearing by heart. The Bloodgrave had no chance of finding her there.

Suddenly, she heard an angry roar, followed by a terrific explosion. She turned and saw that in his rage, the Bloodgrave had blown off the roof of the house. To her horror, the walls of the manor house burst into flames.

CHAPTER 3

WIZARD AND FIRE

This was too much for Tara, who collapsed on the ground, sobbing. She didn't see the Bloodgrave, whose mask had turned a terrible black, roast one of the Mud Eaters with a fiery ray, order the others into the car, and speed off. All she knew was that Isabella, Mangus, and Tachil had just died a horrible death, and it was her fault.

Unable to console his mistress, Manitou was distracted by the sound of someone softly calling to him, and went to investigate. Tara didn't even notice him leave.

A few moments later, the dog returned in the company of a funny little man in a blue tunic that was slit up the side and covered with silver dragons. His golden eyes were half hidden by an improbable thatch of white hair, making him look like an old owl. He wore silver slippers with curved-up tips, their shiny material crisscrossed with little waves.

"Tara? Look at me, please."

The girl started. She'd been so devastated by pain that she'd lowered her guard, and the Bloodgrave had found her! Ready to do battle, she glared into the very gentle eyes of the strange man peering down at her. Was he a friend or enemy?

She spotted Deria behind the odd little man, and leapt to her feet.

"Why didn't you come back sooner?" Tara screamed. "Because of you, Grandma, Tachil, and Mangus are dead, and the Bloodgrave tried to catch me! You abandoned me! I hate you!"

"A Bloodgrave? But . . . but . . . " stammered Deria, completely thrown by the girl's fury. "Stop it, Tara! Calm down."

"After everything she's undergone, I think this child needs some rest," said the old, owl-like man. "We can question her later." Gesturing as if he was tossing sand at Tara, he recited, "By Somnolus, I bid you sleep, your slumber dreamless, calm, and deep."

Tara could feel a spell being cast on her, but she turned on the old man like a fury, fists clenched. No way was she giving in. She didn't need sleep, she needed answers—lots of answers! Resisting with all her might, she used her anger and pain to counter the wave of sleep that threatened to overcome her. To the wizard's and Deria's great surprise, Tara remained standing, defying them.

"Don't bother trying!" she raged. "I don't want to sleep. My grandmother and the others just died because of me, so you're going to give me some answers! Who am I? What's going on? And why did that Bloodgrave guy want to kill me?"

Eyes wide with astonishment, the old man answered her as clearly as he could.

"If that Bloodgrave had wanted to kill you, Tara, you would be dead by now. I don't think that's what he was after. I have a hunch he wanted . . . hmm . . . to kidnap you. Yes, that's right, kidnap you."

She was speechless.

Relieved that Tara had stopped yelling at her, Deria agreed.

"Chemnashaovirodaintrachivu is right, Tara. You have to trust him. Now tell us what happened. When we saw the fire we thought you might be hurt or worse, and we're relieved to see that you're okay. But you say that my companions and your grandmother are dead. How? Did your attacker kill them?"

So *this* was the famous Chem-amajig who was supposed to be so powerful? He sure didn't fit what Tara imagined a high wizard would look like. His hair was all tangled, and his robe clearly displayed the remains of his last meal. Facing the monstrous Bloodgrave, this old guy wouldn't last a minute, she thought.

Seeing Deria waiting patiently, Tara told her what happened. How she had hidden the bodies in the attic and had escaped through the dog's secret trap door. How the Bloodgrave master had blown up the house in his rage and then left, probably when he saw them coming.

She was about to go on when a strange object passed between them and the shining moon. A low-flying cloud? No, it was Tachil!

Heart pounding, she sprinted out of the woods.

Separated by the explosion, the three bodies were floating along with the wind. In a few minutes they would drift over the village. She absolutely had to stop that. Concentrating, she ordered them down.

The old wizard was surprised to see the scorched bodies descend without Tara making a gesture or saying a word. But he said nothing to Deria, who emerged from the forest behind him and didn't see anything.

"Are they dead?" asked Tara in a small, shaky voice as the wizard carefully examined them.

"No. They were protected by the levitation field you created around them. When the Bloodgrave blew up the house he must've blown off the roof, unaware that he was saving their lives. You saved them by hiding them up in the attic. I'll look after them. Follow us."

The old wizard cast a spell, and the bodies slipped from Tara's control to obey him. He did this so casually that he rose a few degrees in the girl's esteem.

But the sight of the manor hit Tara like a body blow. The roof that the Bloodgrave master had blown off lay on the ground, split in half. Every window had shattered in the explosion, and flames were destroying what remained of the walls.

The wizard nodded his bushy head, took a deep breath, and roared: "By the Elementus you are hereby bidden to let us see those forces hidden."

All the flames immediately coalesced into a single place in the ravaged building.

"I'll be darned," gasped Deria. "A fire elemental! We've got a big problem on our hands."

"What . . . what's that?" blurted Tara.

"It's a fire spirit. There are thousands of fire, earth, water, and wind elementals on all the worlds. The Bloodgrave summoned this one to commit as much damage as possible. Try to imagine a fire that is intelligent and destructive, and you have a fire elemental."

It was true. To Tara's amazement the flames gathered into a gigantic scarlet shape with a flickering head and two arms. Great! Now fire was taking human shape!

Spotting the wizard, who looked very small next to it, the burning elemental leaned close, displaying a mouth full of sharp teeth, each of which was a tiny flame.

"Aaaaah!" it crackled. "Chemnashaovirodaintrachivu, you old pile of flammable garbage, what do you want? Why are you interrupting my dinner?"

"This doesn't have my authorization," cried the wizard. "Leave the manor house alone!"

"But you didn't summon me, you trash heap, so you can't banish me until I've eaten everything up."

At that, the elemental casually picked up a section of wall and tossed it into its infernal mouth, where it disappeared.

"I'm warning you," the old wizard answered quietly. "Leave now or suffer the consequences."

Tara screamed. Without any warning, the elemental had shot a jet of flame at the wizard's small figure. His robe began to burn, and he vanished in a thick cloud of smoke. She was about to rush over to him when he reappeared, wearing only silver long underwear and blue socks—and looking very angry.

"Odd bodkins!" he roared. "One of my nicest robes! And my best magic shoes! You're going to pay for that!"

The elemental was surprised that its fire hadn't vaporized the wizard, but it recovered quickly.

"So what do you plan to do, you ridiculous bundle of rags? There isn't enough of that cursed water around to hurt me. And there aren't any water elementals in the area."

"Oh, but water won't be necessary!" said the wizard. He waved his hand at the building's rubble and shouted: "By Vomitus spit up what you've devoured, and restore the manor within the hour."

He had hardly recited the spell when the elemental started to gag, then vomit. Dozens of chunks of debris spurted from its mouth, flying back to their proper places on the manor walls. And the more the elemental vomited, the smaller it got.

"Mercy!" it gasped. "Please stop!"

But the wizard was relentless. When the creature was reduced to a twitching red homunculus, he recited another spell, and a bottle of water appeared in his hand. He calmly sprinkled it on the remains of the infernal fire being, and the bottle and the elemental disappeared together with a dull *crack!*

The wizard rubbed his hands with satisfaction. Then, ignoring the fact that he was still in his underwear, he said: "By Fixus mend both tile and rafter, and cap the house forever after."

The crumpled roof pulled itself together and flew up to settle snugly atop the manor walls.

Dumbfounded, Tara realized that everything was completely back to normal. No sign of the fire remained except a puddle of water by the front door. Talk about efficient restoration work!

Even Deria was impressed.

"Magnificent," she said. "Masterful! Tara, did you hear the formula he chose?"

"Yes. He said, 'By Vomitus—'"

"Aaaah!" cried Deria, "Don't say it! Not until you've mastered your powers. You could cause a disaster. I really don't feel like puking up my dinner, if you don't mind."

"Oops, sorry! But why did you ask me if I heard it?"

"Because it was a very clever thing to do. To defeat a fire elemental, you usually need to have a lot of water, or a water elemental. Since Chem didn't have either he attacked the elemental's weak point."

"Its weak point?"

"Fire feeds on what it consumes. This elemental had become huge because it had 'eaten' half the manor house. So by forcing it to disgorge everything it had swallowed, Chemnashaovirodaintra-chivu weakened it to the point where he could defeat it easily. A very subtle tactic."

"I mainly thought it was terrifying," muttered Tara, still shaken by the vision of the wizard going up in smoke.

"Oh, that was nothing!" remarked Deria casually. "He's a high wizard and completely fireproof. But those elementals aren't very intelligent. Too empty-headed."

"Mmm, also arrogant and conceited . . . serves 'em right," growled the wizard, who was still quivering with indignation. "Now, let's review everything that happened here."

Raising his hand, he said: "By Memorus display the recent past so we can make a plan, and fast."

Blurry shapes materialized out of nowhere, startling Tara. Before her hovered the ghosts of the monsters that had attacked them! The scene she had lived through a few minutes earlier was being magically replayed. But the images of the monsters attacking Isabella began to flicker and waver, and then disappeared. The wizard tried to get them back, but in vain.

"By Gelisor's rotten fangs," he muttered in annoyance, "this spell really isn't ready for prime time! Tara, you'll have to describe what happened in detail later, because the Memorus isn't stable enough. Meanwhile, I'm going to take care of your grandmother."

Tara was about to answer when they heard a siren in the distance.

"Rats!" exclaimed Deria. "It's the fire department! They must've seen the smoke!"

Tara thought fast.

"Deria, can you summon fire without it being an elemental?"

"Yes, of course. We can always summon ordinary fire. It's much easier than summoning an elemental. Why?"

"They've seen the smoke, so we're going to have to give them some fire."

Deria's eyes widened.

"Gosh, you're right! Here it goes: 'By Flamus, give me fire. A lively blaze I now require.'"

A pile of blazing logs immediately appeared on the lawn at a safe distance from the forest and the manor, sending up a column of dark smoke.

"Perfect!" approved Tara. "I'll let you explain why you built a fire in the middle of our yard at two o'clock in the morning. See you later!"

The wizard had already entered the manor with the bodies. When Tara came in, she saw Tachil and Mangus sitting on the staircase, looking glassy-eyed and holding their heads in their hands.

Mad with joy, she cried, "You're awake!" which made the two servants grimace and cover their ears.

"What . . . what happened?" groaned Tachil, whose breath was being squeezed out of him by Tara's energetic hug.

"Deria will explain everything," said the girl, now kissing a groggy Mangus. "After she finishes with the firefighters, that is. I'm really happy you're okay. I'm going to see Grandma."

She left the dazed servants and raced up to Isabella's bedroom. To her surprise, her grandmother wasn't there, nor was the wizard. After a moment's thought she left the room and headed for the basement, where, yep, she'd guessed right: he'd taken her down to the Chemistry Chamber.

This was a place Tara didn't much like, where her grandmother conducted all sorts of strange, noisy, and often stinky experiments. It was sealed from any natural light, and completely circular. Even the furniture was round. There wasn't a single angle in the place except for the big pentagram faintly glowing in the middle of the room. Tara had never seen it before, because it was normally covered with a round carpet.

"Er, can I help?" she whispered, nervously chewing on her forelock.

The wizard turned and looked at her thoughtfully.

"No, I don't think so. But you must avoid all contact with the floor while I'm treating your grandmother, so please go sit on the table."

For once, Tara obeyed without asking questions.

Chem finally noticed that he was dressed only in his underwear. Grumbling at the elemental—Tara caught the words "insolent," "swaggering," and "a good lesson"—he conjured himself a midnight blue robe, and a pair of silver slippers appeared on his feet.

Carefully standing outside the pentagram, he pushed Isabella's body to its center, then took off his shoes and socks.

To Tara's great surprise, the wizard then levitated and went to hover above Isabella's body. He waved his hand and recited some spells, and rays shot from each of his fingers and toes. The twenty beams of light struck the pentagram.

It was very impressive.

"By Transformus, I illuminate you, Isabella!"

With each word, the pentagram glowed more brightly.

"By Illuminus, I transform you, Isabella!"

This sparked a flash of light so bright that Tara was sorry not to have sunglasses.

"May the Rigidifus be banished, I command it!"

At that, the light began to turn pinkish. Hovering motionless, the wizard observed it carefully. When it turned a deep blood red, he raised his arms and cried: "By Vivus, this formula is the right one!"

A deafening explosion followed. Isabella's body glowed briefly, and the whole chamber went dark.

Tara felt a little panicky. The room was pitch black and there wasn't a sound to be heard.

Then a slightly irritated voice broke the silence.

"By Demiderus, would somebody please turn on the light?"

"Grandma!" shouted Tara. She was beside herself with joy, but didn't dare move without the wizard's permission.

"Tara'tylanhnem, is that you? What the—?"

"One moment, my dear," came the wizard's voice in the darkness. "I will shed light both on the room and your situation."

At his command, a glow lit up the scene, softly at first, then stronger, revealing Isabella seated in the center of the pentagram.

"Chem?" she asked in surprise. "What are you doing here?"

"Well, let's just say—"

"He saved your life!" burst in Tara. "May I get down now, Master?" Tara couldn't pronounce the wizard's name, and "master" was a term of respect that seemed to suit him. If he didn't like it, that was just too bad.

"What? Yes, of course."

Tara jumped down and ran to hug her grandmother.

Isabella was surprised by the display of affection and awkwardly patted Tara's back. Seeing this, the old wizard frowned. The girl clearly gave all her love to her grandmother, but the latter didn't return it—or at least didn't show it. And Chem knew how dangerous it was to deprive a child of affection. He would have to talk to Isabella, and soon.

He was thinking about this and putting on his unusual shoes while the girl told her grandmother everything that had happened. At that, Isabella hugged her granddaughter tight. This time the wizard's eyebrows went up instead of down. All right, he thought, all is not lost.

But the woman quickly got a grip on herself. She was a little unsteady when she stood up, and Tara helped her, but she shook off the girl to walk alone. The wizard caught Tara's look of sadness and sighed.

When Isabella was sure that Deria, Tachil, and Mangus were all okay, she went upstairs to her office, followed by Tara and Chem.

"Tara'tylanhnem, would you mind going to your room, please? Chemnashaovirodaintrachivu and I have important things to discuss." Before Tara could answer, the wizard spoke up: "No Isa, she's staying."

Isabella was about to protest, but she yielded wearily, while looking at the wizard with annoyance.

"Good," he said calmly. "Come over here, Tara, and let's see what your grandmother has taught you."

"She hasn't taught me *anything*, Master! I don't know the first thing about spellbinders, attacks, or those elementary thingies."

"But you do know that we're spellbinders?"

"Yeah, I kind of figured that one out," said Tara sarcastically. "You might say I saw it at work when my grandmother hit me with a forgetting spell and it wound up nearly killing both of us."

The wizard looked uncomfortable.

"Hmm, we'll see about that later. For now let's start at the beginning, with the basics. There are a great number of peoples in the universe, living more or less at peace with each other. Like humans, these people have children, parents, grandparents, great-grandparents, great-great-grandparents . . . anyway, the races live a long time. Their basic needs and limitations are the same everywhere: to eat, sleep, study—"

Tara was on familiar ground there, and she interrupted the wizard.

"Do you have schools for spellbinders, like on television?"

"Ahhh, your television! No, we don't have schools for spellbinders. You need only read a book of spells once, and it becomes part of your mind forever. We don't need to study."

Tara's eyes widened in surprise. What? No need to study? Betty would love that!

Isabella shot the old wizard a look of irritation and spoke up.

"But we need to constantly study to make sure that our presence doesn't harm or endanger the worlds where we live," she said. "That takes a lot of work. And specialties are not learned in books but in practice, and that takes a lot of work too."

Unruffled, Chem continued.

"Tell me, dear, based on what you've seen on television and in your movies, what do you know about spellbinders?"

At this, Tara started to flounder. The old wizard was so odd, she didn't quite know how to answer.

"Well, you have cauldrons, and you mix potions, there's black magic and white magic, and . . . "

Chem was making such a horrible face that Tara's voice gradually faded away.

"Fire and brimstone!" the old wizard raged. "Nonspells are always trying to codify what spellbinders do, and it's always twaddle! Cauldrons and potions exist, but they aren't important! We are *masters of spells.* And magic isn't black or white; it's just a tool that depends on who is using it. If you slice your bread with a knife, that's good, but if you stab somebody with a knife, that's bad. But the knife isn't good or bad; it's just a knife. Zounds! Your grandmother hasn't taught you *anything*!"

"Well, duh! That's just the problem," said Tara. "And who are those Bloodgraves? You haven't talked about them yet."

She had touched on a sore point, and the wizard grimaced.

"The Bloodgraves are pretentious, arrogant spellbinders who think they're powerful enough to be masters of the universe. They dress only in gray and hide their faces behind a mask so no one will know who they are. They have declared themselves our enemies and are constantly battling us for control of our worlds."

Now it was Tara's turn to grimace. "Why do they have such a weird name?"

"In the language of our primitive ancestors, we were known as 'Those who know how to bind spells.' That was a little long, and over time it became shortened to 'spellbinders.' Those who lacked our powers were called 'non-spellbinders.' That got shortened as well, to 'nonspells.' A spellbinder named Druidor Bloodgrave decided that the nonspells should be our slaves. The hunter-elves defeated and killed him, but not before he acquired followers. When they decided to challenge us, the gray spellbinders called themselves Bloodgraves in Druidor's honor, and dug up those ridiculous old names. For heaven's sake, Isabella, you could at least have warned her against the Bloodgraves."

"I didn't teach Tara'tylanhnem anything because her father made me swear that she would not be a spellbinder and would lead a normal life. To protect her, I was even prepared to hide her gift from the High Council."

"*What?*" the old wizard almost fell off his chair. "That's unacceptable! How could you conceive of such a thing? It's forbidden!"

Though no longer under the petrifying spell, Isabella was as still and rigid as a statue.

"I gave my word," she simply said.

"That's no reason! We have laws, Isabella, laws created to protect the nonspells and also to protect us. We aren't outlaws, like the Bloodgraves. Do you have any idea how much harm Tara could have done?"

"But it didn't happen!"

"Enough! That's no excuse! Or do you think you are above the law, Isabella? Are you declaring yourself to be a Semchanach?"

(Semchanachs, Tara would learn much later, were spellbinders who rejected the authority of the High Council. They weren't necessarily Bloodgraves, and could use magic as they pleased, provided it didn't harm anyone. If it did, they were mercilessly tracked down by the hunter-elves.)

Isabella looked as if she'd been punched in the face.

"No, of course not!" she shot back. "I've never tried to evade the Council's authority. I obey its orders, as you know better than anyone. But Chem, I swore a blood oath!"

Now it was the old wizard's turn to stiffen.

"A blood oath! Are you joking?"

"Certainly not," she said, pulling up the sleeves of her robe and moving her bracelets aside. Each of her wrists bore a red glyph in the shape of a horizontal number 8. The wizard turned pale and took a step back.

"If Tara'tylanhnem becomes a wizard, I will die," she said as she covered up the glyphs.

Stunned, Tara stared at her grandmother. What was she talking about?

The old wizard was thinking so hard, Tara almost expected to see smoke come out of his ears.

"Well that changes everything," he said gravely. "I didn't know. Did that happen when you—"

"Yes," interrupted Isabella, nodding meaningfully toward the girl.

Tara understood perfectly: more blasted secrets! But now she had a secret as well—about her mother—and had no intention of sharing it.

"In that case we have a serious problem," said Chem, giving Isabella a worried glance. "How much time would you need to protect the property and the girl?"

"Not more than about ten days, if you can lend me Padimo and Glivol. The thing is, I don't have all the necessary ingredients here."

"Hmm, I see. And it would be too dangerous to take Tara with you, I imagine. All right, here's what I suggest: I'll take your grand-daughter with me for ten days. She will accompany me to OtherWorld, to the Royal Castle of Travia. That way I'll be able to protect her. And then I'll send her back to you."

He made an odd gesture in the air, stretched out his hand, and raised his voice: "Let what I have declared be recorded."

Tara jumped when she heard an incredibly high-pitched voice chirping, seemingly from the empty air. It spoke so rapidly it was as if the words were stuck together: "Verywell, HighWizard. TheHigh Councilherebyrecordsthedecision. Thenoticewilbepublishedinthe officialCouncilgazette"

Chem frowned, rubbed his ear, and fiddled with something in his hand.

"No, I want this decision recorded in executive session," he specified. "No point in telling everybody that the child will be on OtherWorld. Simply advise the other members of the Council. Oh, and also Master T'andilus M'angil, the head of our secret services."

This time, the disembodied voice was incredibly low, and spoke very, very slowly: "Veerrryyy weelll, Hiiiggghhh Wiiiizzzzaaaar-rrrddd, iiittt wwwiiilll bbbeee dddooonnneee."

The wizard sighed, annoyed at the bad connection. When he lowered his hand, Tara saw something in it sparkle and realized that he had been communicating by means of a kind of crystal ball, which he now put in his pocket.

Isabella hadn't moved during this entire exchange.

"I could keep Tara'tylanhnem with me," she said soberly. "Now that I know how the Bloodgraves operate, I can repulse them."

The old wizard looked at her, noting the dark circles under her eyes and her slightly trembling hands.

"I think you're very tired, Isabella. Better for the child to come with me. It will be less of a burden if you aren't worried about her."

Isabella hesitated, but then admitted how fatigued she was. She took a deep breath and looked at her granddaughter.

"I can't always express things the way I'd like to, but I love you deeply, Tara'tylanhnem, and I want the best for you. But Chem is right. I can't protect you if you're with me."

Tears came to the girl's eyes. She knew that her grandmother loved her, in her own way. But there's a huge difference between knowing it and hearing it said, as she was discovering.

"I love you too, Grandma."

Well aware that Isabella didn't like to be touched, Tara did nothing. But when her grandmother opened her arms, she joyfully ran to hug her.

"Well, well," said the old wizard with great satisfaction. "That's one good thing taken care of. Now Tara, it's very early, and you have hours of missed sleep to make up. Go to bed. We will leave for OtherWorld later."

Tara left the office, her mind still buzzing with questions despite her fatigue. She understood clearly that the wizard was bringing her to a different world tomorrow. And she remembered what her mother had told her, that she was imprisoned in the Gray Fortress on OtherWorld. Perfect, she smiled to herself. The wizard was taking her exactly where she most wanted to go.

As Master Chem went upstairs to the guest room he also had plenty to think about during what was left of the night.

By what incredible coincidence had the Bloodgraves attacked the Duncan family? After all, the High Council itself knew nothing about this unrevealed young spellbinder. And how had Tara managed to redirect the deadly ray? Only a wizard of an extremely high level could have countered an attack like that. Even Isabella hadn't been able to.

Also, Tara had been remarkable in resisting his Somnolus spell. True, he hadn't cranked it up very high. He hadn't wanted to knock her out for two weeks, just two hours. Still, she had stood up to him.

Finally, those infernal Bloodgraves wanted the girl. They wanted her so badly they were willing to send two of their own, including the famous Magister, their leader, to kidnap her.

It was all very interesting. Yes, very, very interesting.

CHAPTER 4

MASS-LESS TRANSIT

The next morning, Tara thought about the ghostly vision of her mother and the terrible attack as she pulled on the second leg of her jeans. Suddenly, an awful thought struck her, leaving her hopping in place. What if it all had been a dream? She quickly finished dressing and ran downstairs.

To her great relief, she found the old wizard in the kitchen cheerfully chatting with Tachil, Deria, and Mangus over cocoa. So she wasn't nuts after all—spellbinders really did exist.

She plopped down next to the wizard and poured herself a big mug of hot chocolate.

"Morning, Deria, Mangus, Tachil. Good morning, Mister . . . er, Master," she said quickly, remembering there was no way she could pronounce the high wizard's name.

"Good morning, Tara," said Chem. "How are you feeling this morning? Not too stiff?"

She was surprised to realize that in fact she felt very sore. When she moved, muscles she never knew she had complained loudly.

"I am, actually. Why?"

"Because you used your body's energy to do all the things you accomplished yesterday. When you levitated your grandmother, it's as if you were really lifting her. You carried, you ran, you used your power, and your body suffered the consequences. We try not to use magic too often, at least those of us who aren't especially gifted, because it burns up a lot of energy and we could die of exhaustion."

"But I could never have lifted my grandmother without magic," Tara protested. "She's a lot heavier than I am."

"Ah, I can see you're Isabella's granddaughter all right! You want a logical explanation, don't you? And you're quite right. If you'd had a wheelbarrow, for example, you could have put Isabella in it and moved her, right? Well, magic is a little like that. It's a tool. Magic lets you take your twelve-year-old strength and multiply it. To use your power, you unconsciously drew on the forces that exist all around us. Spellbinders are able to use this life force for their own purposes, and normal humans can't."

Great, thought Tara. Now Chem was spouting "May the Force be with you" stuff. All this spellbinder business had been lacking was a *Star Wars* tie-in. Still, she was riveted. So that's how magic worked. She tried to visualize the concept.

"So we're a kind of motor and the fluid around us is like gasoline, is that it? We run on it, and it gives us power. And the better the motor, the greater the power."

The wizard looked at Tara, then pounded her on the back so hard, her cup of chocolate almost went flying.

"Remarkable! Just remarkable! Tara, you have a wonderful gift for simplifying the most complicated things. Ah, Padimo isn't going to like this. He always gets tangled in circumlocutions when he tries to explain the nature of magic. A motor and gas—exactly the metaphor we were after!"

Isabella entered, scowling at the racket.

"Well, well, what's going on here?"

"What's going on is that your granddaughter is remarkable," said the delighted wizard. "Simply remarkable."

Tara was flattered that Chem liked her analogy but thought he was making too much of it. And speaking of magic, it was time she got a few things straight.

"Tell me, Master, when are we leaving?" Tara asked.

"Soon. And you won't be alone. Deria will join us on OtherWorld at Travia Castle. She insisted on going along as your protector. She's a trained magus, so we had the court take her on as its weather wizard. Your grandmother's assistants will stay here to help her prepare the manor's defenses."

"Terrific!" said Tara with an enthusiasm that surprised Isabella, who'd though she might refuse to go. "What do I have to do now?"

"First, finish your breakfast. Deria will help you pack your bags. Then we'll go to the Portal and transfer to Travia. By the way, it might be useful to take your great-grandfather with you. He'll be a perfect familiar, since he can't be identified in his present form."

To Tara, it sounded as if the wizard was speaking Martian, and she stared at him blankly.

"By Demiderus, Isabella," he growled, "don't tell me she doesn't know about your father, either?"

"No, of course not," she snapped. "Manitou, come in here!" she commanded in a ringing voice that made Tara jump.

A moment later, the big black Labrador padded into the kitchen. Isabella hugged him then turned his muzzle toward the girl.

"Tara, I'd like you to meet your great-grandfather. Manitou, you're going to accompany Tara to OtherWorld. You'll pass as her familiar, which will allow you to stay with her and protect her. Can you handle that?"

The dog wagged his tail and barked once.

"Alack the day!" said the old wizard sadly. "There's been no improvement, I see. Maybe this will help. 'By Interpretus the wall between our species breach, so we can understand each other's speech.'"

When the dog barked again, it was with a very different voice.

"*Woof!* I mean, of course I'll go with her. Blasted mutt! He's stronger than I am, and his instinct overwhelms me. But I'll do my best. OtherWorld's magic vibrations may help me stay in my human mind. I hope so, anyway."

Tara fell to her knees in front of the dog.

"Manitou? I mean, Grandpa . . . er, Great-grandpa?"

"Just call me Manitou. it's simpler. It's such a pleasure to think and act like a human being! You have no idea how I've suffered not being able to chat with you during my rare moments of lucidity."

Isabella looked down at him regretfully.

"I'm sorry, but no one has been able to replicate the formula of your spell yet," she said. "And since the shock of the transformation erased your memory, all we can do is keep searching."

"Yes, I know," said Manitou, nodding. "Oh! The dog's instinct is coming back again. Tara, I'll meet you in the yard later."

He gave the astonished girl a little nuzzle and went out.

"But, but—" Tara stammered.

"Sad story," said the wizard somberly. "He managed to discover a spell that gave him eternal life. Problem is, it also changed him into a dog. So he's immortal, but in the shape of a Labrador retriever. And you can't just take him along as your dog, because only familiars are allowed in the Castle."

"What's a familiar?"

"Every spellbinder has an animal companion called a familiar. It's his or her sign or mark, in a way. The spellbinder and the familiar can communicate. Isabella's familiar was a tiger, and it was killed when your father and mother died. As you see, she hasn't replaced it."

"*A tiger?*"

"Don't worry, familiars aren't dangerous to spellbinders. Deria's magpie Mani is her familiar. It's been Mani's job to keep an eye on you when Deria wasn't able to. All right, I see that you've finished your breakfast. Why don't you go upstairs and get ready?"

Tara had been carefully studying the magpie to see what made it different. She was startled when it flew to the table, landed on a loaf of bread, and saluted her by dipping its wings. Then it swiped a piece of her toast.

"Wow! Did you see that?" she exclaimed. "That was great!" Then she turned to her grandmother. "Grandma?"

"What is it, Tara'tylanhnem?"

"Is there anything else I should know about?"

Isabella hesitated for a moment then said, "No, except that I will be leaving for Peru in an hour. To protect the manor I need some sorcery objects that I don't have available here, and I must go get them. Mangus and Tachil will stay at the house. But don't worry. Chemnashaovirodaintrachivu will always know how to reach me."

This news made Tara uneasy. Peru was so far away.

As she was pondering this, her grandmother continued: "I want to say that I'm very happy you're under the high wizard's temporary protection. I'm sure you are going to enjoy yourself at the Castle. The rulers of Lancovit are charming people, and all should go very well. It will be like spending the rest of your vacation in another country."

Tara's mind was racing and she was about to ask more questions, but her grandmother's serious expression dissuaded her.

"I hope so, Grandma. I'll see you later."

With Deria's help, Tara's suitcase was soon packed. She was about to take it and her purse downstairs when Deria stopped her.

"No, leave them here for the time being. I'll bring them over to the count's later. Nobody must know where you're going, and the sight of suitcases might reveal our high wizard's plan."

"So should I just go downstairs like this?"

"Yes. I'll be along in a moment."

Tara went downstairs reluctantly and found Chem and Isabella waiting for her. Her grandmother looked even more serious than usual, but now that she had told Tara she loved her, the girl understood that it was a mask to hide her feelings.

Tara hugged her tight and kissed her. An embarrassed Isabella returned the hug then stepped back.

"You will be going to Travia Castle, which is the capital of the Kingdom of Lancovit," she said. "Castle etiquette isn't as strict as in Omois, which is the biggest human empire on OtherWorld. But I'm counting on you, Tara'tylanhnem. You're the seventh spellbinder in a long and glorious line, and I want you to bring honor to the Duncan name. Never forget that."

Though Tara had sworn to herself that she wouldn't cry, tears started rolling down her cheeks.

"I'm going to miss you, Grandma. I love you."

Isabella shot a look of annoyance at the old wizard, who was discreetly dabbing at his eyes. To Tara she murmured, "Me too, Tara'tylanhnem. Now go."

"All right, let's get moving," said the wizard. "It's time we were off." He had conjured a big blue handkerchief with dancing dragons, but they quickly got out of the way when he raised it to blow his nose.

Tara looked at Chem with some skepticism. Everything that she had seen about magic up to now left her pretty cold. Because of magic she'd been deprived of her mother for ten years, and now she had to leave her family, her friends, and the place where she had grown up. And the old wizard seemed awfully frail to be defending her against the monstrous Master of the Bloodgraves.

Tara turned to Chem, expecting something spectacular—like thunder and lightning and rearranged molecules—but he simply took her hand and they walked toward Besois-Giron Castle. Manitou followed, barking like mad.

"Confounded Isabella," he muttered. "Can't even show she's sad when saying goodbye. Gets on my nerves."

Tara said nothing until they reached the castle. She'd suddenly remembered what she had heard while crouching on the mantelpiece. Isabella had suggested—no, she'd *ordered*—that Fabrice go to OtherWorld. With a little luck, Tara would see her best friend there.

When they reached the castle, the wizard didn't bother ringing the bell. The gates opened all by themselves.

"Magic?" asked Tara, very impressed.

"No, electronic," he answered, pointing to the electric eyes on either side of the gate and the surveillance camera above it. "The count installed them a few days ago."

Count Besois-Giron was waiting for them at the castle forecourt. An impressive figure, he was totally bald, and his large, beaked nose made him look like a plucked falcon. He was holding a scepter.

"Welcome, High Wizard! Leaving us already?"

"Alas, yes. As you know, I love your wine, and I'm practically catatonic at not being able to drink some. But I have to take Tara and Manitou to OtherWorld. Your son is already there, isn't he?"

"Yes indeed," said the count proudly. "He transferred two hours ago."

"Perfect, perfect. We better go right to the Portal then. We still have a long way to go."

The Transfer Portal was located in one of the towers overlooking the valley.

Tara was a *Stargate* fan, so when she looked around for the Portal, she expected complex equipment, humming generators, and busy technicians. But there was . . . nothing. Just a big empty room hung with five tapestries woven with mythological scenes. One showed unicorns with what looked like dwarves. The second, giants carving—or were they eating?—blocks of stone. The third, men in green with pointed ears. The fourth, spellbinders in gray and blue robes around a pentagram like her grandmother's. The fifth tapestry showed little multicolored creatures at a party, beneath a scepter.

"Stand in the center of the room, please," said the count.

"Come here, Manitou," said Tara. The dog obeyed for once and came to sit next to her. Chem could feel the girl's small hand tighten in his, and he gave her a reassuring smile.

The count went to stand under the tapestry depicting the small creatures. He placed the scepter he was holding in a hollow on the wall, where it fit perfectly. He then waved goodbye to his guests, stepped out of the room, and closed the door.

As soon as the latch clicked, the scepter began to glow. Rays of light from the four other tapestries, each a different color, formed a rainbow over the travelers.

In a strong voice, the old wizard said, "The Living Castle of Travia."

They vanished.

Tara felt a shock and a twinge of nausea, then found herself standing in an identical room, but one with an occupant that looked nothing like the old count. It had only one eye, sported bright orange hair, stood seven feet tall, and was waving a piece of paper in one of its four hands. Tara would have drawn back in panic, but Chem held her firmly.

Armed guards in blue and silver livery were eyeing them carefully, their sharp lances at the ready to skewer intruders. Tara gulped as they glowered at her and decided not to budge without permission.

"High Wizard, what a pleasure to see you again!" said the Cyclops in a high, fluty voice, waving them forward. "Count Besois-Giron announced your arrival, and I had just enough time to come greet you. Really, it's amazing how many things I have to do!"

A bell rang, and the Cyclops became even more agitated.

"By Demiderus! More arrivals already! Quickly, quickly! Move on so I can clear the way."

The Cyclops seemed so frazzled that Tara almost laughed. He hadn't let Chem get a word in edgewise and was already pushing them out of the room with the frantic energy of a hen who had lost her chicks.

"That's our steward," said Chem with a sigh. "He panics every time a visitor comes to the Castle, and since people are constantly coming, he's in a permanent tizzy. Come along; I'm going to introduce you to our administrator, Lady Kalibris, so she can register you."

"Register me for what?"

"No one is allowed to be in the Castle without accreditation. Since you are my temporary guest, you will be accredited to Level 6. You'll be allowed to visit some areas of the Castle, but not others. Lady Kalibris will explain the Castle's rules and etiquette, tell you where you sleep, inform you how to be presented to Their Royal Highnesses, and so on."

"Presented to Their Royal Highnesses?" yelped Tara. "What are you talking about?"

"Don't worry, Tara," he said kindly. "The Living Castle is a gigantic entity, a kind of beating heart that regulates the kingdom's circulation. But etiquette here isn't too strict. If you say or do something silly, you can explain that you just arrived from Earth."

The old wizard waved Tara's other questions aside for the time being, having decided to first show her around the Castle.

Wide-eyed, Tara saw people busy everywhere. Floating in midair, young spellbinders were beating the rugs, but in an unusual way: they had them fly outside through high windows and shake themselves. Suits of armor (some of them with *really* unusual shapes) shook off dust by rattling themselves with a loud clanking. The interior of the Living Castle was magnificent, but it was hard to tell how it was constructed because everything was in constant motion. Landscapes on the walls and ceiling appeared, disappeared, and changed, according to the Castle's whim. At the moment it seemed to be in a good mood, because the landscapes were full of sunshine, meadows, and twittering birds. They looked so real that Tara almost bonked her head against a wall a few times when she leaned close to take a better look. Farther on, she drew an amused glance from Chem when she tried to jump over a stream that didn't exist. And she stopped at the end of one corridor, mesmerized by the sight of horses, unicorns, and little animals joyfully gamboling around her in the company of beautiful damsels blowing kisses to the spellbinders. It looked so real that Tara caught herself waving back.

Then she suddenly screamed, released Chem's arm, and leaped backward.

A dizzying abyss had just opened beneath their feet. At its bottom a giant insect with multiple legs, claws, and mandibles was looking up at her with a hungry eye—quite a few eyes, actually. Before she could retreat, the animal started racing up the crevasse wall at terrifying speed. But just as Tara opened her mouth to scream, Chem took her hand, unconcerned by the poison-laden claws threatening her.

"The Living Castle is certainly in fine fettle this morning!" he groused. "Don't worry, it does that to all the new arrivals. You're in no danger; those are just illusions. Come along."

A Castle that played practical jokes—great! Tara felt she didn't share the Living Castle's sense of humor, but she obediently followed the wizard. To be on the safe side, she decided to keep her eyes tightly closed until she figured they were past the abyss.

When she cautiously opened one eye, Tara was shocked all over again. She had just seen a spellbinder heading full tilt toward a desert and cactus landscape with a solid wall behind it. But he just waved his arm and went right through it! Chem was walking slowly enough for Tara to reach out and touch the wall, which felt completely solid. Had she imagined it? But a few moments later she saw a female spellbinder casually fly straight at another wall and go through it just as easily.

All right, message received loud and clear. The stone walls here weren't actually walls, and you could pass through them without any problem. The trick, obviously, was to know how. The familiars accompanying the spellbinders must have also known the trick, because the walls yielded to them too. Still, Tara couldn't help gritting her teeth each time she saw a spellbinder or a familiar heading for what looked like an inevitable and brutal collision.

The high wizard's pocket didn't stop ringing during their entire walk. Tara saw Chem pull out a fist-sized crystal ball. It was clearly the local equivalent of a cell phone, but one that would've made Earth geeks green with envy. Not only could the ball project perfectly clear sound and images of the person calling, but it didn't drop calls every two minutes! To Tara's amusement, the exasperated wizard finally waved his hand over the ball three times, switching it off.

Chem and Tara barely avoided being run down by a battalion of brooms that were sweeping the hallway, swaying to the tune of a flute being played by a sweaty spellbinder. A little farther on, another spellbinder was trying to order a water elemental to take its dirty water outside. The irritated elemental retaliated by releasing a huge wave of soapsuds.

This time, Tara decided she wasn't going to budge. She'd been fooled once, by the crevasse, and she didn't want to look stupid a second time. So she was very surprised when hundreds of gallons of cold, soapy water crashed down on her. Soaked and spluttering, she then found herself surrounded by fish and corals, including a huge shark that was looking at her hungrily. She staggered to her feet, shrieking. The Castle realized that she was frightened and replaced the underwater seascape with a pretty meadow. Nimbly hopping around the puddles, Chem caught up with her. He was followed by an excited Manitou, who energetically shook himself, soaking Tara all over again.

"Why didn't you get out of the way of the water, dear?" Chem asked.

"Because I thought it was one of those lousy illusions again," snapped Tara, literally foaming at the mouth.

The young spellbinder who had unleashed the deluge came running. "I'm terribly sorry!" he exclaimed. "I'll fix things right away!"

He waved his hands at Tara and yelled, "Dry!"

A warm wind filled the hallway, immediately drying everything and everyone in it. But Chem scowled at the young man.

"'*Dry*'? What do you mean, '*Dry*'? Couldn't you come up with a spell with a little more style? Something like, 'By Cleanus and Dryus, the rose and the thistle, make the pretty young spellbinder clean as a whistle'? What will people think if we start saying things like, 'Dry'? We're *magicians*, for heaven's sake, not washerwomen!"

Ignoring the young spellbinder's embarrassed apologies, Chem stomped off down the hallway, followed by Tara, who was trying hard not to laugh. The old wizard looked so offended!

As they turned a corner, an affectionate mop suddenly wrapped itself around Chem's head, who in turn started spluttering and hiccuping as he tried to get it off. A frantic, red-faced spellbinder ran to free him, and this time Tara couldn't contain her laughter. With his hair now standing on end, Master Chem looked more like an owl than ever!

They continued their walk, seeing pages and squires racing this way and that, and Tara began to grasp how enormous the Living Castle was. When they passed a row of warrior statues in dramatically aggressive poses, Chem quickly pulled her to one side. Under Tara's astonished eyes, one of the statues came to life, stretched, and shook off the dust covering it. (In the process, it evicted a pair of resident spiders who felt the neighborhood was getting a little too lively.) The other statues did likewise, in a great creaking of marble, and Tara found herself dodging the huge bodies. The statues clearly didn't bother noticing whether someone was in front of them.

A sudden noise caught her attention, and she was alarmed to see people bending over, as if they were having terrible convulsions.

Her heart skipped a beat. Were the Bloodgraves attacking?

"What're we gonna do?" she yelled at the wizard.

He gave her a look of surprise, while fighting a persistent hiccough.

"Nothing special *hic*! Just do like everyone else when he passes you."

The cause of the courtiers' convulsions was approaching, and she realized that the people weren't vomiting but respectfully bowing to a . . . Tara gasped, hardly able to believe her eyes. The thing before them wore a chic bonnet with a splendid yellow plume and a handsome blue cape held by a beautifully engraved silver brooch. This artistic ensemble covered a creature with the head of a lion, the body of a goat, and the tale of a dragon.

The thing gravely greeted the old wizard, who nodded, then peered searchingly at Tara before going on its way.

She whispered: "By Demiderus, as my grandmother would say, what the heck was *that*?"

"Haven't you ever seen a chimera before? That's Salatar, the king and queen's first counselor. A very cunning old rascal. If he asks you any questions tomorrow, be careful how you answer. Chimeras can't be beat when it comes to worming information out of people."

Tara was too busy straining to see the departing chimera to reply, and Chem had to tug on her hand to get her moving again.

Still hiccoughing, he led Tara through a normal door into a normal office—meaning one whose walls didn't change every five minutes. A huge desk littered with papers filled half the room, a powerful computer stood off to one side, and two very uncomfortable-looking chairs faced an executive armchair worthy of a multinational corporate CEO.

The wizard waved her to one chair and took the other. But after squirming for a moment, he roared between two hiccups: "Lady Kalibris! *hic!* We aren't a pair of kitchen scullions being reprimanded *hic!* Give us some decent chairs, by Demiderus! *hic!*"

"Oops, I'm so sorry, I was practicing!" spoke a voice. "The more uncomfortable the chair, the more ill at ease the guilty party feels. Of course it's different for you."

A second voice chimed in: "By Transformus new chairs quickly, please, so my guests can recline at their ease."

Tara felt something moving beneath her, and she suddenly sank into a soft easy chair.

Lady Kalibris appeared, and to Tara's amazement she saw one body, two legs, two arms, and—she gasped—two heads!

The heads leaned close, observing her carefully.

"So this is the—" said the first head.

"— famous Tara'tylanhnem Duncan," said the second.

"Welcome, dear."

"We're pleased to meet you."

"We are Lady Kalibris. I am Dana Kalibris," said the first head.

"And I am Clara Kalibris," said the second.

"Did you have—"

"—a good trip?"

"Yes, thank you. Lady . . . ladies," stammered the fascinated girl.

"She is very—"

"—well mannered. Isabella has—"

"—done a good job, I see."

"Tell us, dear Chem, what exactly—"

"—happened? Our informa—"

"Chem? Chem?"

Talking at once and interrupting each other, the two heads spoke to the old wizard, who was turning an alarming color. He gave an even bigger hiccup, and Lady Kalibris barely had time to pull Tara and Manitou to safety.

After a hiccup stronger than the ones before, Master Chem started to swell. Under Tara's horrified eyes, he grew and grew. His face changed, lengthened, and grew monstrous fangs. His arms and legs stretched. Blue and silver scales appeared on his body. A sharp crest rose on his back, ripping his robe. Claws the size of swords sprouted from his fingers. His enormous wings began to beat, blowing papers everywhere.

In the old wizard's place now stood a terrifying dragon, and Tara and Manitou couldn't repress moans of fear.

"Ouch!" howled the monster when it banged its head on the ceiling and brought several chunks of stone crashing down.

"Tara? Lady Kalibris? Where did you go?" rumbled the dragon, in a voice so low that the walls shook.

Tara almost burst into tears. Enemies had obviously cast a spell on the wizard, and now he was going to devour them all! Manitou was trying desperately to squeeze even farther beneath the furniture.

Then Lady Kalibris came out from under her desk, and both her heads bravely confronted the dragon.

"You should be—"

"—ashamed of yourself!"

"Shape-shifting right here in our office—"

"—and trampling half our papers!"

"So change yourself back—"

"—and make it snappy!"

The dragon looked sheepish.

"I'm terribly sorry," he rumbled. "You know that happens to me when I get the hiccups."

"Yes, we know!"

"But didn't Shaman Night Bird gave you some medicine—"

"—to control that?"

The dragon hung its head.

"I hate the taste of that stuff! It's yucky!"

"Well, that may be reason enough for you, but—"

"—it doesn't cut it with us!"

"All right, all right, I'll start taking it. Stand back, and I'll change. 'By Alakazam transform this state, from my dragon to my human shape.'"

Within seconds, the dragon began to shrink, losing fangs and claws, wings and scales. The old wizard appeared in its place and quickly snatched a robe that materialized and wrapped it around himself.

Tara suddenly realized that she had stopped breathing some time ago. She took a deep breath, wondering how many more shocks her nervous system could stand.

Lady Kalibris seemed satisfied.

"Very well then—"

"—as we were saying, we don't exactly know—"

"—everything that happened back on Earth."

Chem cast a spell, and the two armchairs he had flattened popped back to their previous shapes. He sat down in one and gazed kindly at Tara, who cautiously remained huddled behind the desk.

"Come here, Tara," he ordered gently, ignoring Lady Kalibris for the time being. "I'm not going to eat you!"

"I'm not so sure about that," she said in a trembling voice. "After all, you just changed into a dragon!"

"No, I didn't."

"What do you mean you didn't?"

"I changed *back* into a human. A dragon is what I am."

All things considered, Tara felt that behind the desk was a fine place to be. Solid. Massive. No reason to leave it—ever—because the wizard had obviously blown a major gasket.

"Okay, sure," she said sarcastically. "You're a dragon and you turn into a human. And everybody knows all about it."

"You don't seem to believe me," he said. "I can show you, if you like!"

"*Nooooo!*" three voices shouted at once, and their cry rent the air.

"If you say you're a dragon, fine—you're a dragon," said Tara very quickly. "I have *no* problem with that."

"Then come out from behind that desk and sit down. And reassure Manitou. I don't eat children, and I don't eat old spellbinders who've turned themselves into pooches."

Tara cautiously walked to the armchair, while giving Manitou a look of regret. The dog was no fool, though, and absolutely refused to come out.

Chem looked at the girl perched at the very edge of her chair, ready to flee at any moment, and sighed.

"I have been the head of the High Council of Wizards for hundreds of years," he said. "I have trained generations of wizards and spellbinders to master their magic. You humans have gifts that we find fascinating. And we dragons live so long! Do you know what our worst enemy is?"

"Hunger?"

"Insanity," he said. "We risk going insane. Those who do, rampage like a plague through other peoples' worlds, destroying everything in their path, until they are killed like mad dogs. And since we're somewhat bigger than dogs that can take several years. When we roamed the Earth, some of those crazy dragons decimated entire human peoples. They are the main reason that you invented armor, and especially spears. It's the only weapon that can bring down a mad dragon."

Tara gulped, feeling very ill at ease. How did one know when a dragon had gone nuts? When it bit off an arm or two? It was just another thing for her to worry about.

The dragon wizard continued: "To avoid that kind of . . . problem, we take special pains not to sink into madness."

"And what if you fail?" asked Tara, now engrossed in the story.

The answer was heavy and implacable: "We die."

"But that's not about to—"

"—happen here!" said Dana and Clara, who had started picking up their papers.

"Because this is—"

"—a real madhouse—"

"—in the true sense of the word!"

"You're right," said the wizard with a smile. "Here, the humans are the crazy ones. But let's talk about our little Tara. She was revealed at . . . how old were you when you first used your gift?"

"I was nine."

Chem gave her a surprised look, but made no comment.

"Oh, really? Very well. Her grandmother Isabella was attacked by a— sorry, by *two* Bloodgraves, including their famous leader, Magister, the source of all our problems. Tara behaved admirably. Not only did she manage to escape, but she redirected a kind of new ray that can both petrify and carbonize back at the Bloodgrave who fired it. Finally, her familiar isn't really a familiar, but her great-grandfather who has come along to protect her."

"What an—"

"—incredible story!"

"I can give you further details later. For the moment the only thing we know for sure is that the Bloodgraves would give a lot to capture her. So I took her with me while Isabella puts the necessary precautions in place. It was the best I could come up with."

"Well, that's obviously—"

"—the right tack to take. Those—"

"—idiots wouldn't try anything here!"

"They're all mouth—"

"—and no trousers!"

"Ladies, please!" the wizard interrupted. "Can we register the girl for her accreditation under the name she has chosen for herself, Tara Duncan?"

"Tara, short for Tara'tylanhnem? That's—"

"—sensible, very sensible. We like the name."

The data was entered into the computer, which didn't operate quite like most computers. Lady Kalibris simply sat down in front of it, and Clara said, "Computer!"

To Tara's surprise, the computer turned itself on and spoke.

"Yes, my lady?"

"Human spellbinder registration," stated Dana. "Name: Duncan. D-u-n-c-a-n. First name: Tara. Age: twelve. Section: Unicorn South Wing."

"Data entered. Paying visitor or invited guest?"

"Guest of the High Council," said Chem. "Isabella also gave me some pocket money for Tara for these few days. She'll have fifty gold immuta-credits to spend."

"Data entered. Familiar?"

"Black Labrador. Name: Manitou. M-a-n-i-t-o-u."

"Accreditation?"

"Level 6, blue, black, yellow zones. Green and red zones forbidden."

"Registration complete."

The computer ejected two shiny, transparent rectangles.

"This is your accreditation," said Lady Kalibris to Tara. "Hold out your hand, please."

Somewhat cautiously, Tara reached to take the card, but Lady Kalibris seized her wrist and recited: "By the Fixus, may this accreditation within our walls give authorization."

Tara felt a kind of tingling at her wrist and was astonished to see that the accreditation card was now under her skin! When she rubbed it she felt only her skin, yet she could see the card clearly. She was also surprised to see that it had a photograph of her. The accreditation card also displayed a handsome white unicorn beneath a silver crescent moon.

Lade Kalibris did the same with Manitou's front right paw.

"There you go," said Clara with a smile. "This way you can't—"

"—lose it. Everybody in the Castle must carry an accredi-card. The moon and unicorn is the emblem of Lancovit. Anyone can go through doors, but you can't go through walls without an accredi-card. And if your card expires—"

"—you're trapped, because the walls will close in on you."

"You have the right to go everywhere except the red and green zones."

"Those are reserved for the royal family, the high wizards, the commander of the Royal Guard, and the Royal Treasurer. On your night table you will find—"

"—a book explaining life in the Castle: schedules for breakfast, lunch, afternoon tea, and dinner; the infirmary; the armory; and in particular the—"

"—rules of etiquette. Caliban will—"

"—take you to your room. Be careful—"

"—not to say anything about your adventures on Earth. Caliban should—"

"—be here any minute. Enjoy your vacation with us!"

The two heads had just finished saying this when a boy with a shock of black hair burst in, out of breath. (Didn't spellbinders ever comb their hair? Tara wondered.) He was followed by his familiar, a handsome red fox named Blondin. The boy's gray eyes widened to see the disorder in the room, then lit on Tara.

"Hi!" he said with a big grin. "I'm Caliban, but you can call me Cal!"

"Hello," she said, a little intimidated by the boy's energy. "My name's Tara'tylanhnem, but I prefer Tara."

"Yeah, I can see why," he said, his grin widening. "You sent for me, Lady Kalibris?"

"Tara is the guest of Master Chemnashaovirodaintrachivu. She will be in the South Wing, Unicorn Section guest quarters. Can you show her to her room?"

"No problem. I'm in the South Wing too, right next door. C'mon! Don't you have any bags?"

"They'll be along later," said the wizard. "Before you go, Tara, I want you to make a note of my crystal number. You never know when you may need it."

At Chem's command, a small piece of paper with glowing numbers floated into her hand.

"Please memorize it," he said. (From Cal's wide-eyed look, it was clearly unusual to be given a high wizard's private number.) "Have fun, Tara. I'll see you soon."

"Goodbye, Master Chem," she said, bowing politely. "Goodbye, Lady Kalibris."

Tara and Cal went out, followed by Manitou, who cautiously gave the dragon wizard a wide berth.

"The high wizard's private crystal number, eh? That's the first time I've ever seen it handed out like that," said Cal, not expecting an answer. Once out of the office, he asked, "So, what did you think of Lady One-Too-Many?"

Tara giggled. "The administrator? How is it that she has two heads?"

"She's a tatris. Her species has two brains in one body, which makes things complicated when they disagree. So you're the high wizard's guest, eh? Are your parents here too?"

Tara hesitated for a moment then said simply, "No. They're both dead."

The boy stopped short in the middle of the hallway, almost tripping a courtier wearing a yellow jerkin covered with purple feathers and green fur-trimmed slippers, who glared at them.

"I'm really sorry. My tongue works a little too fast sometimes."

"That's okay. You couldn't have known. My grandmother Isabella raised me all alone but she didn't want me to be a spellbinder. I found out about that just recently."

"Oooh, so you don't know anything about Travia or OtherWorld?"

"I don't know anything about *anything*!"

A wide smile lit up Cal's face.

"That's great! Finally someone who won't put on airs and parade her knowledge. I think you and I are gonna be pals, Tara."

Tara wanted nothing more than that, but right now she had a specific question in mind, and Cal seemed very well informed.

"What's a blood oath?"

He looked at her curiously.

"A blood oath—wow! Do you know any warriors?"

"Eh, no," she said, intrigued. "Why?"

"A blood oath is sworn during battle, when two warriors are hurt by the same enemy. If one is dying, the other will swear on their mixed blood to seek revenge or do anything else the dying person asks."

"I see," said Tara thoughtfully. "So if one of the warriors made the other swear that his son or daughter would never become a wizard—because that's what got him killed, say—what happens if the oath is broken?"

"The person who swore the blood oath dies."

She took a deep breath. Isabella had sworn a blood oath, which meant that if she, Tara, used her power, she might kill her grandmother! Well, given what she had suffered because of magic these last few days that was not going to be a problem. It was hardly likely that she would want to use her powers ever again.

"Hm, thanks. And do you know something called the Gray Fortress?"

The boy thought for a moment, then shook his head. "No, I don't. What is it?"

"Oh, nothing. Just something I heard about."

Tara hoped that Cal would know the place where her mother was held prisoner, and was disappointed.

Suddenly she felt an odd sensation, a kind of tickling between her shoulder blades, as if somebody were staring at her back. She spun around and glimpsed a fleeting movement and a flash of gray cloth.

To Cal's surprise, she raced off in that direction, but when she reached an intersection of two hallways, nobody was there.

"Hey, what's going on?" asked Cal, who had followed her.

"Nothing," said Tara, frowning. "Tell me: these robes and tunics, you know, the things people wear here, what color are they?"

"We don't wear any particular color, except for the high wizards. In Jaffar they wear red, green in Brandis, purple and gold in Omois, and blue here, because the Castle colors are silver and blue. Why?"

"Just curious. So nobody wears dark gray?"

It was now Cal's turn to frown.

"Only Bloodgraves wear that color. That's why they're also called the gray spellbinders. There's no rule against it, but people avoid dressing like them."

Tara took a deep breath. "Yeah, that's what I figured."

"Am I going to get an explanation?"

Tara flashed him a bright smile and said, "I forgot to tell Master Chem something. Will you excuse me for a moment?"

A very curious Cal peered at her, but agreed.

"Go ahead; I'll wait for you here."

Tara sprinted back to Lady Kalibris' office but found it empty.

Darn! she thought. Couldn't these spellbinders stay put for just a moment?

She went back to where Cal was waiting.

"Master Chem wasn't there. Any idea where he might be?"

"Well, in his office, I guess."

"Oh yeah, right! I should've realized he'd have an *office*. Since he's a dragon, I stupidly assumed it would be a cave or a cavern. Do you know the Castle well?"

Cal's shoulders slumped.

"Inside and out, believe me," he said gloomily. "I've been Master Sardoin's apprentice for the last two years. He specializes in magical mathematics and spatial localization, so he's had me materialize and dematerialize at least a thousand times in every corner of the Castle, supposedly because I must always know where I'm landing. Except for forbidden zones I know it like the back of my hand."

"Great then, let's go. You can show me the way."

The first time Tara passed through a wall, it left her feeling creepy for a good ten minutes. Cal showed her how to spot passages, which were marked with the Lancovit moon and unicorn symbol. You waved your accredi-card, the unicorn let you pass, and the wall melted away. You could also use a regular door, of course, but there were many more passages than doors.

When they reached the wall outside Chem's office, Tara noticed it was marked by a tiny unicorn statue but also by the wizard's personal symbol, a dragon. Each statue stood in a little niche. Tara, who didn't know quite how to proceed, knocked timidly on the wall. She was startled when both the unicorn and the dragon came to life.

"Who goes there?" roared the guardian dragon.

"It's a girl, can't you see?" snapped the unicorn. "What do you want, my child?"

"Er, my name is Tara Duncan and I want to see Master Chem as soon as possible."

"I'll tell him," grumbled the dragon. "And you"—to the unicorn—"don't open the passage until you get my order."

"Yeah, yeah, sure," said the unicorn, rolling its eyes.

Tara was so fascinated by this that she didn't immediately notice the return of the dragon, who looked surprised.

"The high wizard will receive you right away. You may enter."

"Go ahead, Tara. I'll wait for you out here," said Cal, who didn't want to seem indiscreet.

She gritted her teeth and walked into the wall, which politely gave way. Whew! She was through, but good grief! How much she preferred the good old-fashioned doors on Earth.

Tara was amused to see that for Master Chem's office, the Living Castle had created a cave landscape with stalagmites and stalactites. A large heap of gold coins and precious stones stood where the old wizard probably rested between meetings.

A noise made her glance up, and she backed away when she saw that Chem had reverted to his dragon shape. He stood twenty feet tall and was smiling at her with his sharp teeth. Like all dragons, he was exceedingly fond of gold and jewels. With the wave of a claw, he made his treasure disappear.

"So little Tara, to what do I owe the pleasure of your visit?" He seemed relieved to see that Tara had no interest in his gold.

Tara decided to get down to brass tacks instead.

"There's a Bloodgrave in the Castle!" she said.

CHAPTER 5

APPRENTICE SPELLBINDERS

"Ouch!" roared the dragon, who had banged his head in surprise. "What did you say?"

"I said there's a Bloodgrave in the Castle. I just glimpsed part of his gray robe."

"What?" Chem roared again, making the walls shake. "In the Royal Travia Castle? In my domain? Do you mean to say that those sawed-off runts in gray nightshirts dare to challenge me on my home ground? *I will track them down, I will find them, I will break them, and I will eat their hearts! This is war!*"

Tara decided not to argue with him, not at all.

"Right—war. No problem. But it would be nice if you could stop yelling," she added politely, pulling her fingers from her ears. "So while we're waiting for the festivities—destroying, crushing, eating their hearts, and so forth—what can I do to help?"

"Nothing," said the dragon. "Just keep me informed of anything that strikes you as unusual or strange. And if you ever see that twerp in gray rags again, let me know right away."

Tara shrugged helplessly. The old wizard was asking a lot, since *everything* in this world seemed unusual and strange to her.

"I don't know why a Bloodgrave would walk around the Castle in a gray robe," she remarked. "Wouldn't that be the best way to get caught?"

"He's defying me," rumbled the dragon, also shrugging his shoulders, which fanned a small tornado, since the shoulders in question were attached to twenty-foot wings. "The Bloodgraves are among us, and we have no way of knowing which of us has joined their alliance. He also wants to frighten you. Let you know that he's here, watching you."

Tara shivered. In regards to her that was a complete success. She *was* frightened.

"But isn't it possible to recognize them? From their size or their build?"

The dragon sighed, barely containing a blast of fire so as not to burn Tara to a crisp.

"You don't understand, I see," he said. "By Alakazam transform this state, from my dragon to my human shape."

Tara turned pale. Standing in front of her instead of the dragon was a powerful Bloodgrave, the dark gray of his robe stretched across broad shoulders. He was taller than the old wizard, and a mirror mask hid his face.

Before she could scream, the Bloodgrave waved his hand and the mask disappeared, revealing Master Chem's face—but looking thirty years younger! Even his voice was different. His hair was no longer white but brown, and his eyes were green instead of gold.

"The reason we can't identify the Bloodgraves is that they could be any one of us," he explained. "With magic we can change our bodies and our appearance, and fool people. You see?"

Still rigid with fear, Tara nodded. Satisfied, Chem reverted to his dragon shape. Tara briefly wondered which she was more afraid of, the enormous dragon or the Bloodgrave. Right now it was about even.

"If the Bloodgraves wear gray, what would their base be called?" she asked. "You know, like their headquarters?"

"No idea," rumbled the dragon. "And believe me, if I knew I would have destroyed them a long time ago."

So Master Chem didn't know about the Gray Fortress either. Tara would apparently have to find it by herself.

With the old wizard's warning of caution ringing in her ears, Tara rejoined Cal, who led her to her room.

"So, did you get to talk to Chem?" he asked, struggling to contain his curiosity.

"Yeah, I did," said Tara laconically. "Hey, this Castle of yours is huge! Is my room still far?"

"All right," said Cal, who caught on fast. "I can tell you don't want to answer, so I won't ask any questions—at least not now. Here we are! If her ladyship would be so kind . . . "

When the wall opened before Tara, she saw a comfortable lounge with large windows, sofas and armchairs, and little round coffee tables. To her delight, there was also a soda fountain and *two* fireplaces! Despite the summer heat, the Living Castle had given the room a winter landscape of snow and pine trees that made you feel like snuggling close to the fire. It crackled and smelled pleasantly of smoke, even though it didn't exist.

There were stairs at each end of the room. One led up to the Unicorn dormitory, the other to the Phoenix dormitory.

"This is our common room, where we hang out," said Cal. "Your room is over in the Unicorn dormitory. Come on."

Tara was surprised. "Don't you have individual rooms?"

"We're just apprentices, wizards' assistants," he said gloomily. "In other words, we're on-call drudges. We only get our own rooms when we reach the next level and become wizards. The higher your level, the bigger your room. Master Chem's is especially big because he reverts to his natural shape when he sleeps."

"You mean his dragon shape?"

"Right. Which annoys One-Too-Many, because he sleeps in the middle of his flammable old scrolls. She claims he snores and is gonna set the Castle on fire someday."

He paused in front of a wall.

"Okay, show your accredi-card and tell the Castle that you're inviting me in. Otherwise I'll be trapped. I'm not allowed into a girl's room without her permission."

Tara did so, and they entered.

The room was fairly small and almost entirely filled with a canopy bed with blue velvet curtains, and a wardrobe made of a wood Tara had never seen before: it was pink with turquoise grain. The furniture rested on a thick carpet of blue grass and a sprinkling of little white flowers. She could see gently rolling hills in the distance.

"The Castle likes you," said Cal with satisfaction. "This is Mentalir, the unicorn country. You should see a herd of them any moment now."

In fact, some young unicorns came to prance around the bed a few moments later. Though delighted, Tara resisted the urge to stroke their velvety muzzles, knowing that she would only touch a stone wall.

"You're in luck," said Cal with a chuckle. "The Castle once got angry at a count from the Marches of the East—that's between Gandis, the land of giants, and Hymlia, the land of dwarves. He was very arrogant and had insulted the queen. So the Castle produced the most nightmarish landscapes on the planet. After sleeping amid snakes, spiders, scorpions, and all of OtherWorld's monsters, the count gave up and left after three days!"

Tara, who didn't like bugs, shivered. She wouldn't have lasted ten minutes!

A thick, leather-bound book lay on Tara's marble night table. The gilt lettering announced quite a program: *On the Etiquette, Mores, Customs, Laws, and Obligations of the Royal Castle.*

"Now you have to introduce yourself," said Cal.

"Introduce myself? To whom?"

"To your bed, of course."

Tara stared at the canopy bed and figured Cal was pulling her leg. But he looked perfectly serious.

"Oh, I'm sorry," he said with a grin. "I keep forgetting that you don't know OtherWorld. Just stand in front of the bed and say your name. From then on it will recognize you. You'll be the only person who can get into it, except for the administrator and the steward.

Unless you invite somebody in, of course. You do the same thing for your wardrobe."

She walked over to the bed and said, "Tara Duncan!"

The curtains parted with a silky rustle, revealing a fluffy duvet and fresh sheets.

"The bed curtains are kept drawn at night, because we can't always control our power when we're asleep," explained Cal. "To keep us from flying around the Castle, we sleep in canopy beds with the curtains closed. When you're more advanced, you can get a bed without curtains, but I know lots of kids who pretend not to control themselves so as to sleep in them longer! Come on, I'll show you the bathroom."

The Living Castle had decorated the spacious white-tiled bathroom with a calm lake and a beautiful water sprite, who sang as she combed her long green hair.

A noise brought them back out to the bedroom. Tara's suitcases had arrived. They floated in one after the other and landed near the bed.

"Perfect," said Cal, rubbing his hands. "Let's see if I get it right this time. Go stand over by the wardrobe and say your name."

Somewhat cautiously, Tara did so.

The wardrobe responded by opening its two doors and its three drawers.

Cal stood in front of it and spoke: "By Putawayus, this I say: I want these clothes put away!"

He clapped his hands, and a whirlwind of clothes burst out of Tara's suitcases and went to neatly put themselves away in the wardrobe. Within seconds it was full, and it closed its doors and drawers.

"Hey, that's too cool!" said Tara admiringly. What was it that you said, exactly? 'By Putawayus, this I say: I want these clothes put away!'"

At those words, the wardrobe practically exploded. The doors flew open and the clothes violently shot out just as a group of girls entered the room. A bathrobe draped itself around the leader's head, blinding her and producing a series of frightened yelps.

Terribly embarrassed, Tara rushed over, blurting apologies. The girl, a brunette taller and older than Tara, was furious to have shown how scared she'd been. She looked Tara up and down, dark eyes glittering with hostility.

"You little twit!" she hissed. "Are you out of your gourd, firing your duds around like that? I'm telling Lady Kalibris about this, and you'll see!"

"I'm terribly sorry," said Tara. "I didn't do it on purpose. I apologize."

"Get out of my way!"

Tara, who didn't dare use magic to put her things away, started picking them up, under the other girls' mocking looks.

When the tall girl saw that Tara was settling into the room, she yelled, "You! Come here!"

"Me?"

"Yes, I mean you, you little idiot! I want this room, so beat it, or there'll be trouble!"

"Oh, cut it out, Angelica," said Cal, planting himself in front of her. "You know perfectly well that she isn't going to leave."

"And what the heck are you doing in the Unicorn wing, Cal?" she answered, eyes narrowed. "You aren't allowed in here!"

"Oh, yes I am," he said. "I have a perfect right to be here. Administrator Kalibris and High Wizard Chemnashaovirodaintrachivu both asked me to bring Tara here and help her get settled. You're just an apprentice spellbinder, Angelica, so you sleep in the dormitory like the rest of us. You're the one who ought to beat it."

Tara saw Angelica tighten her fists in fury and for a moment thought she was going to attack Cal. But the tall girl got a grip on herself.

"You'll get what's coming to you one of these days, you garden dwarf! Come on, girls, we'll let these two idiots pick up their rags. Meanwhile, let's go see my master and tell him what kind of pinheads I'm getting for neighbors. He'll give me this room!"

With a last venomous glare, Angelica stormed out, followed by her little entourage.

"Whew! I was afraid she was gonna punch me."

"Me too," said Tara, still shaken by the encounter. "Who is she?"

"She's High Wizard Brandaud's daughter—daddy's little sweetheart. She thinks she knows everything, even though her magic gift developed late, and she lords it over everyone. A real pain in the butt. She's sixteen and is apprenticed to Master Dragosh, the most powerful spellbinder after Master Chem. Angelica got scared when your clothes attacked her. She didn't expect it."

"That makes two of us! What happened, exactly? Why did my clothes pop out again? They'd been put away properly."

Cal looked at her with respect.

"You reactivated the putting-away spell. Specifically, you ordered your clothes to put themselves away *again*, as if you were going to pack your suitcase. But you didn't specify where you wanted them to go, so they just zoomed about everywhere."

Tara started feeling panicky.

"Are you saying that when I recite a magic formula, it works right away? That's awful!"

"Are you kidding? It's terrific! We can do lots of things with this gift of yours! Usually it's a heck of a job to get a spell to work. You have to make a real effort of will to succeed. With you, it's, like, instinctive. Listen, sweetie, you can't tell anybody about this!"

"*Sweetie?* Don't you *ever* call me that again, understand? Anyway, I can't use magic; it's forbidden!"

"Ah-ha!" said Cal, his eyes bright. "I get it! That business about the blood oath applies to you, doesn't it?"

"Yes," she admitted reluctantly. "If I use magic, my grandmother will die. So be very careful when you do magic when I'm around."

Cal thoughtfully chewed on his lip.

"But blood oaths aren't absolute, Tara. They depend on who swears them, and especially on the context. Have you ever used magic in your grandmother's presence?"

"Yes."

"Did she keel over dead?"

"No."

"Then the conditions must be very specific. Come to the library with me, and I'll give you a book on the subject."

Ah, the library—excellent. It would certainly have maps and atlases. An ideal place to research the Gray Fortress.

"How long are you staying here?" Cal asked.

"About ten days."

"Then don't worry."

"All right, but first . . . "

"What?"

"First help me put my things away."

The two did the job quickly. Just as they were finishing, they heard a bell.

"Great!" cried Cal. "It's lunchtime. C'mon!"

Grabbing Tara's hand, and waving his accredi-card at every wall in his path, Cal dragged her to a large dining hall. She was relieved to see that it wasn't where the king and queen and their court ate. Instead it was for the guards, stable hands, gardeners, spellbinders, low-ranking courtiers, washerwomen, and tailors—in a word, all the people who helped run the Castle under Lady Kalibris's direction.

Tara grinned when Deria, who was deep in conversation with a handsome guard, winked at her. Knowing she had an ally in the place made her feel much better.

In a corner of the room, bowls of various shapes and sizes had been set out for the familiars, and Manitou and Blondin promptly ditched their young masters and ran over to them.

Lady Kalibris called for silence.

"Good afternoon, ladies, gentlemen, and spellbinders. I have the pleasure of introducing our new mages and apprentices. Master Den'maril has finally chosen an apprentice, Robin M'angil. This means he will no longer be bothering you at the drop of a hat, since Robin will be running all his errands." She pointed, and a tall, fine-featured boy with light eyes and hair stood up, blushed at the laughter that greeted him, and quickly sat back down again.

"We also have a new weather wizard. From now on, if you hang your sheets out to dry and it rains, you can blame Lady Deria."

Deria stood and waved with her inimitable grace while shooting a chilly glance at Kalibris, whose humor she didn't enjoy.

"So much for the wizards and apprentices. Now for the other professions . . ."

Tara was listening to what Lady Kalibris was saying when a boy plopped himself down next to her, jostling Cal.

"Tara? Is that you?" the boy exclaimed in astonishment.

"Fabrice!" she whispered in delight. "I was right; you really are here!"

"You two know each other?" asked a surprised Cal.

"We sure do," said Fabrice. "Tara, I can't tell you how happy I am. When my father sent me to OtherWorld, I almost spilled the beans to him about your gift. But since you're here, you must've finally told your grandmother everything, right?"

"Well, more or less," she stammered, pained at having to hide the truth from her best friend.

Cal, who wasn't especially interested in their meeting, was getting restless.

"I wish she'd hurry up," he groused, as the administrator went on with her announcements. "I'm hungry!"

As if she'd heard, Lady Kalibris's two heads nodded and announced that lunch was served. Tara expected that the food would appear by magic, but instead an army of young pages and squires ran in carrying roast meats, grilled fowl, thick, spicy soups, vegetables dripping with melted butter, huge wheels of cheese, pastries, and mounds of candy and chocolate.

"Bon appétit, my friends," Lady Kalibris said with a smile—two smiles, actually.

She recited a spell, and a slice of meat floated obediently onto her plate, where her silverware began cutting it up.

Cal had already piled three slices on his plate and was eating as fast as he could. As soon as a dish came within reach, he grabbed a couple of helpings of everything (except vegetables). Tara and Fabrice laughed to see their friend stuffing himself as if he hadn't eaten for days.

Tara battled with her cutlery, which insisted on feeding her like a baby. She was finally able to seize the fork and eat on her own, though the utensil quivered with indignation in her hand.

She asked Fabrice to tell her how he got to OtherWorld, and he was happy to oblige. He, too, had been surprised by Lady One-Too-Many, but not by the Cyclops steward, whom his father had told him about. And he didn't like the chimera. All told, Fabrice was enchanted by magic and was eager to start working with the wizard he would be assisting, Master Chanfrein.

Then it was Cal's turn. He said he was the youngest of five children who were all spellbinders, like their parents. And he was in no hurry at all to start his service with Master Sardoin.

"I don't get it," he complained. "After all, my mother is the best of the licensed thieves, and I'm already a very good thief myself. So why should I have to work for a high wizard?"

Tara couldn't believe her ears. "You're a *what*?"

"I'm a thief. Well, I will be when I'm a little older."

"What do you mean by 'thief'?" asked a surprised Fabrice.

"Er, someone who steals things."

"I know what a thief is," snapped Fabrice. "But on our planet we don't usually boast about it. It's not a very admirable profession. On Earth, people who steal go to jail!"

"Oh, you mean *that* kind of thief!" exclaimed Cal. "No, no! We're one of the robber clans. We work for the Lancovit government."

Now Tara was completely lost. "What would the government want with a bunch of thieves?"

"Ah, but not just any thieves! We're *licensed* thieves. We only carry out very specific missions. Suppose a wizard comes up with a very dangerous formula, and a kingdom or empire decides that the formula will help it conquer its neighbors."

"All right, so what?"

"The Lancovit government would call on my family to steal the formula. We then give it to the other countries. That way everybody has it, and balance is restored."

"Okay, I get it," said Fabrice. "And your mother is a licensed thief, a sort of female James Bond. Is that it?"

"James Bond 007—your movie spy? No, he isn't nearly good enough. My mother could steal his socks and his underwear while they were dancing and he wouldn't realize it until he went to bed!"

Though he admired 007, Fabrice decided to let that one pass.

"But why do you say that you're also a thief?"

"I will be one," Cal answered proudly, "when I finish my training."

"Your training?" Fabrice was impressed now. "What kind of training?"

"Want a demonstration?"

"If you don't mind, sure!" he said, sounding skeptical.

"I don't mind at all," said Cal with a shrug. "After all, you'll be my victim."

Just then, Cal's fox Blondin, who had been quietly eating at the other end of the room, decided to cut loose. He jumped up on one of the tables, provoking shrieks from the women and curses from the men.

Fabrice turned back to Cal and said, "Okay, go ahead."

"I already did," he said calmly.

Under his friends' astonished eyes, Cal then proceeded to pull out three handkerchiefs embroidered with the Besois-Giron monogram, several sticks of chewing gum (one looked pretty old), a pink hair ribbon, a gold barrette, a stub of a pencil, an eraser, two coins, and a small brown notebook.

"I'm guessing that the barrette and the pink hair ribbon aren't yours," he said sarcastically.

"Wow!" exclaimed Fabrice. "No, they're Tara's."

"The old chewing gum isn't mine!" she protested, patting her pockets. "As for the rest ... that was incredible! I didn't feel a thing!"

"Neither did I!"

Cal wiggled his long, slim fingers.

"It's an exercise we learn very young. You distract people's attention somehow—I used Blondin, but it can be anything—then grab whatever you're after. It's easy!"

Impressed by Cal's technique, Tara and Fabrice peppered him with questions for the rest of the lunch, eager to learn more about the life of a licensed thief's son. They were skeptical about half of his supposed adventures—they didn't for a minute believe his battle with the winged adder, his stealing the forbidden scroll from man-eating slugs, and other memorable confrontations—but most of the stories were plausible, and they began to look at the young thief with real admiration.

From time to time, Tara could feel Angelica's icy stare on her. The tall girl had pointed her out when she entered the dining hall and had been furiously whispering to a redheaded girl next to her.

After stuffing themselves with cakes and candies, the three friends left the hall. Tara was at a loss for what to do next, but Cal quickly clued her in.

"Whatever you do, don't knock yourself out," he said. "If Master Chem says you're on vacation, then you're on vacation! If anyone wants to see you, your accredi-card will let you know."

"What do you mean?"

"The high wizards communicate with us through the cards. They might call and tell us where to meet them, for example. If nothing is going on and a wizard hasn't given us any instructions, that means they don't need us for now. Personally, I just like to laze around as much as I can, or train. Want to see the Castle grounds? They're great. Fabrice, are you on duty this afternoon?

"No, I'm free," he said with a smile. "I don't start with Master Chanfrein until tomorrow."

"Great! Let's go, then. You'll see, the grounds are wonderful."

Tara had to admit that Cal was right. Magic had colored the trees' branches and foliage, so red trunks and blue and yellow canopies stood out against pink and black flowers visited by birds of so many colors they looked like flying rainbows.

While chatting with her new friends, Tara gazed around at the strange flora and fauna. She suddenly saw a little red mouse with two tails being chased by an orange cat with big green ears. At least that's not so different from Earth, she thought; cats chase mice here too. But then, just when the mouse seemed trapped, it gave an odd little twitch, and vanished. An instant later, the cat vanished as well. Then the mouse reappeared a few feet farther on—right in front of the cat, which had anticipated the move and reappeared in front of it. Furious, the little mouse nipped the cat's nose and ran into a hole under a tree. The frustrated cat climbed up to a branch to watch the hole.

Another of OtherWorld's peculiarities, Tara sighed. Even the animals here use magic. Perfect. I'm not about to go outside alone, she decided.

Cal took the kids on a walk through some of the quiet, dense forest surrounding the Castle. But the grounds were so extensive that they could see only part of them.

OtherWorld had seven seasons, he explained, and a year lasted fourteen months. Magic tended to change the climate very violently, and you never knew if a day would bring 100 degrees in the shade, or ten feet of snow. As a result, OtherWorld's plants and animals were highly adaptable. Animals could grow fur in a single night, or change color from brown, green, blue, or red to pure white after a snowstorm. And the snow itself wasn't always white. In the mountains of Hymlia it had a reddish tint because of the presence of magic iron, a mineral mined by the dwarves. So in snowy weather the animals there ran the gamut from carmine to crimson.

None of the high wizards summoned the spellbinders. Cal was delighted to lounge around at his ease, and Tara and Fabrice took in the marvels of life on OtherWorld.

For his part, Fabrice tried out the riddles he'd been creating.

"My first is a lonely number, my second is its neighbor, my third is a collection of males, my last is the fifth letter of the alphabet. The answer is someone who runs the place."

"That's clever, but I've got it," said Cal. "*One + two + men + E =
one too many* = One-Too-Many, our two-headed Lady Kalibris."

"Okay, try this one," said Fabrice. "My first is a kind of grain
used to make flour, my second is a negative reply, my third is short
for mister, and my fourth is who we are. The answer is the word for
an animal found on Earth."

"I know!" Tara exclaimed. "*Rye* is a kind of grain, a negative
reply is *no*, *sir* is short for mister, and who we are is *us*. *Rye + no +
sir + us* = rhinoceros!"

"Hey, that's not fair!" protested Cal. "I don't know all the animals
on your planet."

"I see I'm dealing with connoisseurs," said Fabrice with a grin.
"Just you wait; I'll come up with something more complicated!"

They spent the afternoon walking and talking until dinner,
which was as lavish as lunch.

When Tara got back to her room after saying goodnight to the
two boys, she noticed that the wall to the Unicorn dormitory was
open. Apparently Angelica still hadn't gotten a room of her own,
and the girls were gathered around the bed from which she presided.

As Tara passed, the tall girl looked up and glowered at her.

Teeth brushed, Tara dove under her cozy duvet to read. First she
memorized Chem's crystal number, then she leafed through the
etiquette book. She learned that she wasn't allowed to dig holes in
the Castle (which didn't want to look like Swiss cheese) or eat the
walls (no chance of that; she was probably allergic to Maliciosa, the
Castle's magical building material). Levitation was allowed except
in the Throne Room. Weapons, magical or not, were forbidden
within the Castle walls. This included dwarf war hammers,

enchanted elf bows, and unicorn horns, which were to be left in a basket at the entrance to the Throne Room. (Unicorns could unscrew their horns? Who knew!) Creatures with non-retractable claws and fangs were asked not to make the slightest aggressive move toward their Majesties, as the Castle guards were kind of jumpy. Creatures with tentacles were to keep several yards away from the sovereigns, since most tentacles caused terrible rashes. Gnomes were not to tunnel up into the Throne Room, but were to arrive by the surface like everybody else. Imps were not allowed to play tricks ever since one accidentally changed the current king's ancestor into a pig. That king lived to a ripe old age, but no one was able to change him back, which is why one Castle portrait shows a fat, shaggy boar wearing a crown.

Running in the hallways was discouraged—it tickled the Castle—except in case of emergency, such as war, invasion, or surprise attack, magical or otherwise. This last possibility gave Tara cause for concern.

Luckily the book wasn't very thick and every line that Tara read magically imprinted itself on her mind. What a practical gizmo! She thought with annoyance about Isabella, who'd made her struggle with her grammar and math books. She was able to finish before the ten o'clock bell, when she turned out the light. The room changed the landscape around her bed to a calm, starry night with a gentle breeze, and it slowly rocked her to sleep.

Her last thought was for Angelica and her little entourage.

"I hope she snores and keeps them awake all night!"

CHAPTER 6

THE VAMPYR

Tara had barely started her breakfast with Cal and Fabrice when her accredi-card started buzzing and vibrating.

"Good morning, Tara," came a voice from the photo of Master Chem that had appeared over hers.

"Er, good morning, Master," answered Tara, who found it odd to be talking to her wrist.

"Did you sleep well?"

"Yes, I did. How about you?"

"Very well, thank you. As soon as you finish your breakfast, go to your room, put on the ceremonial robe you'll find there, and meet me outside the Throne Room."

"M-me?" stammered Tara anxiously. "Why?"

Seeing the wizard's stern look, she didn't dare protest. "Okay, Master Chem."

"Very well. I'll see you soon."

"Did you hear?" she asked the two boys with a sigh. "I have to finish breakfast and then go put on some sort of fancy robe to be presented to the king and queen. But I don't want to be presented to anybody."

"Hey, it's supposed to be a great honor; you should be flattered," said Cal, amused by his friend's discomfiture. "And don't mess up. High wizards hate it when people are late, and I won't even mention Grand Chamberlain Skali. He's a real terror."

With that kind of motivation, it took Tara mere minutes to finish breakfast, slip on the blue-and-silver robe she found on her bed, and race down to the Throne Room.

There, she was able to marvel at the finest example of Lancovit architecture. Because of the sometimes imposing anatomy of the kingdom's subjects, a gently sloping ramp led from the main court-yard to the Throne Room instead of a stairway. The room's white-and-gold walls rose to a silver-trimmed blue ceiling with such airiness that it was hard to believe they were supporting tons and tons of stone. The Living Castle was discreet here, letting the room's fantastically carved walls dazzle its visitors without adding illusory landscapes.

The dwarf artisans and architects had outdone themselves, and shimmering banners representing the peoples ruled by Lancovit further enhanced the magnificence of the setting.

The Count of Peridor's kingfisher, the Duke of Drator's wolf, and the Count of Sylvain's crow faced the golden lions of Prince Marc Steel-Hand, the noble descendant of Ronveau Iron-Hand (who had grafted on a replacement for the hand he lost in the Starlings War), the Count of T'al's squirrel, and Lancovit's moon and unicorn emblem.

Long independent, the six human regions were united four hundred years earlier by Mérié Muréglise, the current king's ancestor, during the war against the trolls and the Edrakins.

Animated, enchanted tapestries recounted the exploits of Lancovit's heroes and the king's forebears. Randalf the Valiant's quest; the theft of the Great Worm's treasure and the worm's terrible revenge; the four bewitched rings of Brigandoon; the magic horn that Ronveau Iron-Hand used to call the elves for help and thereby win the Great War; the saga of beautiful, flame-haired Mariander; and Mérié's battle and the defeat of the evil Edrakin leader.

Tara was startled to see that one of the tapestries showed a story she knew well, that of Beauty and the Beast. Did that mean it had really happened? That one of the Lancovit kings had lived under such a curse?

Near the entrance to the room, Master Chem was deep in conversation with a human man whose gorgeous physique made the women of the court swoon. Next to him, the wizard looked, well, wizened.

Another high wizard, who resembled an enormous pat of butter, was clearly waiting for his apprentice; he kept turning bulging red eyes to the hallway. A third wizard, who was talking to the tall, fine-featured boy that Lady Kalibris had introduced to the assembly the day before, startled Tara when he turned around: he had glittering eyes, long white hair, and pointed ears. If that's not an elf, she said to herself, I'm a vampire bat.

When Angelica walked in with her master, Tara was surprised again. The tall girl's master was a *vampire!* He was tall and thin, and had glowing red eyes and long, black hair pulled back. His curled lips revealed two white, fang-like canines in a rictus that gave Tara the shivers.

Cal leaned close to her, and whispered, "Those are the high wizards of Lancovit. That one is Master Dragosh, a vampyr, spelled v-a-m-p-y-r; his apprentice is our beloved Angelica Brandaud. Next to him is Master Den'maril, an elf; his apprentice is Robin M'angil. Facing you is Master Sardoin, my master; as you see, he's human." Sardoin was looking at the vampyr the way a rabbit might look at a snake, afraid he would be its next meal. "Lady Kalibris, whom you've met, is a tatris; I don't know who her apprentice is. There's also Master Patin, a cahmboum, c-a-h-m-b-o-u-m. The new one over there is Lady Deria, a weather specialist. The muscle-bound human is Master Chanfrein, Fabrice's master. He's also our head trainer, and he took the aerial polo team to the championship twice in a row. Master Night Bird is a human and our shaman." Like some Native Americans, the medicine man wore his black hair in braids and dressed in buckskin. "His apprentice is Monica Gottverdam." (Pretty blue-eyed blonde, with eyes only for her master.) "There's Lady Boudiou, a human." (Gray hair, pleasingly plump, but she looked sad and gazed steadily at Tara.) "Her apprentice is Carole Genty." (The redhead Angelica was whispering to when Tara arrived.) "Over there you can see Lady Sirella; she's a mermaid." Floating in a water bubble, Sirella had blue hair and green skin, and was so beautiful it took Tara's breath away. "Her apprentice is Skyler Eterna." Good-looking and well aware of it, Skyler was eying the girls in a lordly way. "And of course you know our famous Chemna-shaovirodaintrachivu, who doesn't have an apprentice right now."

Just then, the dragon wizard rose to speak.

"Today we will be presenting our guest, young Tara'tylanhnem Duncan, Isabella Duncan's granddaughter," he said. A murmur ran through the assembled high wizards, and their attention increased. Tara gathered that her grandmother was well known on OtherWorld. "She is spending a few days' vacation with us, but must obey Lancovit Castle and OtherWorld's laws, like all its inhabitants."

Tara frowned. From what she'd read in the etiquette book, Lancovit laws didn't seem very complicated. The planet did have one big advantage over Earth, though. If you committed a crime here, you were turned over to the scary telepaths known as Truth Tellers. They had the power to read a suspect's mind, and it was impossible to hide anything from them. If the Tellers convicted you, you were taken to their icebound planet to serve out your sentence surrounded by beings who constantly monitored your thoughts. For that reason, very few crimes were committed in the kingdom, or in the rest of OtherWorld.

A sudden trumpet fanfare announced that the king and queen were approaching the Throne Room.

"I need your attention for just one last matter," said Lady Kalibris, who was letting one of her heads do all the talking, to save time. "We know you love your familiars, but housekeeping has complained about having to clean hair and feathers from the canopy beds. Also, Shaman Night Bird tells me he's treated a number of cases of asthma this year. So from now on your familiars will no longer be allowed to sleep in your beds."

A murmur of protest arose at this, and Kalibris made an appeasing gesture.

"However, so that you can keep them nearby, we have set up perches, kennels, nests, and all sorts of sleeping furniture in a corner of the dormitories. That way, your familiars will never be far away."

Just then, a magnificent gray panther padded into the room. The little monkey perched on Skyler Eterna's shoulder went into hysterics and the boy had a hard time calming it down.

The panther merely yawned, indifferent to the excitement it was causing. Fabrice overheard Angelica saying that the master of such a handsome familiar must be a very interesting boy.

Imagine their surprise when a slim girl with curly brown hair entered instead. She was red with embarrassment and clearly dying to be anywhere but there. Also, she stuttered.

"I-I-'m sorry I-I-I'm late," she mumbled.

Lady Boudiou, who was the nearest, reassured her.

"Don't worry, the presentation hasn't started yet. You're Lady Kalibris's apprentice, aren't you? What's your name?"

"G-g-Gloria D-d-Daavil, but I p-prefer my n-n-nickname, Sparrow."

Tara thought the nickname suited her perfectly. Angelica glared at the girl, who practically wilted, but Tara flashed her a smile—to be contrary, and also because she pitied her.

For Tara, the rest of the ceremony unfolded in a kind of fog as she struggled not to stumble, stutter, and especially not to gape at King Bear and Queen Titania.

The sovereigns were of medium height with brown hair, and looked to be in their fifties. They were dressed in beautiful, dark-blue-and-silver spellbinder robes that fell to their feet.. Their smiles were friendly.

Catching sight of Tara, the queen was startled. She'd already seen those distinctive, deep blue eyes, that sheaf of golden hair with the strange white strand, and the bright smile before—but where? Feeling curious, she asked her a few questions.

"Are your parents happy that you're here on OtherWorld as Master Chem's guest? It's a great honor, you know!"

"My parents are dead, Your Majesty," Tara said quietly.

"Oh, I'm so sorry," said the queen, pained. "I didn't know. Do you have any family? Siblings?"

"Just my grandmother, Your Majesty." (Also my great-grandfather, thought Tara, but there was no way to explain a dog to the queen!)

"You'll see, we're like a big family here," said the queen with a gentle smile. "I know you're not spending much time with us, but you'll soon start thinking of the other apprentices as your brothers and sisters." (Angelica, my sister? Not likely! Tara thought.) "Please consider the king and me as substitute parents. The happiness of our apprentices matters a great deal to us. If you need anything at all, don't hesitate to come find us. We will always be available."

"Thank you, Your Majesty," said Tara, moved by the queen's sincerity. She took a deep breath to drive away the tears that rose to her eyes.

Seated on a pillow next to the thrones was Their Majesties' First Counselor Salatar, the monstrous chimera. He abruptly jumped down to stand in front of Tara, and delicately sniffed her ceremonial robe.

"I sense power . . . and . . . danger. Is it wise to provoke the forces of evil so close to their Royal Highnesses?"

Tara was so terrified, she didn't move an inch—especially since she'd noticed tiny flames coming from the chimera's mouth. When he spoke, Salatar spat fire!

Master Chem, who was observing the presentation, quickly trotted toward the thrones. The courtiers murmured in surprise, and the queen's delighted young ladies-in-waiting whispered that this was the most interesting official presentation in years.

"Your Highnesses!" cried the old wizard, slightly out of breath. "As I said last night, our young friend here is the granddaughter of our powerful ally High Wizard Isabella Duncan, a mainstay of our earthly monitoring program. Tara Duncan is spending a few days of her vacation with us and will soon return to Earth. Your first counselor has displayed his usual subtlety in detecting the power of Tara's gift, but she represents no danger to the throne."

"Come on, Salatar, stop terrorizing the girl," ordered the king, frowning at him. "We have offered Tara our hospitality, and we are not about to take it back."

The chimera hesitated, then, with a powerful leap, returned to his cushion.

"So be it," he grumbled. "I yield to Your Majesty's demand, but I would like my disagreement be noted in the daily record."

The queen rolled her eyes and smiled kindly at Tara, who was still in shock and was having trouble even opening her mouth.

When the presentations were over and Tara could rejoin the others, Angelica shot her a nasty look. The queen had also spoken to the tall girl, but not with such warm affection. How had this little twit managed to attract powerful figures' favor so quickly? Angelica wondered.

"That chimera is more paranoid than the worst secret agent on Earth," said Master Chem with annoyance. "But if Salatar thinks you might be dangerous, I don't want you wandering around the Castle with nothing to do. I'd rather you stay with me for the time being. Do you mind?"

Tara simply nodded. She didn't mind at all. Anything was better than finding herself nose to nose with the chimera.

"Fine," said the old wizard with satisfaction. "Let's go to the daily meeting in the conference room."

The topic of the day was the Castle forest. The high wizards managed the trees, and they needed a fertilizer to restore soil depleted by the trees' incredibly rapid growth. Master Den'maril, the elf, created a mushroom that, when it rotted, would yield a fertilizer rich enough to satisfy the Growers, the spellbinders charged with the growth of the forest. (Loggers cut trees. Growers grow them.)

What most surprised Tara was the length and complexity of the creation process. The elf wizard apparently had to take into account all sorts of factors before he dared release his mushroom into nature. And here she thought magic could solve everything in the blink of an eye!

While he was working, Den'maril knocked a test tube off the table but caught the falling glass tube long before it could hit the floor. The elf smiled to see Tara's astonishment at his incredible quickness.

Master Chem had been turning the pockets of his robe inside out for a few minutes, as if he had lost something. The old wizard asked Tara if she would mind serving as his temporary assistant, assuring her that the job wouldn't involve performing any magic.

"With pleasure, Master Chem," she answered politely.

She soon realized that she had made a terrible mistake.

The problem was that the old dragon forgot *everything*. Chem's memory was so crowded with his centuries of existence that he focused only on important things. From that fateful moment on, Tara spent all her time racing to the four corners of the Castle, looking for whatever the wizard had forgotten. And good grief, how big the place was!

Delighted that the high wizard had found a new victim, the pages, grooms, and other servants grinned mockingly to see Tara sprinting along the hallways. (This tickled and annoyed the Castle, and the hallways began to quiver and undulate under the girl's feet.)

As a result, Tara had very little free time to spend in the library. And to her great disappointment, the librarian, a cahmboum, didn't know of any Gray Fortress. She did check out a few books on the Bloodgraves so as to read up about her enemies.

Fortunately, she was free after lunch, as the wizards were meeting about the war that had broken out between two factions of dwarves in the Hymlia Mountains. So Master Chem turned Tara over to Cal, who invited her to tour the Castle along with Sparrow and Fabrice.

"It's huge," he said, pointing at the Castle's imposing entrance. (Tara nodded vigorously. Huge it certainly was! They should install people movers in the hallways.) "But there are lots of secret or forgotten passages that let you go from one place to another. C'mon, I'll show you the Training Hall. We're supposed to work out there for at least an hour a day, so you may as well know where it is."

Having spent the whole morning running around, Tara didn't see the point of further exercise, but her friends were enthusiastic, so she went along. Once out of the great Council Room, they took some hallways that couldn't have been used very often. In spite of the cleaning spells, they were full of dust and spider webs, which Tara and Sparrow didn't much like.

They were about to emerge opposite the Training Hall when Cal suddenly gestured to them to quickly hide.

They could hear two voices whispering.

"And there were four more last year!"

"That was quite a haul."

"It certainly gave the high wizard trouble! The parents held him responsible."

"Well, he was! Him and that stupid policy of his."

"We're counting on you!"

"Don't worry, I know what I have to do."

"All right. See you later."

The three young spellbinders barely had time to sink back into the shadows and hold their breath before Master Dragosh passed by. Deep in thought, the vampyr didn't see them.

They looked at each other. They had just overheard a very strange conversation. Cal was wide-eyed and seemed very agitated.

"Come along," he hissed. "Let's go in."

The Training Hall consisted of a huge arena divided into sections and surrounded by bleachers for the spectators. A few courtiers were fencing, and Master Chanfrein was giving a lesson in what Tara guessed was a kind of martial art.

"Did you hear what he said?" asked Cal.

"I did," answered Fabrice. "He said, 'Dragon glides and tiger bites.'"

"No! I mean Master Dragosh, not Chanfrein!"

"Oh, sorry," said Fabrice. "He seemed very pleased about something. Do you know what he was talking about?"

"A few months ago, at the end of the year, four apprentices disappeared from the Castle. Nobody knows what happened. One evening they were there and the next morning, *poof!* no one."

"Really?" whispered Fabrice, fascinated. "So what then?"

"The high wizards cast all sorts of spells around the Castle to protect the apprentices. The secret services are apparently on high alert, but they haven't found any clues so far."

"You think they were talking about the disappearances?" asked Tara. "Why did they say it was quite a haul?"

"I have no idea, but I'm going to keep an eye on Dragosh to find out what he's hatching. And I'll let you know."

Fabrice was about to protest that he wanted to be involved as well. Before he could speak, however, he felt a presence behind him. Turning, he found Angelica looking at them thoughtfully.

The tall girl had apparently come to work out. She was wearing tights and a leotard and spent some time sparring. They noticed that when she beat her opponents, Angelica seemed to enjoy inflicting as much pain as possible. Tara decided never to confront her without a complete suit of armor, a bulletproof jacket, a sword, and maybe a few hand grenades.

They were within Angelica's hearing, so they changed the subject. Tara was interested in Sparrow.

"Why did you come in so late?" asked Cal. "You almost missed Tara's presentation."

"Yes, I know. M-m-my father is s-s-sick. He has abracadarthritis. I was d-d-dropping off s-s-some tests at the infirmary, and I didn't notice the t-t-time."

"One of my uncles got it, and he was out of commission for three weeks," he said sympathetically. "Is your father going to be okay?"

"Yes. We hired a specialist who t-t-treated him in t-t-time, though he c-c-cost us a fortune."

"What the heck is abracada— whatever you called it?" asked Tara.

"It's abracadarthritis, and it only affects spellbinders," answered Cal. "Too much magic exhausts the body, and the surplus magic lodges in the joints. The inflammation eats away at the cartilage, and you wind up unable to move. It isn't fatal, but it's dangerous and hard to cure when it's caught late. Luckily, there are treatments. The problem is that most people first think they're just stiff, or have tendinitis."

Tara, who was already sore and whose joints ached, shuddered. No question about it: magic definitely wasn't for her.

Gazing admiringly at Sparrow's panther, Fabrice asked, "So tell me, how did she choose you?"

"N-n-no idea!" she said, blushing. "I-I-I was in the g-g-garden crying, and she just appeared—*poof!* She's helped m-m-me a lot. Haven't you b-b-been chosen yet?"

"No. I don't even know how you go about it."

"You don't do anything," said Cal, affectionately stroking Blondin's reddish fur. "It's like losing your baby teeth, or growing up. It just happens."

"You're lucky," said Fabrice enviously. "How do you recognize a familiar?"

Cal explained: "They have golden eyes, that's one characteristic. And a familiar chooses you as much as you choose it. You can only have one. Some people are chosen when they're young, others older. Angelica, our national viper, is crazy worried 'cause she's sixteen and hasn't been chosen yet. You should've seen her face when Blondin chose me last year, right in the middle of the High Council meeting!"

Fabrice sighed and looked at the beautiful panther.

"May I pet her?" he asked Sparrow.

"Ask her p-p-politely, and you'll see. Her n-n-name is S-h-Sheeba."

"May I, beautiful Sheeba?"

The panther gracefully slid her head under Fabrice's hand. Stroking her, Fabrice wore an expression that was close to ecstasy.

"I have a riddle for you, lovely Sheeba, but it's tough. My first is the twelfth letter of the alphabet or a raised subway, my second is the sound of hesitating, my third is a town in Belgium, and the answer is what you are."

The three friends racked their brains, and Sheeba gave an interrogatory purr. Sparrow finally got it.

"I know!" she cried. The letter is L, so the subway must be an *el,* we say *eh* when we hesitate—b-b-believe me, I know—and the B-b-Belgian town is *Ghent. El + eh + Ghent* = elegant!"

Just then, Tara's accredi-card buzzed, and she stepped away to take Chem's call. The old wizard urgently needed a vial of Pllops drool from the deadly poisonous blue-and-white frogs that live in the Centaur plains.

When she got back to the Training Hall, Cal looked angry, and Fabrice and Sparrow were pale.

"What's going on?" she asked

"That witch Angelica told Master Dragosh that we weren't training enough, so he's decided to make us practice spells for an extra hour."

"After what we heard, do you think it could be a trick to cast a spell on us or kidnap us?" asked Fabrice worriedly.

"No. The others were abducted at night, not in daylight. And I can't imagine Dragosh kidnapping us in front of everybody. Just the same, I'll ask all the apprentices to come watch the class. That way, we'll be in numbers."

Robin and Skyler answered the call, and though they weren't invited, Angelica brought her cohorts Carole and Monica.

To be on the safe side, the Castle made the walls soft and covered the entire hall with fire-resistant blue foam. To protect the bleachers, it furnished them with big cushions.

When Master Dragosh entered the Training Hall, he was surprised to see so many people in attendance.

"Well, young spellbinders, I see that everyone feels the need to review the basics. Very well, let's begin. Miss Genty?"

He aimed a rigid index finger at the young redhead, who timidly came forward.

"Let's see what you can do. Cast a Decoratus spell on your robe, please."

"A Decoratus, Master?"

"Yes, like this." Making a circle around his robe, Dragosh cried, "By Decoratus adorn yourself, with symbols proper to myself." Brilliant, strange hieroglyphics immediately appeared on the wizard's robe.

Bravely, Carole said, "By Decoratus adorn yourself, with symbols proper to myself."

Nothing happened.

The vampyr rolled his eyes and sighed.

"It's not enough just to *say* the spell, young lady. You have to *think* it too. Show her, Angelica."

The tall girl recited the spell in an affected voice, and a complicated pattern promptly appeared in her robe.

Carole turned red and shouted, "By Decoratus adorn yourself, with symbols proper to myself!"

This time, her effort was rewarded with a half-dozen symbols.

Fabrice, Sparrow, and Cal had been watching carefully and were able to do the same feat without difficulty. Fabrice's robe displayed tigers and lions; Sparrow's had flowers; and Cal's had leaping foxes. Skyler's produced swords and lances, and Robin's robe bore scenes of trees and plants.

Tara, who was wearing the plain spellbinder tunic she'd put on after the ceremony, found all this fascinating. Clearly, using magic wasn't all that simple. To harness the power, you had to concentrate. Glancing down at her robe, she idly thought that it would look nice decorated with horses.

Everyone jumped as a thunderclap rumbled through the hall, and Angelica screamed. Her robe was now covered with shiny, threatening snakes. Chickens, turkeys, and ostriches adorned those of her friends. The high wizard's robe bore a horrible, grinning skull, and Tara was astonished to see beautiful silver horses prancing across hers.

All the robes had been transformed. Sparrow's glittered with crowns, scepters, and jewels, and Robin was alarmed to see elf warriors doing battle where his peaceful forests once stood.

Horrified, Tara was at a loss as to what to do, and her anxiety caught the vampyr's attention.

"May I ask what you think you are playing at, young lady?"

"I wasn't playing at anything, Master. I'm very sorry. I didn't mean to."

"Not meaning to is hardly a good way to cast a spell," said Dragosh. "Wanting to, on the other hand, is something else entirely. It seems you wanted to impress your friends by demonstrating your talent. All right, let's see how good you are."

The vampyr went to stand in front of Tara, pointed at the horses on her robe, and said, "By Decoratus make these symbols vanish, and from this robe all patterns banish."

The silver horses trembled and disappeared.

"Now, young lady, make them reappear!"

"But, but . . . " stammered Tara, who didn't want to perform any magic.

"Do as I say!" he roared.

Yelling at Tara certainly wasn't the best way to make her obey. Anyway, her grandmother had been a far tougher adversary than the vampyr. Tara took a deep breath and stilled her mind. Deliberately *not* using any magic, she said, "By Decoratus adorn yourself, with symbols proper to myself."

To her great relief, nothing appeared on the robe.

Dragosh, who didn't realize she had done this on purpose, smiled fiercely.

"I've cast a spell on you and, as clever as you are, you won't be able to undo it any time soon. People will think that you're one of those spellbinders who can't incant a spell correctly. That will teach you to disturb our class."

Then he gestured angrily at the group and shouted: "By Decoratus, grace my students' attire with any pattern they desire."

Except for Tara's, all the robes reverted to their original designs.

Ignoring the triumphant sneers from Angelica and her clan, Tara went to sit on a bleacher cushion and watched the rest of the class as an ordinary spectator. Secretly, she was very pleased at not having used magic!

For the next hour, Master Dragosh had the apprentice spellbinders work on the patterns of their robes, making the colors appear and disappear at will. Then he made them levitate, mercilessly criticizing their maneuvers and sending them roughly bouncing against the walls when they didn't follow his orders quickly enough.

By the time they left the hall under the wizard's malicious red eyes, Cal was close to mutiny. He knew that Tara hadn't deliberately done what she did, but the other spellbinders gave her a wide berth as they walked by. The only exceptions were Robin, who patted her on the shoulder, and Fabrice and Sparrow, who were their usual friendly selves.

"I'm sure that creep has something up his sleeve," said Cal sourly, as he tore into a half-dozen warm meat pies he'd "liberated" from the kitchen. "He had no business humiliating you like that, for heaven's sake. And enchanting your robe so everybody would think that you can't cast spells, that was really low!"

"We've gotta do something!" snapped Sparrow.

"Hey, you aren't stuttering," said Fabrice.

Sparrow blushed and explained, "I don't stutter when I'm angry, and right now I'm *really* angry. Listen, Tara, we don't have to take this lying down. I know how we can support you. Watch this."

She stood up and clearly said, "By Decoratus make my symbols vanish, and from this robe all patterns banish."

The glittering designs on her robe promptly disappeared.

"Hey, too cool!" exclaimed Cal. "You're right. We'll show that old sadist what we can do!"

Cal cast a forceful Decoratus, and his leaping foxes vanished. Fabrice had a little more trouble, but he was able to wipe out his tigers and lions on his second try.

Tara was so touched by their support, she had tears in her eyes. Then she said, "You're real friends. Thank you. I have to avoid doing magic because it might put my grandmother's life in danger, but if I do it in small doses I don't think there's much risk. So just for you I'm going to reveal the truth. Watch this."

With the merest glance at her robe, she covered it with hundreds of sparkling, prancing horses.

Cal was deeply impressed. "Wow! You actually managed to counter his spell! That's a real coup!"

Sparrow, who looked oddly uncomfortable when Tara had spoken of truth, was astonished. "Only a master has the power to counter another master. How did you do it?"

"I don't know," said Tara. "It was as if I suddenly understood what he was doing. It was just real clear. So what I did was to kind of suppress my magic. And there are a few other things I have to tell you."

Everything Tara had been keeping to herself came spilling out in a rush: the nighttime attack by the two Bloodgraves, her grandmother petrified, the high wizard in dragon shape, the clothes flying around her bedroom (Sparrow chuckled at the idea of Angelica with a bathrobe on her head), and finally the Bloodgrave she glimpsed in the hallway. But Tara kept her biggest secret for herself—that her mother was still alive.

She felt hugely relieved when she finished telling her story. Her three friends, on the other hand, looked as if the ceiling had fallen on them. They were staring at her, dumbfounded.

"Good grief, you were really brave!" said Fabrice admiringly. "I would never have thought to go down the trap door with the dog."

"Neither would I," said Cal. "And you say they wanted to kidnap you, right?"

"If they wanted to kidnap her," said Sparrow slowly, her brain racing, "it would mean she would have disappeared."

"Well, duh!" said Cal sarcastically. "Of course she would have disappeared!"

But Fabrice grasped what Sparrow was suggesting.

"She would have disappeared," he said, "just like the four apprentices last year!"

The others exchanged astonished looks.

"My god, you're right! You think there's a connection?"

Tara thought hard as she chewed on her white forelock.

"In any case, Dragosh is mixed up in it, one way or another," she said.

The dinner bell interrupted their cogitations.

"Oh, we'd better go," Tara said.

She jumped up, but Fabrice held her back.

"Aren't you forgetting something?" he asked, pointing to her glittering robe.

She smiled. "You're right! I almost forgot."

Tara made her horses disappear so casually—almost without thinking about it—that Fabrice felt envious. He'd already realized that his book learning wouldn't be of much use to him on

OtherWorld, and that while his gift was real, it didn't seem very powerful compared to Tara's.

When the friends entered the dining hall, the other apprentices' eyes all went to their unadorned robes. Angelica made a nasty crack about Tara having pets who followed her around like puppies.

After dinner Tara returned to the library to borrow some books on OtherWorld life and customs, such as the blood oath, and bid her friends goodnight. After brushing her teeth, she spent some time helping Sparrow get settled in the apprentices' dormitory.

Right away, Tara noticed that Sparrow's clothes were quite beautiful. That struck her as odd, since the girl had said her parents weren't wealthy. The fabrics were . . . strange. Nothing in their textures or colors looked like anything on Earth. Sparrow explained that what Tara thought was white fur was actually glavie, a plant that grew in the mountains of Gandis, the land of giants. The bluish leather of a pair of pants was really the tanned hide of a splendital, a kind of giant scorpion found in Smallcountry, the land of gnomes and imps. The silk had been woven by aragnes, a species of giant spiders raised by gnomes, who also used them for riding.

After hearing Sparrow's explanations, Tara decided not to ask what her own robes were made of. She didn't want to find out that the beautiful fabric had been woven from the snot of some weird animal.

Once Sparrow was settled, Tara climbed into bed to read her interesting book. She learned that the blood oath was indeed a warrior custom. If a warrior's friends were killed as a result of treachery, the survivor had to swear to avenge them or to carry out any task that they gave him. If the survivor didn't keep his promise, he died—the spirit of the dead came and carried him off. The curse could only be lifted by a blood relative of the dead person, provided that he or she was not the reason for the oath.

"Rats!" Tara swore.

That meant that she herself couldn't cancel her grandmother's promise. She had to find a blood relative of her father to release Isabella from her word. Manitou couldn't do it because he was her grandmother's father. And even if Tara found her own mother, she couldn't do anything, either.

"Rats again!"

From what she'd gathered from the overheard conversation between her grandmother and the count, Isabella had promised Tara's father that she would never become a wizard. Yet Isabella had encouraged her to use magic to free herself from the paralyzing Pocus spell. This meant that she could use some power, but without knowing what might endanger her grandmother's life. Great!

Tara yawned as she closed the book. Rocked by a warm breeze under a peaceful landscape of desert dunes glowing silver in the moonlight, she slipped into a deep sleep.

At the next morning's meeting, the vampyr merely smiled on seeing the four apprentices' identical plain robes.

They worked on an aqueduct project led by Master Den'maril, and Tara got to learn yet more passages through the Castle as Chem's errand-girl. If this went on, she would know the blasted building like the back of her hand, she thought. The Castle had a lot of fun putting oceans, trenches, streams, and canyons under her feet, and she had to restrain herself from tripping, retreating, or jumping. Her only consolation was that the Castle played the same jokes on all the young spellbinders, pages, and stable hands—not to mention a few courtiers, who were helpless victims of its teasing.

The afternoon was given over to physical training, and Sparrow challenged Tara to a friendly bout of judo. Repeatedly thrown by the slim and seemingly fragile brunette, Tara got to savor the pleasures of gravity in half a dozen rough landings.

Master Chanfrein hid a smile as he watched Tara spitting out the sand she'd eaten in her latest fall and decided to change exercises. He was curious to see how an Earth girl would handle herself in an unusual environment.

He asked the apprentices to follow him to an enormous chamber in a part of the Training Hall that Tara and Fabrice hadn't seen before. Once inside, she realized that it was impossible to tell up from down or right from left in the chamber. This was partly because all four walls were completely covered with vegetation, but mainly because it had no gravity! Tara stepped in, took off, and to her alarm started floating away.

Suddenly a small black box with a big eye, a tiny jet engine, and two wings came to hover in front of her, crying, "Aim, aim!" Below it, a slightly bigger one was yelling, "Shoot, shoot!" A third maneuvered around to get a good angle on her while repeating, "Zoom, zoom!"

"Don't worry about them," explained Cal, who was comfortably hanging onto a tree. "They're called scoops, and they broadcast our exercises to video screens outside the hall."

Tara cocked her head and flashed her most dazzling smile. The scoop practically hummed with excitement.

"Your attention, please," cried Chanfrein. "You are bound to encounter situations in which you can't use magic. In that case you have to make use of your environment. Let's see how you manage here. You have only one goal: to immobilize or neutralize your opponent without magic, just by using your brains. Cal, show Fabrice and Tara how to do it."

Cal braced himself against the tree and leaped, using his momentum to knock Fabrice to the center of the space. The boy hung suspended there in mid-air, helplessly thrashing around without being able to move an inch.

Tara quickly grasped the game's central feature: unless you had something to hang onto or push against, you lost, because you couldn't move.

At one point, Cal was bumped by Tara and spun around, and also found himself in the center of the chamber. He then did something very strange.

He spat.

It was crude, but effective. It only moved Cal's body about an inch backward, but that was enough for him to reach and grab onto Fabrice. Momentum brought them close enough to the walls so that they could seize them.

Some pages and other spellbinders were training in the hall, and Chanfrein decided to recruit them, creating two teams. The Alpha team would consist of Cal and Fabrice, plus Skyler, Carole, Bea, and Tricia. The Gamma team would be Tara and Sparrow, plus Jane, Tanguy, Mo, and John.

Tara carefully studied the layout of the chamber and its strange vegetation, then signaled to Sparrow and the others to join her behind a grove of trees that would hide them from their opponents' eyes.

"Listen," she said. "Cal is very individualistic, and Fabrice is awkward with weightlessness. I don't know the others, but I imagine that the Alphas and Gammas are pretty equal. But if we work as a team, we should be able to trap them. Take off your robes."

Sparrow stared at her in disbelief.

"You want us to d-d-do what?"

Tara flashed her an evil grin.

"Don't worry, I have no intention of sending you out there naked, though I'm sure it would completely rattle the boys, and the scoops would probably make you a star. I just want you to give me a robe—assuming you're wearing something underneath, of course!"

"I'm w-w-wearing shorts and a shirt," said Sparrow, blushing. "B-b-but what do you want our robes f-f-for?"

When Tara told them, her teammates erupted in admiring laughter. It was a downright diabolical plan, they said, and no one had ever tried it before.

"All right, let's go," said Tara. "We have to eliminate Cal first. He's probably the most dangerous person on their team."

Cal, Fabrice, and the rest of the Alphas planned to attack by splitting into two groups and shoving their opponents to the middle of the chamber where there weren't any trees or walls for them to hold onto. So they were completely taken by surprise when Sparrow suddenly came flying toward them at the end of what looked like a rope and shoved Cal into the center of the chamber.

Buzzing with excitement, the amazed scoops started filming the whole scene.

Fabrice drifted to a branch and turned around to figure out what was happening. Meanwhile, John went to grab another tree and sent Mo soaring to neutralize Carole.

Suddenly Cal understood the trick. Tara and the Gamma team had tied their robes together and were now using them as ropes, with a solid anchor at one end and a flying player on the other.

"Hey, that's cheating!" yelled Cal. "You can't do that!"

"Sure they can!" cried Master Chanfrein, smiling at the Gamma team's ingenuity.

Tara, who was stronger and heavier than Sparrow, chose anchors that allowed her to shoot the agile brunette off in any direction she wanted.

After a few minutes' chase around the chamber, Fabrice tried to liberate Cal. But Tara had anticipated his move and sent Sparrow flying toward him just in time. The smaller girl grabbed Fabrice's heels and pushed him into the center of the chamber. He wound up floating near Cal, but not close enough to touch him. Meanwhile Cal was spitting in every direction, but without result.

While Tara and Sparrow were dealing with Fabrice, Tanguy and Jane neutralized Bea. This left only Skyler and Tricia, who had taken refuge in a corner of the chamber they hoped was out of the Gammas' reach and were desperately trying to free their teammates.

Tara assigned Tanguy and Jane to make sure Skyler and Tricia couldn't get near the other floating Alphas, while Mo anchored himself to a tree as close as he could get them. The two Alphas had decided to imitate their opponents, and were feverishly trying to knot their robes together. But Mo didn't give them the chance. He and John linked up with Tara and Sparrow to make a four-person chain. Skyler and Tricia, who thought they were safe in their refuge, now saw Sparrow hurtling toward them. Tricia dropped the robes and Sparrow briskly propelled her to the center of the chamber. She then did the same to Skyler, who found himself floating helplessly before he realized what had happened. The entire Alpha team had been eliminated!

Like demented paparazzi, the feverish scoops crowded around the triumphant winners while a few filmed the disappointed faces of the losers.

"Well done, Gamma team!" shouted Chanfrein. "Congratulations on a very clever plan!"

They grinned at the trainer's praise as he slowly restored gravity, and everyone sank gently to the ground.

"And the winner is . . . the Gamma team!" Chanfrein proclaimed.

Laughing and joshing, the two teams left the hall, surprised by the applause that greeted them outside. Many of the Castle denizens had followed the match live, and flat-screen TVs were now rebroadcasting action shots of Tara's trick.

The story quickly made the rounds of the Castle, and Cal and Fabrice were a little grumpy during dinner. Tara acquired the reputation as a clever tactician, which made Angelica grit her teeth.

The next day, Tara and half the Castle were awakened by an incredible racket. Intrigued, she quickly slipped on jeans and a T-shirt under the light blue spellbinder robe she'd gotten into the habit of wearing.

Cal, Sparrow, and Fabrice, who were just as curious, joined her. Tracking the source of the noise, they were astonished to see a dozen cages containing some very strange beasts. Leaping around in their cages, they shed greasy feathers and shrieked insults at everyone within range.

"I'll be darned!" exclaimed Cal. "Harpies!"

Harpies were hybrids, and female. Their heads and chests were human—Fabrice could hardly bring himself to look at their bare breasts—but their lower body was that of a giant eagle with sharp talons that dripped with a sticky liquid.

"Don't get near them, whatever you do!" shouted Cal as a curious Fabrice seemed about to approach. "Harpies are a plague in OtherWorld. The high wizards are studying them, but their poison is deadly, and so far no one has come up with an antidote."

"Yikes!" exclaimed Fabrice, retreating cautiously. "Why do they scream like that?"

"Oh, that's how they communicate," said Cal. "They don't know how to speak normally, and if you want to get their attention you have to talk the way they do. Watch this."

Cal stepped a little closer and yelled: "Hey, you rotten crow droppings, daughters of crushed worms and cow flop!"

The harpies settled down immediately. One of them hopped to the door of her cage, leaving a trail of smelly feathers behind, cocked her head, and croaked.

"Rhooooo, dinner's just been served, sisters! Check out the yummy little mongrel yapping at us!"

But Cal kept his cool. Bowing sarcastically to the greasy bird-women, he said, "You half-plucked old chickens, you crud-bottomed harpies, you eat with your feet and you'd make a jackal vomit!"

"Not too bad" said a second harpy, hopping closer. "But your swearing isn't punchy enough. Try something like this instead."

The harpy fired a curse that made Cal and Fabrice blush, and Tara and Sparrow gasp.

"Ah, you see?" shrieked the harpy with satisfaction. "It's a matter of getting the right rhythm. Let's try this one."

The next volley of curses sent Sparrow stumbling backward, hands over her ears. But Tara bravely stood her ground.

A harpy off to one side spoke to her.

"Yellow hair, white strand, watery eyes. You're the Duncan offspring, aren't you?"

Surprised, Tara nodded.

"Er, yeah."

"I have a message for you from the Master of the Bloodgraves. Come closer."

Tara stepped forward, while carefully keeping her distance.

"What do you want to tell me?" she asked.

The harpy looked her up and down scornfully.

"Can't you even talk properly, you spellbinder squirt, you sick traduc snot?"

Tara had no idea what a traduc was, much less a sick one, but she understood that she would have to swear back at the harpy if she wanted to communicate with her. And the swearing called for both style and rhythm.

"You moth-eaten hunk of carrion meat," she shouted, "your breath would gag a hyena at twenty paces, and you reek worse than traduc turds!" (Hey, if it stinks, might as well use it.)

"I like your style, yellow head," cackled the harpy. "So I'm sorry I have to do—*this*!"

With a violence that shook the whole cage, the bird-woman lunged at the cage door and popped it open.

Before Cal could react, the harpy flew at Tara, burying her under a mass of filthy feathers. The second harpy was about to escape when Fabrice reflexively kicked the cage closed, almost knocking her out. Then Sparrow welded the lock shut, yelling, "By Mixus quickly seal this cage, weld its bars against their rage." Meanwhile, Cal rushed over to Tara.

On hearing the commotion, Masters Chanfrein and Dragosh burst into the room. The trainer fired a paralyzing Pocus, and the vampyr a deadly Destructus, but it was too late. When they lifted the dead bird-woman off Tara, they saw deep claw marks on the girl's body, oozing poison.

CHAPTER 7

THE DEMONS OF LIMBO

Stunned by the harpy's assault, Tara didn't feel any pain until the poison reached her bloodstream. When it did, it felt like liquid fire coursing through her veins, and she screamed in agony.

First Counselor Salatar, who had witnessed the whole scene, now leaped forward. With Cal and Fabrice's help, the chimera gently eased Tara onto his back before she fainted, wrinkling his elegant cape in the process.

As the courtiers stared in amazement, Salatar nipped in the bud any possible comments about his role as a beast of burden.

"If I hear even one crack, that person will pay a little visit to the Castle dungeons. Understand?"

Deeply worried, the chimera bore Tara to the infirmary. It was actually a state-of-the-art hospital, where magic and earthly science combined to save people's lives. Shaman Night Bird struggled against the poison all night long, but despite his great talent, without success. It was slowly paralyzing the girl, and since no antidote existed, there was nothing he could do to stop it.

Interrogated by T'andilus M'angil, Cal told the grim-faced secret services chief what he had discovered. The cage holding the harpies had been sabotaged, and its lock filed through. Master Dragosh had unfortunately been too efficient. His Destructus spell had killed the bird-woman instantly, so they couldn't question her. The other harpies claimed not to know anything about the attack, and a Truth Teller brought in on an emergency basis confirmed it. Master M'angil was furious, and was interrogating every person in the Castle. The cages had been checked when they arrived, so only someone in the Castle could have sabotaged them.

By morning, tortured by a thirst that water couldn't slake, Tara began to feel she was dying. Their eyes red, Master Chem, Sparrow, Cal, and Fabrice had watched over her all night long.

As she sank deeper into unconsciousness, she suddenly heard a velvety voice that she immediately recognized. She struggled to open her eyes and was startled by what she saw. The mirror mask of Magister, the Bloodgrave master, had appeared on the white infirmary wall!

"Ah, Tara, I see you received my message," chuckled the apparition, its mask turning blue with satisfaction.

Master Chem leaped to his feet.

"How dare you project yourself here, Bloodgrave!" he shouted, gesturing angrily at the apparition. "You'll pay for this!"

The image wavered briefly then spoke again: "Don't even try. You can't locate me. But I have a proposal for you, and I would advise you not to turn it down. Do you want this child to live? I can treat her; I have an antidote that can save her. But for her to get it, you have to give Tara to me."

"Never!" roared the dragon wizard.

"Er, Master Chem, don't you think Tara should be the one to decide?" suggested Cal. "After all, it's her life."

The old wizard glared at him, but Cal stood his ground.

"Tara?" asked Chem very gently. "Caliban is right. This has to be your decision."

"I . . . I don't want to die," she mumbled, confused and feverish.

"We don't have the antidote," he said. "If you want to live, we have to hand you over to Magister."

"Whatever . . . whatever you say," she said weakly, and passed out.

"Very well, Magister, you've won," said Chem darkly. "I won't play games with the girl's life. Tell me your conditions."

"Having you bow to my demands will be one of my life's great joys," he gloated. "Bring the girl to the Transfer Portal Room in an hour. I will send one of my assistants to pick her up. Oh, and one more thing. Don't try to use him as a bargaining chip in exchange for the antidote. It won't work. I will abandon him without a moment's hesitation, and the girl will die. Is that clear?"

"Quite clear."

The image vanished in a peal of scornful laughter.

Chem waited cautiously until he was sure that the apparition could no longer hear or spy on them. Then he turned to the young spellbinders.

"This time, we don't have any choice," he said calmly. "We're going to have to use forbidden magic!"

Sparrow, Cal, and the shaman turned pale.

"What's forbidden magic?" asked Fabrice.

"The magic of Limbo. We're going to need the help of a demon. It's extremely dangerous, so you should all leave now."

"Out of the question," countered the shaman brusquely. "She's my patient. I managed to keep her alive all night, and I'm not going to abandon her now."

"We won't leave her either," said Cal. "Tara's our friend, and she would do the same for us. Tell us how we can help."

The old wizard seemed about to object, but he realized that he had very little time. Besides, Tara's friends' help could be valuable. He sighed.

"Caliban, you're a good thief, aren't you?"

"Yes, I am," he said without false modesty. "Why do you ask?"

"One of the harpies has laid an egg. It's immature, but she kept it. Do you think you could steal it from her without getting scratched?"

Cal smiled broadly.

"Do you mean can I fool those stupid, greasy things? You must be joking, Master. You'll have your egg in two minutes." He rushed out of the infirmary.

"Perfect," said Chem. "Now it's your turn, Sparrow. You know where my office is, don't you?"

"Yes, M-M-Master."

"I can't leave Tara's side, so I'm going to give you a difficult mission. I want you to get me a cursed book the Bloodgraves have been after for years. It's called *The Forbidden Book*. Here's what you're going to have to do; listen carefully. First, I'll reprogram your accreditation card so my wall-door will let you in. On the upper left-hand bookcase you'll see a book called *Comparative Anatomy of OtherWorld Fauna*. Take it down and put it on my desk. Tap three times on page 3, and then ten times on page 20. Be careful not to make a mistake."

Sparrow nodded, looking serious.

"My desk will shift aside, revealing a glass staircase," Chem continued. "Go down it, skipping the fourth and seventh steps. At the bottom you will see two fire snakes. Crawl between them on your hands and knees. Whatever you do, don't walk between them standing up; they'll cut your head off. This passageway will bring you to *The Forbidden Book*, which is on a pedestal. Walk around the pedestal and pick up the flat stone hidden behind it. Quickly replace the book with the stone; you'll have less than a second. When you've done that, climb the stairs, this time skipping the second step from the bottom, then the fifth. In the office, pick up the anatomy book without touching its pages and put it around the forbidden book to hide its cover, and bring all this to me. Do you need me to repeat that?"

There certainly was no risk of anyone stealing Chem's forbidden book!

"No, Master, I understand," Sparrow said firmly. She was so frightened, she had lost her stutter. "Tap three times on page 3 and ten times on page 20, skip the fourth step and then the seventh, replace the book with the stone, bring it upstairs skipping the second and fifth steps, put the anatomy book around the forbidden book, and bring them to you. Got it! I'm on my way."

As Sparrow ran off, Chem turned to Night Bird and to Fabrice, who wasn't quite sure how he could help.

"Take Fabrice to the forest and dig up three kalorna roots," said Chem. "Use the boy as bait."

"Exactly what do I have to do?" asked Fabrice a little nervously.

"Not a thing," said the shaman with a faint smile. "Kalornas hide underground when they sense danger. But if you sit quietly without threatening them, their curiosity will bring them back up and I'll be able to capture them. Let's go."

With a wave of his hand, Chem levitated Tara in the center of the room, floated several finely engraved goblets around her motionless body, and put burning herbs in them. Though unconscious, the girl softly moaned in pain, and each moan made the old dragon wizard tremble. He began his preparations by magically reinforcing Tara's defenses.

There was a sudden commotion outside, and Cal burst into the infirmary carrying a large, gray egg.

"Hooo-boy!' he crowed gleefully. "The harpies didn't like that one bit, but I was able to get the egg. Anything else I can do for you?"

"No, thank you," said the wizard. "This is perfect. Are you sure you want to stay, Caliban? It will be terribly dangerous, you know."

"The question is, do you need us?"

"To be honest, yes, I do," said Chem with a sigh. "You are Tara's friends, and I'll need you to hold her hands as tightly as you can, and not to let her go for any reason. Think you can do that?"

"I can't speak for the others," said Cal, "but as far as I'm concerned, I won't let her go."

The shaman, Fabrice, and Sparrow returned at the same time. The kalorna roots were wriggling in a jar, and Sparrow had successfully retrieved *The Forbidden Book*, though her singed hair suggested that it hadn't been easy.

To Chem's question, Tara's other two friends answered the same way Cal had. They wouldn't abandon her, they said, and would stay no matter the risk.

"Very well," said the wizard approvingly. "So let's begin. Shaman Night Bird?"

The shaman indicated that he was ready. Chem opened *The Forbidden Book* and put the kalorna roots in the goblets around Tara. As a ring of red smoke rose around them, they all chanted together: "By *The Forbidden Book*, we seek your aid. Allow us to cross through Limbo unscathed. Guide us through the demonic sphere. Our hearts are pure, we have no fear!"

The room disappeared in a deafening thunderclap, and they all found themselves floating in a vast, empty gray plain. There was nothing to see except for a sickly purple sky, a few clouds wondering how they wound up there, and rocks that seemed to have been abandoned millions of years before. The whole scene was so depressing that the travelers felt their morale sink.

When they'd started out, Cal had been holding Tara's right hand, Fabrice her left, and Sparrow her head, but they now found themselves empty-handed. Their bodies had lost all substance—they had turned into ghosts!

"What's going on, Master Chem?" asked Cal in a voice verging on panic. "What do we do now?"

The old wizard looked annoyed.

"Drat! I assumed that our bodies would follow us, but apparently only our minds made the trip. Be very careful. Whatever happens to our minds here will also happen to our bodies back on OtherWorld. All right. According to the book, we will soon encounter the ruler of this part of Limbo. His mansion should walk by in a few minutes."

"Hey, where am I?" asked Tara, who had suddenly woken up and couldn't understand why she was floating in empty space. "I don't hurt anymore. Did you cure me?"

"No, unfortunately," said the old wizard. "We don't have an antidote to the poison. Our minds are in Limbo, which is why you aren't feeling any pain, but our bodies are still back in the infirmary."

He paused and looked around.

"Aha! Here comes the Demon King's mansion now. Watch your step, everyone, and don't respond to provocations."

Yikes! thought Sparrow. What kind of provocations?

Borne on four gigantic legs, a huge, black basalt mansion was striding toward them. As it got closer, they could tell it had been built by someone who had seen a house only once and tried to replicate it without understanding what the openings were for. The doors were up high, and the windows down low. The roof had been mounted on the side of the walls, leaving the upper floor exposed to the elements.

The old wizard nodded at the group to follow him, levitated, and without hesitation flew through the mansion walls, followed by the shaman and the four friends. Despite the grimness of the situation, Tara loved being able to fly, even though passing through the wall really did make her feel like a ghost.

Once inside, they were seized by terrible vertigo. All the colors that had been stripped from the gray plain were locked in a terrible battle with each other. On the left-hand wall and part of the floor, a brilliant yellow was trying to sneak up on the adjoining wall's vivid red. On the right-hand wall, a tough blue was launching an offensive against a fearful white, which retreated before the threat. The black ceiling extended tentative tentacles that sometimes got drawn into the other colors' skirmishes.

In the exact center of the room, floating in space, was an opening through which the gray plain outside could be seen. This opening was obviously the focus of all five colors' attention, and they were spreading across the floor, falling from the ceiling, and erupting from the walls in their efforts to reach it. Master Chem and his group had to advance very cautiously so as not to get caught up in the confrontation.

"Hey!" Cal suddenly cried. "We're becoming solid again!"

And in fact their bodies were very gradually acquiring mass.

"By Baltur's bowels!" cursed the wizard. "The demon has cast a spell that sends visitors into the colors' trap and imprisons them there. We're neither fully material nor immaterial anymore—we're somewhere between the two. Problem is, the colors will be able to touch us, and what is worse, capture us!"

"What . . . what are we g-g-gonna d-d-do?" cried Sparrow in a panic.

Chem looked at his hand, which was now only faintly translucent.

"The demon has trapped the colors in his mansion, and they're battling each other to get out through the magic opening in the center," he growled. "Their plan is probably to stick to us and ride outside with us. So don't touch the walls, or they'll catch us. And we have to hurry; otherwise we won't be able to pass through walls anymore. Follow me!"

By some mysterious sense, the colors could hear the old wizard's voice. They were now still—and watchful. Red suddenly shot toward Chem's feet, and he was just able to avoid it. But this brought the wizard close to black, which saw its chance. A long black tentacle dropped from the ceiling, and Chem had to jump backward to avoid it. Following him, Tara, Cal, Sparrow, Fabrice, and Night Bird zigzagged at top speed around the traps the colors laid for them.

Suddenly, Fabrice cried out. He hadn't been able to dodge blue, and his hand was slowly turning color.

Distracted by Fabrice, Sparrow was touched by red, and her leg turned purple. As he tried to free Fabrice, Cal was touched by yellow and black. Chem was unable to duck white and red. First blue, then white caught Night Bird. The more they struggled, the tighter the colors stuck to them! Tara, unable to dodge yellow and red, saw them color her skin. But instead of mixing and becoming orange, they began fighting right on her body.

"Colors, listen to me!" Tara shouted. "I know how to free you! We aren't going to leave the mansion without seeing the Demon King. So there's no point in trying to get out by sticking to us, because he will never allow you to leave. But if you listen to me, you'll be able to escape on your own."

For a moment, she thought the colors didn't hear, because they continued their pointless fighting. But then red stopped to listen, yellow ignored black, and white and blue quit waving their tentacles.

"You have to work together," continued Tara. "Otherwise it will be impossible for you to use the exit, and you'll go on fighting until the end of time. So please line up in order: white, yellow, red, blue, and black. Then stand in front of the opening in the center of the room. Go on!"

Reluctantly at first, the colors obeyed. Despite some shoving and grumbling, white lined up with yellow, then red, blue, and finally black. At first nothing happened, and Tara felt a twinge of panic, thinking she'd made a mistake.

But then the colors started whirling around each other with a sharp whistling sound, and a gorgeous rainbow lit up the room. United at last, the colors joyfully poured through the central opening and burst outside, brightly coloring the entire plain.

"Wow, that was a stroke of genius!" shouted Fabrice, startling them all. "I was afraid I was going to live out my life as a little blue man!"

"Is everybody okay?" asked Master Chem, who was examining himself all over, to be sure the colors hadn't left any marks on his skin.

"T-T-Tara!" Sparrow suddenly cried. "L-L-Look at your throat!"

Tara looked down, but she couldn't see what the others found so surprising: an unusual design had appeared on her throat. Before departing, the colors had apparently left her a thank-you present. Each color had deposited a bit of glowing hue: yellow, gold; blue, sapphire; white, diamond; red, ruby; and black, ebony. Together, they formed a striking, jewel-like pattern. It was at the base of her throat, and she could cover it by raising her collar.

"Whoa!" said Tara, impressed. "I hope that won't be on my skin when I get back to Travia."

"I'm sorry, but as I said, everything that happens to us here also happens there," said the wizard. "But this means that if you ever need the colors, just call their name, and they'll come."

He paused.

"I doubt the Demon King will be happy that we released the colors, so roll up your collar, Tara, and let's go inside before he realizes it—and before we're too dense to pass through walls."

Master Chem flew through the wall, quickly followed by the others. They landed in a large hall, skidding to a stop so as not to bump into the fearsome black dragon that awaited them.

Tara stumbled backward. She remembered what Chem had said about dragons that went crazy—and any dragon who lived in a house like this one had to be seriously deranged.

All around them, swarms of demons were writhing, drooling, cursing, and generally making an infernal din. They came in all types, sizes, and colors. Some were so disgusting that just looking at them made the four young friends nauseous.

Ignoring the deafening racket, Chem bowed politely to the black dragon.

"Your Demonic Majesty, you do me great honor by appearing as a dragon. Wouldn't you prefer to take your own shape?"

The dragon answered in a thunderous voice so deep it shook all of Limbo and silenced the crowds of demons.

"Won't that frighten your young companions? I hate the sound of screaming."

So just what were the other demons doing? Sparrow wondered sarcastically. Singing lullabies?

"They've been very well trained, Your Demonic Majesty," said the old wizard patiently. "They won't be frightened."

Tara shot him a look. What did he mean, they wouldn't be afraid? Easy for him to say! They were already terrified.

The black dragon disappeared and the Demon King materialized in his normal shape. Tara didn't scream at the sight, but only with tremendous effort.

The Demon King was an enormous mouth with a long, disgusting, purple tongue dotted with large black spots, set on an oozing white ball bristling with tentacles. Each tentacle had an eyeball at its end, and the variety of eyes was amazing. They were red, green, and blue; some were tiny, others enormous.

Taken all together, it was enough to make you toss your cookies.

The demon settled comfortably on a sort of throne, licked himself with his huge tongue, and turned his hundreds of eyes to Master Chem.

"What can I do for the powerful High Wizard Chemnashaovirodaintrachivu?" he asked. "It's been an eternity since I've seen humans in my dimension. The last time was about a dozen of your years ago, I believe. A young spellbinder came to me seeking power. I was happy to give it to him, and the results exceeded his hopes!"

"You knew very well what you were doing when you gave Magister demonic power," the old wizard snapped. "He's gone crazy and is completely out of control. He has become so powerful that he wants to dominate all our worlds. He hurt this girl in his quest for power, and you are as responsible for her condition as if you had wounded her yourself. You know the terms of our agreements. Ever since the last great war, when we dragons and spellbinders defeated you demons, dragons don't attack demons and demons don't bother dragons!"

Now this was interesting, thought Tara, carefully noting what the two opponents were saying.

"That wasn't our choice," thundered the Demon King bitterly. "And you imprisoned us in a limbo we can only leave when you call us, like servants!"

But Master Chem stood his ground. The demon calmed down, then spoke again.

"Anyway, this girl is human, unless I'm very much mistaken," he purred malevolently. "She's certainly no dragon. And I'm pretty sure our agreements don't cover humans."

"Attacking our humans is the same as attacking us," the wizard responded stoutly. "I demand reparation."

"Nice try, but it won't work," said the demon with a chuckle. "I know the terms of our agreements as well as you do, Chem. We have conventions, and we respect them. Or do you want a new war between demons and dragons to establish new bases for negotiation? If so, I'm at your disposal."

The noisy swarm of demons suddenly began paying close attention. Shaman Night Bird visibly paled.

Master Chem had no choice.

"No, I don't want that," he said reluctantly. "I will merely ask that Your Majesty donate his skills to treat the girl."

"*Donate?* You must be dreaming, old lizard! You may be hiding in human shape but your dragon duplicity shines through. I never do anything for free. But let's suppose I did treat her. What would my reward be?"

"I have a nice, fresh harpy egg that can be transferred here immediately. That's a good price for a vial of harpy poison antidote."

The mass of tentacles began to shake with laughter.

"Harpy poison? Really? You must think I'm an idiot. I have no interest in your egg. What about your Escalidos pentacle? I know you retrieved it a century ago, and I could use it."

The old wizard scowled. Tara didn't know what an Escalidos pentacle was, but it was apparently pretty valuable.

"Oh, very well," Master Chem said with ill grace. "My pentacle in exchange for a vial of antidote."

The Demon King gazed at the wizard thoughtfully, licked an eyeball, then let his tongue loll out with amusement.

"I would have taken your pentacle with great pleasure," he said and sighed. "But I don't have the antidote you're speaking of, alas. And if I don't have it, nobody does!"

"So why are we even discussing this?" asked Cal angrily before Chem could speak.

The Demon King opened a huge mouth amid his tentacles and began to laugh again.

"Why, for the pleasure of seeing the great Chemnashaovirodaintrachivu give in, of course! I was wondering how far he would go to save the little human girl."

Now Tara was angry as well. The demon was mocking the old wizard and clearly enjoying his discomfiture.

"Then go to the devil if you can't help us!" she cried. "Let's leave, Master Chem. This babbling blob talks a good game, but he doesn't actually have any power. You would've done better to approach someone really powerful."

"Aha, the little girl has teeth and knows how to use them," said the Demon King, furious at being insulted in front of his entire court. "So you don't think I'm powerful, eh? Well, we'll see about that. Go on back to your world. You'll be thinking of me very, very soon. *Sparidam!*"

The spell hit the group like a hammer blow, blasting them out of Limbo like wisps of straw. They barely heard the Demon King's roar of fury when he discovered the colors capering freely about on his plain.

In a flash, the travelers' disoriented minds were rejoined with their bodies in the Travia Castle infirmary.

When she reentered her body, Tara noticed that something had changed. She was still aware of the burning poison that was slowly killing her, but she was now able to keep the pain at bay. In fact, she felt fine. She jumped up, not realizing that her body was hovering above the infirmary floor.

Cal was just able to grab her just before she banged her head on the ceiling.

"Hey, what d'you think you're doing?" he asked in surprise. "How do you feel?"

"Great!" she replied joyously. "I feel wonderful! Oh, look: the color pattern came back with me."

It was true; the design on her throat glowed like a baroque, wild jewel.

Shaman Night Bird came over and passed his hand in front of the girl's face, then looked at his palm and read it.

"I don't understand," he said, looking disconcerted. "The poison is still in her system, but she doesn't seem to be experiencing its effects. Very odd."

"Demon humor is very peculiar," said Chem somberly, who was very worried. "Tara challenged the Demon King's power, and, since he was unable to cure her, he must have done something to help her fight the poison's effects. But if she doesn't get that antidote very soon, she will die."

"We don't have any choice, then," said Cal thoughtfully. "Tell me, Master, are those Bloodgrave masks solid, or just illusions to hide their faces?"

"They're illusions, otherwise they couldn't breathe. Why?"

"Because I have a plan, but I'm going to need your help."

In a few words Cal told the group what he wanted to do. The old wizard was completely against the idea at first, but he quickly realized he had no choice but to go along.

When the image of the masked Bloodgrave master next appeared on the infirmary wall, everything was in place. Tara was lying unconscious on a floating stretcher, with only Master Chem present.

"So, are you ready?" asked Magister gleefully.

"She's dying, you vicious Bloodgrave," snapped the old wizard bitterly. "I'm going to take her to the Portal Room now. But you'd better give her the antidote immediately. Otherwise, we'll have done all this just to transfer a corpse."

Magister leaned over the stretcher to peer at the girl. Tara's face was flushed with fever, and she was delirious.

"Then hurry up," he ordered the wizard. "My assistant is leaving now and should reach you in less than thirty seconds."

Pushing the floating stretcher ahead, Chem reached the room just as Magister's assistant was materializing. Cautiously, the Bloodgrave cast a spell to reveal any invisible wizards ready to attack him, but there was only Tara and Chem. He checked that no one was lurking under the stretcher, but there wasn't room for anyone to hide down there.

"It's useless to try to follow me," he warned. "My destination Portal is simply re-sending me somewhere else."

"I won't try," said Chem, "but please get going. She's dying."

The Bloodgrave nodded then shouted, "Sylvine Forest!"

They disappeared.

Tara and the Bloodgrave materialized in a forest clearing, and he shouted, "Tylerthorn!"

They disappeared again, this time materializing in a room where the Master of Bloodgraves was waiting, a small vial in his hand.

Magister approached Tara and was raising her head to help her drink when the seemingly unconscious girl suddenly grabbed him—with four hands!

Before the astonished Bloodgrave knew what was happening, his masked face was sprayed with a dark powder. He gave a terrific sneeze that practically bent him double. He dropped the vial, but one of Tara's extra hands caught it.

The other Bloodgrave rushed over to help, but Tara yelled, "Go to the devil, both of you!" She was about to cast a Pocus, when *poof!* both Bloodgraves disappeared.

Tara wasted no time wondering what had happened. Instead she shouted, "Travia Castle!"

The Portal obeyed, and Tara and her unexpected partner disappeared in turn. That partner turned out to be none other than Cal, who had somehow made himself flat enough to lie hidden under Tara on the stretcher.

The moment they appeared at the Castle, Master Chem took the vial and immediately made Tara drink it.

After waiting a few minutes, Shaman Night Bird passed his hand over the girl's face, read his palm, and nodded with satisfaction.

"She's cured," he announced, as laconic as ever. Then he packed his things and left.

Fabrice, Sparrow, and Cal whooped with joy.

"My plan worked perfectly!" exclaimed a radiant Cal. "I was pretty sure they would check that no adult wizard was magically hiding near Tara. So I used a thief technique where we compress our chest so much that our bodies take up very little room. They didn't think to lift Tara up, and when the Bloodgrave master approached, he got a handful of black pepper in his eyes."

"Pepper?"

"Yeah. I needed a substance that Magister couldn't detect, but one that would blind him long enough for us to grab the vial and get out of there. But I still don't understand why the two Bloodgraves disappeared."

"What do you mean, disappeared?" asked Chem, frowning.

"Well, yeah," said Cal, shrugging. "All at once, *poof!* No more Bloodgraves. Then Tara activated the transfer, and here we are!"

"You saved my life, Cal," said Tara very seriously and unexpectedly planted a big kiss on his cheek.

The boy stammered in embarrassment but was rescued when a young page came to get them. The king and queen had gotten word of Tara's miraculous rescue and wanted to ask her about it.

Led by the page, Tara and the old wizard walked to the Throne Room. The king and queen were holding court, but the moment Tara was announced they indicated that they wanted to speak with her privately. The courtiers stepped back while listening closely.

"My dear girl," said the queen kindly, "you've apparently had a terrible adventure."

"Yes, Your Majesty. But Master Chem and my friends saved my life. And Cal was incredibly brave to go to the Bloodgraves with me."

An anxious murmur ran through the assembly, and Salatar, the chimera, sat up on his cushion.

Tara told the whole story, including how she acquired the jewel-like design on her throat. (This sparked some jealousy among the assembled girls. From their envious looks, Tara had unwittingly launched a new fashion statement.) She had just reached the point where they were in the demons' hall in the topsy-turvy mansion, when she said, "We were frozen with fear, Your Majesty, because we didn't know that . . . "

Tara stopped dead. Under her horrified eyes the two sovereigns had started to shiver and turn blue, and frost was covering their hair and eyebrows.

"Whhhhhhhhhhat . . . what's happppppening?" the king managed to say through chattering teeth.

Sparrow, Cal, and Fabrice were stamping their feet and shivering. Tara looked around and became very frightened.

Everyone in the Throne Room was blue with cold. The shivering courtiers anxiously blurted questions to each other, their hair covered with frost.

Salatar, who hated the cold, roared when he saw his strange body covered with frost.

"By my ancestors!" murmured Master Chem. "Tara! Don't say another word without my permission." Then, to the king and queen: "Your Highnesses, I think I know what is happening!"

He turned back to the frightened girl.

"Our dear friend the demon gave you a little present, Tara. Kindly say this aloud: 'We are gently warmed by Their Majesties' kindness.'"

For a moment, Tara wondered whether the old wizard had lost his mind, but she obeyed.

"Er, we're gently warmed by Their Majesties kindness.'"

Immediately, the sovereigns and the rest of the assembly thawed, and pleasant warmth replaced the bitter cold.

Salatar, sodden hair falling into his eyes, jumped down from his cushion.

"Would somebody care to explain this to me?" he asked in a dangerously calm voice.

"During our adventure in Limbo, we unfortunately challenged the Demon King to cure Tara," admitted Master Chem, feeling very awkward. "He couldn't do it, so he gave her the gift of a new power. Whenever she uses a metaphor now, it actually takes place. I suspect this happened when Cal said the two Bloodgraves disappeared when Tara yelled 'Go to the devil!' at them. I imagine they were quite surprised."

"They weren't the only ones," grumbled Cal, mopping his face with a handkerchief. "Do I understand this right, that whenever Tara says something like, 'I'm burning up,' or 'I'm hot to trot,' she might make toast of us?"

"That's about it," admitted the old dragon.

Grinning at Tara, Cal said, "Well, sweetie, you better purge your vocabulary of metaphors if you don't want to turn us into shish kebabs."

Rigid with fear, Tara stared at him and gulped.

Sparrow, who was drying her brown curls and watching her friend with concern, asked, "B-B-But we c-c-can c-c-cure her, c-c-can't we? C-C-Control the runaway magic? Otherwise, her life will b-b-be a nightmare!"

"It will take all the high wizards' combined power," said Salatar, "and there aren't enough of you. You'll have to go to Omois."

"Omois?" asked the king, who had been listening carefully. "I don't like having to ask the Empire for anything. Besides, do you think that the empress and the emperor would let you enlist their high wizards' power to cure our little Tara?"

"Yes, Your Highness," said Chem. "That's part of the high wizard covenant. Regardless of our political differences, if one of us is in danger or is hurt, we close ranks to save or cure them."

"That's perfect, then," said Salatar, who finally saw a way to rid the court of Tara's dangerous presence. "In that case, you have carte blanche to go cure the girl."

"We won't be able to leave right away," said Chem, to Salatar's annoyance. "We will need some time to prepare. I propose that we go in . . . let's say a week; that should work. In the meantime Tara will be very careful, won't you, dear?"

Careful was putting it mildly! Tara was being so careful now that she didn't say anything, just nodded.

Though she was feeling fine, Tara elected to stay in her room rather than risk freezing or frying anyone. Nervous courtiers gave her a wide berth along the way.

That evening, she rejoined her friends. Another trip to the library hadn't yielded anything, and she was feeling discouraged. OtherWorld was huge—one and a half times as big as Earth. She would never be able to find her mother!

"I heard what happened," said a concerned Deria, who had joined the group. "Are you all right? I wanted to visit you, but Master Chem prevented me."

"Oh, Deria!" wailed Tara. "I'm so scared! I have to watch every word I say!"

"Come here, darling," said Deria kindly, taking the girl in her arms. "Don't be frightened. Power is only dangerous if you don't know how to control it. And you'll learn, trust me."

As Tara dried her tears, Cal chimed in enthusiastically: "During the High Council meeting tomorrow, can't you say that we were all mute with admiration at the demon's power? With a little luck the masters won't be able to speak and we'll have the whole day free!"

"C-C-Cal, you should b-b-be ashamed of yourself!" scolded Sparrow. "P-P-Poor T-T-Tara has enough p-p-problems as it is."

"That's all right," said Tara, smiling weakly. "If I don't use any metaphors, I should manage not to hurt anyone. I just have to watch it."

But when she went to bed after dinner, she felt very worried. She fought sleep as long as she could, and when she yielded, she was tormented by nightmares. She saw hordes of demons overpowering the world and turning people into slaves. But the worst of all came when the monstrous demon commander removed its helmet. The demon had deep blue eyes and long golden hair with a strange white strand. It was her! *She* was the queen of the demons!

When Tara awoke the next morning, she felt frightened and exhausted. So she didn't immediately notice what had happened to her room. She sleepily stumbled a dozen steps toward the bathroom before realizing that she'd previously crossed the small space in two or three. When she actually opened her eyes, she gasped.

Her room had grown—a lot! It now featured a handsome desk, a living room with a sofa and a couch, a fireplace, and a glittering chandelier. Her canopy bed was twice its previous size, with richly carved posts. On the walls, the Castle was projecting majestic landscapes, in keeping with her new status. Tara blinked. Well, here's hoping my magic hasn't hurt Grandma, she thought, because I have a real wizard's bedroom now.

She opened the wall with a wave of her accredi-card just as Angelica was passing with the other apprentices. When the tall girl saw Tara's new décor, she practically choked with rage.

Master Chem knew Tara was worried about her grandmother, so he contacted Isabella in Peru and confirmed that she was feeling fine. The old wizard took the occasion to tell her that Tara would be staying on OtherWorld for another ten days or so. Isabella was concerned and asked why, and Chem told her a barefaced lie. He said that Tara had been invited to Omois with the other wizards, and that he wanted to show her that wonderful country. Isabella raised no objection, especially since she hadn't yet found everything she needed to protect the manor house against the Bloodgraves.

The delighted wizard reassured Tara that her grandmother was fine and that she was being allowed to spend more time on OtherWorld.

Feeling relieved, Tara went to look for her friends. After the morning Council session, they were mostly free that afternoon. Not completely, however; Master Chanfrein assigned them to the stables, to ride the animals that needed exercising. Familiars weren't allowed there, so the young people had to leave them behind.

At two o'clock sharp they entered the stables and peered around. At first, Tara couldn't see the horses very well, but when she got closer, she saw they had what looked like big blankets on their backs. When one of the blankets moved and rose up, she realized that she was looking at . . . a wing? *Winged horses?* Her heart began thudding in her chest.

Attracted by the noise, the pegasi stuck their heads out of their stalls, looking the spellbinders over as carefully as the young people were examining them. Tara quickly realized how they differed from horses—besides having wings, of course. For one thing, the pegasi seemed very calm and let the spellbinders stroke them without reacting to their excitement. Also, when Tara hesitantly reached out her hand, she discovered that their hide felt different from a horse's. Their coat was softer and much thicker, probably to protect them against wind and cold at high altitudes. Their wings were very long, with firmly seated feathers. When one pegasus gave her a friendly bump to encourage her to keep petting him, she noticed that his head was very light. Like birds, pegasus bones were probably hollow. This considerably reduced their mass, though not so much that they couldn't carry a rider's weight.

Cal laughed to see Tara and Fabrice marveling at them. Sparrow, on the other hand, knew about pegasi and had even seen a couple of aerial polo matches.

"Hey, guys!" shouted Fabrice. "What do you get when the pegasus polo team has to go to the bathroom? Aerial manures!"

As the others groaned, he continued. "What happens when a pegasus farts at high altitude? It breaks the sound barrier!"

"Fabrice! Stop it!" shrieked Tara and Sparrow. Cal, on the other hand, just grinned.

Master Chanfrein appeared.

"Ah, our beginning riders," he said. "Good, good. How many of you have already ridden before—any kind of animal?"

They had almost all ridden something before: a horse, a pegasus, and for two of Angelica's blushing and giggling friends, a unicorn.

"Perfect," he said. "Here are the saddles."

The saddles had a form-fitting safety belt to keep the rider from falling off. It could be released with just the click of a button, if necessary.

The saddles, which were held in place with three straps, were designed to leave the pegasus's wings completely free. One went around the animal's chest, and the other two cinched the saddle to its back. Stirrups fit the rider's feet, and the bit and bridle were just like a horse's.

"I'm going to take out Danguerrand for a demonstration. Then you'll each choose a pegasus and we'll go for a ride."

Chanfrein opened a stall and led one of the pegasi out. The animal was so graceful, its feet barely seemed to touch the ground. To her great surprise, Tara saw that it didn't have hooves, but more like cat's paws, with sharp, retractable claws. A hoof wouldn't have been practical for perching in trees, and evolution had responded accordingly. The pegasus spread its wings to make it easier for Chanfrein to saddle it.

Everyone came out of the stables to watch them take flight, and Fabrice and Tara were astonished by the power of the pegasus's takeoff. Within a second it was a dozen feet in the air. It flew like an arrow to the end of the field, galloped first in the air then on the ground, vaulted easily over trees. It even did a loop the loop, which made the two earthlings gasp. Graceful and quick, the pegasus appeared to carry Chanfrein's weight easily.

Cal nudged Tara to attract her attention.

"So what do you think?" he asked with a hint of mischief.

"They're magnificent!" she said ecstatically.

"Hey, they're just big flying animals; nothing to get excited about."

Tara was about to protest when she realized that Cal was kidding. She was thinking of a snappy comeback when she became aware of something exercising a strange, powerful attraction on her.

Cal was baffled to see Tara heading for the forest, like a sleep-walker or a blind person. Deaf to his shouts, she was listening to a voice singing in her mind.

"Come to me," said the voice. "Don't be afraid. I am here. Come! Come to me!"

Cal alerted Fabrice and Sparrow, and they all followed her.

They tried to keep Tara from entering the cold, dark forest, but failed. With surprising strength, she shoved them aside and disappeared into a grove of trees. In a panic, Sparrow yelled for Master Chanfrein. Cal and Fabrice plunged into the forest on Tara's tracks.

She now heard nothing but the cajoling, caressing voice, which led her to a sun-dappled clearing. Suddenly, a huge winged form swooped down from the sky.

Her friends screamed.

CHAPTER 8

THE FAMILIAR

Tara looked up, met the pegasus's strange golden gaze, and felt something deep inside her click. Weeping with joy, she threw her arms around the winged familiar that had just chosen her.

She would never be alone again. She would never again be judged, but instead supported, loved, and helped. She and her familiar would form a single being, a single spirit, united forever.

Alerted by Sparrow, who by now was in a complete panic, Master Chanfrein immediately knew that the big white horse wasn't from his stable. Landing next to it, he exclaimed, "A pegasus? Where did it come from? What's going on here?"

"Oh, it's nothing, Master," said Angelica maliciously, who ran up panting. "This girl enjoys being the center of attention. She's not one of us. She probably saw the pegasus and—"

No one would ever know what Angelica was going to say. Spurred by Tara's anger, the winged stallion strode menacingly toward her.

Angelica yelped and ran to hide behind Chanfrein. "Look at that!" she cried. "She's trained it to attack me!"

Chanfrein examined the pegasus carefully. When he noticed its golden eyes, he shouted, "Tradilan trash me, it's a familiar!"

Seeing Tara's hand on its flank, he asked, "Did it choose you, girl?"

"Yes, Master. He says his name is Gallant."

A strange hint of calculation appeared in the trainer's eyes.

"That's good. In fact that's very, very good! So your familiar is a pegasus, eh? That's terrific!"

As the young spellbinders looked on in astonishment, Chanfrein started jumping and dancing around.

"This is a real secret weapon!" he cried jubilantly. "It's gonna make that Tingapore donkey jockey swallow his spurs! C'mon, kid, let's get you a saddle and see what you can do."

Still feeling stunned by everything that had just happened, Tara followed him, her hand on the powerful stallion's neck.

"If looks could kill, you'd have died long ago," Cal whispered while pointing at Angelica, who was pale with fury,

"Oh, Cal, it's incredible," said Tara with a deep sigh. "Gallant chose me—*me!*"

"This actually gives us a problem with Manitou," he said, frowning. "Someone's bound to remember that your familiar was supposed to be a dog. And nobody can have two familiars."

Fabrice, who was listening, spoke up.

"Has anyone really made the connection between you and Manitou, Tara?"

"No. That is, I don't think so. He doesn't follow me around, he snores all day long and goes out at night. Why?"

"Do you think he's lucid enough to pretend to be mine?" asked Fabrice.

"I don't know, but I can ask him. You want him to pretend he's your familiar?"

"Yeah, while I'm waiting to be chosen myself. You can't risk attracting even more attention, and two familiars is one too many."

"It's a good idea. Let's try it."

Master Chanfrein treated Gallant very differently from the other pegasi. For one thing, the bridle he brought out didn't have a bit. Instead, the two reins were fastened to the nose band. For another, he didn't try to put it on himself. He first showed it to Gallant, then handed it to Tara. Gallant immediately lowered his head so she could adjust the crownpiece and the browband.

The trainer then showed her how to put on the saddle, cinching it tight enough to keep it in place, but without squeezing the horse.

Meanwhile, three stable hands had saddled the other pegasi. The spellbinders led their mounts out of the stables and headed for the exercise arena.

Gallant's presence was a constant in Tara's mind now. After telling her his name, the pegasus hadn't said anything else, but he vividly communicated his feelings to her, as she did hers to him. He was happy to be there, the saddle wasn't heavy, and he was eager to fly with her.

Teasingly, she mentally told him that she imagined her first flight would be on a broom, like some old fairy-tale witch. Gallant's indignation made her laugh. How dare she compare him, a stallion of the skies, with an uncomfortable stick of wood? He sent her images of herself perched on a broom, trying desperately not to fall and wincing in pain after only a ten-minute ride.

Tara had to admit that Gallant was right. Riding a broom couldn't be a lot of fun.

"Okay, we're ready," said Chanfrein, after checking everyone's cinches and headstalls. "How many of you know how to transform your clothes?"

"I do!" answered Angelica.

"So do I," said Cal.

"M-M-Me t-t-too," Sparrow stammered.

"Then you know what clothes to wear." Turning to Angelica, he said, "Show your friends."

She waved her hand from top to bottom and commanded: "By Transformus, I want a riding outfit, pants, a shirt, and riding boots."

Immediately, she was wearing black riding pants and boots, and a black-and-white shirt.

"By Transformus, I want a riding outfit, pants, a shirt, and riding boots."

Cal and Sparrow cast the spell at the same time and laughed to see that they had both chosen brown boots and tan pants.

Except for Fabrice, who briefly wound up in a nightshirt, the others' transformations went pretty well. Sparrow knew that Tara was reluctant to use her magic, so she conjured her a pair of pants and boots.

Unlike the others, Tara's pegasus knelt to help her climb on. Once in the saddle, she took the reins and before she even had time to think, found herself thirty feet in the air.

The feeling was incredible. She flew toward the sun, breathlessly watching as people and places shrank below her. She was riding a pegasus! And he obeyed her slightest wish, almost before she even thought it.

With a burst of laughter, she banked in a steep turn, brushing by Cal, who didn't look quite at ease. Neither did Sparrow, who was clutching her reins, terrified of falling.

Experiencing Gallant's feelings so strongly and sharing the sensation of freedom was so intense, it brought tears of joy to Tara's eyes.

Fabrice, grinning like a maniac, shouted to her: "Pretty neat, isn't it?"

Cruising alongside Tara, Fabrice sat his pegasus well. He was a very good rider back on Earth, and the two of them had often gone out together in Tagon. The count owned a half-dozen horses, and Fabrice and Tara used to ride them every Saturday. But this was something else!

Gallant's powerful muscles rippled under his white coat and his wings beat steadily. But Tara was sorry not to have braided her hair, which whipped her face with the stallion's every move. She had the same thought about the pegasus's long mane, which wrapped around her hands. Next time, she would braid his mane as well.

Master Chanfrein flew up to them on Danguerrand. Watching Tara carefully, the trainer was delighted. He'd never seen anything like it: girl and horse were flying as one. He had a plan for Tara, and if he didn't pull it off, he would eat his helmet!

After an hour's flight, Chanfrein had the whole spellbinder group return to the ground. Then, being a believer in *mens sana in corpore sano*—a sound mind in a healthy body—he made them spend a weary hour cleaning tack, grooming the pegasi, putting hay in the stalls, and straightening the stables. When they were done, he gave them permission to go back to the Castle.

Gallant was put in a stall without a lock and was free to come and go as he pleased. Because of his size he couldn't go to Tara's bedroom, of course, which saddened them both.

As the spellbinders walked away from the stables, Tara found herself on the verge of tears. Leaving Gallant was causing her almost physical pain. It didn't last long. Despite the stable hands' efforts, the pegasus walked out of his stall and joined her just as she reached the Castle.

Heads turned as the imposing stallion walked by, and everyone gathered as an embarrassed Tara tried to make him understand that he had to go back to the stables.

Her embarrassment turned to horror when she saw Master Dragosh making his way toward her through an excited crowd of courtiers—followed by the king, the queen, and the chimera.

When Dragosh saw the reason for the excitement, he bared his canines in a sinister rictus. Tara thought he looked ready to bite her. OtherWorld vampyrs apparently didn't fear sunlight, because Dragosh was paying it no mind.

"Well, young lady, what have you done to attract attention now?" he hissed malevolently.

"I haven't done anything!" said Tara defensively. "It's just that Gallant can't stand not being with me."

"That animal has no business being here, young lady. Take it back to the stables right away. You will be punished."

Frowning, the queen was about to remind the vampyr that Tara was a guest, when Cal spoke up: "He's her familiar. She was just chosen!"

A murmur of surprise greeted this statement. Such a big familiar! Very unusual! The king and queen exchanged a smile of delight.

The vampyr was surprised as well but quickly recovered.

"That it's her familiar is neither here nor there. The fact remains that this animal may not enter the Castle. So take it back to the stables, young lady. The punishment stands."

Tara felt a fierce, abnormal rage slowly rising in her mind. Something inside her hated being contradicted. Was this miserable little vampyr daring to cross her? He would learn the price of opposing her. Driven by the demonic rage, she was about to speak when a booming voice stopped her.

"What's going on here?"

Old Master Chem was making his way through the crowd. His eyes widened to see the king and queen, Tara, the pegasus, the vampyr, and the chimera, its tail slowly sweeping back and forth.

"Nothing that I can't handle, Chem," said the vampyr calmly.

Still, Tara could see how much the wizard's intervention annoyed him.

Master Chem paid him no attention. Staring at the pegasus's golden eyes, he instantly grasped the situation.

"My word, you've been chosen by a pegasus!"

Tara tried to restrain the abnormal fury boiling within her and coldly answered, "Yes . . . Master."

"May Dragondor dash me, this is really something! What were you going to do?"

"She was just returning to the Castle, Master," said Cal, ignoring the vampyr's menacing look. "Gallant couldn't stand being separated from her. You know how it is in the beginning; the attraction is almost irresistible. So he left the stables and caught up with Tara just as she was about to enter the Castle. Master Dragosh wants to punish her because he's sure she deliberately attracted Gallant here to show off. But that's not true. He only followed her!"

"Regardless of the reason why this animal is here, it still can't enter the Castle with her," said the vampyr firmly. "It must go back to the stables!"

"Can't enter the Castle?" asked the old wizard in surprise. "Why ever not?"

"Yes," chimed in the queen severely, "that's exactly what I was going to ask."

For a second, the vampyr looked stumped. Then he said, "Well for one thing, it's much too big!"

"Bah, that's nothing," said the dragon wizard. "I'm a good twenty feet tall in my natural shape. Besides, if my memory serves, Tara's grandmother was chosen by a ten-foot Bengal tiger. It obviously runs in the family! Here is what we did in those days."

He pointed at the pegasus and said: "By Miniaturus shrink the winged horse, so it can accompany Tara as a matter of course." As she watched in amazement, the pegasus shrank and shrank until it was the size of a German mastiff—still big, but quite acceptable.

"To return it to its normal size," Chem kindly informed her, "simply say: 'By Normalus it would be wise if you regained your normal size.'"

And the pegasus grew again.

"Go ahead, Tara, try it," said Fabrice.

"Don't bother," hissed the vampyr. "This 'guest' of yours can't control her power! You saw what happened in the Throne Room."

At that, the courtiers cautiously backed away from Tara. They were in no hurry to experience her power again.

"That's irrelevant," said the old wizard, frowning. "She can control her magic perfectly if she's careful."

Tara knew she could change the arrogant vampyr into a squeaking little mouse with a twitch of an eyebrow if she wanted to. Giving Dragosh a contemptuous glance, she said: "By Transformus, I want my clothes, with my usual robe on top of those!"

No sooner said than done: jeans and T-shirt promptly appeared along with Tara's robe. With an imperious snap of her fingers, she decorated her robe with hundreds of glittering horses. Finally she turned to the pegasus and said: "By Miniaturus shrink my winged horse, so it can accompany me as a matter of course."

The pegasus shrank once again.

"Heh, heh!" chuckled the old wizard, pleased but also a bit surprised by Tara's casual mastery. "I don't think the girl's doing too badly! Let her keep her familiar, since she just proved she's able to take care of it!"

Tara's rage reluctantly gave way to joy. With her mind suddenly clear again, she very nearly embraced Chem, but remembered just in time that kissing the High Wizard of Lancovit simply wasn't done. She bowed gratefully instead. But she did hug her pegasus, who was feeling a little dizzy after his repeated changes of size.

Tara shot an icy look at the vampyr, whom she no longer feared, turned, and proudly climbed the Castle steps. The king and queen were peppering her with questions, followed by the courtiers who had witnessed the scene.

The story spread like wildfire, and many people came to see the miniaturized pegasus.

After taking a shower, Tara explained to Manitou that he would now be going with Fabrice. At first, she thought he didn't understand, but her great-grandfather made a tremendous effort and managed to speak.

"Idiot dog!" he muttered with difficulty. "He's stronger than I am, and I can't fight him. You're my granddaughter, Tara. I don't want to leave you. I want to stay and protect you!"

Once again, Tara felt the strange rage that erupted when somebody crossed her.

"You don't have any choice, great-grandfather," she said coldly. "I have Gallant, and everybody knows my familiar is a pegasus. You're of no use to me."

"I understand," sighed the big Labrador sadly. "I'll go with your friend. Anyway, the stupid dog will be happy to play with a boy for a change."

Gallant, who was in permanent contact with Tara's mind, expressed his strong disapproval. He didn't like the way the girl was treating her great-grandfather, and he let her know it.

His compassion melted her abnormal rage. Tara suddenly realized how it pained her great-grandfather to abandon her, and she hugged and petted him as she expressed her thanks.

From then on, Manitou followed Fabrice like his shadow. Nobody noticed that the dog didn't have golden eyes, and he seemed to get along very well with his new friend. In any case he quit sleeping all day and started joining in his human companion's activities like the other familiars.

The king and queen were fascinated by Gallant and often asked Tara to bring him to their private apartments. She found herself increasingly struggling against the irritation that the sovereigns' affection caused her.

When rage or contempt overwhelmed Tara, Gallant struggled to help her. They both knew it wasn't normal, but something in the girl prevented her from mentioning it to her friends or to the dragon wizard; something that absolutely didn't want to make itself known.

Tara was no fool. She understood that the Demon King had put a spell on her that was changing her behavior. Did it mean that she too would turn into a demon? Despite her best efforts, Tara's demonic rages grew stronger.

One afternoon, her friends decided to tell her more about OtherWorld, magic, and spellbinders.

The four of them got together out on the Castle grounds. Since Cal was born on OtherWorld and had already been an apprentice spellbinder for two years, he was the best person to describe the magic planet.

"All right, let's see what I can tell you," he said thoughtfully. "Spellbinders have always lived among nonspells. We have found their traces even among cave dwellers. The spellbinders didn't realize that they were different, of course. Most of them helped nonspells, usually by treating their illnesses. But some others took advantage of them by pretending to be gods."

Catching Tara's look of surprise, Sparrow chimed in. "That's right. Among the Aztecs, the gods Quetzalcoatl and Tezcatlipoca were both usurped by spellbinders."

"Among the Egyptians, it was Isis, Osiris, Anubis, and Seth," said Fabrice, happy to show off his book learning. "For the Romans, Jupiter, Juno, and Minerva. For the Greeks, Zeus and Aphrodite; Thor and Odin among the Vikings. Because of those impostors, the High Council wizards created a special police force to prevent spell-binders from passing themselves off as gods. As soon as a false god tried to seize power on Earth, he was tracked down and imprisoned or destroyed."

"As mankind evolved, the spellbinders evolved as well," continued Cal, now comfortably stretched out on the grass. "Finally the day came when they were numerous and powerful enough to want to dominate the nonspells. But it didn't work—"

"—because of rivalries between different spellbinder factions, and they nearly destroyed Earth with their lousy wars," said Sparrow, who disliked conflict. "Then the dragons appeared. They came from another dimension. From another time. From other worlds they ruled. Strange worlds where elves, trolls, giants, imps, gnomes, tatris (Lady Kalibris's people), vampyrs, changelins (were-beasts), and chimeras lived. The dragons were fighting a terrible war with the demons and decided to conquer Earth with an army of elves, giants, and others. The aim was to keep the demons from using it as a base, since the main rift between our world and Limbo is located on Earth. But Demiderus, a wizard of genius, assembled an army of spellbinders who used their magic powers to oppose the invaders. The dragons were very surprised to discover that humans knew magic."

"More than surprised," said Cal, laughing. "They took a pounding, and it stopped their conquest in its tracks. The dragons realized that rather than fighting the spellbinders, they were better off joining them to defeat the demons. So they offered our ancestors a pact. The dragons agreed not to invade Earth, if the spellbinders would promise not to try to dominate it and help them defeat the demons. To train the spellbinders and increase their power, the dragons suggested that they come to OtherWorld, where magic was much more powerful than on Earth. At first, the spellbinders thought this was a trap, but over the years they realized the dragons were sincere. So they agreed, and the dragons cast a forgetfulness spell on Earth. It erased the memory of the centuries of invasion from the nonspells' memories. What remained were legends about vampyrs, elves, and other magical peoples.

"Thanks to the alliance, and especially thanks to Demiderus and four other unusually powerful wizards, the demons were defeated and imprisoned on their worlds, in the demonic world called Forbidden Limbo. Magic seals were placed along the rifts, and Atlantis, the main island where the primary rift was located, was drowned in the ocean." (Atlantis! thought Tara. She'd read about the Earth legend of a mysterious island with a very advanced civilization that had vanished beneath the waves of the Atlantic Ocean. Now she understood what had really happened.) "Only the five original high wizards or their descendents can penetrate them; no one else. At the same time, the dragons created openings—portals—that allowed communication and travel between OtherWorld and Earth. The spellbinders moved permanently to OtherWorld, as did many nonspells."

Fabrice continued: "The very few spellbinders who chose to stay on Earth had to swear that they would never use their powers in the presence of nonspells, and never to profit from them."

"The special police created to track false gods was merciless and efficient, so it was now given a new mission," said Sparrow with a shudder. "Under the high wizards' orders, the elf police was charged with tracking down and punishing offenders. They were the ones who eliminated Druidor Bloodgrave, which is why Bloodgraves hate elves. Along with a few high wizards who remained on Earth, they keep an eye on the nonspells and see to it that no demons try to escape from Limbo. As Cal said, the major rift between Limbo and our world is located on Earth."

"Lots of different peoples live on OtherWorld," said Fabrice, "and not just spellbinders and the nonspells who moved here and now live in the planet's kingdoms, republics, and empires like Lancovit, Brontagne, and Omois." He ticked off the peoples on his fingers. "Elves live in Selena; dwarves in the mountains of Hymlia; giants in Gandis; unicorns in Mentalir; imps, gnomes, and goblins in Smallcountry; vampyrs in Krasalvia; trolls in Krankar, and so on. So that we can understand each other, an Interpretus translates everything we say."

"And talk about politics!" said Sparrow, rolling her eyes. "Omois is the most powerful of the human kingdoms, empires, or republics. It is jointly ruled by Empress Lisbeth'tylanhnem T'al Barmi Ab Santa Ab Maru and her half-brother Sandor T'al Barmi Ab March Ab Brevis. The empress hasn't been able to have any children, even though she's had several prince consorts. Her brother Danviou T'al Barmi Ab Santa Ab Maru disappeared a dozen years ago, and the question of succession will come up soon, because under Omois law, her half-brother can't rule alone. He must always rule with a full member of the imperial family, because the empress is the direct descendent of Demiderus, one of the five high wizards who imprisoned the demons."

Tara shook her head, overwhelmed by the flood of information.

"Yikes, it's so complicated! Kingdoms, empires, republics, dwarves, elves, vampyrs, dragons, tatris!"

"It's so complicated that the rest will have to wait for another day," said Cal, standing and brushing himself off. "Because now it's time for kitchen duty. After that, we'll go take a spin with the pegasi."

Gallant looked up with delight. Sparrow, who got dizzy riding a pegasus, was much less enthusiastic.

The apprentice spellbinders had kitchen duty three times a week, which allowed them to refine their spell casting on a small scale.

That day's operation was being supervised by Master Dragosh, Tara noticed. Under his firm leadership, dinner rolls, meats, vegetables, and pastries were replicated and then quickly carried to the dining halls to fill the many hungry stomachs in the huge Castle.

"All right, time for the new crew to take over," Dragosh ordered. "And remember, no eating before dinner!"

Skyler, Robin, and Carole gratefully yielded their places to Cal, Sparrow, and Fabrice, who began to replicate what the cooks brought them.

Tara knew she could use magic to help her friends if she needed to. When Gallant chose her, she'd asked Master Chem to contact her grandmother to make sure that meeting her familiar hadn't laid Isabella out stone cold. Fortunately, she was fine. But Tara still preferred to avoid magic; she'd seen how the demonic fury inside her boiled up when she turned on her power. So she grabbed an apron and with a sigh started peeling carrots for the pot of soup simmering in front of her.

Despite his itchy fingers and ravenous appetite, Cal managed to restrain himself until the moment when the cook took a beautiful mulberry pie out of the oven.

"I'll take care of that one," he said innocently, and the unsuspecting cook handed it to him.

Cal set the hot pie on the table and muttered, "By Duplicatus, I want three pies, just like this one, but a larger size." Three mulberry pies appeared, and one promptly vanished . . . into Cal's mouth.

"C-C-Cal, be c-c-careful," hissed Sparrow. "D-D-Dragosh is watching you!"

"Ow, that's hot!" said the young spellbinder, who'd burned his tongue. "Don't worry, I'm a thief. The vampyr who's gonna catch me in the act hasn't been born yet. You want some?"

Tara was mournfully staring at a mountain of carrots and thinking that if she were a rabbit, she'd be in heaven. A sudden cry of rage made her jump. She just had time to see three things— Dragosh grabbing Cal by the scruff of the neck; the pie falling from his hand; and Sparrow leaping back in fear—before a thousand gallons of hot leek soup flooded the kitchen.

The vampyr slipped and fell in the sticky, brownish liquid, releasing Cal, who raced off. The soup swamped the kitchen's pots, pans, and skillets, put out the burners, half drowned the cooks and their helpers, and only stopped just before it reached the door.

Tara, wide-eyed at the scale of the disaster, couldn't suppress a nervous laugh.

"You, you . . . " roared the incensed vampyr, who was dripping wet and trying to stand on the slippery floor. "You did that on purpose, I know it! You're going to clean up this whole mess, and with a mop and a bucket! No magic, or I'll . . . "

Dragosh was so enraged that words failed him, and he flew out of the kitchen in pursuit of Cal. Drenched in soup, the other kitchen workers were glaring at Tara. She shrugged. The vampyr had frightened her, so he got what he deserved. Cal was gone, and Sparrow and Fabrice had vanished, so Tara started mopping and sluicing the soup down the drains alone.

A few minutes later, Master Den'maril's apprentice, Robin, came by. He was very surprised to see Tara on her hands and knees, wiping the floor.

"What the heck are you doing?" he asked.

"I'm mopping the floor," she said through gritted teeth. She was so furious that she had to struggle to keep her magic from blowing up the kitchen and half the Castle. "And the more I mop, the more I feel like Cinderella."

"I see," said Robin, approaching her cautiously. "And who is the evil stepmother who made you mop the floor?"

"The evil stepmother is a horrible vampyr who's always tormenting me. I admit I sort of drowned him in soup, but it's not my fault. He scared me!"

"Ah, I get it," Robin said sympathetically. "And is there any special reason why you aren't using magic to clean the kitchen?"

"Can't do it," she said tersely. "Not allowed."

"Well, in that case I'll do what any knight errant would do for a damsel in distress." With an elegant gesture, he said: "By Cleanus, I demand, make this kitchen spic and span!"

A tornado instantly swept through the room. In the blink of an eye the pots scrubbed themselves clean, the soup disappeared, and the plates flew onto their shelves. Within moments, the kitchen was as clean and dry as if nothing had ever happened. Deeply impressed, Tara thought that Robin would bring joy to the heart of every housewife on Earth.

She wanted to hug and kiss him but fought the impulse since she was still soaked with soup from head to foot.

"Thank you!" she cried with delight. "You've saved my life!"

Robin made a sweeping bow. "At your service, lady fair," he said. With a tip of an imaginary hat, he went out.

Tara shook her head and laughed, but deep down she was terribly worried. Since coming back from Limbo she'd been very careful about what she said and had managed to avoid using metaphors. But she flew off the handle too easily, and her abnormal rage made her want to hit, hurt, or destroy anyone who annoyed or crossed her. Worse, the influence of the demonic spell only seemed to be growing.

Still feeling very concerned, she went to take a shower and scrubbed herself for a good quarter of an hour to get rid of even the faintest whiff of leeks. She got dressed and went down to the dining hall.

Lunch was nearly over, and everyone had heard about the incident in the kitchen. As Tara headed for the table with her friends, muttered comments followed her.

"She's dangerous," whispered Angelica to her little entourage. "She isn't one of us, and she has no business being in the Castle. One of these days she might hurt someone, maybe even kill them."

"She shouldn't be allowed to do magic," whispered someone else. "She can't control it. She's reckless."

"She's a weirdo," said a third. "Who knows where she's from?"

And so forth.

Tara kept her temper, ignored the whispers, and went to sit down next to Cal.

"Don't pay any attention to them," said Cal loudly enough to be heard. "They're just gutless cowards. And they're jealous because your gift is more powerful than theirs."

"That's right," added Fabrice. "If Master Dragosh hadn't grabbed Cal, everything would've been fine. I was just replicating a gallon of soup—"

"—and I replicated a thousand!" interrupted Tara glumly. "*I hate magic!* It's dangerous. Not only do I risk killing my grandmother, but I can't control it. As soon as I get home I'm gonna ask her to take this blasted magic away forever."

Cal, Sparrow, and Fabrice stared at her in shock.

"What are you s-s-saying?" asked Sparrow. "You d-d-don't have the right! It's your g-g-gift, and it's dumb—"

"—to react like that," finished Cal. "Just because you can't control your magic doesn't mean you should give it up completely! You're so gifted, Tara!"

"No, I know I'm right," Tara interrupted. "Besides, I'm putting you at risk. I heard what Angelica said. She said I might be dangerous to you, and she's right."

"No, she isn't," said a voice. "Your gift is very precious, Tara. And you shouldn't give it up because of a few nasty gossips."

Tara turned to see Robin standing there, watching her.

She gave him a warm smile. "I want to thank you again for what you did in the kitchen," she said. "Without you, I'd probably be cleaning the place all night."

Robin shrugged off the compliment. "It was nothing. Any one of us would've done the same thing."

"That's right," said Fabrice, who didn't seem especially pleased by Robin's sudden turn in the limelight. "Master Dragosh was chasing Cal, and we were chasing Master Dragosh."

"I really better avoid him for the next few days," said Cal. "He looked pretty angry."

"Come on! He was so furious, smoke was coming out of his ears," said Fabrice with a chuckle.

"No, that was soup; it was still steaming," said Tara with a hint of a smile.

"He had celery up his nose, a piece of carrot in his ear, and was dripping soup everywhere, while screaming for Cal."

"We had n-n-no t-t-trouble following him," said a giggling Sparrow. "He left s-s-soup t-t-tracks all over the c-c-castle."

"And got chewed out by the steward for making such a mess," said Fabrice. "His face turned so red, I thought he was going to have a heart attack."

"Yeah; it's crazy what a *souper* wizard the guy is," Cal concluded.

The friends looked at each other and burst out laughing.

"Oh, man, I wish I'd seen that," said Robin, wiping his eyes.

"Stop it!" said Tara, still laughing. "My stomach hurts!"

That evening, the five gathered in the dormitory common room to get to know Robin a little better. Angelica and her friends were off in a corner, chatting.

"It was s-s-so funny," said Sparrow, remembering the soup-soaked vampyr. "Lady K-K-Kalibris told me that s-s-she'd m-m-met M-M-Master Dragosh in the hallway, and s-s-she mentioned—"

Angelica, who'd been eavesdropping, suddenly snapped.

"Are you ev-ev-ever g-g-gonna f-f-finish y-y-your s-s-sentence?" she shouted, imitating Sparrow's stutter. "It's maddening enough to make a normal person blow up!"

She'd barely finished her tirade when Tara's magic slipped off leash and struck. Angelica started to blow up. She got bigger and bigger, and floated up toward the ceiling, screaming in panic.

Dumbfounded, the young spellbinders looked up to see her wedged between the ceiling beams.

The Castle was so surprised that the walls wavered and the landscapes disappeared for a moment. But it quickly gathered its wits, as well as its sense of humor. It created a blue sky for Angelica to float in, along with a few birds and some puffy white clouds. It also made the floor disappear. Overcome with vertigo, Angelica closed her eyed and screamed even louder.

"Jeez Louise, she's never gonna stop!" said Cal, plugging his ears. "She must have a hundred gallons of air in her lungs. Let's haul her down before my eardrums burst."

Cal, Skyler, and Carole levitated and tried to lower her but they failed, even when pulling with all their might. Angelica was as buoyant as a helium balloon, and stuck tighter to the ceiling than two-week-old chewing gum. They didn't dare cast any spells for fear of making her situation worse.

"Nothing works," said Skyler as he landed. "We can't get her unstuck. We better get a high wizard."

"Maybe if we had some sort of serving utensil," mused Cal. "You know, one of those flat things you use with a pie—or a tart."

"Angelica is not a tart!" exclaimed Carole. "That's mean, Cal! We've got to do something!"

After ten more minutes of fruitless effort, they finally called Lady Kalibris. Her powerful magic got Angelica unstuck from the ceiling but couldn't deflate her or get her down to earth.

Tara watched with some pleasure as Angelica was tied to a rope and towed to the infirmary in front of the whole Castle.

"I can't believe you did that!" whispered Sparrow to Tara when Lady Kalibris had taken Angelica away. "What a pain in the neck that girl is, anyway. Serves her right!"

"Hey, you aren't stuttering," said Cal.

Sparrow blushed happily.

"Gee, you're right! Let's see: 'Peter Piper picked a peck of pickled peppers; a peck of pickled peppers Peter Piper picked!' I can't believe it! I'm not stuttering anymore. That's fantastic!"

She started dancing around the common room with Sheeba, who looked just as happy as she did.

"But how did it happen?" she asked. "Mom took me to the best medical spellbinders in the kingdom and they all said they couldn't cure me!"

When Tara answered, it wasn't her speaking, but the demonic thing that controlled her mind and sparked her rage: "Angelica needed to be taught a lesson, and her mocking your stutter made me want to kill her."

Taken aback by the brutality of the statement, Sparrow gaped at her for a moment. But she decided that her friend was joking, and smiled.

"So you're the person I have to thank. It's fantastic!"

To her astonished friends, Sparrow now recited: "When a fox is in the bottle where the tweetle beetles battle with their paddles in a puddle on a noodle-eating poodle, this is what they call a tweetle beetle noodle poodle bottled paddled muddled duddled fuddled wuddled fox in socks!"

"Brava!" cried Cal. "That's amazing!"

"It's by an Earth writer called Dr. Seuss. Want to hear more?"

Cal was enthusiastic, but he wasn't crazy.

"Er, no thanks. That was very good. Congratulations again!"

Sparrow never stuttered again.

Lady Deria, who didn't much like Angelica either, was very amused by what had happened. She'd been keeping an eye on Tara and spent as much time as she could with her, talking about magic and powers.

One day when they were in the training room, Deria was working out with an exercise sword, slashing the air with total concentration. As Tara admired the precision of her movements, she reflected that she was glad to be Deria's friend. She wouldn't care to be her enemy.

Deria said to Tara later: "You know, Tara, I've known you ever since you were a little girl, and I never suspected that you had magic powers. But when I saw how powerful your gift was, I knew it was important for you and for OtherWorld for you to be able to use it." Deria didn't know about the blood oath, and Tara didn't tell her. As the days passed, Deria encouraged Tara to use her magic as much as possible. There was nothing better than practice, she said. Tara gradually let herself be tempted. It wasn't much, she thought to herself, just a few exercises. Changing her hair color, for example (red didn't suit her at all, and neither did brown), changing the color of her pegasus's coat (Gallant really hated the green polka dots and purple stripes she made him wear one whole afternoon), or improving her wardrobe (that was hardly conclusive, and it was awkward to put on a shirt with one sleeve on one side and three on the other). But because of the abnormal rage that boiled up when she was crossed and which amplified her magic, Tara was careful not to use her magic around her friends. It was safer—for them.

The Bloodgraves hadn't tried anything since the harpy attack. Not a scrap of gray cloth had been seen. Tara hadn't learned anything in Lancovit about the Gray Fortress, and she was impatient to continue her research in Omois.

If she hadn't been on a mission, she might have enjoyed her stay on OtherWorld more. Aside from the chimera and the vampyr, the people were pretty nice. The chimera had a nasty habit of popping up when she least expected it, staring at her from a distance, then disappearing. It got on her nerves. As for the vampyr, he looked at Tara the way a cat looks at a particularly appetizing canary. Except he didn't realize that this canary could be a lot more dangerous than the cat.

Aside from those vexations, she and Fabrice were fitting in well, and the tall, handsome earthling had drawn plenty of girls' looks.

One afternoon Fabrice burst into the library looking furious.

Cal was levitating, trying to chase a recalcitrant book. When he grabbed the wriggling tome, he saw Fabrice's expression and said, "What's up with you? You look like someone who bit into a plum and found a family of worms having dinner in it."

"That's pretty much it," grumbled Fabrice. "I was just ambushed."

"Really?" said Cal, who immediately came down to earth. "Tell me about it."

Fabrice plopped down onto a chair.

"Do you know those two bimbos who are always gossiping with Angelica?"

"You mean the two looky-looks?"

"What the heck is a looky-look?"

"A big bird with golden feathers that spends all its time parading around and clucking. They're very easy to catch. You just set up a mirror in the forest, and within ten minutes you'll have half a dozen of them admiring themselves in it."

"You're pulling my leg," said Fabrice.

"Not at all," said Cal very seriously, though a dimple in his cheek gave him away. "I think the description fits Angelica's friends perfectly. So?"

"Well, your looky-looks cornered me when I was playing with Manitou, and they asked why I hung out with losers like you."

Cal started to laugh. "Is that all? You must really interest them. What did you tell them?"

"Nothing. I was so surprised I couldn't think of a thing to say. But Manitou came to my rescue. He put his muddy paws on their nice clean dresses, and they took off."

Cal scratched the dog behind the ears, producing a moan of pleasure. "Now that's a good doggie!"

"Er, remember, that's Tara's great-grandfather," said Fabrice. "How about a little respect, okay?"

"Has he spoken in the time he's been with you?"

"No."

"Then that makes him a *very* good dog," said Cal, stroking Manitou's silky head. "And speaking of dog, I saw what you did last night."

"Last night?" asked Fabrice cautiously.

"Yeah. Either I dreamed it, or you let Manitou into your canopy bed."

"Listen, I don't dare let him sleep in his kennel. What if he suddenly comes to his senses? So he sleeps at the foot of my bed—and man, does he snore!"

Cal laughed. "Personally, I don't care, but don't let Lady Kalibris catch you."

That night Cal had trouble sleeping because he'd had too much dinner—mulberry tarts were served again, and he ate four of them—and he decided to go out for a walk.

Passing Fabrice's bed, he chuckled to hear Manitou snoring, then slipped out of the dormitory. On the way he noticed that Robin's bed curtains were open.

He was about to duck into one of the passages that led out of the Castle when he heard voices. Squeezing into a recess, he saw the silhouettes of two people next to the dormitory wall.

"What are you doing here?" asked a woman.

"I could ask you the same thing," hissed a voice that Cal immediately recognized. It was Master Dragosh!

"It doesn't seem very healthy for a vampyr to be roaming the Castle hallways in the middle of the night," said the woman coldly.

"Come now, Lady Deria! You know that I feed only on animal blood. Human blood doesn't interest me."

"All I know is that you have no business being around the apprentices' dormitory, Master Dragosh. So I suggest you leave before I tell the high wizard about your odd habits."

The vampyr bowed to the young woman.

"Then allow me to accompany you back to your room," he said with icy politeness. "Since our rooms are next to each other, you'll be able to see me go into mine."

Having no choice, the young woman agreed, and they left together,

When Cal stepped out of his hiding place his heart was pounding. What was the vampyr up to? Was he in league with the people who had attacked Tara's grandmother? She had sent Deria to protect her granddaughter, and Cal got the impression that this was exactly what she'd been doing.

Reluctant to wake Fabrice, Cal decided to wait until morning to tell him, along with Tara and Sparrow. Their little group would have to be on its guard; they would figure it out tomorrow.

It was a decision he would bitterly regret.

Because the next morning, Fabrice had disappeared.

CHAPTER 9

VANISHED!

"Tara was the person they were after," said Cal somberly. "I'm sure of it!"

The three friends had gathered in Master Chem's cavern office.

"That seems clear," said the wizard, who was pacing back and forth. "Tell me again everything that happened since yesterday, Cal."

The young thief didn't need to be asked twice.

When Fabrice didn't get up, Cal said, he'd gone to take a shower. He then went back to his friend's bed and called to him, thinking he hadn't heard the eight o'clock bell.

No answer.

Now worried, Cal knocked on the canopy bed frame, but no one stirred. So he'd gone down to the dining hall, where Tara and Sparrow were waiting.

"Cal, what's wrong?" exclaimed Tara, upon seeing his anxious face.

"I don't know yet. Have you seen Fabrice this morning?"

"No, why? Isn't he up?"

"I knocked on his canopy bed, but he isn't answering, and I'm not allowed in without permission. Also, something very strange happened last night."

He then told them what he had seen.

"See Lady Kalibris swiftly and speak to her!" said Sparrow. She had developed a fondness for the letter S since she'd stopped stuttering, and it led to some strange turns of phrase. "Fabrice might have the sniffles, or be sick with something."

"She's right," said Tara. "This isn't normal. Let's go."

Lady Kalibris had come to supervise breakfast. When she learned that Fabrice hadn't gotten up, her two heads exhibited worried frowns, and she rushed to the boys' dormitory.

Despite the straightening-up spells, the dormitory looked pretty much what you'd expect from boys. Odd socks hovered here and there, seeking their mates; unfinished models sprawled next to puzzles with missing pieces; and a pair of sneakers tried to hide the holes in its soles. All this amid a vague smell of stinky feet.

Lady Kalibris opened the curtains of Fabrice's bed.

It held only a pillow and a cushion indented with the shape of Manitou's body.

Fabrice's spellbinder robes were all hanging in the closet.

"He couldn't have gone far in pajamas," muttered Lady Kalibris in perplexity. "I'll have the Castle and the grounds searched. Meanwhile, go eat your breakfast. And thanks for alerting me!"

With heavy hearts, the three friends obeyed.

Moments later, High Wizard Chem interrupted the meal when he entered the dining hall accompanied by Lady Kalibris. He cleared his throat, and his magically amplified voice silenced everyone.

"I have some strange, sad news to announce. This morning one of our apprentice spellbinders, Fabrice Besois-Giron, disappeared. We think he may have been kidnapped, as several of our apprentices were last year."

An anxious murmur ran through the hall.

"The Castle is now on high alert," continued the wizard. "If any of you saw or heard anything, come to my office after breakfast so we can discuss it. We will do our best to clear up this mystery. Thank you for your attention."

As Chem was talking with Lady Kalibris, Sparrow whispered to Cal, "You ought to come forward right away about what happened last night!"

"Why me?" asked Cal, who was never very comfortable with authority. "I'm sure Lady Deria told Master Chem about it. What if he asks me what I was doing up in the middle of the night?"

"Don't be so self-centered, for heaven's sake," cried Tara indignantly. "Even if there's a chance you'll be punished, Chem has other things to worry about besides your little affairs. Fabrice is our friend, and he's disappeared. We can't abandon him!"

Feeling disgusted, Cal put down his fork. It went over to spear a piece of cheese and offered it to him, but he shook his head.

"All right, I'm going. Anyway, I'm not hungry anymore."

In the wizard's huge office, Cal related the odd nighttime conversation he had overheard.

"That's curious," Chem said thoughtfully, "because neither Master Dragosh nor Lady Deria told me about this incident. Though I'm not sure you could call it an incident. My wizards are free to wander wherever they like. But Besois-Giron's disappearance does cast a different light on it."

Tara agreed.

"I don't know that much about magic yet," she said, "but let's imagine somebody wanted to kidnap me or Fabrice. What would they have to do to grab us?"

"Well, at least they would have to be able to see you. Fabrice seems to have been kidnapped in the dormitory, because the Memorus showed a brief flash in his canopy bed."

"But we were all asleep," said Cal. "How do we know Fabrice wasn't lured outside?"

"A kidnapper could only do that by kidnapping a familiar and using its hair or feathers to attract their human companion. I was under the impression that young Besois-Giron didn't have a familiar."

Tara and Sparrow exchanged looks.

"Well, that is . . . not exactly," said Tara.

The old wizard straightened in his chair. "What do you mean 'not exactly'?"

"Well, when I was chosen by Gallant, we thought it would look suspicious for me to have two familiars. Fabrice didn't have one and was feeling left out, so I loaned him Manitou."

Chem couldn't believe his ears. "You *loaned* him your great-grandfather?"

"Er, yeah, sort of."

The wizard looked bothered, but then he sighed and muttered something like, "Ah, children!" Then he said, "In any case I don't think Manitou could have been the link, since his kennel was too far from Fabrice's bed to affect him."

A very embarrassed Cal now spoke up.

"What if . . . what if Manitou slept right on Fabrice's bed? Would that be a problem?"

For a second, Tara thought the dragon wizard was going to start hiccuping in surprise, and she quickly examined the desk. Okay, all was well—there was plenty of room underneath to shelter the three of them in case of a fit of transformation.

But Chem managed to control his hiccuping and didn't turn into a dragon. He was furious, however.

"By Demiderus! When we make rules, doesn't *anyone* in this Castle follow them? We didn't forbid familiars in the canopy beds because of hairs or feathers, but to keep them from being used as vectors by hostile spellbinders. Anyway, what matters isn't the magical link, but how close the animal is to the person to be kidnapped. The apprentices who disappeared last year were probably kidnapped with the use of their familiars. It's your fault that your friend disappeared. You should've come to see me right away to warn me that Fabrice was breaking the rules!"

Cal felt terribly guilty and sank into the depths of his chair. But Tara exploded, barely containing her fury to keep from turning the dragon into dog food.

"So you've been telling us more lies!" she yelled. "When are adults going to learn to trust us? If you'd told us how the apprentices were kidnapped—and especially why we aren't allowed to keep our familiars with us—Fabrice would never have disobeyed your orders. It's *your* fault! Anyway, you'd better tell everybody the truth, because I'm sure Fabrice wasn't the only one letting his familiar sleep with him!"

The dragon wizard seemed astonished at being reprimanded. He must not be used to having his orders challenged, thought Sparrow, who was scared he would turn them into toads to teach them manners. But Chem had no intention of punishing them.

"I know," he said, pacing back and forth. "We considered doing it, but we decided not to say anything because everybody was already so upset. Anyway, thanks to you I now know how Besois-Giron was kidnapped."

He paused and turned to Tara.

"Tell me, Tara. Even though we forbade it, I suppose you told your story to your friends, haven't you?"

"Yes," she said defiantly, refusing to feel guilty. "I couldn't keep such a secret to myself. So they know what's going on."

Cal, who had been thinking hard, spoke up somberly: "All this means just one thing: the traitor is one of us!"

Chem nodded.

"I realize that," he said. "Only a high wizard or the most advanced spellbinder could have accomplished this. First the harpy cage was sabotaged, then Besois-Giron was abducted. But I really can't see by whom."

"You know Master Dragosh well, don't you?" asked Cal casually.

"Mmm, what?" asked the wizard, lost in thought. "Safir Dragosh? Yes, I know him very well. Why?"

"He has a strange attitude," said Cal. "He seems to hate Tara. Also, he was prowling in the hallways the night Fabrice disappeared."

"No, it couldn't be Dragosh," said Chem firmly. "I trust him completely. He wouldn't be capable of doing such a thing."

Tara had seen dozens of movies in which the good guy says that he absolutely trusts the bad guy, usually adding that he couldn't hurt a fly. At that very moment the camera shows the bad guy chopping someone to pieces. So she was far from convinced by what Master Chem was saying.

"Listen, children, I don't think you can do much more for the time being," he said. "Let me take care of this."

Once outside the office, Sparrow turned to Cal.

"So what do you think?"

"I think we should take turns watching our friend the vampyr to see what he does, who he talks with, what he eats—"

"No!" she said with a shudder. "Not what he eats!"

"All right then, who he eats with. Are you guys willing?"

"Of course, but it won't be easy," answered Tara. "What if Lady Kalibris or Salatar catches us?"

"We'll just have to be careful. If we can prove Dragosh is guilty, Chem can hold his feet to the fire to make him say where he hid Fabrice."

"You're right," said Sparrow firmly. "We'll set it up. We can take turns watching his room until midnight or one o'clock. If he goes out or does something unusual, we'll follow him."

But though they watched Dragosh's room for hours, the vampyr never left it.

That same day, an impressive array of protective measures was taken in the Castle, which didn't make the three spies' job easier.

By a trick Cal wouldn't reveal, he was able to persuade the Living Castle to create a secret hiding place for them in the wall opposite the vampyr's room. It was completely hidden behind the illusory landscapes, though Tara once broke into a cold sweat when the chimera suddenly started sniffing the wall. But Salatar walked off shaking his head, wondering where the suspicious smell could have come from.

Meanwhile, they had to avoid the guards, sleepless courtiers, wizards, and familiars who wandered the Castle. Not to mention Robin, who seemed to spend so much time outside it that they began to wonder what he was up to every night.

Late the next evening, the whole Castle was jolted by the sound of screaming.

Cal, who was sleepily standing guard behind the illusory landscapes, nearly had a heart attack. Everyone came running, but surprisingly, nothing stirred in the vampyr's room. So Cal was astonished when he saw Master Dragosh down the hall with the other wizards.

The screaming continued, loud enough to wake the dead. It brought Master Chem running too. He had forgotten that he had turned back into his dragon shape to sleep and almost demolished half the Castle and trampled the king and queen, who were also racing toward the noise. The old wizard's hair was standing straight up, and his fangs, claws, and wings had only just shrunk away.

"What in the world is going on?" Chem roared at the enormous red demon who was in charge of security. Half the Castle was staring at the demon in terror.

"Someone tried to go out without permission," the demon answered with dignity. "I apprehended the offender."

He opened his enormous hands, revealing the unconscious body of Angelica.

"Miss Brandaud?" blurted the surprised wizard. "What's going on? And what is that racket we keep hearing?"

Everyone listened, and the people standing closest to the Castle's main entrance cautiously moved away from it. Outside the doors, something was causing an infernal din—shrieking, screaming, and pounding on the panels.

Master Chem gestured to the crowd to step back and ordered the doors to open. He barely had time to get out of the way when a small, glittering lizard flew to attack the red demon.

Roused by the demon's desperate attempts to avoid his attacker, Angelica opened her eyes but promptly closed them again and resumed screaming.

Lady Kalibris was the first to understand what had happened. Using both her voices to make herself heard, she yelled, "Let her go, demon. She's been chosen!"

The demon promptly released the tall girl, who tumbled to the floor. The flying lizard immediately rushed over to Angelica and began to stroke her cheek, while uttering little cries of encouragement. The lizard was absolutely beautiful, with a golden body and glittering wings—the perfect bauble to flatter Angelica's vanity.

She was struggling to gather her wits. Then, her eyes wide with wonder, she announced, "Kimi! She says her name is Kimi!"

"Well, we're all very happy to hear that," said the wizard, who didn't look happy at all. "Go back to bed, everyone, the choosing is over. Go on!"

He bowed to the red demon.

"Thank you for your prompt intervention. We are sorry to have bothered you."

"No problem, it was a good little scrap," said the demon with a smile that revealed an impressive row of teeth. On his body, the wounds inflicted by the lizard were already healing and fading. "I was bored stiff, sitting in my dimension, and this livened things up a bit. I'm happy to come back for guard duty whenever you like."

Bowing to the king, the queen, and the high wizards, the demon vanished in a cloud of sulfur.

Angelica's friends surrounded her, in raptures over the beautiful flying lizard.

Finally, everyone headed for their respective dormitories.

Cal signaled to Tara and Sparrow that he had discovered something. But Lady Kalibris accompanied them back to their rooms, so they had to wait until the next day to find out what it was.

That night, Tara had trouble sleeping. She realized she was starting to enjoy her nightmares. They were all about power and domination, and she was always in charge, giving the orders.

Next morning, Cal had some bad news for the group.

"Master Dragosh is somehow able to come and go without my seeing him. All the racket last night should have brought him out of his room, but it didn't. But when I looked down the hall, who do you think I saw?"

"Dragosh?" guessed Sparrow.

"Bingo! But I was standing right in front of his room, and he never came out. Which means he can come and go without our knowing it!"

"Yikes! We've got a serious problem," said Sparrow. "What do you know about vampyrs? I can tell you a lot about the habits of giants and dwarves, because we lived among them for a long time, but I don't know the first thing about vampyrs."

"I seem to remember that they live a very long time, like human wizards," said Cal. "They raise animals and drink their blood without killing them. They like the blood of sheep, cows, chickens, ducks, and pegasi. The only kind they can't drink is human blood. If they do, it makes them crazy and cuts their life span in half. When they drink human blood they can't stand sunlight and only go out at night. Oh, and they also can't stand the blood of dragons and unicorns. That's pretty much all I remember."

"On Earth, vampires are also able to change shape," said Tara thoughtfully. "Is that true of OtherWorld vampyrs too?"

"Of course, that's it!" said Cal, slapping his forehead. "What an idiot I am!"

He scowled at Sparrow, who had a big grin on her face and was energetically nodding in agreement.

"You're right, Tara!" he continued. "They *can* change shape. They can change into a wolf . . . or a bat! That must be how Master Dragosh can leave his room without our being able to see him. In this warm weather all the Castle windows are open. He can fly in without activating any magic spells, so he doesn't trip the alarm or the anti-mosquito spells."

"That would explain last night," said Tara, thinking hard. "But how can we keep an eye on a guy who can fly? And we can't go out at night anyway."

Looking gloomy, the three friends were racking their brains when Gallant raised his head and whinnied joyously. He stroked Tara with his wing, then flew out the window to perch like a cat in the enormous oak tree that loomed over the south side of the Castle.

Cal, Sparrow, and Tara were trying to understand what he was up to when Sheeba also ran outside and climbed the oak tree. Then

Blondin scurried through a hole in the wall, reappeared out on the grass, and ducked behind the oak, leaving only the tip of his muzzle showing.

Sparrow, who was the most intuitive of the three, suddenly got it.

"They're geniuses! Our familiars are geniuses!"

Cal and Tara were staring at each other, unsure of what their friend meant, when their eyes lit up at the same instant.

"They're going to be our lookouts!" they said together.

The familiars had found the answer. They were much freer to come and go than the young spellbinders—and who better to follow a flying animal than another flying animal? Standing watch became a lot easier, because when Blondin wasn't watching, Sheeba or Gallant was.

But Master Dragosh didn't seem to fly anywhere special. He simply fluttered around the Castle without entering any particular room. The three spies finally decided that he was an insomniac, or that he liked moonlight, or that it was something vampyrs did, exhausting themselves by flying here and there all night long.

Tara was feeling so worried about Fabrice that she had chewed halfway through her white forelock, and Cal didn't know what to do to reassure her.

For her part, Sparrow was also going through a difficult period. She had a secret that she couldn't share, and it was eating at her.

She had already almost given herself away several times—when she unpacked her clothes, for example. Tara was smart enough to know that the person Sparrow claimed to be didn't have the means to pay for those kinds of clothes. Sparrow had noticed her reaction and had almost told her the truth. She liked Tara, but something still stood between them, and she knew that her friend was aware of her distance.

For his part, Cal noticed that Angelica's flying lizard seemed to spend a lot of time around them. Whenever he turned his head, Cal would spy the tip of a glittering wing, a golden eye, or a scaly claw. In the beginning, he thought the little familiar was just curious. But as the business continued, he laughed when he realized what was going on.

They were watching the vampyr, and Angelica was watching *them*.

Angelica was nasty, but she wasn't stupid. She clearly understood that Tara was powerful, even though she had trouble controlling her gift. She also was in no doubt as to the identity of the person who had blown her up. Finally, she felt she had less influence over the other apprentices than she'd had the year before. A terrible hunger for revenge began to build in her.

So Angelica sent her flying lizard to see what the three were up to. She hoped to catch them red-handed doing something wrong so she could turn them in. And if she could do worse, she wouldn't hesitate.

Lying in bed, she often wondered how she could get rid of her rival.

One approach would be to get Tara in trouble during a session of the Council. Another would be to leak information only the high wizards had, to make Tara look like a spy. But Angelica's trap had to be perfect, so no one would suspect her of having set it. And the apprentices were all too close for her to act without being noticed.

One evening, she was mulling over revenge fantasies when she suddenly sat up. Yes! She knew what she would do!

Angelica glanced toward Tara's room and gave a nasty chuckle. That girl will rue the day she'd ever set foot on OtherWorld, she thought.

CHAPTER 10

HIGH WIZARDS AND EVIL SPELLS

The following day, Tara awoke with a feeling of . . . emptiness. As if something had been taken from her.

She spent nearly all day wondering about it until the moment she absentmindedly grabbed her white forelock to chew on it and missed by a couple of inches. Someone had cut her hair—or at least a strand of it.

Tara mentioned it to Sparrow, who just laughed.

"You've been so worried about Fabrice, you never quit chewing on that silly strand. I'm not surprised it's shorter."

"Look, I know somebody cut it," Tara said firmly. "I don't know who, why, or how, but I know how long my strand is, and last night it was different, and—"

She was interrupted by a sudden burst of excitement at the door to the common room. An excited Cal rushed in, holding a sheet of paper.

"Listen to this!" he shouted. "Thanks to our dear Tara here"—
Cal grinned at her—"we've asked the Omois high wizards for help.
'I am therefore announcing that the Omois High Council has
agreed to receive us in Tingapore to help cure the poor child of
her attacks of demonic magic. The Lancovit high wizards *and* their
apprentices are hereby invited to the Imperial Palace.' You heard it
here first!"

A lively hubbub filled the room. Cal walked over to Tara and
Sparrow. Besides hair problems, they'd also been discussing the
lives, mores, and customs of OtherWorld, some of which struck
Tara as totally weird. Female dwarves, for example, weren't allowed
to shave until they reached the age of 250. And lady elves couldn't
have more than five husbands.

"Did you hear that?" Cal asked, eyes shining with excitement.

"We aren't stone deaf, so your stentorian voice was strong
enough for us to perceive it," said smiling Sparrow, who was having
a minor *s* relapse.

"I hope the trip is soon," said Tara. "My gift has been acting very
strangely the last few days and I'm really worried. Where are we
going again, Tingapore? That's in Omois, right?"

"You really don't know a thing, do you?" came a chilly voice
behind her. "Tingapore is the *capital* of Omois, and its Palace puts
this pathetic Castle in the shade, believe me."

Her hissing lizard perched on her shoulder, Angelica was scornfully looking down at Tara.

Cal was about to protest but Angelica had already turned and
left.

"What a pest that girl is!" he snapped.

"What's she so excited about?" asked Tara.

"Once you're cured, we'll get to visit the sensational, fabulous, extraordinary, unique city of Tingapore, since the Imperial Palace is right downtown. The high Omois wizards probably want to impress us, so that we—Lancovit's talented and good-looking apprentice spellbinders—will want to work for them."

"Tingapore! That's so cool!" said Sparrow, her eyes shining. "They say there's more business done there than in any city on the planet. All the races go to Tingapore to trade. I absolutely must crystal my mom and get her to send me some extra creds."

She turned to Tara. "Did your grandmother give you any money for this sort of occasion?"

Tara was about to say no when she suddenly remembered what Chem said when she registered.

"Yeah. I have fifty of those gold thingies, I think."

Cal looked like he was going to choke.

"*Fifty gold immuta-creds?* Is your grandmother a millionaire, or what?"

"Why, is that a lot? And why are they called immuta-creds, anyway?"

"With fifty gold immuta-creds you could live in the fanciest resort in Omois for months. Each gold cred is worth three silver ones, and each silver cred is worth twelve brass ones. Fifty gold immuta-creds would be . . . lemme see . . . about what a skilled worker could earn in two years. My dad gave me ten brass creds, which is really chintzy. That might just buy me a giant scorpion-hide belt or a few pounds of Boom Bars, those candies that explode in your mouth. They're called 'immuta-credits' because they're immutable; they can't be forged or transformed. Spellbinders can't replicate them or change their value, which avoids inflation problems. What about you, Sparrow? How much do you have?"

"I have ten silver creds," she happily announced, "and I plan to spend it all in Tingapore!"

"I don't need that much money," said Tara. "We can share it."

"You'd really do that?" asked Cal.

"Well, sure. Why not? You're my two best friends. Besides, what do I need to buy?"

Cal was delighted. "You're gonna eat your words when we get to Tingapore! But a promise is a promise!"

"Did you guys go on any trips last year?" Tara asked.

"Man, did we ever!" said Cal, remembering happily. "We went to Earth to Novel York, for a secret conference arranged by the nonspells."

"Don't you mean New York, in the United States?"

"Yeah, that's it. There's a Portal on top of one of your skyscrapers, the Chrysler Building. Really tall and handsome, with lots of shiny chrome everywhere. After the conference we had a couple of days to visit nonspell cities, and it was great. But the trip was cut short when High Wizard Chemnashaovirodaintrachivu had a little problem."

"Really? What happened?"

"We were admiring the view on top of another skyscraper, the Empire State Building, when Master Chem noticed a pretty girl wearing a scarf. The wind blew the scarf away, and Chem caught it just before it went over the guardrail. The girl was really grateful. But her hunky boyfriend came back with a couple of sodas just then and saw Chem putting the scarf around the girl's neck. He blew up, called him a dirty old man, and wanted to punch his lights out. Chem was so startled, he reflexively turned into a dragon."

The two girls began to laugh.

"No kidding? Right on top of the Empire State Building?"

"That's right. We had to erase the memory of the previous ten minutes from all the nonspells on the observation deck and get the heck back to OtherWorld. The High Council called Chem on the carpet and really chewed him out."

Tara could well imagine the boyfriend's surprise when the doddering old man suddenly showed his fangs. "The guy must've been scared to death, don't you think?"

"I don't know, 'cause he fainted, like a lot of the other nonspells. Chem was furious at being attacked, and he decided to let the boyfriend keep his memory. So the guy distinctly remembered roughing up an elderly gentleman who suddenly turned into a dragon. As we were leaving, I saw an old lady trying to bring him 'round. When he opened his eyes and saw the old lady slapping his cheeks, he must've figured she was the dragon in disguise, 'cause he ran away screaming."

By that point, Sparrow and Tara were limp with laughter.

At last, the day of the trip to Omois finally arrived. Bags were packed, and everything made ready. Angelica drew some sarcastic remarks from Cal, who claimed she'd packed enough clothes to outfit a family for a whole year. Tara miniaturized Gallant so he could stay with her during the transfer.

As they lined up at the Portal for the trip, the Cyclops steward was freaking out, as usual.

"Come along, let's have some order here," he barked. "We need discipline! Four at a time. One, two, three, four—go!" He ran behind a desk with a little, smoked-glass screen, and yelled, "Omois Imperial Palace!"

The people, their baggage, and the wizards' essential papers all vanished.

Tara again felt that vague nausea she felt during her first transfer. When she looked around she blinked, dazzled.

The Imperial Palace's arrival hall was at least ten times bigger than Lancovit's. Gleaming statues of people wearing loincloths or kimonos sewn with precious stones stood in the four corners of the room. The tapestries that allowed the transfers were so bright, they looked as if they had been woven only the night before. Gold—or a substance that looked very much like it—glittered on every wall.

"Wow, do you see that stuff?" blurted Cal, his future licensed thief's fingers itching.

"Kinda hard to miss," said Sparrow sarcastically. "It's every-where!"

But at that point Cal noticed the reception committee and decided not to touch anything—or even look. A hundred four-armed guards had two hundred sharp spears pointed right at the spellbinders' belly buttons.

"What . . . what's going on?" squeaked Sparrow.

"We're in Tingapore, all right," said Robin, looking around. "I recognize the Palace Portal Room. Those are the Imperial guards. They're a little paranoid, so don't make any sudden moves."

Behind a desk like the one at Lancovit stood a young woman who was stunningly beautiful, once you got used to her three sets of arms. Very useful when carrying packages, Tara thought to herself, but probably a drag when doing your nails. The young woman bowed graciously, ordered the guards to stand aside, and greeted them:

"Welcome to Tingapore. My name is Kali and I am the Palace administrator. Please follow our hospitality delegate, who will show you to your rooms. I hope you enjoy your stay with us."

A teenager with a crown of shiny black hair stood next to her. Bowing, he politely introduced himself: "My name is Damien. Be so kind as to follow me."

The Palace's decor was sumptuous, magnificent, and showy. Walls of green marble whose dark veins flowed like rivers gave way to walls of marble yellow encrusted with luminous mother of pearl. Bridges soared over interior gardens. The empress was fond of animals, and many of them roamed the Palace freely. These included vrrirs, large, six-legged, white-and-gold felines that lived in a world of enchanted illusion. Instead of the Palace's chairs and beds, they saw fallen trees and comfortable stones. And when the courtiers stroked them, they felt only the caress of the wind. They were magnificent prisoners, blind to reality.

Precious carpets covered the floors, golden statues stood guard, the hallways went on for miles, and banks of windows admitted bright summer sunshine.

The Omois spellbinders wore robes cut from a kind of animated purple and gold fabric that changed pattern with their moods. The bright colors sharply contrasted with the Lancovians' sober blues and silvers.

The two girls were fascinated, but Robin and Cal traded snarky comments that included words like "peacocks," "show-offs," and "bling." But they dropped their criticism when they reached their rooms. In Omois, it wasn't the Palace that was alive, but the doors. Damien stood in front of the first one, and an enormous eye blinked open.

"Yes?" said a mouth that appeared under the eye along with an ear.

"Damien, apprentice spellbinder to High Wizard Lady Auxia. I am escorting these guests. Open the door, please."

The eye blinked, registering the young spellbinders' faces, and disappeared. An arm shot out where the ear had been and opened the door to a magnificent suite of rooms.

The mouth reappeared and spoke: "You may enter. Welcome, guests of Their Imperial Majesties. Here are your rooms."

They were *private* rooms, the kind you give honored visitors.

Each spellbinder had a suite consisting of a bedroom, a living room with a work table, a couch, and several chairs, and a bathroom whose tub was practically the size of a swimming pool. Comfy baskets with cushions had been set out for the familiars, and Blondin plopped into one with an audible sigh. In one corner a huge crystal panel, a sort of flat-screen TV, was showing a war between heavily armed dwarves and elves, who were shooting their arrows so fast, they were a blur. Everything was incredibly luxurious.

Sparrow, Cal, and Robin happily took possession of their rooms, and the boys tested the mattresses by bouncing on them. Tara, who was worried about her upcoming exorcism, hardly budged.

Damien informed them that they could visit each other until lights out, which was half past midnight for guests, except in the event of a banquet or other special occasion. An ifrit, a flying djinn in the empress's service, would come to take them to the dining room. Because the Palace was so big, it was easy to get lost. Familiars were not allowed to wander in the Palace alone; they had to stay with their companions.

The high wizards went into a meeting as soon as they arrived, so their apprentices had a couple of free hours to get settled. Closing doors was simple, Damien explained. You simply said your name, and each door recognized you, the same way they let you in. The spellbinders' accredi-cards had been programmed when they arrived. Some areas, of course, were forbidden.

Damien added that he hoped that they would enjoy their stay in Tingapore and went off to greet other guests.

When they had all been recognized by the various doors, the young people gathered in Tara's room.

"So, what do you think?" asked Cal.

"I think it's fantastic!" said Sparrow enthusiastically. "I've never had such a big room before!"

"We could have sea battles in the bathtub, it's so big," said Tara with a grin. "But don't you think it's a bit much?"

"Absolutely," said Cal loyally. "Our Royal Castle is a lot less pretentious than this one."

"Who heads their High Council?" asked Tara. "A dragon, like Master Chem?"

"No," said Robin, who seemed well informed. "Omoisians don't like the other races much. The High Council is chaired by High Wizard Lady Auxia, a cousin of Empress Lisbeth and Emperor Sandor."

There was a knock on the door, and Tara cried, "Come in!"

The suitcases glided in, and the spellbinders hurried to their rooms to hang up their things.

Tara sighed. Reluctant to use her magic, she began putting her clothes away. Without really shaping the thought, it occurred to her that it would be a lot faster if her power cooperated. At that, her white forelock crackled and a tornado of clothes burst from the suitcases. In response to her unformulated thought, they rushed to put themselves away on the hangers and in the dresser drawers as Tara gaped, slack-jawed.

The last dresses were hanging themselves up when Tara's magic malfunctioned. It happened just as Sparrow came into the room, and she found herself buried in clothes. The ones that had already been put away shot out onto the bed, the furniture, and into the bathroom. A number of socks dangled from the chandelier, completely out of reach. Tara's sneakers landed on top of the dresser.

Sparrow fought free of the clothes wrapped around her head, then helped an embarrassed Tara put them away. She even levitated to retrieve the socks from the chandelier and the sneakers atop the dresser.

"I don't get it!" said Tara in annoyance. "I didn't activate my magic!"

"I know the feeling," said Sparrow sympathetically. "I've had that same kind of frustration."

Tara's eyes widened. "You mean that you too—"

"No, no!" interrupted Sparrow. "My gift has never been as powerful as yours. I meant my stuttering problem. Sometimes just when I thought I'd whipped it, it came back worse than ever. But this time it's gone for good. I'm sure you'll be able control your gift is well."

"I dunno," said Tara as her shoulders slumped. "There are times when I think I was a lot happier before I was a spellbinder. I had two good friends, Fabrice and Betty, and I went to a normal school with normal kids. This stupid magic has caused me nothing but problems, and I *hate* what's happening to me. I have furious and violent feelings sometimes—deadly, even."

"You're exaggerating," said Sparrow firmly.

"What?"

"You're always complaining. Don't you realize that Angelica would give all her fancy duds to have a quarter of your gift? That without magic, Gallant would never have chosen you? That you have good friends here too—not just me and Cal, but also Robin, who really likes you? Yet here you are, whining that three of your lousy socks won't obey you. I think you're very unfair!"

Having shy little Sparrow lecture her left Tara speechless. Then she smiled ruefully.

"About that sock, I can't seem to find its mate. And you're probably right, but—"

"What do you mean, 'probably'? I *am* right. Period. And you know it as well as I do. So quit whimpering, and let's instead figure out how to spy on Master Dragosh, so we can find out what he did with Fabrice."

"Not Master Dragosh. Master Chem."

Sparrow almost dropped the dress she was hanging up.

"*What?* Master Chem? You suspect him of being a Bloodgrave?"

"No," said Tara with a smile. "I suspect Master Chem of using my healing situation to set a trap for whoever kidnapped Fabrice!"

"Who's setting a trap?" asked Cal, who had just come in.

The two girls nodded meaningfully toward Robin, who was right behind him, and Cal changed the subject.

"By the way, do you know when we're going into Tingapore? I'm anxious to see the town."

"First, the high wizards are going to deal with Tara's situation" said Robin, who knew the schedule for their stay. "If all goes well, she'll be cured tomorrow morning. Lady Auxia suggested that we then visit the empress's summer palace and the market bazaar, then come back here. The Omoisians have also arranged a visit to their amusement park. Apparently they cast an anti-vomit spell before you go on Death Mountain or the Endless Tunnel."

The two boys' eyes shone with enthusiasm.

"Mmmm, if you don't mind, Sparrow and I will wait and see what shape you're in when you come back before we go," said Tara.

Though she didn't show it, Tara was feeling more and more worried. What if the wizards couldn't cure her? Worse, did she really *want* to be cured? She sometimes marveled at the strength of her power, and sometimes she feared it.

Robin knew Tingapore very well, because his father had been stationed at the Lancovian embassy in Omois. He was a pleasant boy, cheerful and straightforward, and got along with Cal very well. He often had them in stitches with his descriptions of the Omoisian court, whose etiquette was very strict.

When you met the empress and the emperor at an audience, he said, you were supposed to bow three times, cross the quarter mile across the throne room in a dignified way, and only speak when spoken to. Moreover, you could only answer, "Yes, Your Imperial Majesty," or "No, Your Imperial Majesty."

"So what do you say if they ask you how old you are?" wondered Cal. "Anyway, Master Chemnashaovirodaintrachivu isn't just a spellbinder, he's one of the high wizards on the OtherWorld High Council. He shouldn't have to bow to anybody."

"That may be, but it doesn't excuse him from court etiquette," said Robin. "In fact, it applies to him in spades."

Then he very casually asked, "Speaking of high wizards, why are you all watching Master Dragosh so closely?"

His question was met with complete silence.

Then Cal asked cautiously, "What makes you think we are?"

"Oh, nothing special—except that your familiars are constantly on his heels, that you watch him as if he'd swallowed the canary, the cat, and the cage, and that he dislikes Tara to a degree remarkable for a more or less normal master."

"And what exactly are *you* up to every night, prowling the Castle hallways?" Cal shot back

Robin gave a tight smile.

"Ah, I didn't realize you'd noticed. I've a small problem. I suffer from claustrophobia."

"What's that?"

"It's a fear of being in tight spaces. So when I start to feel the walls closing in on me, I go sleep in the forest. I have a special authorization that allows me to go out without triggering the alarms."

"In the forest, at night?" asked Sparrow with a shiver. "Aren't you afraid?"

"No, not at all. To me, the forest is a friend."

The three friends looked at each other in perplexity. Should they share their suspicions with Robin? Together, they turned to Tara.

She took a deep breath and spoke: "We're watching Dragosh because he was outside the dormitory door just before Fabrice disappeared."

Robin's eyes widened. "How do you know that?"

They decided to tell him at least part of the story. When they were done, Robin looked very thoughtful.

"That seems very odd," he said. "A traitor tries never to be noticed. He has to keep to the shadows and remain undercover so he can carry out his plans. Revealing himself would blow his cover. He'd be of no further use to whoever was running him. I think we should be looking elsewhere. The guilty party is often someone you don't suspect."

Tara agreed. She'd read enough books where the criminal turned out to be the last person she suspected. And speaking of suspicions, she thought Robin's language had a strangely military flavor.

But Cal didn't like having his hunches challenged.

"So you have experience in this kind of situation?"

Robin looked up and Tara felt he was about to say something, but he kept quiet.

"You don't, do you?" continued Cal. "Any more than the rest of us. Master Dragosh's attitude is suspicious. When Deria caught him near our room, he sounded very embarrassed. And what about the conversation we overheard before that, huh? Isn't that a clue? Besides, he was around when the other apprentices were kidnapped last year."

Robin looked thoughtful. "To catch the culprit we have to discover his motive."

"You're right," agreed Sparrow. "What's the common denominator? What do all those apprentices have in common? Cal, you were there last year. Any ideas?"

"Not a one. They were all very different. There was a girl, Brida, who was quite gifted. A boy, Erik. A somewhat arrogant elf, T'ane. And a dwarf girl, Fafnir. After the disappearances, Hymlia, which sends its dwarves afflicted with magic to the Castle, and Selenda, the elf country, both announced that they were temporarily keeping their citizens home to avoid problems."

Tara found this very interesting.

"Are you saying that only humans were affected?"

"Not exactly. More that the ones who served high wizards were special targets. Master Chem didn't say so, but I heard my parents talking about it. Lots of young spellbinders have disappeared all over OtherWorld, and nobody knows what happened to them."

"In that case, we have to figure out what connects the disappearances," said Tara. "Cal, you know the apprentices better than we do; can you try to learn as much as you can about each one who disappeared? Robin, you're familiar with Tingapore; talk to people here and find out if there were also disappearances from the Imperial Palace. Sparrow, you move around easily and you're discreet; see if you can listen to what the high wizards are talking about."

"And what do you plan to do?" asked Cal.

"I'm going to wait here until you give me all your information," she said, and took a deep breath. "Then I'll go confront Master Chem."

"Well, I'm happy to leave you that part of the plan," said Sparrow, who was terrified of the dragon wizard. "Anyway, I just heard the dinner gong." At Omois, gongs rang the hours. "So let's go eat, gang!"

Cal grinned at the thought.

An ifrit, whose purple body ended in a spiral instead of legs, was patiently hovering outside their door and led them to the banquet hall.

They discreetly made their way to their table. A sumptuous dinner was already laid out, with enormous golden trays and fine porcelain dishes. Cal and Robin looked hungrily at the feast awaiting them. Many dishes were set on . . . nothing. The food floated in the air right above the table.

Tara soon discovered that appearances didn't necessarily match reality. She helped herself to some very ordinary-looking white rice, and it set her mouth on fire for half an hour. After gulping a gallon of water, she began to watch what the others ate and cautiously followed suit.

The dishes tasted strange; not bad, just unusual. The sauces were spicy and though the vegetables looked familiar—beans, grains, and root vegetables—they had very different tastes and smells. A kind of string bean tasted like an unlikely combination of broccoli and banana; a yellow tomato like cauliflower with sardines; and the red oyster plants like peaches in honey.

They also got Boom Bars, the candies Cal liked so much. When Tara put one in her mouth, it first melted and then exploded, releasing all its flavors. She also saw Soothsuckers, odd blue and white, frog-shaped lollipops that contained a secret message. When you licked away the frog's stomach or back, a message appeared that told your fortune.

To Tara, the magic sucker announced: "Your anxiety is high because danger is nigh." She frowned; that wasn't exactly breaking news. Cal's Soothsucker told him he would be wrong. Robin's said that he would reveal himself, which he seemed to find alarming. Sparrow cautiously declined to try one.

All the Soothsuckers were the same color, so you didn't know what flavor you were getting until you tried it. Tara experimented successively with orange steak, almond cherry, chocolate camembert, lemon-breaded fish and red-chili plum, and pepper apple. The problem, of course, was that you had to eat the whole thing if you wanted to get the magic sentence.

Cal told her that the lollipops were the creation of the P'abo, imps who loved to play tricks. They had been inspired by the Eastern Valley centaurs, who had gotten into the habit of licking the backs of blue-and-white frogs called Pllops. They were extremely poisonous for the other races, but their venom gave centaurs pleasant dreams and sometimes visions of the future.

Tara loved Tzinpaf, a sparkling apple cola with a hint of lemon. But she hated Barbrapo, an acrid, yellow, fermented drink that gave her the shakes.

While they were eating, Tara accidentally knocked a basket of dinner rolls off the table, and Robin surprised her by catching the falling rolls before they could hit the floor. She seemed to remember seeing someone else display such unnatural speed but, after a moment's thought forgot the incident.

The banquet ended with an array of stuffed chocolates—a universal treat, apparently. Then a beautiful, dark-haired woman stood up to speak. It was Lady Auxia, high wizard of the Omois High Council and the empress's cousin.

"My dear friends, allow me to welcome you to Tingapore!"

A burst of applause from the high wizards interrupted her. She nodded graciously, then continued: "As we do whenever you visit us, we put our entire infrastructure at your disposal. But there is a new development this year, or rather an exception. Our dear empress and emperor have agreed to lend the high wizards of Lancovit our skills to cure a young spellbinder who is suffering from demonic magic. Once her case is treated, our beloved rulers have asked that the Lancovit apprentices be presented to them. This is unique in the annals of the Palace and worthy of note. Their Imperial Majesties are paying you a great honor."

A murmur of surprise greeted this statement, but Cal—who was deciding whether to eat a ninth chocolate stuffed with bitter orange—noticed that the Omoisian apprentices near them didn't seem surprised.

"Their Imperial Majesties would also like to see a demonstration of skills by the leading apprentices from each palace. Selections will take place tomorrow as soon as our young guest is cured. Thank you for your attention." She sat down.

Tara turned to Damien, who was deep in conversation with Angelica.

"Excuse me, do you have a common room, like in Travia?"

Interrupted in mid-sentence, he answered with ill grace. "No, none of our rooms are common. However, we have a Discussarium!"

"Ooooh, you're so lucky!" purred Angelica. "A real Discussarium! I'd *love* to see it."

Damien bowed to her—they must all have backaches, thought Tara, from bowing right and left all the time—and said, "It would be my pleasure to take you there, beautiful Angelica!"

Cal rolled his eyes, and chirped, "Oooooh, lovely Tara, would you accord me the favor of your presence and accompany my unworthy self to the Discussarium?"

"I'll be happy to," answered Tara, stifling a giggle. "What's a Discussarium?"

Damien glared at Cal. "It's a place where we hold discussions and inform ourselves," he said loftily. "But it would be best if I showed you. Follow me!"

Cal leaped theatrically to his feet, yanked Tara's chair out so fast she almost fell on her face, then bowed and said: "Kindly rest your dainty hand on my manly arm and we'll follow our gay companion along the mysterious meanders of this ancient Palace!"

Contemptuously ignoring the Travia apprentices' jibes, Damien led the way, with Angelica close on his heels.

"Please forgive them," she said through gritted teeth. "They're immature, second-rate spellbinders. Our poor masters have been forced to admit practically anyone these last few years."

"I understand," Damien answered quite seriously. "But if that boy continues to provoke me I might forget the rule and teach him some manners."

"The rule?"

"Lady Auxia, our high wizard, has forbidden us from fighting duels with you."

"Duels?" Angelica didn't understand. "What do you mean, duels?"

"If our honor is defied or insulted, we issue a challenge. We aren't allowed to issue deadly challenges, of course"—Damien's tone suggested this was something he quite regretted—"but we can inflict enough pain that the loser will remember it for a long time."

Angelica seemed to find the notion fascinating.

"Really? You're allowed to fight with magic? That's unbelievable!"

"Why unbelievable?" asked Damien, surprised. "Aren't you allowed to?"

Angelica shook her head.

"No, of course not! It's absolutely forbidden."

"Then what do you do when somebody threatens you? You train under real-life circumstances, don't you?"

Angelica glanced behind her, but the others were too close for her to be able to say what she had in mind. So she simply slipped her arm under Damien's, to his delight, and murmured: "Our customs are very different from yours. We can talk about all this in the Discussarium. I have lots of questions to ask you about these . . . duels."

The Discussarium was a large hall full of many small tables with chairs around them. The hall was very crowded—and totally silent.

Tara could see people arguing and waving their arms, but to her astonishment, she couldn't hear them.

"This is a Discussarium," said Damien, who found Tara's surprise gratifying. "Come along; I'll demonstrate."

To Angelica's great annoyance, Damien showed Tara to a seat, grumbled when Cal plopped down next to her, and then sat down himself. He was followed by Sparrow, Robin, Carole, and Sil, a fat Omois apprentice who brought a supply of chocolates, as if he were afraid he might run out.

Damien then announced loudly, "We are in place."

A sphere of silence immediately isolated them from all the other groups.

"There you go," he said, smiling brightly. "Now I'll show you what we do when we disagree about some subject. Let me think . . .

He thought for a moment and then said, "I've got it! How well do you know Lancovit history—specifically the story of King Tarien the Beast and Queen Beauty? It happened about five hundred OtherWorld years ago."

Tara pricked up her ears. Beauty and the Beast? Like on the Throne Room tapestry?

"They had a son and a daughter. Do you know the daughter's name?" asked Damien, in a tone that suggested he didn't think they could answer such an easy question.

"Isabella!"

Sparrow's prompt answer took him aback.

"Very good. But let's say I disagree, and I claim that the name of their daughter was Katiane, say."

He raised his voice and spoke: "Voice?" A resonant voice answered, seemingly from nowhere: "Apprentice Damien?"

"What was the name of the daughter of Their Majesties Tarien and Beauty, in Travia, capital of Lancovit, in the thirtieth century, please?"

"Isabella, Apprentice Damien."

"Thank you."

He turned to the others.

"There you are! We can talk without disturbing other people. And when we aren't sure of something, we can call on the Voice to resolve the issue. We can also watch movies, listen to music, read, sing—or work, of course."

Tara's eyes lit up. This was exactly what she needed! Maybe the Voice would know where the Gray Fortress was.

"Bravo!" said Angelica enthusiastically. "Your Discussarium is very advanced! We don't have a Voice, and our silencing screens are much less sophisticated. What a luxury! I should ask my parents to send me to work for one of your wizards. I really don't understand why they stuck me in Travia Castle."

"Maybe because nobody else wanted her," Cal evilly whispered in Tara's ear.

Robin followed up on Angelica's comment,

"Speaking of Travia, there have been a lot of strange incidents there. One apprentice disappeared recently, and four others last year. Has anything like that happened here?"

Damien and Sil looked at each other, then Sil spoke up.

"We don't know anything about it, but apparently there were several disappearances last year. My parents didn't want me to come to the Palace, but the emperor passed a law requiring young spellbinders to work under a high wizard or a more experienced spellbinder, and not in their home towns. Supposedly to avoid magic accidents. So we didn't have any choice."

"Do you know who disappeared?" asked Robin casually.

Sil shot a crafty look at Damien and then said, "Nobody this year, at least so far. And we don't know the ones who disappeared last year. But my sources tell me that their parents got a message."

They were all now hanging on his every word.

"How do you know?" asked a surprised Damien. "You never mentioned this."

"I never mentioned it because nobody ever asked me. But my mother was part of the team that investigated the abductions, and I just happened to be passing by her office at home, and I overheard her talking with a crystalist." Tara knew that crystalists were OtherWorld journalists who broadcast the news though crystal screens or balls. "The guy had learned from one of his sources that the victims' parents got a message saying they didn't need to worry about the kids, that they were fine, and that they would be returned later. The message also said that they would get regular updates. My mother was so furious that she threatened to have the crystalist arrested for obstructing the investigation and putting hostages' lives in danger. In fact, she threatened him so severely that he wound up agreeing not to broadcast the information."

Robin was leaning so far forward he practically fell onto the table. "That's a vital piece of information," he said. "Thanks for telling us." He excused himself and left somewhat quickly.

This suddenly reminded Cal that he had an assignment. "Oh, I see some friends of mine. I'll be back later."

"As far as I'm concerned he can stay with his friends forever," growled Damien, who was still smarting at Cal's flipness. "Anyway, now that we're among civilized people, let's talk about civilized activities. You wanted to learn more about duels, didn't you, Angelica?"

From the way Angelica looked, you'd think she actually wanted to kill him. But she controlled herself.

"I'm sure this is a topic that wouldn't interest our friends," she purred. "Why don't we go discuss it, just the two of us? Elsewhere . . . in private . . . *somewhere else.*"

But Damien was oblivious to the hint.

"But it's an excellent custom! I'm very surprised you don't have the right to use it in Lancovit. That's quite backward!"

"No it isn't," protested Sparrow, who didn't take criticism kindly. "Omois is the one that's backward. Duels have been forbidden for more than two hundred years in most OtherWorld countries. I don't understand why such a barbaric custom is still allowed here!"

Damien was starting to find the Lancovit apprentices a pain in the neck. For the moment, the only one that hadn't contradicted or annoyed him was Angelica. He made a quick decision and rose stiffly to his feet

"In that case, since you find our customs barbaric, I'm going to go discuss them with the only person among you who approves of them."

Clicking his heels, he bowed to Angelica and asked her to accompany him out of the circle. They went to sit at another table. Carole hesitated for a moment but when Angelica waved her over, obeyed without argument.

That left only Sil, Tara, and Sparrow. The latter also stood up and decided to go hang out with the high wizards who were talking with their opposite numbers.

Tara continued quizzing Sil, but didn't learn much beyond the fact that he didn't share his chocolates and thought he was very smart.

The moment he left, Tara spoke up.

"Voice? Do you know a place called the Gray Fortress?"

She waited, her heart pounding. After what seemed a very long silence, the Voice announced: "Gray Fortress. Name given to the headquarters of the Bloodgraves in OtherWorld year 3457, named for General Bloodgrave, who launched the movement. The general advocated that spellbinders enslave nonspells and colonize the Earth. After his death the Bloodgrave clan was dissolved by the hunter-elves."

Tara took a deep breath. So the Gray Fortress really existed!

"Connection between Magister and the Gray Fortress, and localization."

"Magister, Master of the Bloodgraves, revived the sect a dozen years ago. His identity remains unknown. His face is masked and his body covered by a gray spellbinder robe. The Gray Fortress was located in the mountains of Hymlia but was completely destroyed. No link found between Magister and the Gray Fortress. End of report."

Tara's hopes died. Magister must have rebuilt the Gray Fortress somewhere else on OtherWorld. She clenched her fists. She wasn't giving up. She'd find the answer somehow!

That night before lights out, everyone gathered in Tara's room for a council of war.

With great self-restraint, Tara and Sparrow managed not to giggle when they saw Cal's camouflage-patterned pajamas.

His eyes bright, Robin seemed very pleased with what he had learned.

"People don't know much," he said, "but I was able to pick up some disturbing coincidences between their abductions and ours."

"What are they?" asked Cal, who was wondering why the two girls seemed so tense when they looked at him.

"All the kidnapped apprentices were either very talented or had unusually powerful gifts. More to the point, they were all the children of wizards on the High Council!"

"Yeah, that's what Sil told me after you guys left," said Tara. "He even claimed he tried not to be too good because he didn't want to risk being kidnapped. Then he changed his story and said his parents weren't important enough for him to be taken."

"Same pattern in Lancovit," said Cal. "Gifted or powerful apprentices, all the children of high wizards. Except for the female dwarf. What can we conclude from this?"

"That you'll never be kidnapped?" suggested Sparrow mischievously.

"Very funny! No, I mean seriously!"

Tara grabbed her white strand and started to chew it, to the great annoyance of Gallant, who hated the habit. She stroked the pegasus, then startled him when she exclaimed: "Rats!"

"What?" cried the other three, who'd been equally startled.

"I don't get it! When Magister, the Master of the Bloodgraves, tried to kidnap me"—Robin jumped again; he had missed that part of the story—"he said he wanted to give me the Power. What Power? And why me? What's the connection between Fabrice, high wizards, kidnapped apprentices, the Bloodgrave master's plans, and me? That's bugging me."

"I think we're missing part of the big picture," said Sparrow thoughtfully. "I spent some time around the high wizards, and they don't have any clues. They're all very worried about the kidnappings. They're also concerned about the presentation to the empress tomorrow. They don't understand why Her Imperial Majesty wants to see a demonstration by the apprentices."

Robin, who was starting to realize that Tara was really very pretty, spoke to her: "I'm mostly worried about you. I hope the wizards know what they're doing. Curing a demonic gift isn't all that easy." Tara flashed him a bright smile.

"I trust Master Chem completely," she said calmly. "I'm not worried in the least."

Which was a bald-faced lie, of course. Tara wasn't able to get to sleep until very late that night and around four o'clock in the morning had to admit the truth to herself.

She wasn't sure she wanted to be cured.

The thought terrified her.

CHAPTER 11

THE DEMON OF METAPHORS

Tara got no breakfast the next morning. Like a patient before surgery, she would undergo the exorcism on an empty stomach. Resisting an urge to flee, she followed the ifrit that came to fetch her.

The hall she entered was padded and painted red, which didn't reassure her—was that to hide any blood that might be shed? The spellbinders were sitting in a circle on comfortable cushions. There were at least a hundred high wizards present.

Lady Auxia took the floor. "Welcome, child. Come stand in the center of our circle, please."

Tara silently obeyed.

"Now show us what is happening to you," Auxia said in a slightly condescending tone. "I'm having trouble visualizing the extent of your problem."

Tara looked up with an ironic smile. So the high wizard had trouble visualizing the problem, eh? She would understand soon enough.

"Well, the demon's welcome was as chilly as a cold shower," she said. "We took to our heels, but his arrogance so stunned us, we were frozen like statues."

Tara had barely finished the sentence when her white forelock crackled and a cascade of ice-cold water flooded the hall. A powerful wave washed over the Omoisian wizards, pinning them to the walls and half drowning them. No sooner did it retreat but the second metaphor struck. Their legs started flailing, and the hall was suddenly full of screaming wizards running around like lunatics. Finally, the third metaphor froze them in whatever posture they happened to be at the moment. Some were lifting their legs, others were jumping. The Omoisian wizards were left stupefied and statue-fied.

Fortunately, Tara's magic wasn't powerful enough to immobilize them for long, and they managed to free themselves from the spell.

The Lancovians had activated their magic shields as a precaution and were floating in clear bubbles above their stunned, soaked, and chilly Omois colleagues.

All trace of Lady Auxia's condescension was now gone. Pulling long, wet hair away from her face, she exclaimed, "By my ancestors! This is terrible!"

"Yes, it is," agreed Master Chem, who was drifting high and dry overhead and struggling not to laugh at the dripping wizard. "It really is terrible. Do you think we can cure this unfortunate child?"

Auxia nodded. "I'm sure we can. Let me just dry myself off and we'll begin the operation."

The Omois spellbinders flushed away the water, then conjured blasts of warm air, leaving themselves disheveled but dry. Tara now had their complete attention. They hadn't realized they would be dealing with something so powerful.

All the wizards took up positions around Tara and closed their eyes. A huge face soon appeared in the air above her head. It was the joint incarnation of their combined minds, and they spoke through its mouth.

The face chanted, "By Extirpus, demon, resistance is vain. Leave this girl's body and cause her no pain!"

As the power of the wizards' spells grew, Tara felt herself getting hotter. It didn't really hurt, but it was extremely unpleasant. The pressure grew and grew, and the huge face above her twisted in pain. Suddenly she saw something emerging from her body. A tiny demon was twisting its way out of the astonished girl's chest. It grew larger and larger, eventually becoming as big as the huge face.

"Hey, what's up with you guys?" the demon screamed. "Back off and show a demon a little respect, okay? All you do is dish me!"

The metaphor immediately became reality, and hundreds of dishes came crashing down around the spellbinders. Hot bean stews, steaming sauerkraut, and roast chickens with baked potatoes spattered the wizards who ran this way and that, dodging a deluge of potted meats, sausages, white beans, truffles, cream cakes, custard sauce, and ice cream.

The huge face now seemed truly furious. It roared, "*Demonus, vade retro!*"

"Heck! Can't even have fun anymore," said the demon. "Cut it out!"

The high wizards' robes were immediately cut to ribbons, and the wizards desperately snatched at scraps of fabric to preserve their modesty. This must have rattled some of them, because the big face overhead briefly wavered.

"Don't let yourselves be distracted!" thundered Master Chem. "We've got to continue—we're almost there!"

The face stabilized and firmly resumed reciting its incantations.

The demon cackled and threw its knockout punch.

"No reason for us to fight like cats and dogs or squeal like stuck pigs! I've seen you drunk as a skunk, so don't get on your high horse! I'm as stubborn as a mule, as clever as a monkey, and as proud as a peacock. All you'll get from me are crocodile tears!"

A succession of loud *plops!* was heard, and the high wizards, despite their resistance, shrank smaller and smaller until they became cats and dogs lost inside their tattered robes. As they hissed and barked angrily at the demon, the second metaphor struck. Paws changed shape, skin turned pink, tails corkscrewed, and a hundred pigs ran grunting around the room. Tara had to bite her lip so as not to laugh, but a moment later she was holding her nose. The pigs had turned into a hundred smelly animals with black-and-white stripes. An instant later, the skunks swelled enormously and started stamping their hooves, first whinnying in fear, then braying. As the demon howled with laughter, the mules were replaced in turn by chattering monkeys, parading peacocks, and, finally, weeping crocodiles.

When they'd struggled to regain their human shapes, the hundred enraged wizards confronted the demon.

"Destroy that demon!" screamed Lady Auxia. *"Now!"*

The face above Tara convulsed, and a beam of light shot from its eyes and struck the laughing demon. This time, the wizards' fury was stronger. The demon struggled to open its mouth to blast them with some new metaphor, but the huge face didn't give it a chance. The beam of light intensified, relentlessly battering its head. The demon screamed, writhed, and tried to speak again, but it was too late. It first began to fade, then exploded in a cloud of viscous bits and pieces that spattered all over the wizards.

At that instant, the feeling of rage and fury that had been boiling in Tara ever since her adventure in Limbo disappeared. She was free!

The high wizards opened their eyes again, and the huge face disappeared.

"Bravo, everyone!" said Master Chem, draped in a ragged robe so cut up that his underwear showed. "That was a monumental struggle, but it was terrific!"

High Wizard Auxia, suddenly embarrassed that everyone could see her purple-and-gold lingerie, zapped away the slimy stains and conjured herself an over-tunic. Having regained a more dignified appearance, she turned to the girl.

"Now, Tara, kindly say something using a metaphor. Preferably something innocuous."

As Tara opened her mouth, she noticed the wizards tensing up.

"I guess that demon really got our goat!" she said cautiously.

A collective sigh rose from the wizards, none of whom started to bleat.

"Very good!" said Master Chem jovially. "I think we've done it. Our little Tara is cured!"

A joyful hubbub greeted this declaration, and Tara felt hugely relieved. She could now speak freely, without fear of frying, freezing, or transforming her friends.

"That's perfect," said a smiling Lady Auxia. "Now let's go to the Training Hall to select the apprentices who will have the honor of demonstrating their skill to Their Majesties. I suggest that our young friend Tara participate as well, now that she is cured."

Chem frowned. "I'm not sure that—"

Auxia cut him off. "Their Majesties will certainly want to see the girl who was saved by our talent from such a powerful demon," she said firmly. "We put our lives in danger and even so, we still nearly failed. I'm sure you wouldn't want to displease them, after what the Empire has done for you."

The old wizard knew when he was licked. "Certainly not, Lady Auxia," he said, bowing. "Our Tara will be delighted to participate in the contest."

"Perfect," she said with a smile. "I will send ifrits to fetch the young people. We meet in the Training Hall in five minutes."

Chem bowed again. "Just as you please, my lady."

Tara was about to speak up, but Chem signaled her to keep quiet and later whispered to her not to worry, that she could use her magic without it affecting her grandmother. So she followed the high wizards to the Training Hall. It was identical to the one in Travia, but of course much, much larger.

Sparrow joined her, looking oddly nervous. Sheeba seemed jumpy too, which was surprising, because the panther was usually pretty placid. Knowing that Tara hadn't eaten anything, Sparrow brought her a bottle of Tzinpaf, three morning buns, and a chocolate bar. Tara gratefully wolfed this down while describing everything that had happened. Sparrow also brought her a Soothsucker that announced, "A trap out there is closing fast. Oppose it now or be caught at last." *Great*, thought Tara, *I just love the surprises this world has to offer.*

Gallant kept restlessly spreading his wings as if he were about to take off. This attracted even more attention to Tara, since no one had ever seen a pegasus familiar before.

"Good grief, will you keep still!" she hissed. "What's gotten into you?"

The tension was almost palpable, and Gallant made a valiant effort to calm down.

At last the high wizards took their places in the bleachers and the tryouts began. A panel of four apprentice spellbinders lined up and the wizards fired commands at them.

"Flowers!"

The apprentices cast spells and made magic passes, and flowers appeared—lots of flowers. Blue, red, violet, yellow, and some that were all those colors combined. Other flowers, with big mouths full of sharp spines, hopped and leaped about, snapping at the wizards.

"Animals!"

New spells and new passes treated the spectators to a giant, golden, gobbling bird like a turkey ("Hey, it's a looky-look," said an amused Cal), a blue-and-white frog, a six-legged stag with no antlers, and a tiny, pink, furry animal whose head was hard to tell from its tail ("I'll be darned, it's a snaptooth!" whispered Sparrow. "They're very rare").

One of the apprentices obviously had a sense of fashion, because his looky-look's color exactly matched the bouquet of flowers he had just created.

"Trees!"

Trees immediately shot up out of nowhere and grew to the ceiling. Tara now understood why the hall was so high.

The big looky-look was prancing about near the little snaptooth when it suddenly got a bad surprise. The pink fur ball abruptly doubled in size, opened a pair of terrifying jaws, and swallowed it whole. It then stuck out a huge blue tongue and licked its chops with a satisfied *burp!*, leaving only a few drifting, golden feathers. Pulling in its tongue, the tiny fur ball started stalking the six-legged stag.

The high wizards signaled to the apprentices who'd created the frog and the stag that they were eliminated. The stag barely escaped a tragic fate when its creator made it disappear from right under the astonished snaptooth's nose.

This left the two apprentices who had conjured the looky-look and the snaptooth. The wizards looked at them and shouted, "Portal!"

The first apprentice panicked and froze. The second waved his fingers as if sketching a door in the air and illuminating it. Then he recited: "By Transferus, Portal, open wide. Transfer me to the other side."

A spark briefly glowed at the end of his index finger, but then went out.

With nods to each other, the wizards dismissed the two apprentices and made all their creations disappear, just as the pink fur ball attacked an aggressive flower and started chewing on its petals.

The next four apprentices stepped forward. New flowers, new animals, new trees. The animals conjured were extremely varied: a moose with two heads, one at each end; a fox that hopped around like a kangaroo; a giant rabbit that disdained carrots and preferred to hunt wolves; a whole series of felines that made Earth tigers look like pussycats—half insect and half mammal, they were equipped with an array of claws, antennae, and pincers; and finally some pegasi whose colors made Gallant whinny: green with faint orange stripes, and silver with red or blue polka dots.

But each time the apprentices came to the Portal challenge, things got complicated. One candidate was so tense he almost threw up on the high wizards and was able to run outside only just in time.

Two of the Omoisian apprentices were finally able to create Portals, but they looked pretty dicey. Lady Auxia tartly remarked that she wouldn't use them if her life depended on it.

The competition also involved tests of speed and artistic creativity: making balls, jewels, and various objects appear, and decorating the hall in different colors.

The Lancovit apprentices did quite well, cheered on by their high wizards: Deria, Boudiou, Dragosh, Chem, Sirella (floating in her bubble), Den'maril, and the rest. When Angelica's turn came, Tara thought that she would do her best so as to be presented to the empress. Curiously, Angelica seemed to botch her presentation. She was eliminated, but departed with a small, superior smile at the corner of her mouth. Cal was also eliminated. When the high wizards shouted "Cakes!" he decided it would be fun to squirt them with whipped cream. "We are not amused," one said stiffly.

The judges' verdicts weren't always understandable. They sometimes eliminated apprentices who had created wonderful things while favoring others who seemed to have less talent.

Damien, who came in late, appeared on a panel with the last three Lancovit spellbinders: Sparrow, Robin, and Tara.

Damien looked serious and focused. When given the order "Balls" he reacted like an ace sharpshooter. He moved his hand like lightning while muttering a few words, and six multicolored balls popped into the air. Tara was so fascinated she almost forgot her own demonstration. She closed her eyes and concentrated, and a multicolored swarm of balls started dancing in front of her. When she opened them, she first noticed that Damien was glowering at what she had created, and that Sparrow was trying not to laugh. Then she realized that hundreds of balls were bouncing and jumping around her.

People—especially the Omois wizards and apprentices—were staring at her in such amazement that she lost her focus and also her hold on the balls, which fell to the ground. Good grief, she thought to herself, she'd visualized three balls, not three hundred! With the demonic gift gone, she was obviously going to have to learn to control her magic all over again.

Lady Auxia cleared her throat and spoke: "Very interesting! This girl really has excellent potential. All right, it's time for your familiars, please!"

Each apprentice created a circle within which their familiar leaped, danced, or flew. (Damien's familiar was a kestrel.) Gallant cordially disliked the flaming hoop; he flew a little too close and singed a feather.

Tara had no intention of performing magic in front of the empress so she made sure to be slower than Damien, Sparrow, and Robin. Given the lack of control over her blasted gift, she couldn't afford to be chosen.

It didn't work out that way.

When Lady Auxia read out the list of successful apprentices, Tara heard her and Sparrow's names, and moaned. Sparrow didn't seem all that happy either. She was an excellent spellbinder, she loved magic, and she liked having her talent recognized. But she had a secret, and was worried about appearing before the entire Omois imperial court. What if somebody recognized her? Cal, on the other hand, was delighted and laughed at his two friends' long faces.

The apprentices were told to go freshen up and change their clothes.

Back in their rooms, they found that the Lancovit high wizards had left them a present: new ceremonial robes cut from a beautiful fabric that they could decorate any way they pleased. Tara took a quick shower, carefully fixed her hair, and pulled on her robe. She slightly enhanced the glittering silver pattern of pegasi and horses, making them practically come to life. And she made sure to bare the shining colors pattern at her throat.

When Sparrow saw her, she couldn't help exclaiming, "Tara! You look fabulous!"

"Thanks. You look pretty good yourself!"

Sparrow had also worked on her robe, and it set off her darker skin and eyes very attractively.

Cal and Robin joined them and they went down together to the heart of the imperial palace, the Double Throne Room. What they found looked more like a grandiose cathedral.

Tara commented: "I would have bet that the decor would be overwhelming!"

That was certainly the word for it. The walls gleamed, and on the animated tapestries unicorns leaped, giants ripped chunks of stone from the mountain and ate them, imps gamboled, elves hunted, and wizards cast spells. There was enough gold around to rival Fort Knox, and it was bright enough to blind you.

A majordomo with a face so impassive it could have been carved from granite—it was gray with small white specks—appeared and asked them to follow him. When everyone was gathered round, he explained court etiquette.

"The apprentices who were not selected for the demonstration are to stand on either side of the two thrones," he said. "Those who were chosen will remain here at the entrance to the hall. When their names are called they will enter two by two, take fifteen steps and bow, take another fifteen steps and bow again, and take a final fifteen steps and bow. Their Imperial Majesties may do you the honor of asking questions. Answer with either 'Yes, Your Imperial Majesty,' or 'No, Your Imperial Majesty.' At their command you will perform your demonstration. When finished, you will bow again and, without turning your backs on Their Imperial Majesties, go stand next to the other apprentices. Is that clear?"

They all nodded, suitably impressed. Satisfied, the majordomo led them to the threshold of the hall and gave them a final piece of advice.

"Remember, not a sound during the demonstrations! It would be disastrous if one of the selected apprentices lost his or her concentration. Magic that escapes its conjurer can have dangerous consequences, and Their Imperial Majesties' guards are trained to react in a split second. We would like to avoid any regrettable accidents—to you."

Cal gulped when he saw the menacing-looking guards, who were armed with swords, knives, and all sorts of cutting and chopping implements. He decided he wouldn't move a muscle.

Though the hall was huge, it was three quarters filled with a noisy, chatting crowd of courtiers.

The apprentices went to stand facing each other on either side of the throne. Cal winked at Sparrow and Tara, who were looking greener by the second. A deafening trumpet fanfare announced the empress and emperor of Omois, and the entire room bowed as one. Tara and Sparrow were so far away that the two rulers taking their seats on the imposing thrones looked like dolls. The high wizards, arrayed in a half circle, chanted spells and levitated, to sit cross-legged in the air.

Two Omois apprentices were called and the presentations began.

In showing off their talents to the entire imperial court, the apprentices displayed wonderful creativity. Jewels shaped like butterflies materialized and fluttered around the hall, landing on the amused courtiers' heads. Glittering eggs cracked opened to reveal smaller eggs, which revealed yet smaller eggs, eventually yielding tiny birds made of precious stones that began to sing when the last shell cracked open. Shining salamanders appeared to leap at the jeweled butterflies, which took off all together in a dazzling flight.

A surprised murmur arose from the crowd when one of the apprentices showed Emperor Sandor a simple, black, wooden disk.

When he reached for it, the apprentice whispered something, and the emperor gestured to one of his guards. The soldier took the disk and set it on his chest, where it stuck without apparent support.

Fast as lightning, the young spellbinder caused razor-sharp throwing stars to appear and hurled them at the guard. The empress couldn't retain a gasp of horror. But just as the metal points seemed about to skewer the man, the black disk intercepted each of the five throwing stars and did it so quickly, it was practically invisible. Not a single one got past it. Wow! thought Cal, a super-bulletproof vest that was light, compact, and effective.

Finally it was their turn. With Sparrow at her side, Tara walked a few steps and bowed, took more steps and bowed again, accompanied by envious murmurs from young women who were leaning closer to better see the beautiful pattern glittering at Tara's throat. From the comments she could overhear, Sparrow realized that the fashion launched at Lancovit was about to sweep Omois.

Tara found herself facing the empress.

When she looked up, she had a shock. She knew her! Or rather she seemed strangely familiar at second glance. Yet Tara had obviously never met her before. What an odd feeling . . .

The empress was very impressive. Tall and slim, she sat on a throne shaped like the symbol of the Empire, a purple, hundred-eyed peacock whose proud beak rose above her. Despite an impassive face, the empress's deep blue eyes seemed kind. She was wearing seven different-colored robes, each one shorter than the last. The top robe was white, sewn with jewels that ranged from white to ruby red, and made a shimmering ripple every time she breathed.

She had no doubt dyed her hair, because its subtle dark scarlet perfectly matched her robe and throne. Held only by the imperial crown, the hair enveloped her in a sumptuous living cape and tumbled to her tiny feet, which were shod in sandals with fine ruby straps.

Next to her sat the emperor, his shorter blond hair in a thick braid resting on his right shoulder. He was equally impassive, and he looked at Tara coolly. His posture was more military, and he wore an embossed-steel breastplate over his imperial robes. A simple gold crown circled his head, and a saber with a finely engraved pommel lay at his side. He looked dangerous. Dangerous and competent.

The majordomo announced them: "The guest of High Wizard Chemnashaovirodaintrachivu and the apprentice of Lady Kalibris: Tara'tylanhnem Duncan and Gloria Daavil. Young ladies, you may conjure the object of your choice."

Tara decided she really liked the empress's style. Let's see, she has such wonderful hair, she thought, how about a golden snood strewn with sapphire flowers to match her eyes? Nah, too banal. She can do better that that. Then she got an idea . . .

Tara looked at Gallant while visualizing a glass and gold statue of a pegasus poised to take flight. Her white forelock crackled, and the audience gasped in surprise when a splendid statue materialized.

Tara had noticed that people in Omois liked big things, but in this case she may have gone a bit overboard. The glittering statue was enormous, with each muscle and hair limned in glass and gold. As a whole it was breathtakingly elegant.

For her part, Sparrow had decided to play up to the emperor, so she created a beautiful cigar box with a built-in humidor, decorated with centaurs and unicorns. A ghost of a smile appeared on the imperial lips, and she knew she had chosen well. Her box was less impressive than Tara's present, but Sparrow was still pleased with herself.

The majordomo signaled to the guards to take the gifts away, then spoke again: "Thank you. You may now present your familiars."

Gallant and Sheeba approached the thrones. The majordomo was about to have them go into action when the emperor spoke.

"Wait a minute," he said in a deep bass voice. "That's a pegasus! Why is your familiar so small?"

How could Tara answer him, since she was only allowed to say yes or no? She looked over at Chem who nodded that it was all right.

To be on the safe side, she bowed before saying anything.

"He is indeed a pegasus, Your Imperial Majesty"—or was it "Majestic Highness"? She couldn't remember!—"I miniaturized him so he could come indoors with me."

"Ah, very interesting," he exclaimed in his unusual voice. "But that means you have an unfair advantage over your friend here. Would you mind restoring it to its normal size?"

No problem, she thought.

"I'd be happy to, Your High Majesty." Turning to Gallant, she said, "By Normalus it would be wise if you regained your normal size."

The magnificent pegasus grew to its full size, looming over the admiring assembly.

"Hm, I can see why you made him smaller," said the emperor as he looked Gallant over carefully. "He's very big, even for a pegasus."

"Yes, Your Imperial Majesty."

"Very well, show us what you can do. But given your familiar's size, please start alone. We will see your friend perform after you."

"Yes, Your High Majesticness."

Tara sounded confident, but she was actually very nervous. She could easily conjure flaming hoops for a small pegasus, but creating one for a full-size winged horse was something else again. She glanced nervously at the hall's flammable, coffered ceiling, and regretted that Omoisians so loved building with wood, especially wood that was rare and dry.

The others must have picked up on her anxiety because Tara noticed that Sparrow looked tense, and the spellbinders were suddenly watching very closely.

Tara took a deep breath and looked upward, and a huge flaming hoop appeared. Gallant leaped into the air and flew through it without his vast wings even brushing the hoop's edges.

It was a spectacular scene, and Tara was heaving a sigh of relief when she suddenly felt a sharp pain at her neck. It abruptly broke her concentration.

To her horror, the flaming hoop expanded and started to fill the hall with a terrific fireball that Gallant was barely able to avoid. But the crowd thought she had done this deliberately, and everybody applauded.

Despite the pain, Tara managed to regain control of her magic. She was able to extinguish the flames, which were getting dangerously close to the wooden ceiling, as Gallant returned to the ground.

When a pegasus is frightened, it bristles, and when Gallant landed, still trembling, next to Tara, he looked like a huge ball of feathers. She wiped away the sweat running into his eyes. They had barely avoided a catastrophe!

CHAPTER 12

DEADLY VORTEX

The empress and emperor were satisfied and had Sheeba perform with Sparrow. Then Tara miniaturized Gallant, and the two friends left as another pair of apprentices took their places.

Once back with Cal and Robin, Tara was finally free to touch her neck. To her horror, her hand came away covered with blood.

"What happened to you?" Sparrow screamed.

"I don't know," she said. "I was trying to maintain the flaming hoop when something stung me. I lost my focus and very nearly killed Gallant and set the palace on fire."

"You mean you didn't do that on purpose?" exclaimed Cal, wide-eyed. "It was a terrific show."

"I didn't do any of it," Tara said bitterly, who was in pain. "I have no idea what happened."

When Robin examined her wound, he got a surprise. "That's a blood fly sting!"

"A what?"

"A blood fly, an insect that mostly bites cattle. There's no way it could have gotten into the Palace by itself. There are insect-repellent spells all over the place."

"Someone was trying to make you lose your concentration, and I think I know who," said Cal, who was scanning the crowd. "Wait a moment." Quick as a fox, he darted off between the spellbinders and courtiers, and disappeared.

Robin couldn't stand the sight of Tara in pain, so he put his hand on the sting and said: "By Healus, let the pain be gone, let Tara's wound be cured anon!"

To her great relief, Tara felt the pain fade, then disappear. She gave Robin a warm smile, which seemed to embarrass him.

Cal came back, muttering angrily.

"The little brat was careful to stay close to the thrones. She knows that if I get my hands on her—"

"Who in the world are you talking about?" asked Sparrow, baffled by Cal's doings.

"Angelica! I'm sure she's the one who planned this. That's why she did her best not to be selected. She was holding something in her hand when she came into the hall. I didn't pay any attention at the time, but I'll bet it was a blowgun. Just wait until I catch her."

In spite of her intense dislike of Angelica, Tara didn't want Cal tackling a girl who was twice his size and a much better spellbinder. Somewhat reluctantly, she decided to calm things down.

"But you don't have any proof, Cal. You can't go around accusing people without proof."

"You want proof?" he asked, glowering. "Wait here. I'll give you proof!"

Ignoring her protests, he again disappeared into the crowd.

While Tara's group was arguing, the two apprentices performing for the imperial couple were asked to create Portals, those magic passageways created by the dragons and later used by spellbinders to travel great distances. (For short trips, levitation, flying carpets, and "Transmitus" spells were perfectly adequate.)

The exercise was somewhat dangerous. A poorly mastered Portal could escape its creator's control and send everybody somewhere else—possibly to a place from which no traveler returns.

The hall was completely silent.

The two apprentices seemed to know what they were doing, and together they said: "By Transferus, Portal, open wide. Transfer me to the other side."

Vague, luminous shapes shot from their fingertips and coalesced into two Portals opening in a yawning void.

Suddenly a scream in the crowd rang out, shattering the spellbinders' intense concentration and causing a catastrophe.

As with Tara, one of the apprentices lost his hold over his magic. The Portal he had just created escaped from his control and literally exploded, tripling in size in a second. The resulting shock wave very quickly became a swirling vortex. The Portal started spinning out of control, threatening to swallow the entire Palace! Chandeliers, candles, spears, and chairs—anything that wasn't nailed down—were already being sucked into the whirlpool. People ran around screaming and the guards dragged the empress and the emperor away to safety. Master Chem, Lady Auxia, and the other high wizards furiously chanted spells, but without effect. Long beams of destructive energy were now shooting from the Portal and sowing panic. A terrible wind arose, growing from a gale to a thundering tornado that centered on the Portal.

Someone bumped into Tara. Then, before she realized it, the wind blasted her in front of the apprentice who was desperately trying to master his Portal. Suddenly she had a flash of inspiration: she knew what he had to do!

Struggling against the sucking force, she shouted to the boy: "Listen to me! You have to concentrate on the vortex! Try to miniaturize it, then close it. If you can master the vortex, you'll regain control of the Portal. We can do it together!"

The boy was white as a sheet. Without looking at her, he obeyed. Together, they stretched their hands toward the expanding whirlwind and said: "By Miniaturus as quick as we think, may the vortex irreversibly shrink!"

Nothing happened.

Not only did nothing happen, but Tara sensed a kind of rejection, a negative power that opposed their efforts. And that power was coming from the thrones! One of the high wizards was trying to keep them from closing the Portal! Master Dragosh was firing lightning bolts into the whirlwind. Was he doing that to close it or to strengthen it?

To her horror, Tara saw a familiar suddenly sucked into the swirling void, to the anguished scream of its human companion. And like an evil entity, the Portal was coming closer in spite of all the wizards' efforts.

Suddenly the boy next to her yelled as he began to slip, drawn into the whirlwind. Tara seized his arm, but the young apprentice flailed around so violently, he shook her off. She wasn't able to grab him again and watched with mute horror as he was sucked into the vortex. The boy's legs thrashed around for a moment, and then he was gone.

Tara herself was now just a few yards from the Portal and could feel its pull on her increasing. She lay flat on her stomach, desperately trying to hang onto something, but the blasted Omoisians covered everything with slippery marble, and she continued sliding.

The high wizards intensified their efforts and the hole suddenly stabilized and even began to shrink, but too slowly, much too slowly. Tara was about to be sucked in as well.

Suddenly something grabbed her feet, stopping her slide. But when Tara turned around to look, she almost fainted. Holding her ankles was a gigantic beast, a terrifying combination of a lion, a bear, and a bull.

Tara was about to kick free when the beast yelled: "Stop! It's me, Sparrow!"

Tara thought she was losing her mind.

"Sparrow?"

"For heaven sakes, concentrate on closing that infernal Portal. You almost had it!"

Held tight by Sparrow, Tara gritted her teeth and focused all her power on the yawning void. Slowly, she forced it to yield. The thunder gradually died away and the Portal disappeared.

Cal and Robin rushed over to Tara and Sparrow, followed by Master Chem. Tara groaned when she stood up. Sparrow had been so afraid of losing her, she'd practically crushed her ankles.

Tara turned to her friend, who looked like the classic fairy-tale Beast: ten feet tall, covered with thick fur, and armed with claws and fangs as long as knives. (*Note to self: never, ever annoy Sparrow again,* thought Tara.)

"What the heck happened?" Tara asked, as she massaged her legs. "How did you turn into that big hairy thing with teeth?"

"I don't know," moaned Sparrow, whose spellbinder's robe was desperately stretching to accommodate her new bulk. "I didn't know what to do to help you, then all of a sudden something happened. I started to get bigger and stronger—strong enough to break through the edge of the whirlwind. I saw you sliding, I grabbed you, and that was it."

Poor Sparrow seemed totally freaked out by what had happened to her. Even Sheeba, her fur standing on end, was sniffing at her distrustfully.

A sudden blare of trumpets made everyone jump. All the courtiers bowed at once, and the Travia wizards and apprentices watched as the empress and the emperor returned to their thrones.

Though apparently impassive, the empress was pale with rage. She had wanted to join in the battle, but her guards had dragged her to shelter without asking her opinion. She had decided that the captain of her guards was due for a very long rest—maybe spreading pegasus manure on a rose garden somewhere.

"Tara'tylanhnem Duncan, I want to thank you for what you did," she declared. "It wasn't very smart, but it was very brave. The wizards would have quickly mastered the danger, and if my guards hadn't decided to move me to safety"—she cast an icy glance at the captain, who turned pale—"I could have helped them close the Portal. They must have forgotten that I am not only the empress, but also the Imperial Spellbinder."

Tara frowned. That title sounded familiar. Where could she have heard it before?

"You saved many lives and prevented great damage to our palace," she continued. "I therefore wish to reward you. I will grant whatever you ask of me."

Tara bowed.

"I'm deeply honored by the favor, Your Imperial Majesty, but I can't choose right now. My mind's still exhausted from the struggle against the Portal and I'm not thinking clearly. Can I give you my choice some other time?"

"Ah, a favor," said Emperor Sandor, who'd been listening closely. "That's a good idea. So our Empire now owes you a favor."

Put in that curious way, the phrase sounded vaguely menacing.

"Well, a *small* favor," said Tara, who didn't want to create a diplomatic incident.

"No, no!" the empress protested, waving Sandor off. "I have spoken. I will grant whatever you desire. But to set a limit on this imperial favor, let us say that it will be valid until you come of age"—the woman wasn't a politician for nothing; an adult's desires are very different from those of an adolescent—"and it must concern only you. It is not transferable. Does that suit you?"

Feeling a little lost, Tara knew she had to give some sort of answer. And from the look on Master Chem's face, she had just been granted something very precious.

"That suits me perfectly, Your Majestic Imperialness. I thank you on my behalf and on behalf of Lancovit."

"Very well. Now, will someone kindly inform the unfortunate parents of the boy who was killed by his own Portal? As a sign of mourning we will not hold an audience this afternoon. But before retiring, we have another question for you, Tara'tylanhnem. It's about the beast standing next to you. Is that another familiar?"

Feeling awkward in her huge carcass, Sparrow was shifting nervously from foot to foot, which looked pretty funny.

"I think I can answer your question, my dear," said the emperor. "If I'm not mistaken, this is the result of the curse on Tarien the Beast, who was once king of Lancovit."

Sparrow bowed her big, hairy head and stared anxiously at her enormous claws.

"I guess that's right," she said nervously. "I'm one of his descendents."

"Ah, I thought your name sounded familiar!" exulted the emperor. "Does our imperial court therefore have the honor of receiving Princess Gloria of Lancovit, known as Sparrow?"

As her astonished friends looked on, Sparrow bowed her head further, and big tears ran down her furry cheeks.

"Yes," she murmured.

"This is an unexpected pleasure," Sandor said, purring like a large, vaguely malevolent cat. "The Lancovit ambassador should have alerted us to your presence in our modest Palace. We would have welcomed you with the ceremony due your rank."

"Stop tormenting that child!" Master Chem suddenly shouted, causing a scandalized murmur among the courtiers. "Her parents asked her not to reveal her title. Besides, she isn't a hereditary princess, but a member of a collateral branch, so there's no reason to make a fuss. And now I must ask you to excuse us, but the morning's events have been extremely upsetting and I must look after my apprentices. We extend our condolences to the unfortunate parents of the dead boy. We will convene the High Council in extraordinary session as quickly as possible. We thank you again for your great kindness, but I think we will return to Lancovit right away."

The emperor glared at him but said nothing.

The high wizard had none too subtly reminded the emperor that because of his position on the High Council, Chem wasn't answerable to him. And that if the princess wanted to remain incognito, that was her business, not his.

Led by Master Chem and Lady Auxia, the apprentices headed for the Portal Room, whispering excitedly.

Suddenly Cal noticed a slumped figure in a corner of the hall, sobbing bitterly.

"Master Chem!" he exclaimed.

"What is it now?" snapped the wizard irritably.

"Er, I'm not sure," said Cal hesitantly, "but I think Angelica has a problem."

Rolling his eyes, Chem told Lady Auxia to go on ahead without him. Followed by Tara, Sparrow, Cal, Robin, and Carole, he went back into the Throne Room, walked over to Angelica, and pulled her to her feet.

The tall girl's eyes were red with weeping, and she seemed dazed.

"Kimi, Kimi, where are you?" she babbled.

The wizard frowned. "Is it your familiar?" he asked, not unkindly. "Are you looking for your familiar?"

Angelica's eyes seemed to have trouble focusing on his face.

"Yes, it's Kimi. Where is she? She's not in contact with my mind anymore."

The wizard looked grave. "I think I saw a familiar being swallowed by the Portal. I'm terribly sorry, dear, but I'm afraid your Kimi was sucked into the whirlwind. Come along, we'll take you to your room."

Suddenly Angelica saw Cal, who was looking at her sympathetically. With a roar, she ran over and started pummeling him.

"He's the one!" she said, hitting him with all her might. "It's his fault! I'm going to kill you!"

Cal was too surprised to avoid Angelica's punches, but Sparrow reacted instantly. She grabbed Angelica with a paw and lifted her three feet in the air where she struggled, unable to get free.

Clearly fed up with all the agitation, Master Chem yelled, "What is going on here? Why in Demiderus' name did you attack Caliban?"

"It was him!" yelled Angelica. "He was trying to look under my robe. He frightened me and that's why I screamed. That broke the two boys' concentration, the Portal exploded, and Kimi . . . " She burst into sobs again.

They all looked at Cal, who had turned the color of a ripe tomato.

"That wasn't what happened at all!" he stammered. "I wasn't looking under Angelica's robe! I was just trying to prove that she was the one who sent the blood fly to bite Tara, so she would lose her focus and cause a catastrophe."

"A blood fly?" asked the wizard, who was now completely at sea. "What in the world are you talking about?"

"Show him, Tara," said Cal.

Tara lifted her hair away from her neck to show the bite mark, which was gradually fading but still visible. "When I conjured the fireball and it expanded, you all thought I was doing it on purpose, but in fact I almost killed Gallant and burned the Palace down. A blood fly bit me right in the middle of my demonstration. Luckily I was able to keep control of my magic. Cal figured that Angelica had planned the whole thing and wanted to prove it."

"Search her!" said Cal, pointing at Angelica. "When I was trying to search her pockets—and not look under her robe—I felt something pointed."

Angelica thrashed around like a lunatic, yelling that no one would search her. But while the wizard hesitated, Sparrow held her firmly and looked through her pockets. With a claw, she pulled out a small glass cage with a girl's sock inside.

A heavy silence fell over the group. Even those who were inclined to defend Angelica, like Carole, were now looking at her with dismay.

"I'll be darned!" exclaimed Tara. "That's the sock I couldn't find!"

"And this is an insect cage," said the wizard calmly. "Can you explain it, Miss Brandaud?"

"It was for my flying lizard Kimi!" she shouted. "I fed her bugs. This doesn't prove anything. It's just nonsense!"

Suddenly Sparrow had a flash of understanding.

"That's it" she exclaimed. "It was her lizard! She must have sealed up a couple of blood flies with Tara's sock and ordered Kimi to release them during the demonstration. The flies would know Tara's smell and would make a beeline for her and sting her. Kimi was probably still flying, looking for a second chance since the first sting hadn't broken Tara's concentration. She was in the air and not able to grab onto anything, so that's why she got sucked into the vortex."

Sparrow turned her muzzle to Angelica, who had gone completely white.

"You killed your own familiar!" she said accusingly. "You and your scheming are responsible not only for the death of the apprentice spellbinder, but also for Kimi's death."

For a moment, Tara thought Angelica would deny everything. But the loss of her familiar and the terrible guilt she must have been feeling overwhelmed her, and she started crying again.

The old wizard had turned the color of marble, white and green. He could instantly foresee all the political complications the incident was going to create.

"Let's go," he growled. "We have to talk about this, but not here. You're all going back to Lancovit. Pack your bags and transfer immediately to Travia. I'll stay here to take care of any problems."

Deeply shocked by what had happened, the six apprentices did as they were told. They didn't notice a shadow camouflaged in one of the hanging tapestries. Shedding its colors, the figure took the shape of a small, slim man in black who thoughtfully watched them leave. If they had known the Omois secret services better, they would have realized that he belonged to them—and would have been extremely concerned.

Omois High Wizard Lady Auxia was waiting for them. She was first surprised, then alarmed when she saw Master Chem's grim face and the way the apprentices were clustered around Angelica, who looked ill.

"What happened?" she exclaimed. "We were waiting for you! Was there another problem?"

The old wizard forced a smile but it must not have been very convincing because Lady Auxia looked even more worried.

"No, nothing at all," he assured her. "Just a little matter we had to settle. My guest and our apprentices have been deeply shocked by this regrettable incident. My fellow wizards and I think that it would be a good idea for us to return to Travia, so—"

"Ah, but that's not possible!" interrupted a panicky Lady Auxia. "I just got a call from our security chief. An investigation into the circumstances of the accident has been opened. The head of the guards told us that they found a blood fly in the palace. It's now being studied to see if it's carrying any viruses or toxins intended to assassinate our sovereigns." Tara unconsciously touched her neck and felt a bit nauseous. "This is all extremely awkward. The head of security insisted that we seal all the Portals. No one is being allowed to leave Omois for the time being."

Shoot, thought Tara, the darned secret services were too fast!

"The Omois secret services' paranoia is none of our affair," said the wizard threateningly. "Am I to understand that they intend to hold members of the Lancovit High Council against their will?"

"But none of this involves you!" said Lady Auxia, wringing her hands. "You were due to stay with us a few more days anyway, so what does it matter?"

Chem was about to reply when he noticed Carole hurrying toward Damien and the other spellbinders. Before Carole had a chance to say anything, Chem thundered, "Miss Genty!"

"Master?" she turned in surprise.

"In my office, immediately! With Caliban, Tara, Robin, Sparrow, and Angelica. *Now!*"

"Er, Master Chem?" said Sparrow timidly.

"What is it?"

"You don't have an office here."

"Oh, that's right," he grumbled. "Lady Auxia, would you mind lending us your office? One of my apprentices lost her familiar in the accident, and we need to talk it over privately."

"Of course!" she said, relieved at not having to argue with the old wizard. "Follow me, please. Should I have our medical master called?"

"No, I don't think that will be necessary," said Chem, who was still very annoyed. "I will take care of her and also deal with Sparrow's situation."

"Ah yes, Sparrow, the princess Gloria," murmured Lady Auxia, glancing sideways at the huge beast. "Do you think you'll be able to reverse the curse? The poor girl must be terrified."

In fact, the poor girl was having a wonderful time. She had set Angelica down, but when she flashed her impressive set of teeth, it sent the tall girl into hysterics. For shy little Sparrow, the feeling of power was much more enjoyable than frightening. The small, slim girl had acquired a strong, muscular body. Looming over the others, she saw them back away nervously when she showed her fangs. The feeling was intoxicating.

Lady Auxia led them to her office and then discreetly withdrew, quietly closing the door.

Chem waited for a few moments, gesturing to the young people not to speak. He then astonished them by casting a spell that made the walls transparent. When he was satisfied there was no one outside in the hallway, he let the walls become opaque again and sat down behind the desk.

"All right, we're alone," he said. "Let's start with Sparrow's situation. Princess, I want you to concentrate on transforming your body. Visualize it becoming normal, that you are no longer the beast, but Sparrow. You will feel your muscles change, your claws shrink, your weight diminish. The transformation is a magic one but it responds to your will."

Sparrow wasn't at all eager to do it, but the old wizard insisted. So she relaxed in her armchair, which creaked alarmingly under her weight, and tried to visualize her old body. Very quickly her fur vanished, fangs became teeth, horns disappeared, enormous muscles melted away, and Sparrow reappeared. You could almost hear her spellbinder robe groan as it struggled to shrink back to its normal size.

"Well done!" said the wizard. Then he turned to Angelica.

"Miss Brandaud, your conduct has been unspeakable," he said curtly. "Not only did your desire for revenge put all your fellow students' lives in danger, but you caused that boy's death. What do you have to say?"

"It was all Tara's fault!" Angelica yelped, with a sideways glare at Sparrow, who could now no longer hoist her into the air. "If she'd lost control of her power, you would've put out the fire and she'd be sent back home to Earth! That's all I wanted. She's dangerous, she can't control her magic, and she'll wind up killing all of us. Isn't there anybody in this palace besides me who realizes this?"

The wizard looked at her as if she were a noxious insect he'd found in his coffee cup.

"Instead of taking responsibility for their own weaknesses, many people prefer to turn on others," he said very softly. "That's why they beat children and women—out of frustration, rage, anger, and especially weakness. But the fact that Miss Duncan is far more powerful than you is no reason for you to take it out on her, Miss Brandaud."

"Then let me leave!" said Angelica defiantly. "Let me go somewhere where I don't have to put up with the presence of a dangerous freak."

"Oh, no!" answered the old wizard. "That's exactly what I'm *not* going to do." Cal, who had started to smile, looked dismayed. "Your punishment will be to remain in Travia and work for Master Dragosh until he is satisfied with your progress. And don't even think of taking any vacations."

"What?" exclaimed Angelica. "That's out of the question! I'm going to call my father and tell him what you're planning. He'll stop you. He'll get you relieved."

"I'll be delighted to give him the reasons for your punishment, Miss Brandaud. You put the imperial court of Omois in danger. What do you think he'll say when he learns that little detail?"

Angelica bit her lip so hard, it bled. She knew what her father would say. That she should've chosen another moment and especially not gotten caught! And with those truth-telling spells, there was no way to hide what had happened. Angelica's tense body relaxed, and her shoulders slumped in defeat.

"Good," said the wizard, satisfied by her surrender. "I am now going to cast a spell on all six of you and—"

"No!" Tara's shout interrupted him. "No spells!"

Chem blinked in surprise but then remembered how angry Tara had been when her grandmother cast a forgetting spell on her. He smiled at her kindly.

"Don't worry, Tara, I'm not going to tamper with your memory. I just want to cast a light spell on all of you to keep you from discussing this regrettable incident with any third party. You will be able to talk among yourselves about what Angelica did, but if someone overhears you—whether by magic or just by being present—the spell will prevent you from talking about it. Is that okay with you?"

"Yes," said a relieved Tara. "It seems important that we not forget what happened. Thank you."

"You're welcome."

He quickly recited the spell before she changed her mind: "By Informatus, the secret we share. May no one else know of this affair!"

A greenish cloud rose from the old wizard's hands, settled on them, and the spell was activated.

"Now Tara, I want you to tell me what happened when you tried to close the hole. And what in Demiderus' name possessed you to rush toward the Portal. I really thought my two old dragon's hearts were going to stop!"

"Well, I knew what needed to be done," said Tara with a smile. (*Dragons have two hearts? Who knew? A lot of knights must have gotten a big surprise!*) "The tornado shoved me into the boy who was reciting spells. I told him what we had to do, and we tried it together, but a kind of negative force opposed us. That was enough for Angelica's familiar to be sucked into the vortex along with the boy. I almost was too."

"Yes, I felt it as well," confirmed the old dragon. "There were more than a hundred high wizards in the hall. We should have been able to control the Portal right away. You're right, it was extremely powerful."

"I knew it!" said Cal, who was still hung up on his dislike for the vampyr. "Master Dragosh kept shooting lightning bolts. I'm sure he was preventing the Portal from closing so Tara would be sucked into it."

"Balderdash and tommyrot!" snapped the dragon wizard angrily. "Dragosh's magical skills are different, that's all. The lightning bolts don't mean anything. Did you notice anything else, Tara?"

"Well, I was trying to save my life, so aside from that, not much."

"Yes, I can understand that. I really thought the vortex wasn't ever going to close. What about the rest of you, children?"

Cal opened his mouth to speak, but a sharp look from the wizard stopped him. All right, got it: no more talking about Master Dragosh. But Cal was still convinced that the vampyr had done something against Tara, and he would eventually find proof, just as he had with Angelica.

"We're no further along than we were," said the wizard with a sigh. "I know you want to help me find whoever has been kidnapping our apprentices, but I don't want you to be mixed up in this. It could be extremely dangerous. And something about what happened today is escaping me . . . "

The six young people waited, but he gave them no further explanations.

Once Angelica and Carole had gone back to their rooms, Tara suggested that everybody meet at her place.

"Sparrow, you were incredibly brave!" she said gratefully. "You saved my life, hanging on to me like that."

"You know, considering how much I weighed at that point, a little howling tornado wasn't gonna scare me!"

"I want to thank you too," continued Tara, looking at Cal and Robin. "You risked your lives trying to help me!"

"We really didn't have much time to think," said Cal with a laugh. "Otherwise we would've taken off and would probably still be running."

Tara smiled, then continued more thoughtfully.

"Master Chem is right when he says that something is escaping us. There's one thing I don't understand either."

"What's that?" asked Sparrow.

Tara looked at the three of them seriously and said, "Whoever was trying to kidnap me has changed his mind. Now he wants to kill me."

CHAPTER 13

MAGNIFICENT TINGAPORE

Tara's three friends couldn't think of anything to say to that. They, too, suspected that the rules of the game had changed.

"Do you really think so?" asked a horrified Sparrow. "Maybe you aren't the one they're gunning for, but the boy who died."

"I don't know," answered Tara wearily. "But if you hadn't shape-shifted, I would be dead. And nobody knew you could do a thing like that."

"I didn't know it myself," said Sparrow. "I'm gonna have to have a little chat with my mom."

Tara smiled at her. "Welcome to the club. My grandmother likes to keep her little secrets too. What am I saying? She's raised secrecy to an art form! I'm sure she hasn't told me more than a quarter of the truth."

Cal said, "Speaking of truth, you sure hid the fact that you're the Princess of Lancovit."

"Not *the* princess, just one of the princesses," Sparrow replied. "My mother is the queen's sister, and we're a collateral branch. My dad is an engineer wizard who specializes in precious and magical minerals. We haven't lived in Lancovit much, mainly in Hymlia, the land of dwarves, and Gandis, the land of giants. My parents figured it would be better for me to be an ordinary apprentice, like everyone else. That's why the issue of my title never came up. And I had no idea that I could shape-shift. That was a major surprise."

"It must have surprised the Bloodgrave who was trying to kill me too," said Tara.

"Yeah, but we still don't know who wants to hurt you," said Cal. "And we especially don't know why."

"You're in someone's way," concluded Robin. "So much so that they tried to kill you right in front of the Empress of Omois."

The three friends looked at Tara with new respect. Cal, as their spokesman, said, "So what have you done to attract a reaction like that? My mom often says she's going to kill me because I exasperate her, and I know a few high wizards who'd be happy to lend her a hand. But you—wow! Someone out there *really* doesn't like you!"

"That's enough!" snapped Sparrow, who could see that though Tara was holding her head high, her hands were trembling. "We aren't sure of anything. Maybe it was just an accident, maybe not. I suggest that we do our best to protect Tara. In fact, I don't think we should leave her alone. I'll sleep with her at night. The bed's big enough."

"I'll be glad to sleep with her too," said a grinning Cal, just before Robin's pillow caught him full in the face.

When the majestic lunch gong rang, the friends had to interrupt the energetic pillow fight they had launched. A purple ifrit led them to the dining room, where everybody was talking about the recent events.

Lady Auxia, who had traded her usual brightly colored robe for one so black it seemed to actually absorb light—and given that she was a wizard, maybe it did—rose to speak: "In memory of your unfortunate fellow apprentice, we are going to observe a minute of silence."

Everyone bowed their head, and Tara reflected that if Sparrow hadn't rescued her, it would be *two* minutes of silence.

Auxia continued: "Because of the ongoing investigation, we initially canceled the visit to Tingapore. But since the Lancovit apprentices aren't yet familiar with our magnificent capital, the empress specifically requested that the visit take place. So please come to the Palace entrance at two o'clock. Our flying carpets will take you to Tingapore and pick you up at five."

A buzz of excitement greeted her announcement.

"Lunch is served. In spite of these tragic events, I hope you enjoy your meal."

Cal noticed that the seat next to Damien was empty. Angelica had stayed in her room. He was still angry at her and secretly hoped she wouldn't find out about the trip into town. It was petty and he knew it, but all's fair in love and war.

Sparrow, on the other hand, was all smiles.

"Tingapore, neat!" she exclaimed. "You'll see, it's terrific!"

Tara was chewing on her white strand and observing the high wizards—Dragosh, Boudiou, Deria, Patin, and Sardoin—and merely nodded, without answering. She was willing to bet her bottom immuta-cred that the guided trip into Tingapore was part of some scheme of Master Chem's, but to what end? Robin didn't seem overly delighted by the news either, and looked worried.

Chem gave them their spending money in case they wanted to buy something and very seriously delivered some final safety instructions.

"Be careful not to bump into anybody," he said, "especially not giants. They're very touchy and have the unfortunate habit of tossing aside anybody they dislike or who gets in their way.

"Don't cast spells on dwarves, on pain of instant death. Dwarves despise all forms of magic, and they punish offenders in particularly horrible ways that usually involve hammers, pincers, and very hot fires.

"Don't touch any animals. Some of them look like cuddly plush toys until they open their mouths, which are often full of sharp teeth. Any number of heedless visitors to OtherWorld have died saying, 'Oh, look how cute this little—'

"Don't eat anything you can't identify. The living seaweed of Peridor, for example, grows in the stomachs of people who eat it and comes out through their brains. Dwarves can eat sacat larvae with impunity, but anyone else could find a swarm of them in their belly. Sacat larvae hatch into poisonous and very aggressive red and yellow flying bugs as long as your finger. Taval nuts drive humans insane. The toxins they contain are reserved exclusively for trolls who, as we all know, don't have any brains." Master Chem smiled to show that he was joking, but Tara had already sworn not to eat or touch *anything* in this crazy world.

"It's best to stay with the high wizards and not wander off by yourselves," he continued. "Slavery still exists in some parts of OtherWorld, and the Salterians are always looking for workers for their salt mines.

"Don't go into holy areas. You could be stupidly mistaken for the sacrifice of the day.

"Bow politely to merchants if you want to buy anything. Bargain if you like, but always patiently, and don't offer more than thirty percent below the asking price." Cal complained that he didn't like having to do math just to know how and what to buy. "Immediately alert the high wizards in case of even the slightest incident. If the problem is more serious, call a police wizard. They are easy to recognize in their red-and-gold robes."

The group was preparing to leave when Angelica appeared, looking defiantly at Master Chem. He couldn't very well order her back to her room, because the others wouldn't understand. But with Cal, Robin, and the old wizard all glaring at her, she cautiously kept a low profile. Angelica's friends gathered around out of sympathy for the loss of her familiar—except for Carole, who had started keeping her distance since the Portal incident.

When lunch was over, Master Chen gave the signal to leave and they finally stepped outside.

"Gee, the Palace is right downtown!" exclaimed Tara, seeing that the walls around its manicured lawns overlooked a busy highway.

"That's right," said Robin. "A spell keeps the noise from bothering the empress and the emperor. That's why we can't hear anything. But just wait until we leave the Palace grounds."

Half a dozen beautiful flying carpets equipped with comfortable chairs (and seat belts!) were hovering by the Palace entrance. Their drivers lowered them to the ground, and the passengers stepped aboard. Then one by one, the carpets flew out through the Imperial Palace main gates.

"*Switchil mum trav ungeran?*" asked Cal.

"Beg pardon?" asked a dismayed Tara.

"*Glentar 'Interpretus' unglar glinucli! Baclar vindus sabul a chahi-clli,*" gurgled Sparrow.

"*A valux . . .* how old-fashioned these carpets are," continued Cal, suddenly intelligible again.

"Okay, I can understand you now," said Tara with surprise, "but for a moment I couldn't understand anything."

"That's normal," explained Sparrow. "The Interpretus translation spell only works within the Palace, so I cast another Interpretus so we can understand each other."

Tara was about to speak when a deafening roar made her look around. The carpets had just entered Tingapore, and the sounds of the city hit them like a living wave.

There wasn't one level of traffic, but eight of them! Stacked on top of each other, carpets, spellbinders, armchairs, stools, cushions, sofas, and beds (for the really lazy) were flying and crisscrossing in every direction. All this traffic was coordinated by ifrits. They looked like the ones in the Palace except they were smaller and their luminous bodies changed colors.

Tara's heart almost stopped when their carpet sped up when the ifrit turned red. Apparently, Imperial red here corresponded to a green light on Earth; gold was yellow, and blue was red. Traffic surged ahead the instant an ifrit changed color. Tara also saw many pegasi zooming among the armchairs, beds, chairs, canopy beds, wagons, wheelbarrows—even a bathtub!

When drivers ran a blue light, they usually didn't get far. A red-and-gold ifrit from the imperial guard would materialize to write them tickets. Pile-ups weren't too serious, because anti-collision spells kept people from getting hurt. Besides, it was hard to dent the radiator grille of a flying carpet.

As they flew deeper into the city, a terrible rainstorm hit. Tara instinctively hunched her shoulders, expecting to get wet but getting a surprise instead. Huge transparent bowls suddenly materialized over the city and hovered to catch the rain. When a bowl was full, it went to pour its contents into the river that flowed through town and was replaced by another bowl.

Paying no attention to the wind and thunder raging overhead, people were shouting, selling, buying (sometimes stealing, which raised a hue and cry), bartering, bargaining, crying, gesticulating, jumping, raging, and laughing in an extraordinary cacophony. Little garbage cans on legs ran hither and yon, looking for litter. When they spotted a piece they rushed over and gulped it down, sometimes pounding each other with their lids for the privilege.

Bright, colorful stores sold everything under the sun. Palaces and mansions outdid each other in luxury and beauty, their gleaming slate roofs forming striking patterns. (Tara's grandmother would probably sniff contemptuously and call it flashy, but the city was pretty fantastic.) It was a feast for the eyes and the ears.

Tara was staring open-mouthed at a sumptuous palace when it suddenly began to waver, then vanished! A broken-down little house stood in its place. A man stormed out of the house and threw his hat on the ground in a fury. He waved his arms, and the palace reappeared!

Robin smiled to see Tara's surprise.

"He must be having trouble mastering his spell. Or else he's a tenant who hasn't paid his rent, and the landlord is blocking his home improvement spell. In Omois, things are rarely what they seem at first."

Tara saw the same thing happen several more times. Splendid houses would suddenly disappear, briefly revealing miserable hovels, then reappear in all their glory. Once it was the other way around: a small house trembled for a moment, showing a glimpse of splendid palace. Cal burst out laughing.

"That must be a spellbinder who's in trouble with the imperial tax authorities. He doesn't want them to know that he owns a beautiful piece of property, so he disguises it as a little shack. Very ingenious!"

The rain stopped as quickly as it had started and the sun came out again. The transparent bowls disappeared.

Feeling somewhat stunned by the noise and traffic, the young spellbinders reached the Central Market, where Robin gave them some advice.

"Omoisians are OtherWorld's businesspeople, and they're better at business than any of the other races. There isn't anything they won't buy or sell, so be careful when dealing with them. They'll offer you any number of things, saying that they're good deals. What they don't say is that they're good deals for *them*, not for you!"

The carpets landed, and the high wizard indicated where to meet in case anyone got lost. Then they all eagerly dove into the crowds.

Robin hadn't been kidding when he said that all OtherWorld came to Tingapore. Tara was able to recognize most of the races: imps (tiny, brown, very agile), gnomes (hunchbacked, bearded, surly), unicorns (white, cloven hoofs, golden horn, doe eyes), vampyrs (she decided to carefully avoid them), fairies (small, talkative, winged, multicolored), chimeras (as at Travia Castle, everyone cautiously stepped aside when they passed), and centaurs (half horse and half man or woman). But she couldn't put a name to a cat-sized creature that sported a snake's tail, lobster claws, and the head of a seagull, or another animal with a crocodile head framed by a lion's mane and the rear parts of a hippo!

The shapes and colors were strange enough, but the smells were overpowering.

Tara had loyally shared her money with Cal, Sparrow, and Robin (over his fierce resistance), so they could all take advantage of the marvels on display.

A seller of magic flutes vied for their attention: "My beautiful, beautiful flutes are silver and gold. The music they make will beguile the most sensitive ear, even if you don't know how to play!"

Next door, a fabric seller was shouting: "I have the finest velvets and the most beautiful silks in the entire Central Market. Feel my muslins, my organdy, my actarus wool, my giant-spider silk."

A leather merchant called: "Come see my merchandise! Look at my beautiful scarlet, purple, and black leathers. They don't fade, they're treated to stand up to rain and hard riding, and they don't stretch out of shape. I've got every kind of leather: baby dragon, snake, fireproof salamander, Earth and OtherWorld cowhide, even deerskin from the elfin forests."

Yet another merchant waxed poetical: "Pots and pans I have for you, for baking, roasting, or for stew. Ovens cast iron or Dutch, for pennies you can cook so much!"

The owner of a pet shop called to them: "Step right up, young gentle people! Come right in and experience the marvels of nature! Chameleon frogs, talking parakeets, tiny fire-breathing dragons, miniature manticores, immortal phoenixes, trained sphinxes, secondhand pegasi! Come in!"

A jewelry seller made eyes at the girls: "Look, young ladies! I have everything you need to set off your beauty, dream stones and love stones, green diamonds and blue sapphires, fire opals, glittering gold, soft silver, and shining vermeil. Look them over, try them on!"

A perfume merchant pulled stoppers from his flasks: "Love perfume, dream perfume, make your boyfriend lose his head, subtle scents, brutal scents, your scent will be all that exists!"

Tara was in a daze. She had never experienced such chaos. Frightened by the noise and the crowds, Gallant, Blondin, and Sheeba stayed close to their companions. Suddenly she noticed Master Chem casually wandering away from the other wizards. Without thinking, she hastened after him, followed by her three friends.

"What are you doing?" asked Sparrow, who'd reluctantly put down the perfume she was sampling to race after Tara.

"Look! Master Chem is trying to sneak off. Let's follow him! Don't lose sight of me!"

That wasn't easy because they had to weave in and out of the dense crowd without attracting attention. After a few moments of this game, Master Chem glanced behind him. Tara, Cal, Robin, and Sparrow just had time to duck behind a peasant's wagon, drawing a suspicious look from its owner.

Chem then stepped into a seedy-looking shop that dealt in spells and magic paraphernalia. The young people crept closer, and Tara stood on tiptoe to try to see in through the magic shop's grimy front window.

"I can't see what he's doing," she whispered. "The window's too dirty!"

"Then clean it," said the ever-practical Sparrow.

"Nothing doing, most of the grime is on the inside. Wait a minute. I can see something, but—"

Tara suddenly crouched down, trembling.

"What's the matter with you?" asked Cal worriedly.

"Master Chem is talking with a Bloodgrave!" she answered, looking very pale. "I can't believe it!"

"My father always says you have to be very careful about appearances," whispered Robin.

"Well, he's definitely with a Bloodgrave!" whispered Cal, who had also taken a look. "What should we do?"

"He's the head of the High Wizard Council," said Tara bitterly. "What are we supposed to do? Go see the other wizards and say, 'Oh, by the way, Master Chem is buddies with the Bloodgraves'? For him to know them is one thing, but to be meeting them in the back of a shop is something else. Something in this business doesn't make any sense."

"I don't know what's going on anymore," moaned Sparrow, "but this is terrible!"

"Listen, we can't hang around," said Robin nervously. "My dad says that when you're in enemy territory you've got to keep moving. We better get out of here, or Chem's gonna catch us!"

Tara's head snapped up. "You're right. Let's go join the others. We have to discuss this calmly. And I *must* talk to my grandmother. She's the only adult I can trust!"

"Same for me," agreed Robin. "I have to tell my dad all about this. Something really out of the ordinary is going on."

Scuttling over hunched down so nobody in the store could see them, the friends went to hide behind the wagon again. This time, its owner strode around to confront them, his four arms crossed on his chest.

"Hey kids, just what exactly d'you think you're doing with my cart? 'Cause if you want to steal it, you've got another think coming!"

Cal looked at the peasant, cast a scornful eye on the wagon, and said, "Why would we want to steal that rickety old thing? We—"

"Look! He's coming out of the shop!" interrupted Robin.

Ignoring the angry peasant, they watched as Master Chem came out, cautiously looked around, then blended into the crowd.

The peasant grabbed each of them by the collar of their robes. "I don't know what shenanigans you're up to, but I don't want any part of it. So get out of my way. Beat it!"

Lifting the four struggling kids high in the air, he gently set them down a few yards away.

"He's lucky I gave my word to my mom," snarled Cal as he dusted himself off, "cause his purse was right at my fingertips."

"Yeah, well I'm glad you resisted the temptation because I don't especially want to face the imperial police," said Robin. "All right, ready to go?"

"Let's move," said Tara. "The sooner we're back, the sooner I'll find a way to contact Grandma."

Suddenly Sparrow whistled, "Wait, I just saw something!"

"What?" whispered Cal.

"It's weird," she said, "but it looks like Deria, and Master Dragosh is following her."

"Oh, great!" complained Cal. "I bet you ten to one that Tara will want to—"

"Let's follow them!" interrupted Tara.

"—follow them," he said with resignation.

They went back the same way they'd come, because Deria was heading for the same store. She entered the dusty magic shop and disappeared. Master Dragosh did what the friends had done earlier: he posted himself near the window and watched.

"Okay, what do we do now?" asked Sparrow with a sigh. She was getting very anxious, what with everybody following everyone else.

"We wait," said Tara, whose mind was working at full speed, "because I think what we have here is the explanation of the mystery."

"Oh really?" whispered Cal. "Then it would be nice if you explained it, because for the moment it's not clear to us at all!"

At that moment Deria came out, closely followed by a man with brown hair and a big nose. He was the same size and build as the Bloodgrave, except that his robe was yellow. The vampyr had just enough time to duck out of sight, and the two passed without noticing him. The four young spies were then surprised to see Dragosh turn into a large black wolf and follow them.

Leaving her friends flat-footed, Tara charged into the shop, followed by Gallant.

It was very dark inside, but she gradually made out an amazing clutter of vials, bottles, stuffed and caged animals, rusty weapons, and broken furniture.

From a corner, a wrinkled old man popped up at the ringing of the entrance bell.

"Good afternoon, Miss," the old man quavered. "What can I do for you?"

Caught short, Tara stammered, "Er, I just came in to see what you sell."

"Oh, that's an old Earth language, if I'm not mistaken," said the merchant, on hearing Tara speak. "Mind if I cast a double Interpretus, so I can understand you? Don't answer in your language, just nod yes or shake your head no."

Tara nodded and he recited the spell "By Interpretus, we each come from a different land, but we want each other to understand."

The merchant smiled. "That should be better. So tell me, what might you need? Do you have a boyfriend?"

"No!" said Tara, blushing. (What a lame question!)

"No boyfriend, eh? That's too bad, because I have some very effective love potions. They can keep a boy interested for a couple of centuries. If you don't want a potion, maybe a trinket of some sort would appeal to you."

"Er, sure, why not?" Tara said politely, who was wondering what her friends were doing and why they hadn't come in yet.

"In that case I have just the thing. It's a ring that makes you older for a few hours. If there's something you're not allowed to do because you're too young, you switch it on and *poof!* you're grown up. It just costs one brass immuta-cred."

Tara was tempted in spite of herself. But she reluctantly recognized that she had problems no spell could solve.

"No, thank you, I prefer growing up normally," she answered virtuously.

The old merchant chuckled. "You're nobody's fool, I see. The last person who bought this ring from me switched it on wrong and aged 150 years all at once. Let me see if I have something else for you. I know! Look at this marvel!"

He pulled a parchment scroll from a shelf and blew the dust off it, which set him coughing for a good minute. Then he unrolled it. To Tara's astonishment, she saw that it was a map of OtherWorld—except that once it was unfolded, mountains arose, rivers flowed, tiny people filled the cities, and animals galloped across the fields.

"It's . . . it's wonderful," said the dazzled girl. "I've never seen any map like it!"

"The map updates itself automatically," explained the merchant, pleased with the impression he'd made. "As soon as a new road is built or a city street renamed, the map displays it. If you're in one place and you want to go someplace else, just ask the map. It automatically knows where you are and indicates it with a red circle. It also tell you the number of days it takes to get somewhere on foot. You divide by three if you're on horseback, and by five if you're riding a pegasus. To get a detailed view of the place where you are, just recite the following spell: 'By Detailus I need information about my specific location.'"

With astonishing speed, a map of Tingapore and all its streets appeared with a red circle floating above it. Tara could identify the city hall, the empress's Palace, the municipal administration building (a dozen times bigger than the Palace!), and the merchant quarter.

"What if I wanted to walk to Lancovit?" she asked

"Unless you have gills, I don't see how you'll manage," said the map snidely. "There's an ocean between us and Lancovit, in case you didn't know. Otherwise, on foot it would take you about two years— if you walk and swim fast."

Well, I'll be . . . a talking map! thought Tara, who liked its sense of humor. It would make a wonderful present for her grandmother, and she decided to buy it.

"What's it worth?" she asked, reluctantly looking away from the fascinating spectacle.

Before the merchant could answer, the map said, "I'm priceless!"

"The map is actually right," said the merchant, who was trying to guess how much money she had. "But I could let you have it for ten gold immuta-credits."

Tara could tell that he'd just plucked the figure out of the air, so she pretended to leave. "I'm very sorry, but I don't have that much on me. My master doesn't want us to walk around with too much money. Actually, you just saw him. He came into your store a few minutes ago: a high wizard in a blue robe with silver dragons."

As Tara moved toward the door, the old man shook his head and started rolling up the map.

"Wait, wait, don't leave! Let's discuss the price of the map. But as to the high wizard, you must be mistaken, young lady. No one besides you has come into my shop for more than an hour."

"Really!" exclaimed Tara. "That surprises me, because I also saw another wizard here, a young woman."

The old merchant shook his head again, but Tara saw a sly glint in his eye.

"You must be confusing this with another shop, young lady. I assure you no one came in here. Now, for the map, I can give you a discount. Let's say five gold creds."

"One silver cred," answered Tara firmly. "Are you sure you didn't see anybody?

"Two gold creds, and I'm losing money at the price. And no, I didn't see anything."

"Hey, that's not nearly enough!" gasped the map in a shrill voice.

"One silver cred," said Tara, ignoring the map's comment. "That's the best I can do . . . unless you saw something."

"One gold cred, and I'm slitting my own throat just to please you."

"I don't want you to lose money, Master Merchant," said Tara politely, "and I value your good health. One silver cred."

The old man moaned. "Eight silver creds, and that's my best offer."

"And that's selling me at a discount!" howled the outraged map.

"In that case, I'm sorry," said Tara with a sigh. "I'm also sorry that you haven't seen anybody in your store for the last hour."

The merchant squinted and then said thoughtfully, "I might remember something, but I now realize that this map is more valuable than I thought. Ten silver immuta-credits."

Tara appeared not to care. "It's too hard to put a value on your recollection. Two silver creds."

"The old wizard came in and he talked with another man, then he left. That's all I remember. Nine silver creds."

"That's only part of the information. What was the nature of the discussion? Three creds."

"Alas, they put a silence shield around themselves, young lady. Eight creds."

"Come on, you're a master of spells. Who could keep you from listening whenever you wanted to? Four silver creds."

"Your old wizard seemed angry at the other man. He reproached him for something that I really didn't hear, and the man answered that it was the wizard's own fault. The wizard said that he had been patient so far, but that all of OtherWorld would declare war on them unless the fids were returned. Then he left. Seven creds."

"The *fids*? I don't . . . Oh, I see! Could it be 'the kids'? And what about the young woman? What did she say?"

"Maybe it was kids. And where are my immuta-credits?"

"We haven't agreed on a price yet," Tara shot back. "Five silver creds for the map and the young woman's discussion."

"Done," said the merchant, giving in. "Show me my credits."

Tara carefully took five silver coins from her purse and held them out to the merchant, but snatched her hand back when he tried to take them.

"She talked with the same man," he said, sighing, without taking his eyes off the money. "She seemed angry, too. It must not have been a very good day for him because as soon as somebody came into the shop, it was to bawl him out. That's all I know. Here's the map. Now give me my creds!"

Tara handed over the coins, which he promptly hid in the vast folds of his blackish robe.

"Good, good," he said with a smile that revealed the stumps of three loose teeth. "What else can I give you, my young gentlewoman?"

"*Give* me!" said Tara mockingly, as she carefully folded the map, which yelped that it had been sold for *much* less than it's worth. "Your 'gifts' are expensive! I have what I need, thank you. Good—"

A terrible racket was heard outside, and Angelica stormed into the store. Catching sight of Tara, she rushed at her, screaming.

"You're gonna pay! It's because of you that I lost Kimi. I'm gonna kill you!"

She shoved Tara against the shelves, which collapsed around her in a terrible crash. The merchant started screaming like a stuck pig.

Angelica, who was stronger and heavier than Tara, slapped her with all her might. Stunned by the blow and truly enraged for the first time in her life, Tara lost control of her magic completely. Her eyes turned entirely blue and she levitated. A tornado arose out of nowhere that blew off the roof and propelled it several yards away, as passersby screamed, and sent Angelica crashing into the merchant.

Cal, Robin, and Sparrow entered the store in turn, closely followed by Deria and Master Dragosh.

Meanwhile, Tara must have decided that the tornado wasn't frightening enough and had conjured a huge set of jaws in which the compasses, squares, machetes, knives, and lances cluttering the store become sharp, gleaming teeth snapping threateningly.

Master Dragosh saw Tara flying right at Angelica, preceded by the voracious jaws, and quickly cast a paralyzing Pocus. The spell closed around the two combatants and immobilized them.

But Tara knew exactly how to counter the Pocus. Defying the vampyr, she visualized the mesh and got rid of it with a scornful twitch of an eyebrow. Then she drove the howling tornado toward the paralyzed Angelica, whose eyes were wide with fear. (The merchant, on the other hand, wasn't looking at anything; he had fainted.)

Tara spoke in an icy voice she didn't recognize as her own: "If you ever try something like that again, if you even *think* of raising your hand against me or one of my friends, there won't be enough pieces of you left to fill a teaspoon!"

"That's enough!" Deria's voice rang out. "Stop that immediately, Tara! I'm not joking!"

Tara's totally blue eyes turned to Deria, and for a moment the others thought their friend was going to vaporize her.

Then Tara wrinkled her nose, shook her head as if to get rid of something, and obeyed. With a gesture she stopped the howling wind and floated gently to the floor. Her eyes reverted to their usual color as the instruments rained down around her with loud bangs, clicks, and crashes.

"That's better," said Deria. "Now, can somebody tell me what is going on here?"

"I don't think this is the best place to discuss it," said Master Dragosh, nodding toward the gathering crowd and the merchant, who was slowly coming to. "Let's transfer the children somewhere else and we'll decide."

Without waiting for Deria's response, he began to recite a teleportation spell, and the air around his fingers started to glow.

"Nooooo!" screamed Deria. "I won't let you do it!"

She raised her hands and a ray of red light blasted the vampyr, who barely had time to raise a shield. Within seconds the two spellbinders were dueling, each firing wizard fire, each sheltering behind a magic shield, then firing another ray that burned everything in its path. Half the store was already in flames.

Astonished, the friends shoved Angelica, who was still paralyzed, under the desk. The terrified merchant hid behind the few display cases still standing.

Suddenly Deria spotted an enormous cauldron hanging directly above the vampyr's head. She said: "By Gravitus, cauldron, fall to your doom. Send this wizard to his tomb!" The cauldron fell, knocking Master Dragosh unconscious.

Before the spellbinders could react, Deria yelled: "By Transmitus help us leave this rubble, and avoid all further toil and trouble." A ray of light shot from her hands, split, and touched Tara and everybody near her. To her horror, the vampyr had gotten to his feet behind Deria and was about to cast a spell. The young woman barely avoided it and yelled something. For Tara, everything faded to black.

CHAPTER 14

IN THE BLOODGRAVES' LAIR

At first, it felt like the rocking of a boat and made Tara feel vaguely nauseated. I really don't like sailing, she thought.

Then her vision cleared, and she realized that what looked like sails hanging in front of her weren't part of a boat but canopy bed curtains. For a moment, she thought she was back at Travia Castle until she realized that the curtains were white, not blue. The room she'd woken up in looked a lot like an infirmary. It was white from floor to ceiling, and its glass-fronted cabinets contained unpleasant-looking instruments. Then she looked down at her robe and was startled to see that the last piece of the puzzle had fallen into place.

Tara thought back on everything she had heard, what she knew, and what she guessed, and she could see it all taking shape. It wasn't a pretty picture. She had done everything in her power to get here, but she hadn't anticipated that it would be as a prisoner, or that her friends would be caught with her.

Around her, people in other beds begin to stir, and she saw Sparrow, then Cal, Robin—and Angelica. Freed from the Pocus, the tall girl was looking around in a panic. "Where are we?" she shrieked. She was answered only with silence.

Gallant preened his feathers. Then, with Sheeba and Blondin, who were yawning, the pegasus headed off to reconnoiter the area.

To the spellbinders' astonishment, Fabrice suddenly entered the infirmary, followed by Manitou. He rushed over to them, and Tara's great-grandfather energetically licked her face.

"Gee, it's good to see you!" said Fabrice. "I've really missed you guys! How did you get here?"

"Hey, wait a minute," mumbled Cal, who was still half asleep. "When did you manage to get free? And where the heck are we, anyway?"

"Free?" said Fabrice frowning. "Er, no, I'm not free. You're the ones who are—"

"—in the Bloodgraves' fortress," interrupted Tara.

"Son of a gun!" an astonished Robin said. "How do you know that?"

"I've had my suspicions for a couple of days now. There were lots of clues, but they seemed contradictory. Then what happened in the magic shop made everything clear. And look at the color of our robes. They're still ours but they've been changed; now they're gray!"

"Would you mind explaining that?" cried Sparrow. "Because I don't get it."

"I guess this is my fault," said Tara, sitting down on her bed. "Even though it was perfectly obvious."

"What was obvious?" snapped Cal.

"Master Chem and Master Dragosh weren't the people trying to kidnap me; it was Deria. She's behind all this. Deria was the one who alerted the Bloodgraves the day I first revealed my gift. She led them to kidnap me. Because of the Memorus, the spell that recreates past events, she couldn't kill me herself without blowing her cover, I guess. So she waited for an opportunity when she wouldn't be suspected. She couldn't know that the spell wasn't working properly. When Magister attacked me on Earth, that's why she took such a long time bringing Master Chem back from OtherWorld. And it wasn't Master Dragosh who was prowling around our dormitory, but Deria. She didn't realize that Manitou was with Fabrice instead of me, and kidnapped them. Finally, it was Deria who met the Bloodgrave in the magic shop. When she saw us there, she must've figured we'd been spying on her and cast a spell to send us here. I'll bet she's the one who cut a lock of my hair one night to prepare her Transmitus."

"But what about the conversation we heard between Master Dragosh and the other wizard outside the Training Hall?"

"If you remember, Master Dragosh never said he had arranged the kidnappings, only that he thought Master Chem's policy was stupid."

"You know, you're right! But Chem went into the magic shop with the Bloodgrave too."

"Well, of course he did," said Tara soberly. "Because it was Master Chem and his fellows—"

"—who created us, in a way," purred a velvety voice.

The young spellbinders jumped. They hadn't noticed the man entering the room. A mirror mask hid his face, and a rich gray robe covered his powerful body.

"What do you mean, 'created us'?" asked Sparrow. Since learning that she could shape-shift, she had lost most of her shyness.

"That fool wanted to create an elite group, against the wishes of his fellow dragons," said Magister with a scornful laugh. "He secretly trained a thousand of us to help him destroy the demons once and for all. But some of us became more powerful and we chose a different path, and he couldn't bring himself to admit the truth. That's what I find especially amusing. He doesn't even know the identity of his worst enemies! Isn't that terrible? Here, we're doing exactly what he did: training the future masters of the world."

"I want to go home!" shouted Angelica. "I have nothing to do with this girl! I'm here by mistake."

"That's correct," said a voice they all knew well. "You shouldn't have been included in the spell. But I doubt it will upset your father. We know he supports our cause." Just then Tara noticed a familiar figure standing near Magister.

"Deria!" exclaimed Tara.

"Good morning, darling." The young woman was smiling. She wasn't masked, and her black-and-white magpie was perched on her shoulder.

Tara didn't smile back. "Why, Deria? What does your betrayal get you?"

Deria's face contorted with rage, losing all its beauty.

"Betrayal?" she hissed. "Who's talking about betrayal? Your grandmother, that crazy old woman, was prepared to let your gift rot. To hide your power, when it should be on display for all to see!"

"Does that mean you aren't the person who tried to kill me?" asked Tara very calmly.

Deria turned pale and took a step back.

"Kill you?" asked a baffled Magister. "What do you mean, kill you?"

"Ask her," said Tara, pointing at Deria. "During my presentation in Omois, one of the apprentices lost control of his Transfer Portal, and it blew up. Someone took advantage of the raging vortex to try to get rid of me. And I suspect it was Deria."

Magister's mask swung toward the young woman, and she turned even paler.

"It wasn't me, Master! I swear it!" Deria's magpie left her shoulder and cautiously flew up to a ceiling beam. "Why would I do such a thing? I'm loyal to you. The girl is talking nonsense!"

"No, what Tara is saying is true," said Sparrow bravely. "When she tried to close the Portal something opposed her, and she nearly died."

"But I didn't do it," Deria protested as the Bloodgrave's mask darkened. "I swear it wasn't me, Master!"

For a moment, the mask became completely black. Deria stumbled backward in terror, realizing she might only have a few seconds to live. But Magister relaxed and his mask lightened again.

"Find out who wanted to kill her and get them," he said sharply. "Take the Hunter with you." By now, Deria was almost white. "Bring me the guilty party—alive, if possible. Oh, and one more thing: because you were living at Isabella's, we didn't want you to go through your Initiation. You were so close to her that she might have discovered that you were one of us. But I think it's essential now. We'll schedule your loyalty oath ceremony soon—very soon."

The order had so shocked Deria, they thought she was going to faint, but she held on.

"Er, excuse me," hazarded Cal, interrupting the discussion. "What do you plan to do with us, now that you've kidnapped us?"

"We didn't kidnap *you*," answered Magister, turning his attention from the trembling young woman. "We only wanted Tara. But I'm happy to see that Her Royal Highness has also done us the honor of a visit."

With mock courtesy, he bowed to Sparrow. Modeling her response on Tara's, Sparrow gave him a brief, regal nod.

"You're all here, so you're going to be our guests for some time. In your case, Your Highness, we'll have to talk with your parents."

"Meaning you're going to ask for a ransom," translated Cal. "I can't say I'm surprised. But my parents don't have any money, so I'll ask again: What are you going to do with us?"

From Magister's attitude, Tara sensed that he didn't like people standing up to him. He nodded his head slightly, and Cal suddenly fell down, clutching his throat and apparently unable to breathe.

Sensing his companion's distress, Blondin flew into the room like a red streak, ready to attack. But Magister waved his hand, and the fox barked once and collapsed, unconscious.

"For starters, we're going to teach you to respect your elders," Magister snarled. "The old dragon clearly doesn't know how to teach the younger generation manners. Then, when that lesson has sunk in, we'll see what we can make of you."

He gave another nod, releasing Cal. The boy rolled onto his side gasping, his face crimson.

"Just one more detail," Magister said with an evil chuckle. "Don't bother trying to use your accredi-cards to reach your masters. We disabled them."

Disappointed, Tara bit her lip. That was exactly what she'd thought of doing.

Magister opened the door, allowing a frantic Gallant and Sheeba to race in, then left.

Before reluctantly following him, Deria gave Tara one last look.

"I had to reveal my allegiance to bring you here," she said. "I hope you'll understand that everything I've done has been for your own good."

Tara just glared at her. The young Bloodgrave sighed, ordered her magpie back onto her shoulder, and closed the door behind her.

The moment they left, Tara's shoulders sagged and she sighed.

Fabrice cried, "Wow! Until now I didn't even know that it was because of Tara that I was here. I had a hunch there was a mistake because of Manitou, but I would never have suspected Deria!"

"She thinks what she's doing is for the best," said Tara wearily. "I'm sure she feels her choice is the right one. I'm terribly sorry to have dragged you into this whole business."

"Don't worry about it," said Sparrow kindly. "We're all together, and that's what counts. I'm happy to be with you. I wouldn't have wanted to let you do this on your own."

"Me either," said Cal, stroking Blondin, who was gradually reviving. Then he made an awkward move and yelped, "Jeez! I'm really hurting!"

"You know, Cal, you shouldn't provoke people who are bigger and stronger than you," observed Sparrow sarcastically. "It's not good for your health."

"You got that right! Next time I'm kidnapped I promise to keep my head down. Meanwhile, would somebody mind explaining the rest of why we're here? I think I missed an episode."

Tara smiled at him and started counting on her fingers.

"Episode 1: the dragons encounter spellbinders on Earth, and war breaks out. Episode 2: they're already fighting the demons, so the dragons decide to ally themselves with the spellbinders and invite them to OtherWorld. Episode 3: together they manage to defeat the demons. Episode 4:—"

Sparrow jumped in and picked up the thread: "Episode 4: Master Chem makes a big mistake. He gives some spellbinders too much power and they turn against him. Those spellbinders misuse dragon wisdom and become the Bloodgraves. Chem meets one in the magic shop to warn him that he is ready to admit to the other dragons what he did, and set all of OtherWorld against the Bloodgraves. Right now, OtherWorld and its rulers only consider them a minor irritant. They don't understand them or the danger they represent."

Tara continued: "Episode 5: the demons realize it was because of the high wizard spellbinders that they were defeated. So they decide to forge an alliance with the Bloodgrave spellbinders. Thanks to the Demon King and his magic, the Bloodgraves are now preparing a plan against the dragons that will allow them to rule the universe!"

"That's completely nuts!" exclaimed Cal. "But do we get to rule along with them?"

"Cal!" shouted Sparrow and Tara at the same time.

"Kidding!" he shouted mischievously. "Just kidding."

"You don't understand," explained Tara soberly, "because you've never been infected by demonic magic, as I was. Did you see Deria's reaction earlier to the Initiation? I'll bet twenty to one that Magister has found a way to infect the apprentice spellbinders with demonic magic."

"You think so?" asked Cal with great interest. "Is it dangerous? Because your thing with the metaphors was pretty funny."

"Cal, it took more than a hundred wizards to cure me," Tara said seriously. "And while I was under the demonic influence I almost killed you all a half-dozen times when you annoyed me. A few more days and you and your jokes would have been on your way to a meeting with infinity."

"Now that's not funny," he admitted. "Not funny at all. So what do we do?"

"I think the Bloodgraves want to turn us against our parents," said Tara with a frown. "The high wizards will be taken by surprise if their own children attack them and won't have time to defend themselves. As a plan, it's both subtle and smart. So we've got to escape this place as quickly as possible and warn the high wizards. By the way, why did it take you so long to join me in the magic shop?"

"That was Angelica's fault!" snapped Cal, shooting a dirty look at the girl sulking in a corner. "Just when you ran into the store, we realized that she was following us and very furious. She rushed in after you, gave you that enormous slap . . . and after that, it's all a bit fuzzy. You launched the tornado of the century right in the poor merchant's shop, Deria and Dragosh showed up and decided to fight OtherWorld War One over again, and *poof!* we all wound up here."

Fabrice was practically rolling on the floor laughing.

"Man, how I've missed you guys! I didn't understand all of what you just said, but I get the feeling things have been pretty lively after I left. Not like here."

"Oh really?" asked Robin. "Why?"

"The apprentice Bloodgraves all think they're super-accomplished," said Fabrice with exasperation. "'Check out my powers, I'm hot stuff' sort of thing. And we're given lots of tests where we have to practice fooling nonspells and manipulating them with illusions. I hate that garbage. Oh, and they're brainwashing us to convince us that the nonspells are supposed to be our slaves. It's totally lame. Can you imagine me telling my dad that he's going to be my slave? He'd knock my block off before the words were even out of my mouth! And the worst of it, not a single person here understands my riddles!"

"What, you mean we're supposed to *work* too?" asked a horrified Cal, who'd picked up on only that part. "Here I was about to say that the only good thing about being kidnapped is that at least you don't have to do anything. Know what? I suddenly feel a powerful urge to punch someone."

"Hey, don't look at me like that," protested Fabrice.

"Don't worry, I didn't have you in mind," said Cal with a faint grin. "You're much too fat for me to punch. I'm not at all sure I'd win."

"Fat, me?" protested the athletic Fabrice. "What do you mean, fat?"

"Come on, boys, cut it out!" said Sparrow. "What were you telling us about this place, Fabrice?"

"It's a kind of laboratory," he answered, scowling at Cal. "We're constantly being given aptitude tests. And what's drilled into our heads is contempt for the races that don't practice magic—and even some that do, for that matter. Almost all the Bloodgraves here look down at me because my parents are nonspells. And to answer the two unspoken questions on your minds: no, I haven't undergone any kind of initiation, and no, you can't escape from here. I tried twice, but it can't be done."

"Oh yeah? Why not?" asked Cal, who was naturally drawn to the idea of escape.

"The place is a real fortress. I have no idea what country we're in, but the building is surrounded by grounds and high walls. Levitation spells don't work outside. And there are chatrixes roaming the grounds at night."

"*Chatrixes*?" exclaimed Sparrow. "They must be crazy!"

"I hate to interrupt," interrupted Tara, "but what's a chatrix?"

"They're monsters," answered Sparrow somberly. "They look like the giant hyenas that lived on Earth in prehistoric times. Their fur is completely black, so you can't see them at night. They can tear your leg off with a single bite. Plus, their saliva is poisonous. If you get bitten but manage to escape, you'll die within two hours, and they'll feast on your carcass. Finally, they're immune to all offensive magic, which makes them pretty fearsome enemies for spellbinders."

Tara shuddered, but said, "Well, we'll just avoid crossing the grounds."

"It isn't that simple," said Fabrice. "There's no other way out."

Fabrice then told them about his arrival with Manitou and how enraged the Bloodgrave master had been when he realized they'd kidnapped the wrong person. He was about to describe a typical day in the Fortress when Cal and Blondin's stomachs rumbled simultaneously, which made everybody smile.

"All right, I get it," said Fabrice with a chuckle. "Come on and eat, and I'll introduce you to the others."

They followed him to a big dining hall where a lot of people were eating breakfast. Hairy things with lots of teeth were running here and there, and Tara recognized Magister's Mud Eaters. She scanned the room, but nobody there looked like her mother. She felt her heart sink. Was she really in the Gray Fortress, the place where Selena Duncan was imprisoned?

They were waited on by nonspells, men and women who wore short black robes with rope belts, and necklaces around their necks. The spellbinders noticed that the nonspells seemed terrified. They never raised their eyes, and the Bloodgraves treated them as if they really were slaves.

"Wow, is it breakfast time already?" exclaimed Cal. "Now I understand why I'm so hungry. How long were we unconscious?"

"No idea," answered Fabrice. "I was just told a few minutes ago to go to the infirmary. That's all I know."

"Rats! I was hoping to figure out what country we were in by the time difference," said Sparrow.

Tara looked over the huge, almost silent dining hall. "Doesn't the architecture give you a clue? On Earth, countries' architectural styles vary a lot."

"Hey, that's a thought," said Sparrow. "How would you describe the Fortress, Fabrice?"

"Well for one thing, it's big," Fabrice said, sitting down with a mug of hot chocolate. "The door lintels are very high, and there are passages going every which way, as if the Fortress had been built by enormous rabbits. There isn't any magic in the walls, and you open the doors using handles. No tapestries, no decoration, no nothing. It's big, drafty, and depressing."

"I've never seen this speckled gray stone before," observed Robin.

"But I have!" exclaimed Sparrow, who was just now noticing the rock walls. "We're in a fortress that belonged to a giant."

"Are you sure?"

"I'm reasonably sure. I've seen this stone before, in Gandis. It's spellblock, so called because it blocks magic. That hides it from spellbinders' eyes, which kind of makes the Fortress invisible. And I think it belonged to a giant because that stone is also the only ones that giants don't eat, so they use it for building."

Tara was wide-eyed. "Eat? You mean they eat rocks?"

"Yes, they do. Giants eat stone, which is why they live in the Gandis Mountains. Dwarves mine precious minerals in the same mountains, and they sell their mine tailings to the giants. There's a lot of business between the two peoples."

"What do the giants sell them?" asked Tara, who found this very interesting.

"Some of the metal pieces that the dwarves create require more strength than they have, so the giants forge them for the dwarves. They also pay with immuta-credits, like everyone else on OtherWorld."

"Hmpf! Dwarves can forge anything they create!" came a loud voice near them. "Dwarves are just as strong as giants. That story about our needing the giants' strength was cooked up to make the giants think we need them. After all, they're our best customers. We have to flatter them a little."

The five friends turned toward the person who had spoken, and Tara made a mental note to never contradict her. She was a dwarf and about as wide as she was tall. Massive biceps seemed about to snap the gold bracelets on her upper arms, which were displayed not in a gray robe like theirs, but a sleeveless jerkin. Her shoulders were so square that you could've balanced two trays of glasses on them. She gave off an extraordinary sense of energy and density.

The dwarf's reddish beard was braided with pretty ribbons, and a dark line on her lower lids accentuated beautiful gray-green eyes. A thick mane of hair, also braided with ribbons, practically reached the floor. The overall effect was striking and pretty exotic.

Fabrice said cheerfully, "This is Fafnir, a dwarf from the Hymlia Mountains who was kidnapped last year."

"Of course I was. I was the best of the apprentices, and those nasty Bloodgraves only kidnap the best."

"Well, we're going to bring the average down," Cal predicted, "because we're here by accident."

The dwarf's beautiful eyes narrowed.

"How so?"

"Well, originally, we—*Ow!*"

"It's a long story," said Robin laconically, who had just kicked Cal under the table.

Sparrow was looking at the dwarf with intense curiosity, and shyly spoke up: "Let me introduce us to you. I'm Gloria Daavil, Princess of Lancovit, but I prefer to be called Sparrow. This is Caliban Dal Salan, known as Cal; Robin M'angil;" (Tara was startled; she hadn't paid any attention to Robin's last name before, but it certainly sounded familiar) "and finally, Tara Duncan. The girl over there who is deliberately not looking at us is Angelica Brandaud. Please forgive my asking, but isn't your being here pretty unusual?"

"You're telling me," the dwarf sighed as she pushed away the remains of the enormous fowl (turkey? ostrich?) she'd been eating for breakfast. "When my fellow dwarves realized I had spellbinder gifts, they banished me. You know how much we dwarves hate magic, and the fact that I was still so young didn't make any difference. And me, not even 250 yet, imagine!"

"I can see that," said Sparrow sympathetically, pointing to her beard. "You haven't shaved it yet, which means that you're still a minor, right?"

"Yeah, that's right," Fafnir said gloomily. "And if I don't get rid of this blasted magic and join the others for my Exordium ceremony in a few days, I'll be banished for life."

Her eyes full of compassion, Sparrow didn't know what to say in the face of such obvious distress. The Exordium ceremony is very important to dwarves. At it, young dwarves have to deliver a speech to be accepted as adults and respected members of their clan. Dwarves hate magic, and if one of them suffers from it, they immediately become outcasts. That's why so few dwarves become high wizards, which is too bad, because their magic is often very powerful.

"But then why were you an apprentice spellbinder at Travia Castle?"

The dwarf's answer shocked them.

"I was looking for a way to get rid of my magic!"

"But you can't do that!" exclaimed Sparrow. "It's like having brown hair or a big nose. You can try changing it, but the results are just temporary."

"Not true, as it turns out. When the Bloodgraves kidnapped me, I was desperate, because in a year of working at the Castle for Lady Sirella, I hadn't learned anything that made me think I could rid myself of magic. No document or manuscript mentioned it. The only reason I've stayed here is because these creeps have a library that's even bigger than the one at Lancovit. It's especially good on forbidden spells and potions. And last week I learned something that gave me hope again."

"What was that?" asked Robin, now completely fascinated.

The dwarf lowered her voice.

"There's a plant called *Rosa annihulus* that grows in the Swamps of Desolation in southern Gandis. All the spellbinders who know about it are scared of it. It's a black rose whose juice can completely eradicate magic. You just boil the petals, swallow the brew, and *bingo!* no more magic, ever! Black roses are very hard to find and they say a curse hits whoever picks them, but I don't care. It's my only hope!"

Cal didn't understand. "If dwarves hate magic so much, why didn't you just pretend to be 'normal'?"

Fafnir frowned.

"Dwarves are honest. We can't tell lies." (Cal blanched at that. To not be able to tell lies? How awful!) "Well, not to each other anyway," she said, correcting herself. "And merchant dwarves have special dispensations. So when my parents discovered my gift, they immediately told the Council about it."

Since she was being honest, Fafnir added, "I might have been tempted to pretend. But my blasted magic isn't controllable. Just throw anything sharp or threatening in my direction and *blam!* a kind of protective force field automatically surrounds me. I tried to get rid of it, but it was nothing doing. I failed. So they banished me."

Even Tara, who didn't especially like magic, couldn't help but shudder at the idea of struggling so hard to get rid of it, and in such a drastic way. "So what are you going to do?" she asked.

"I'm gonna get out of here, find that silly plant, and go home."

"But what about the chatrixes?" asked Fabrice.

"Hmpf! I'm a dwarf," sniffed Fafnir contemptuously. "If I decide I'm getting out of here, nothing's gonna stop me!"

"But that's crazy," Fabrice objected. "You'll never make it! There are way too many of them. And if a chatrix bites you, all you can do is go back to the Fortress to get the antidote, otherwise it's bye-bye!"

"Look, they already tried to make me undergo their blasted initiation," she said, shrugging her muscular shoulders. "It didn't work, and they were furious. So I'm not going to let a bunch of little doggies keep me from leaving."

Fafnir was about to go on when she suddenly stopped, as if listening to something. Then she abruptly stood up and said, "May your hammer ring clear."

Without hesitating, Sparrow gave the polite answer: "May your anvil resound."

The dwarf left without another word.

Very surprised, the five friends watched her walk away. Tara frowned, thinking about the dwarf's odd behavior. Fafnir had suddenly fallen silent and left the table. Why?

Suddenly she got an idea. "Fabrice, what time do the tests begin?"

"There aren't any this morning, just this afternoon. Why?"

"Listen, I have to check on something. Do we have our own rooms?"

"We have individual rooms," he explained. Anticipating Tara's next question, he added resentfully, "But getting together in one is forbidden. If we want to talk, we have to go to the common room."

"Hm, I see." Tara stared at Fabrice so appraisingly that it started to make him uneasy. The others watched as she thoughtfully chewed her forelock. Then she took a deep breath and spoke: "Listen, Fabrice, there are a couple of things that Cal, Robin, Sparrow, and I have to take care of. Why don't you go to that common room and we'll join you there in a few minutes? Just tell us how to get there."

Fabrice frowned, curious and annoyed at being excluded. The other three looked at Tara, baffled.

"It's easy," he said, pointing at the stairs leading up from the dining hall. "Go to the first floor, where the bedrooms are. The common room is just beyond the library. I'll see you there."

He stood up with dignity and walked off, closely followed by Angelica, who was probably hoping to enlist him as an ally.

Tara leaned close to her other friends and murmured: "I'm going to need your knowledge. Does a spell exist that lets you listen in on a conversation without the people being aware of it?"

"Oh, sure," said Cal, "the Indiscreetus. Thieves often use it to get information. Why?"

"And how do you protect yourself against it?"

"With a Shieldus, which keeps anybody from listening."

"Hm, that won't work, then. If we cast a Shieldus, the Bloodgraves will realize we know they're trying to listen to us. We need something else."

Cal, Robin, and Sparrow were staring at her.

Then Tara very distinctly said, "And then Angelica sent Kimi at me to get revenge."

"Beg pardon?" asked Sparrow.

"What?" said Cal and Robin together.

"Do you remember the spell that Master Chem cast on us?" whispered Tara, glancing at the other tables carefully.

"The one that keeps us from talking about the Omois incident? Sure, why?"

"Master Chem said that if anybody was listening to us, the spell would keep us from talking. Which means that as long as we're able to say, 'And then Angelica sent Kimi at me to get revenge,' that means nobody is listening. And if we can't speak, it means that somebody is."

"Well, I'll be darned," said Cal admiringly. "I would've never thought of that! But there's going to be a problem with Fabrice. He's not going to understand if we try to get rid of him each time we want to talk."

"Listen, I think Fafnir wants to escape from here, and I suspect she has a plan that's a lot better than what she said. I want to escape too, and as soon as possible. So let's not worry about hurting Fabrice's feelings. We'll explain when we are all out of here, okay?"

"Yes, ma'am!" snapped Cal, with a sort of military bow.

"No, that's not okay at all," said Robin. "I'd hoped it wouldn't come down to this, but I don't have a choice. I'm going to have to tell you the truth about myself as well. 'And then Angelica sent Kimi at me to get revenge.' I'm not just Master Den'Maril's apprentice. I'm also T'andilus M'angil's son."

"The secret services head!" whispered Sparrow.

"Of course! That's where I'd heard that name!" exclaimed Tara. "I've been wondering for a while now. When I was on Earth with Chem, he said something about your father. When I accidentally transformed your robes with the Decorus, Sparrow's robe displayed scepters and crowns, and if I remember right, yours got covered with elf symbols. And the dinner rolls! Nobody could have caught them! 'And then Angelica sent Kimi at me to get revenge.' But you're not an elf."

"A very pertinent remark," said an amused Robin. "And you're right; I really panicked when you redecorated my robe. If anyone had figured out why elfin warriors were battling across my robe, I was toast. Your deductions are really smart, except for the business about dinner rolls. I don't get that."

"Try to remember. During the lunch at the Omois Imperial Palace, I handed you a basket of rolls, but I dropped it," said Tara, blushing a little. "And you caught them before they hit the ground. I remember thinking that wasn't normal; nobody could've moved so fast. But then I forgot about it."

Robin fixed his light eyes on her. "You have the most observant mind I've ever seen, Tara. It's kind of disconcerting. It's like you're putting all the details of a puzzle together. The Soothsucker warned that I was going to 'reveal' myself. I should've paid attention."

Embarrassed by the compliment, Tara blushed even more.

"Yeah, she'll be a magic detective when she grows up," cut in Cal. "Anyway, you were telling your story."

Robin continued: "'And then Angelica sent Kimi at me to get revenge.' This is a partial disguise, which I put on so I could approach you without the Bloodgraves realizing it. I'm older than you; in OtherWorld years, I'm fifteen. But I'm way behind in my spellbinder training because I had to do my elfin service before coming to Travia. Anyway, the Bloodgraves managed to kidnap me along with you, which is what we'd been hoping for. You see, my father cast an undetectable locator spell on me that only works on an elf. So for the time being, your risking your lives to escape is out of the question."

Sparrow was perplexed. "Why a partial disguise?" she asked.

"Because I'm only part elf," Robin admitted, as if it were some sort of defect. "I'm a half; my mom's human, a spellbinder. My dad cast a spell to hide my elf traits: you know, pointed ears, light eyes, slanting eyebrows. Otherwise, the rest of my body is human enough that you wouldn't notice. And neither would our enemies."

"'And then Angelica sent Kimi at me to get revenge.' All right, nobody's listening," confirmed Tara. "What do you suggest we do?"

"My father said the locator spell would work for several days, but that if he didn't bring the cavalry riding to the rescue within twenty-six hours, I'd be on my own. He also said he needed at least twenty hours for the spell to activate and indicate my location."

Sparrow mulled this over. "The kidnappers probably kept us asleep for several hours, so your father could arrive with help anytime between tonight and, say, tomorrow morning."

"That's right," said Robin. "So let's not go off half cocked. If nothing's happened by tomorrow afternoon, we'll take things into our own hands."

"Let's go join Fabrice," suggested Cal. "He must be chewing his fingernails wondering why we aren't there yet."

In fact, it looked as if Fabrice had chewed right down to his knuckles. He was shooting nervous glances at Angelica, who was sitting at another table. The room wasn't a Discussarium, like the one in Omois, and it didn't have the charm of the common room in Lancovit Castle, but the chairs were comfortable and there was Tzinpaf to drink.

"Ah, there you are at last!" Fabrice cried with relief. "Angelica's gone off her rocker."

"That's nothing new," said Cal breezily. "Don't listen to her. Instead, tell us what she did."

"It was terrible," Fabrice moaned. "She jumped on me, demanding that I tell her what was going on here. At first she was pretty hysterical, but then when she understood that only the best spellbinders were held in this blasted Fortress she stopped screaming. Not a moment too soon either, because in another minute I would've gone deaf. What were you guys up to, anyway?"

His friends looked embarrassed, so Fabrice shrugged and continued.

"All right, you want to know the schedule? This afternoon you'll take tests to determine the level of your magic." Tara rolled her eyes. Tests, what a drag! Especially when she needed time to search the Fortress. "Then they'll evaluate your speed, strength, and agility, both physical and magical. They say it's useless to recite spells or make magic passes. We should be able to visualize what we want and make it happen without any tricks. It's a lot harder than with spells, but they claim the dragons are the ones who need the help of reciting spells, and that the dragons taught us their system as a way of controlling us."

"That's a pretty radical theory," remarked Sparrow, pursing her lips. "But not impossible. Magister didn't recite a spell when he immobilized Cal. And I've noticed that Tara rarely needs to make passes. It's like she visualizes what she wants and *bingo!* it happens."

"Well, sort of," said Tara. "More like I think it, and then my magic works whether I want it to or not."

"In any case it's a terrific advantage in duels," Fabrice continued, "because your opponent doesn't know what kind of spell you cast before it hits him."

"*Duels?*" the four friends exclaimed at once.

"Yeah," said Fabrice, delighted with his effect. "Here they use duels to evaluate spellbinders' relative strength."

"Like in Omois!" said Sparrow. "Except that in Omois, it's pretty unusual. I don't think I'm going to like this place at all."

"Neither will I," said Tara and Cal together.

"Duels? Great!" exclaimed Robin, his eyes shining.

"Oh, you elves, all you like is fighting!" said Cal in disgust.

The words were hardly out of his mouth before he realized he had blundered. Tara and Sparrow jabbed him in the ribs. And Fabrice was looking at him as if he'd lost his mind.

"Er, in case you haven't noticed, Robin is a human, not an elf!" he said.

"Yes, I know," said Cal smoothly, "it was a joke. But Robin enjoys fighting, just like elves. You've missed a lot of stuff since being kidnapped. We even nicknamed him 'Robin Hoodlum' because he almost took a guy's head off who was bothering Tara in Omois. And he's the first to come to her defense against Angelica."

That little fable seemed to satisfy Fabrice.

The morning passed pretty quickly. Fabrice introduced them to several apprentice Bloodgraves, and Tara's theory was unfortunately borne out. They were arrogant, cruel, and impulsive. They enjoyed using their unusual magical gifts to torment the nonspells, giving them invisible slaps or hiding hidden obstacles in their paths for them to stumble over. Tara noticed that the gray spellbinders had a habit of rubbing their chests, as if something bothered them. With a shock, she remembered that the demon had emerged from her own chest. She and the others began to feel very frightened.

Then they watched their first duel—much against their will.

It started when two boys in gray got into an argument. Their voices grew louder with each point they made, until they filled the room.

"Tarda was right!" yelled the first. "It doesn't take even the thousandth of a thousandth of a second to lift the spell."

"And I'm telling you, Tarda was wrong. She didn't take the speed of the counter-spell into account. It can't be done in less than a second."

"Okay, that does it!" screamed the first. "I'm challenging you!"

"Fine with me!" snapped the second. "Let's go to the Dueling Hall."

To the friends' surprise, no adult intervened. Instead, all other spellbinders left the room and Fabrice leaped to his feet to follow them.

"Come on," he yelled, "we have to go watch the duel, it's a rule. But don't worry, it shouldn't be too bad. Those two got here the same time I did, so they haven't been initiated yet."

Sparrow stared at him in disbelief. "What? You mean we have to see this?"

"I thought it was pretty interesting before I heard about that business with the dragons," admitted Fabrice. "Now, let's say it's best to act like everyone else and follow them."

Robin nodded enthusiastically. His elf temperament was excited at the idea of watching the duel, while his human reason felt concerned. He often wondered why his father and mother got married, considering how different they were. He hated just being a *half*. He was enjoying this mission because in his disguise he felt entirely accepted as a human by his friends for the first time.

When the friends reached the hall, all the best seats were already taken, and they had to climb up to the nosebleed section of the bleachers.

The hundred-odd Bloodgraves weren't the smallest group in the hall, which gave Tara the shivers. They must obey a very precise hierarchy, she thought, because the circles on their chests weren't all the same color. They varied from yellow to red, just as their robes went from light gray to a gray so dark it was almost black. You couldn't see the Bloodgraves' masked faces, but their restless hands betrayed their eagerness for the duel to begin. The group gave off a sinister and threatening tension.

The two duelists stood opposite each other and together shouted "Duel!"

Immediately, the floor rose so that everyone could see clearly. A transparent force field surrounded the duelists, isolating them from the rest of the space.

In the movies, duels between wizards are usually fought as a series of transformations: "I turn into a chicken, you turn into a cat. I turn into a dog, you turn into a lion. I turn into a flea, you turn into a monkey. I turn into a crocodile, you turn into an elephant. I turn into a mouse, and uh-oh! You turn into a dragon and try to incinerate me, which is illegal, aaaahhhaah!" and so forth.

But these two boys hadn't seen the same movies as Tara and really seemed to want to tear into each other.

They began in very classic fashion, but they were clearly still in the habit of chanting and gesticulating, and the audience easily recognized two paralyzing Pocus spells. Both managed to break free of the meshes at the same time. First round score: 0–0.

One of the boys made a pass and a pair of magnificent donkey ears popped up on his opponent's head. The whole hall burst out laughing. Furious, the second boy cast a Transvestus, and his opponent's robe vanished, generating catcalls from the boys and blushes among the girls.

Enraged, the offended boy countered with a Detritus, and a ton of manure came falling on the other duelist, who jumped aside to avoid it.

It looked as if magic could be avoided if you were fast and agile enough. In fighting a duel, you had to move like a boxer: graceful, smooth, and quick on your feet.

The two spellbinders had now reached the stage of "I shoot you something dirty, viscous, and stinky," and "I shoot you something just as disgusting back."

Then one of the boys smirked slyly and cast his spell without moving or speaking. At first, his opponent thought the spell had missed him. He wiggled his fingers to fire something, but realized that instead of hands, he now had *fins*! He opened his mouth to yell, his legs stuck together, which caused him to fall, scales covered his skin, and soon an enormous fish was flopping in the middle of the arena, feverishly searching for water to survive.

To admiring applause, the winner sadistically took three turns around the arena while his opponent flopped desperately, trying to breathe. A Bloodgrave finally made the winner restore the unfortunate fish to his original shape.

"That was really interesting!" cried Robin enthusiastically as they left the hall. "Are there often duels like that?"

"Quite a few," said Fabrice with a grimace. "Once or twice a week some boy or some girl will say the wrong thing, and *pow!* it's off to the arena. Duels between apprentices are different when they're arranged by the Bloodgraves, because you can only cast the spells they assign you. In a duel of honor you can cast any spell you like, provided you don't kill your opponent."

"Are we allowed to go outside during the day?" asked Tara.

"Yes. And the Familiars go out onto the grounds a lot, even though it's getting chilly. This is the start of one of the cold seasons."

"Do you think we could go out now?"

"Sure, follow me."

"Wait a sec," said Tara, stopping him. "I want to ask someone to join us."

Seeing the dwarf passing, Tara discreetly called to her.

"Fafnir, do you have a moment, please?"

"Yeah?" The tone was laconic.

"We're going outside, and we'd like you to come too."

The dwarf looked her over, and seemed to be thinking hard. Then she shrugged and said, "Okay."

"Great, let's go."

They walked in silence until they reached the tall trees that loomed over the outside benches and tables. Fabrice was right; it was chilly. But even though the dwarf's arms and legs were bare, the cold didn't seem to bother her.

Tara spoke: "Sparrow, I'm going to ask you to make a great effort. Do you remember the incantation that our wizard recited after the Omois incident?"

"Yeah, I remember it, why?"

"I want you to write it down, but not say it. I want to try an experiment."

Though perplexed, Sparrow obeyed. She produced paper and pencil from a pocket, wrote out the incantation, and gave it to Tara.

Before the others could do anything, Tara said, "By Informatus, the secret we share. May no one else know of this affair!"

As she was saying the words, she powerfully expressed the wish that Fabrice, Manitou, and Fafnir would have access to their secret, while the others would still be protected by the old wizard's spell.

To her great satisfaction, the same greenish fog as at Omois settled over the other three. But then Tara suddenly found herself flat on her back with a blade pressed against her throat.

Feeling the spell touch her, Fafnir had whipped out her knife and pinned Tara so quickly the girl never saw it coming. She was now crushed under the dwarf's weight, and her face was so close, Tara was looking cross-eyed. Maybe I should have warned Fafnir before casting the spell, she thought.

"What in the world did you just do to me?" snarled the dwarf. "Cancel that fast, before I slit your throat!"

The others were paralyzed, not daring to move. When Tara spoke, the movement nicked her throat on the dwarf's blade, but she couldn't help that.

"Wait! It's a protection spell! We witnessed an incident in Omois, and Master Chem told us not to talk to anyone else about it. To be sure we obeyed, he put this spell on us. I noticed earlier that you suddenly stopped talking at one point, so I figured you knew someone was watching us. And I thought we might be able to help each other."

"That doesn't give you the right to cast a spell on me," answered the dwarf, ignoring the bleeding cut. "You're lucky I'm a calm girl. Any other dwarf would have cut your throat first and asked questions later."

She lifted the knife and sheathed it, then jerked Tara upright. The girl tottered for a moment, surprised by Fafnir's strength.

"Anyway, you don't need to use that stupid magic," she growled. "I can sense when someone's listening to me."

"But we can't!" protested Tara. She cautiously touched the knife cut. It had practically stopped bleeding, but by Baldur's horns—her grandmother's favorite curse—did it ever sting! "If we're able to say, 'And then Angelica sent Kimi at me to get revenge,' that means nobody's eavesdropping on us. Check it out yourself, you'll see!"

The dwarf shot her a menacing look and strode off.

Sparrow ran over to Tara, put her hand on the cut, and said: "By Healus, let the pain be gone, let Tara's wound be cured anon!"

The pain eased, and Tara heaved a sigh of relief.

"I'm getting tired of people going for my throat every thirty seconds," she said. "Obviously, I forgot that you're not supposed to cast a spell on a dwarf without permission. Fabrice, I don't know whether Fafnir has gone to check out our story or if she's stormed off in a total rage. Would you do something for me, please? Go up to the first person you meet, and say the sentence, 'And then Angelica sent Kimi at me to get revenge.' If you can do it, it will mean that my magic has outdone itself and I've accidentally extended the protection to the whole Fortress instead of just to us. If you can't do it, it'll mean that it worked."

Wisely, Fabrice decided not to ask any questions and ran off with Manitou. He came back a few moments later, grinning widely.

"I just spent ten seconds in front of a Bloodgrave without being able to say a word. He thought I was sick and wanted to send me to the infirmary. That trick of yours is great. But what's it for, exactly?"

While checking periodically that no one was listening to them, they told Fabrice the whole story, including the tragic episode caused by Angelica. Every so often while they were talking they found themselves unable to say the magic sentence, so they quickly changed the subject, but it wasn't easy. Tara was worried because Fafnir hadn't returned, and she had trouble concentrating.

The dwarf still hadn't reappeared when the lunch bell rang. Well, so be it, Tara thought. They had to prepare their escape, just in case.

In the dining hall she saw Fafnir sitting in the same place as at breakfast, devouring something big that Tara couldn't identify. She cautiously decided to sit down not next to her, but across from her. That way, if the hot-tempered dwarf went for her throat again, she'd have to get across the table first.

Fafnir turned her big doe eyes to Tara, spat out a bone, and muttered, "Information correct. Meeting outside at five o'clock."

Tara nodded.

Lunch passed quickly, and the spellbinders had barely eaten the final piece of fruit when it was time to go to the Testing Hall, where initial evaluations were held. When they entered it, Cal, Robin, Tara, and Sparrow looked around in amazement.

Before them were trees, ropes, bridges, a river, and a lake, all arranged in a commando-style obstacle course. At the top of a very steep hill glinted a jewel on a pedestal.

A mirror-masked Bloodgrave with a clearly female voice came over. What she did next stunned everybody, especially Tara. The Bloodgrave bowed low in front of her and said, "Good afternoon, Your Imperial Highness. Our Fortress is deeply honored by your presence. My name is Lady Manticore. Welcome."

Tara turned around to see who she was talking to, but there was nobody behind her. "Er, I'm sorry, but the Highness around here is Sparrow, not me."

"I know, Your Imperial Highness." She then bowed to Sparrow: "Your Royal Highness."

What has this woman been smoking? wondered Fabrice in astonishment. The local herbs must be pretty potent!

"If you don't mind, Your Highnesses, we're going to test your capabilities. Brida!"

"Yes, my lady?" answered a girl Angelica had been chatting with.

"Show Their Highnesses how we work in this hall. You'll be timed from the moment you cross the starting line until the moment you grab the dream stone."

"Very good, my lady."

The girl gracefully stepped forward and silently traded her robe for a kind of gray leotard. Then she set out.

The group understood the goal of the exercise the moment the first trap was sprung.

Brida was running on a path toward the first rope when a large pit suddenly opened before her, filled with a writhing mass of monstrous white and red worms. She maintained her momentum and jumped, using magic to soar over the obstacle. In a bound she grabbed the rope and swung up to a branch, balanced there for a moment, then dove into the lake. The banks were too steep and slippery to climb out without help, so Brida swam over to some roots and tried to use them to haul herself out of the water.

Suddenly a black tentacle appeared, lazily coming up behind her. Startling the four newcomers, the spellbinders in attendance started to shout: "Brida, look out for the kraken! Look out!"

Sensing the gigantic octopus was behind her, Brida desperately tried to get away from it, and her concentration wavered. Her foot slipped and a black tentacle dragged her underwater, to toss her coughing and spitting at Lady Manticore's feet.

"Not bad, Brida. What mistake did you make?"

"I lost my focus and didn't get out of the water fast enough. I had to keep swimming to keep afloat so I couldn't help myself by making magic passes. That's why I failed."

"Very good. Next!"

The two young spellbinders to go next had no better luck. One fell into the pit with the worms, which became angry at being trampled. The worms are harmless if you don't touch them, but they burn like fire at the slightest contact. The unfortunate boy emerged screaming in pain, his face and hands covered with red blotches. That was enough to motivate the second one, who gracefully jumped over the pit but went down to watery defeat with the kraken.

Then it was Robin's turn. The half-elf easily avoided the pit, practically flew up to the branch, did a perfect swan dive into the lake, and stayed well clear of the kraken while climbing the slippery roots out of the water, to a burst of applause.

Lady Manticore's mask turned a thoughtful blue, and she jotted something in her notebook.

The boy hesitated for a moment and then, skipping the path, grabbed a vine and swung from tree to a tree, flying over the traps.

Lady Manticore nodded and wrote something else in her book. Tara was in despair, because Robin was overdoing it. But the half-elf was too caught up in the challenge and had forgotten where he was. With Tara silently cursing him, Robin continued to gracefully jump, leap, and tumble past the obstacles.

He landed at the foot of the hill without any trouble, to a round of enthusiastic applause. Without losing his focus, he carefully studied the hill and began to climb it. He deftly avoided first an avalanche that threatened to sweep him away, then a waterspout that came out of nowhere. If he hadn't, he would've been washed back down into the lake, right into the kraken's arms.

Once at the top, Robin stopped briefly to examine the pedestal. Then he grabbed the dream stone, backed away, and ran downhill at top speed. Under his feet, the hill began to crack open in a deafening roar. He just had time to levitate onto solid ground before the hill collapsed into a kind of muddy magma.

The Bloodgrave was studying the obstacle course intently. At least Tara assumed she was studying it, because the course and its traps had disappeared.

Robin easily returned to the small group, proudly brandishing his trophy, a dazzling dream stone. He was beaming . . . until he caught Tara's eye and realized what he had done.

Lady Manticore didn't waste any time.

"Come here,"—she glanced at her notes—"Robin, is it?"

"Yes, my lady," he answered reluctantly.

"Stay right there. I need to check on something."

Suddenly Cal fell to the ground moaning.

"Oh, my stomach hurts! My lady, I'm in pain."

The Bloodgrave, who was about to examine Robin, looked down at him. "All right, what's the matter with you?"

"I don't know," Cal whimpered, "but everything hurts. I was transferred here this morning and—"

His attempt at a diversion didn't work at all. The Bloodgrave, who was probably used to panic attacks, cut him off. She leaned over, touched him, and in an icy voice said, "By Transmitus you can go to the infirmary, they'll cure you of this infirmity."

When she turned back to Robin, she was giving off an air of menace so strong, it was almost palpable. He was trying to make himself look small, which, given his size, wasn't easy.

"Did I . . . did I do something wrong?" he stammered as she came closer.

"No, not at all," she said soothingly. "You did everything perfectly. You made your way past all the obstacles and you got the stone—"

"But then why am I—"

"—which is *impossible* for a normal spellbinder using only their physical capacities! I therefore conclude that you're not normal. And here in the Fortress we don't like things that we don't understand. So come over here."

Robin didn't move an inch. In fact he backed away, as if he were very frightened. (He wasn't pretending; he really was frightened.) The other apprentices, who didn't understand what was happening, cautiously got out of Lady Manticore's way.

Then she stepped on what she thought was a rope but turned out to be Sheeba's tail. The enraged panther furiously attacked and would have torn the Bloodgrave to ribbons except that she was able to paralyze her with a spell.

Ignoring the blood dripping from her lacerated arm, Lady Manticore growled, "Everybody, stay right where you are! By Pocus, not a one of you can move until this mystery I disprove."

Tara had experienced paralyzing Pocus spells cast by Mangus and Master Dragosh, but this one was something else again. It glittered with turquoise fire, and its mesh was so tight she could hardly breathe. Gallant was struggling in vain, and Tara realized that she wasn't able to snap her own bonds either. The wizards in Omois had cured her fits of rage, but that also meant she wasn't furious enough to access the power she had when confronting Angelica in the magic shop.

Tara heard a slight noise next to her and realized that it was Fabrice's teeth chattering with fear. Sparrow yelled and tried to shape-shift, but it was too late. Lady Manticore had just touched Robin with her bloody hand. The moment their skin made contact, she screamed: "By the entrails of Isciarus, an elf! And a locator spell! *Alert! Alert!*"

Manticore's magically amplified voice echoed through the entire Fortress, and Bloodgraves immediately materialized all around her. Some were in their work clothes, others in pajamas (in the middle of the day?). One Bloodgrave, dripping with soap suds, held a brush in one hand and was desperately trying to hold up a towel with the other.

A hubbub of voices: "What? What? What's going on?"

Then Magister, with the distinctive red circle on his robe, appeared. From his attitude, you sensed he would pulverize anyone who had disturbed him.

"Who sounded the alarm?" he thundered.

"I did, Master," Lady Manticore quickly explained. "This elf somehow managed to penetrate the Fortress, and I found a locator spell on him. We have to interrupt it right away, but I can't do that alone!"

"Take it easy," said Magister. "Even the most powerful spell needs time to activate completely. The clever people hunting us may suspect which direction to look in, but they still don't know the exact place."

He touched Robin's chest, and the boy flinched at the burning pain. Then Magister made a rough gesture as if he were erasing something, and Robin's face began to change.

His eyes lightened, his eyebrows slanted up to his temples, and his ears lengthened. His hair grew longer, with a few black streaks mixed with the characteristic white elf hair clearly showing his partial human makeup.

"Well, well, well," said the Bloodgrave master sarcastically. "A nasty little elf! Or rather a half-elf. And a nice locator spell. I can see the hand of our good friend Chemnashaovirodaintrachivu in this. If I analyze the spell, I'll still have a few minutes before they find us. But I'm afraid the process will cost you your elf ears, my friend. I don't think I can cancel the spell that quickly without killing you."

The four friends turned pale, and Angelica gave a cruel snicker.

"Nooooo!"

Tara's scream shook the Bloodgrave master, who rubbed his ringing ear.

Struggling like a madwoman to free herself from the Pocus, Tara felt power flowing through her veins. As in the magic shop, her eyes turned completely blue and the spell suddenly yielded with a sharp *snap!* She levitated, looking down on the scene as Angelica moaned with fear.

Magister was astonished when Tara spoke to him, her voice ringing like a gong: "Let him go! Let him go immediately!"

He didn't react, so she mentally repulsed the Bloodgraves crowded around Robin, scattering them like wisps of straw. Some wound up in the trees, others in the arms of the kraken, which was quite startled to have so many people in its lake.

A furious Lady Manticore intervened, screaming, "Wizard fire!"

The Bloodgraves must have devised abbreviated incantations, because a fiery ray shot from her fingers, hitting the shield Tara had just enough time to raise. Tara in turn fired a devastating ray, forcing Manticore to take cover behind her own shield. So far, the score was even.

Tara was surprised that the other Bloodgraves weren't getting involved. After two more assaults, she realized that she would have trouble piercing her opponent's defenses. Using a surge of magic power, she went to hover above the lake. Furious that a girl was standing up to her in front of all the other Bloodgraves, Lady Manticore levitated in turn and pursued her.

At the risk of being captured by the kraken, Tara swooped to within a few inches of the water's surface. Fortunately, the giant octopus was busy with all the Bloodgraves bobbing around it.

Manticore released a fiery ray, but Tara didn't try to counter, merely dodging it. The ray hit the lake like a missile, instantly creating a thick cloud of steam, which was exactly what Tara had hoped for. Hidden by the cloud and moving like lightning, she fired a petrifying ray at Lady Manticore. Hit in midair, the surprised Bloodgrave cursed, lost the power of flight, and fell into the lake with a great splash.

All right, that's one down, thought Tara. Now it was Magister's turn. She whirled to face him, ready for battle.

But Magister hadn't stirred. Legs firmly planted on the ground, he'd been watching the scene with great interest. He now cocked his mirrored head and exclaimed, "Ah, what power! I can feel your anger and your hatred. Go on! Let the anger fill you. Feel your magnificent power!"

For just an instant, Tara was at a loss. *Great, now this guy is doing a Darth Vader number on me.* Repressing an inane urge to laugh, she got a grip on herself.

Her power didn't need incantations to act, but to neutralize an adversary like this one she would have to be creative. A direct attack probably wouldn't work. She stretched her hand toward the lawn and activated her magic. Magister, who was expecting a violent blow and was ready to counter it, was taken aback when steel-tough roots rose from the grass and wrapped themselves around him, enveloping him from head to foot. Tara raised her hand, and a surge of power sent the Bloodgrave into the air, slamming him against the ceiling with a terrible noise. Still trapped by the roots, he then crashed back to earth with a loud *boom!* and lay still.

Tara turned to face the other Bloodgraves, but they didn't move. She quickly freed Gallant and was looking after her friends when Fabrice suddenly yelled: "Tara! Look out behind you!"

As the imprisoned Bloodgrave master lay twisting on the ground, hundreds of little saws appeared, cutting through the roots. He stood up, his mask now a sinister black, and discarded the shredded robe covering his black jerkin. To her horror, Tara realized that the saws had sprouted from Magister's own arms. She had to come up with something, and fast!

She turned the lake into an enormous wave poised above Magister like a giant liquid fist. This time, however, he reacted. He raised his hand and the wave split in two, leaving the astonished kraken stuck up in a tree, still holding a half-dozen Bloodgraves in its tentacles.

Suddenly, Magister fell to the ground, butted by Gallant. The pegasus had cautiously attacked from behind, to try to knock him out. Unfortunately, the Bloodgrave was only stunned, but Tara saw her chance. Turning to the giant trees, she used all her mental energy to tear one out by the roots and bring it crashing down on Magister, who was still on the ground. One of the other Bloodgraves saw the danger and yelled just in time to warn his master. Magister rolled aside, barely avoiding the enormous mass. To his fury, Gallant attacked him again. With a scream of rage, Magister easily lifted the fallen tree and hurled it at the pegasus. Unable to dodge, the winged horse slammed into another tree with a sickening thud.

Tara's heart was pounding faster and faster, and she realized that using so much magic was taking a terrible toll on her body. But she didn't have any choice—she was fighting for Robin's life. If she could just hold on for a few more minutes, the locator spell would activate and Master Chem would find them. Drawing on her last reserves of energy, she again stretched out her hand, firing a ray at the ground right at Magister's feet. An enormous pit yawned open, swallowing a quarter of the hall. But he'd had enough time to incant and now floated unhurt above the abyss.

Tara was exhausted. Had she held on long enough for the dragon wizard to localize them? Since blasting holes in the ground hadn't worked, she thought, let's see what she could do with the ceiling.

She was about to bring a few dozen tons of rocks crashing down on the Bloodgraves' heads when Magister struck. He stretched out his hands and yelled, and a terrible blast staggered her, shattering the shield she'd raised. She tried to recover, but Magister was faster. She wasn't able to counter his second blast and collapsed.

The scene around her began to fade, and someone switched out all the world's lights.

CHAPTER 15

EXIT STRATEGY

For the second time that day, Tara felt like she was waking up on a ship whose heaving and pitching made her sick to her stomach.

The white infirmary curtains around her glowed softly, and she could hear low voices in the distance. Her head was spinning, and she grimaced when she tried to get up.

Gallant was sleeping at the foot of her bed and didn't stir. He was still unconscious, but thankfully seemed unhurt.

Shaking slightly, Tara parted the canopy bed curtains and headed toward the voices. Fabrice, Cal, and Sparrow were standing around another bed, somberly listening to a Bloodgrave wearing a gray-and-white robe, probably a doctor or a nurse.

"Dead," the woman said softly. "It's terrible. I can't believe it."

Tara's heart skipped a beat. *Robin was dead!* She had failed in her attempt to protect him! She walked over to them, tears running down her cheeks.

Cal suddenly noticed that Tara was up.

"Hey, how are you?" he shouted, running over to her. "How are you feeling?"

"I . . . I'm fine," she stammered. "But what's this about Robin? I heard you say he's . . . " her voice failed.

"See for yourself," said Cal, stepping aside.

She stepped close to the bed and stared at Robin, lying deathly pale in the middle of the big bed.

"Oh, Robin, I'm so sorry!" she cried. "It's all my fault. You're—"

"—a total idiot," the body interrupted, opening its eyes.

Tara recoiled in shock.

"But . . . but you're dead!"

The would-be corpse blinked. "Oh, really? Nobody told me. But I hurt pretty much all over, so it could be true."

Now Tara was completely baffled. She turned to her friends. "But she"—pointing at the Bloodgrave—"said he was dead! That she couldn't believe it."

"Oh, we weren't talking about the half-elf," said the Bloodgrave doctor, who finally understood what Tara meant. "We were talking about the kraken. Some of my colleagues are quite emotional. When they suddenly found themselves in the water, they kind of lost their heads. The kraken just wanted to set them back on shore, as it does for everyone who falls in the lake. They thought it was attacking them, and then it wound up in a tree, and it was just all too much. Too bad; I was very fond of that kraken. Oh well, that's life. All right, I'll leave you for a moment. Don't tire my patient out too much."

Smiling from ear to ear, Tara leaned over to hug a somewhat startled Robin.

"So you're not dead! That's great!"

"Ouch! Take it easy. That hurts!"

"Oh, I'm sorry. So what happened? And what about the locator spell?"

Sparrow answered her: "I was able to shape-shift during your amazing battle with Lady Manticore and then Magister, but a Blood-grave paralyzed me. Magister knocked you out, and then he touched Robin's chest and canceled the spell. It nearly killed him. And unfortunately for us, Magister was able to short-circuit the process, so the spell didn't have time to activate. Which means nobody knows where we are."

"Robin was half dead when they brought him here," explained Cal, still shivering at the thought. "It gave me the biggest scare of my very short life. Luckily, their medical shaman is very good."

"Yeah," Robin agreed. "I didn't know half the swearwords she was using, but she saved my life!"

Suddenly Tara started. "What time is it?"

"About five, I think, Why?"

"'And then Angelica sent Kimi at me to get revenge.' Because we're supposed to meet Fafnir in less than a minute. I have to talk to her."

"You go ahead," suggested Sparrow. "I'll stay with Robin. The doctor thinks that if he rests up today and tonight, he should be okay by tomorrow morning."

"Well, I think her prognosis is wrong," he grumbled. "It's going to be a lot longer before I go back to that infernal Testing Hall."

"Oh no!" cried Tara. "You've got to get better very fast. If Fafnir decides to . . . you know, tonight or tomorrow, she won't wait for us, believe me."

Robin smiled weakly. "Don't worry, I won't let you down. Give me just a couple of hours, and I'll be bouncing around the way I did earlier."

"That's enough of that!" snapped Sparrow irritably. "When it comes to bouncing around, you've already done more than your share."

Looking sheepish, Robin wisely closed his eyes.

"All right, I'm heading outside," said Tara, who was now in a hurry. "Cal, are you coming with me, or do you want to stay with them?"

Cal didn't particularly care to deal with the touchy dwarf, especially not in the cold. "Your pegasus is still unconscious," he said. "I'll send him to you as soon as he wakes up."

"Great. Catch you later."

Tara raced outside and Fabrice showed her the way.

When they got there, Fafnir was already pacing back and forth.

"You're late," was her only greeting.

"Our friend got hurt in the Testing Hall. He's resting in the infirmary. I'm sorry to have made you wait."

"No prob," muttered the surprised dwarf. "I didn't have anything else to do, anyway. Is your friend okay?"

"Yes, he's all right. He snuck in here in disguise, but Magister caught him. He's a half-elf."

"An elf?" she hissed. "Snobs and show-offs, every last one of them. I don't like elves."

Tara, who had other things to worry about, said: "'And then Angelica sent Kimi at me to get revenge.' That doesn't matter. We have to talk about your plan."

"Why *my* plan? No way all of you are escaping with me. Out of the question. You'll just slow me down. Besides, I have to get home, and I only have a few days. I don't know where we are, exactly. I have to find a Portal outside the Fortress. Anyway, what would you do in Hymlia?"

"It would certainly be better than here. And you need us to deal with the chatrixes. Don't tell me you were thinking of facing them by yourself."

Fafnir looked at her for a long moment.

"Sorry, but the answer's no," she grumbled. "I thought maybe you had a plan. But I can see you're counting on me to pull you through. It's gonna be hard enough for me to get out alone. All I can promise is to tell the High Council where the Gray Fortress is as soon as I reach Hymlia. Okay?"

"No, that's not okay at all!" exclaimed Fabrice. "We're all very worried about Tara. Magister assigned a Bloodgrave to keep an eye on her ever since she was a little girl. Now that she's in his hands, who knows what he's gonna do?"

"He's been spying on you since you were little?" asked Fafnir in surprise. "Why?"

"I don't have the faintest idea," said Tara with a sigh.

"Then that's one more reason why I shouldn't take you with me," said the dwarf flatly. "If the boss Bloodgrave has his eye on you, you better keep your nose clean. Otherwise you'll wind up like your friend—in the infirmary."

Tara and Fabrice tried to get her to change her mind, but Fafnir wouldn't bend. She'd already gathered her provisions and planned to break out the very next day.

By now, Tara was desperate. She had searched every room she was allowed to enter and a few she wasn't but hadn't found any sign of her mother.

They ate dinner in gloomy silence.

Gallant was slowly recovering from his shock. Each time he saw the Master of Bloodgraves, he bared his teeth and flattened his ears.

By the time Tara was ready for bed her mood was so black she could've painted the whole fortress with it. She was feeling tired, and took a good hot shower. Picking up her robe, she was about to hang it in the closet with the others when she noticed something hard in the pocket. Intrigued, she reached in—and stifled a shout of joy. It was the magic map!

In her panic, she had completely forgotten it. Spellbinder robes' pockets were designed so their contents never got in their wearers' way until they took them out.

Feverishly, she spread the map on her bed and unrolled it.

"Well, it's about time!" the map snapped. "I was simply bored to tears in there. I'm not made to molder away in a pocket, you know."

"Show us where we are, instead of complaining," she ordered.

The map obediently came to life, displaying an image of a fortress in the middle of a vast plain at the foot of a mountain. Gandis! So Sparrow was right; they *were* in the land of the giants!

"How long would it take us to get to Hymlia?"

"That depends. If you walk fast, at least twenty days. If you run, fifteen days, assuming you can keep up the pace. And it depends where in Hymlia you plan to go. Dwarf country is pretty big."

"Mmm," muttered Tara, chewing on her favorite strand of hair. "How about to the Swamps of Desolation?"

"If you go through the forest, it'll take you three days. Two days if you go across the plains, which I recommend because the going is easier."

"I don't want to cross the plains, it's too exposed. I'd rather go through the forest. Show me that route."

The map didn't agree. "If you go through the forest, it could take you much longer because the terrain is rougher. Trust me, I know."

In annoyance, Tara slapped the edge of the map and said, "By Detailus show me my location and the forest route to the dwarfish nation."

The map was tempted to throw a hissy fit, but had no choice but to obey.

After studying the various itineraries, Tara went to bed with a faint smile on her lips. Fafnir was as stubborn as a mule, but she didn't have a map—and they did.

Tara was sleeping peacefully when a strong gust of wind blew her window fully open, rattled the gray curtains, and woke her up. A shadow appeared in the room. Tara didn't have time to be frightened because the shadow turned into a beautiful young woman floating in the air. Astonished at seeing Tara, she exclaimed in anguish: "I don't believe it! That cursed man managed to kidnap you too!"

Though shaken, Tara was overjoyed.

"Mom? I've been looking for you for days! Where are you?"

"Shhh, don't say anything aloud. Just think the words and I'll hear you. I'm upstairs, a few feet over your head. I heard that

Magister had captured some new apprentices and I came to see. I didn't expect to find you here!"

Tara described their kidnapping.

"So he succeeded!" her mother groaned. "That monster succeeded! I thought Isabella and Chem would do a better job of protecting you. We have to find a way for you to warn the dragon wizard, darling. You mustn't stay here. I've seen what he does to children. The ones who stay, change. They become powerful and cruel. You have to get away!"

"Oh, Mom, I'm so happy you're here! I thought you were being held prisoner somewhere else," said Tara, who for the moment wasn't giving a thought to her escape plans. "Can I come see you?"

She felt her mother hesitate, then make a decision.

"Listen very carefully, darling. I'm going to arrange it so Magister calls you in tomorrow morning. He'll probably send a Mud Eater to fetch you. Whatever you do, don't try to provoke him. Play the fool, so he doesn't get suspicious. When the Mud Eater brings you here after the meeting, go back the way you came and look for me in the living room. It's two doors beyond Magister's office. You'll find it easily. Be careful; there are guards."

"All right, Mom. I'll act as if I didn't expect to be called in, and I'll try to see you. What do we do if I can't?"

"In that case I'll come back to your room in thought tomorrow night, and we'll figure something out together."

"Oh, I nearly forgot!" Tara quickly added. "I think that Fafnir is planning to escape. In fact, I think she's going to try tomorrow night. She's a dwarf."

"Really? That's wonderful! I didn't know they had kidnapped a dwarf. What fools! Dwarves can't stand being locked up, so she'll do everything in her power to escape. You can trust her, darling. Dwarves are wise and thoughtful."

"Oh, really? You sure we're talking about the same people?"

"I have to leave you now. Be brave, my darling. See you tomorrow."

"So soon? But . . . "

"I can feel him waking up," her mother said quickly. "I can't risk being caught; not now. Until tomorrow, darling. Be careful."

"Til tomorrow, Mom. I love you."

"I love you too."

The shadow disappeared.

Wild with excitement, Tara wasn't able to get back to sleep until dawn.

When she woke up her heart was singing, and she felt as if she could fly. She danced around the room with her somewhat mystified pegasus, hopped into the bath, carefully washed her hair, and put on her nicest clothes. Her mother! She was finally going to see her mother again!

She carefully folded the map and put it in her pocket, where she also found her remaining immuta-creds and change.

She was heading for the dining hall for breakfast when a Mud Eater stopped her. Tara knew that the Bloodgraves used Eaters for all sorts of little chores that they didn't have time or inclination to do themselves. Mud Eaters were very stupid, so you had to give them clear explanations to be sure they obeyed. This one had apparently been ordered to bring Tara to his master's office the moment she left her room.

Tara decided to act as if she wasn't expecting this and tried to argue. The Mud Eater wasn't having any of it.

"Come now, Master want to see you."

"But I'm hungry!" she whined. "I'll come after breakfast."

Fortunately, the Mud Eater had specific orders.

"Come now, Master want to see you." He took her by the arm and pulled her along.

The area were Magister lived was brilliantly lit up. That's where Tara met her first giants.

Lost in thought, she found herself in front of what she initially took to be columns. Then she saw feet—very large feet. She looked up . . . and up . . . until finally reaching two rigid faces that looked like granite. She had a moment of panic when one of them seemed to crack but realized that the giant was just trying to smile.

She timidly smiled back and followed the Mud Eater into the office.

Magister was sitting behind his desk. Once, when Tara and her grandmother were watching a movie together, Isabella commented that the distance you had to cross to reach the movie CEO's desk was directly proportional to the size of his ego. The Bloodgrave leader's ego must be huge, because the room, modeled after Omois's Double Throne Room, went on forever. When Tara found herself in front of him, though, any temptation to laugh quickly left her.

Magister seemed to be in a good mood, however. Though she couldn't see his face, Tara got the unsettling feeling he was smiling. And his mirror mask was a serene blue.

"Welcome to my humble abode," he said. "Did you sleep well?"

Tara decided to be direct.

"I'm hungry. Your *thing* there didn't want me to eat before I came."

"Well, of course not. I wanted to have breakfast with you. Please, come this way."

The Bloodgrave opened the door to an attractive private dining room where a sumptuous breakfast was laid out. Tara sat down and started eating a bread roll without paying Magister the slightest attention. She knew he expected her to ask questions, so she stayed completely silent. After a few minutes of her studious chewing, the Bloodgrave broke the silence, and she knew she had won the first round.

"So tell me, Tara, do you like it here?"

A question that dumb didn't deserve anything less than a clear, frank answer. "Nah. Not at all."

Magister took a deep breath. "Ah, I see. But you have everything here that you had at Travia, only better."

Tara knew he was trying to draw her into a discussion. But there's no point trying to change a nasty person's mind, so she didn't answer. Instead, she merely shrugged, knowing this would annoy him.

"Do you like your room?" he tried again, awkwardly.

"Nah. I can't be with my friends. I don't like rooms by myself."

That surprised him. Magister was profoundly individualistic and couldn't imagine that someone might prefer a dormitory to a private room. He began drumming his fingers on the table.

"Otherwise, did you find it interesting to take the tests?"

"Didn't have time. You attacked my friend first!"

The drumming increased.

"But I couldn't let anybody locate our fortress! You understand that, don't you."

She countered his drumming with a shrug.

"Come on, I know you're very powerful," he snapped, starting to get agitated. "A lot more powerful than all the other Bloodgraves here. I'm going to increase your power, make you a force in the world, transform you, and—"

"Nah. I don't want to be powerful. I don't like magic."

At that, Magister was speechless. That is, Tara assumed he was speechless, because he certainly wasn't saying anything.

"You . . . You don't like magic?"

The drumming stopped.

"Nah. I wanna go home, to Tagon. I like TV better."

Tara had prepared her strategy while the Mud Eater was dragging her along the hallways. Tara knew a complete idiot at her school back on Earth, named Brutus. All she had to do was say what she imagined Brutus would say, and it would completely discombobulate the Bloodgrave.

"That's . . . curious," said Magister, who was no fool. "With Deria yesterday you were speaking completely normally. I can't believe that the powerful spellbinder who stood up to me in the Testing Hall could be that stupid."

After a few initial passes, the real duel was beginning. Thrust and parry. All right, thought Tara, let's see what we can do.

"Why did she call me Imperial Highness?" she asked.

"What?"

"Lady Manticore, the Bloodgrave who wanted to test us. She called me Imperial Highness. Why?"

Disengagement, thrust. Totally unprepared for the question, Magister didn't know what to answer. To Tara, he looked bothered, exactly the way her grandmother did when she was stuck.

"It must have been a mistake. She probably meant to speak to the Lancovit princess."

"Nah," Tara immediately countered. "Sparrow's only a royal. To me she said *Imperial* Highness. Why?" Slide along the blade and touch!

Magister suddenly remembered that he had a lot of urgent things to deal with, the first of which was to call in a certain blabbermouth named Lady Manticore.

"Well, I see that you've finished your breakfast," he said. "I'll let you get back to your friends. Whatever you may think, I'm sure your stay with us will be very productive. And I promise you'll get all the answers to your questions after your Initiation tomorrow."

This rattled Tara, but she didn't let it show.

"M'murm!" he called, after carefully looking Tara over, who remained motionless.

"Master?" The Mud Eater came in.

"Take Tara to the dining hall. Then bring me Lady Manticore. Immediately!"

"Yes, Master, nice Master, good Master."

"All right, all right, get a move on!"

Tara didn't know how much the Mud Eater could report back to his master, so she was careful not to smile. Just as they stepped out of Magister's office and were about to leave his private apartments, Lady Manticore suddenly appeared.

"Ah, M'murm, you're just the . . . person I was looking for," she said. "Do you know if the master is available? I want to see him."

"Nice Master, good Master await you. You come. Now."

Tara had no way to tell if Manticore had gone pale, but she seemed unsteady for a moment, and her mask turned green.

"Oh really? He asked to see me? Well, here I am. Let's go in."

The Mud Eater hesitated, torn between order number one, which was to bring Tara back, and order number two, which was to fetch Lady Manticore. He wound up not having a choice, because Manticore literally dragged him into Magister's office.

Tara was delighted. She was in her enemy's private residence. All she had to do was to find her mother.

Tiptoeing along, she entered the first room she came to. It was a library, and she saw that it held the kind of books that you don't leave lying around where children could find them—or most adults, for that matter. Lots of stuff on demons, and obscure, not to say frankly infernal magic. *Exactly what I would have expected of Magister,* she thought with a shudder of disgust.

The next room was the bedroom. *Man, does this guy like black!* thought Tara, looking it over. Everything was black, from the furniture to the adjoining bathroom, which was dominated by a huge granite tub with gold faucets—the height of good taste. A hair brush lay nearby. *Hmm, he's blond,* she noticed. Without thinking, she took a few of the hairs. Cops in TV crime shows are able to identify criminals by their DNA, so why not on OtherWorld?

She silently pursued her search. And found her mother in the third room.

She very slowly opened the door. It was a pleasantly sunny room that probably served as a private Discussarium, because there were chairs and tables everywhere.

When Tara stepped in, the pale, lovely young woman stood up, clapped her hand to her mouth, and ran to her.

"Tara? My little girl! My darling, darling Tara!"

"Mommy! Oh, Mommy!"

She hugged her mother so tight, she felt as if she would never be able to let her go again. After a few moments her mother found the strength to step back to look her daughter over.

"You're beautiful, darling! I didn't notice how you've grown. I've missed you, Tara. You can't imagine how much I missed you!"

"I missed you too, Mommy! You look just like in Grandma's pictures. You haven't changed. You look so beautiful!"

Her mother took Tara in her arms again and rocked her. It was a moment of pure happiness that they'd been cheated out of for so long.

Meanwhile, Gallant made the acquaintance of Sambor, the big golden puma that was Selena's familiar. The two stationed themselves by the door, ready to intercept anybody who tried to come in.

Reluctantly, Selena tore herself away from Tara again and they gazed into each other's eyes, golden hazel into deep blue.

"How are you, darling? Magister hasn't hurt you, has he?"

"No. For the moment he must be wondering if I was actually equipped with a brain when I was born because I told him I didn't like magic."

Her mother burst out laughing.

"Oh, I would have liked to have been a fly on the wall when you told him that! Good move, darling. He can't imagine that someone wouldn't want to have power, because that's what magic represents in his eyes."

"Yeah, I sort of got that."

"That cursed man has held me prisoner for ten years," said Selena, biting her lip. "He takes a sadistic pleasure in telling me about his plots to seize power. To protect you, I had to resolve not to try to contact you. At least not until a few days ago, when I learned that he was going to go after you."

Now Tara was confused.

"You mean you let all of us think you were dead so you could protect me?" she said, frowning. "That's ridiculous!"

"My lord, it's like hearing your grandmother," said Selena with a small laugh. "It seemed like the best thing to do at the time, darling. And the threat Magister represents to OtherWorld and Earth is very serious. Not to mention that it's only very recently that I was able to project my vital essence to Earth."

"But you abandoned me!" said Tara indignantly. "I don't care about those threats. You abandoned me!"

Her mother recoiled in shock. "I'm so terribly, terribly sorry! But that's not the whole story. I can't escape from here! You see, when he killed your father, he also kidnapped me."

Tara slumped back against the gray stone wall. She was completely lost.

"Well of course," she said bitterly, as the truth began to sink in. "You didn't die in the Amazon jungle, and neither did Dad. So what really happened?"

"We were living in Lancovit with your grandmother and great-grandfather. I knew that your father was hiding something from me, but in spite of all the love he had for us, he would never tell me about it. One day when you were about two, a man in a shiny mask appeared at our house. I was upstairs and entered the room just as he was about to take you from your crib. Maama, your grandmother's tiger familiar, attacked him, but he killed it. Just then your father arrived and rushed the man in the mask. They fought, and your father was mortally wounded. The man's spellbinders came running, and when he fled, they took me with them. My mother didn't realize I was still alive. And her only thought was for you."

"But why? Why did Magister kill Dad and kidnap you? And why kidnap me now, and not before? And—"

A tremendous thunderclap interrupted her. A high-pitched scream came from Magister's office and a dense red cloud of smoke spread through the whole floor.

"Quick!" said Selena in a frightened voice. "It's getting too dangerous. Get out before he realizes that you're here. I'll contact you again in your room tonight." She kissed her daughter. "I love you."

Before Tara could stop her, Selena went out into the hall. The giant on guard was distracted—he was looking anxiously toward Magister's office—and she was able to slip behind him and into her own room.

Tara left as well, her head full of questions but her heart singing. She'd seen her mother. She'd kissed her mother. Her mother had held her in her arms!

Still on a cloud, she ran down the stairs and through the dining hall. By the time she got outdoors, she was dragging a recalcitrant Fafnir, followed by Cal, Fabrice, Sparrow, and Robin, who still looked very pale and was rubbing his chest.

"Hey! Why d'you interrupt my breakfast?" grumbled the dwarf, who was in a foul mood.

"Yeah, I'm still hungry," said Cal, for whom the meals were sacred. "Besides, where were you? We looked for you—"

Turning to Fafnir, Tara crisply asked, "Do you have a map?"

The dwarf looked at her resentfully. "What business is that of yours? I'm not taking you. Period."

"I asked you a question. Answer it, please."

"No, I don't have a map. Happy now? Can I go back to my breakfast?"

"'And then Angelica sent Kimi at me to get revenge.' Well, I have one."

It took Fafnir a moment to grasp what she was saying. "What do you mean, you have one?"

"Gaze and admire!" With an elegant gesture, Tara pulled the map from her pocket and unrolled it on the grass.

"Hey there, take it easy! I'm delicate!" it protested.

Tara ordered the map to display their location, and it showed them sitting outside, next to the Fortress. Fafnir's jaw dropped. Fabrice, who loved everything that could be read or deciphered, gazed at the map in fascination.

"Hey, we're in Gandis, just as I thought," said Sparrow, looking closely. "My parents and I lived in the land of giants for years."

"Absolutely," said Tara warmly. "According to the map, the Swamps of Desolation aren't very far—maybe two or three days' walk, max. On the other hand, the nearest border with Hymlia, the dwarf country, is a month away!"

"That's right!" agreed the map. "At the very least!"

The dwarf fell to the grass with a cry of despair. "We're in the middle of nowhere!" she moaned. "I thought there'd at least be a town around where I could use a Portal. I'll never make it! And my Exordium is in less than six days!"

"Listen," said Tara. "I have a solution."

"Oh yeah?" asked Fafnir indifferently, caught up in her misery. "You do miracles?"

"Better than that. I have a pegasus!"

Gallant, who was cropping the delicious grass, raised his head upon hearing himself referenced. But he frowned. He had caught Tara's drift and quickly estimated the dwarf's weight.

"Pff, your pegasus is tiny!" hooted Fafnir.

"Tara shrank him so that he could go wherever she did," explained Cal, who found Fafnir's arrogance irritating. "In his normal size he could carry five of you!"

Gallant rolled his eyes and sniffed. Really, five? Come on, let's not exaggerate!

"If you help us escape," continued Tara, "I'll accompany you to the Swamps of Desolation and lend you Gallant so you can get home in time for your Exordium. The merchant who sold me this map said that you divide the time by five if you're traveling by pegasus-back. We'll find this black rose of yours whose juice eradicates magic. Then you fly home on Gallant. Once there, you contact Master Chem right away, he sends reinforcements, and it's a done deal!"

Everyone looked at Tara in dismay.

"Are you saying we're going to cross the land of giants without any supplies or water, with wild animals and all?" wondered Cal. "Have you gone absolutely nuts?"

"He's right," said Sparrow seriously. "You don't know the country. I've lived there, and it can be very dangerous."

"Besides, you won't be able to use your magic," added Fafnir. "As soon as you do, the Bloodgraves will detect it, especially if you create food or weapons. They'll locate you right away!"

"You don't understand!" cried Tara, on the verge of despair. "We have to get out of this fortress right away! We don't have any choice. Magister wants to infect me with demonic magic tomorrow. He killed my father and he kidnapped my mother!"

"What?"

"How?"

"Huh?" said Cal (who was no more original than the others).

"It's too long to explain. Seven of us will be escaping."

"Then we may as well put up signs and send out invitations!" snapped the dwarf. "Seven—that's impossible!"

"In that case, you can forget about your Exordium with the other dwarves, because unless we escape, there's no map and no pegasus."

Fafnir stood up, her eyes glittering with anger.

"And I'm telling you, I can't take you. End of discussion!"

Tara smiled at her sweetly. She had been dealing with stubborn adversaries all morning and she knew what tack to take.

"You have my proposal," she said calmly. "Take it or leave it. I'll wait for your decision. But I wouldn't waste any time, if I were you. You only have six days left! Tick, tick, tick—the clock's running."

The dwarf clenched her fists, glaring at the slender girl defying her. Then she turned on her heel and stormed off.

"Whew!" breathed Sparrow. "I thought she was going to make mincemeat out of you."

"Don't tell her, but so did I," said a very relieved Tara.

"Man, when you want something, you're like a bulldozer!" said Robin admiringly. "You charge straight ahead!"

Tara decided that Robin was praising her determination, and not her manners. But her legs felt shaky after all the morning's emotions, and she had to sit down on the grass.

"So tell us all about it!" urged Fabrice eagerly, who suspected that something big had happened.

Sparrow said, "'And then Angelica sent Kimi at me to get revenge.' Okay, you can go ahead."

Tara decided to stick to the essentials. "I found my mother," she began.

"Hang on a moment!" said Fabrice. "Your mother? Who's dead?"

Tara didn't have time to explain everything. Besides, she felt a little guilty about hiding from her friends the fact that she had been searching for her mother ever since coming to OtherWorld. She decided to keep it short.

"We thought she was dead, but she's actually been imprisoned in this fortress for the last ten years. I found her and we were talking in the apartments next to Magister's when something very loud with colored smoke happened. Mom ran off, and so did I. She's going to contact me again tonight. I don't have any choice. She has to escape with us."

"Well, of course," agreed Cal, who for once liked the idea of having an adult along. "What do you want us to do?"

"We need to get as many provisions as possible. I don't know Fafnir's escape plan yet, but things won't be easy once we're outside. Beg, borrow, or steal some weapons, like knives. Everything has to be ready by this evening."

"A bow and arrows!" declared Robin, who was again rubbing his chest despite Sparrow's look of annoyance. "I need a bow. It's essential for hunting."

Tara realized that she hadn't paid any attention to his condition.

"Oh my goodness, Robin, I'm so sorry," she said contritely. "What with everything I completely forgot to ask how you're doing."

"It itches something terrible," he said with a thin smile. "But aside from that, I'm doing pretty well for someone who almost died yesterday. That Bloodgrave doctor is very good at her job. If she weren't a gray spellbinder, I'd recommend her to my father."

"If you stopped rubbing your chest it might heal a lot faster," said Sparrow.

"Do you think you'll hold up, once we're outside?" asked Tara.

"Don't worry, I'll manage. Give me just a few more hours and I'll be fine."

Tara was far from convinced. He looked so tired.

"So we were saying, a bow," said Cal, pulling out a notebook. "What else do we need? I'm the best at stealing stuff, so I'll take care of blankets, bags, and weapons. I hear they have a good armory here; we just have to find it. Fabrice, I'm going to need your help. I can't steal big things by myself."

"Er, you sure I'll be able to help you?" asked Fabrice, who looked less than pleased at being pressed into service. "You know, for me stealing—"

Cal cut him off: "Don't worry about it, *partner*. I just need a side-kick to be a lookout and help carry things. I'll handle the hard part."

Fabrice rolled his eyes but didn't answer,

"Perfect," said Sparrow. "I'll take care of food. I can deal with that."

"Aside from thinking, I can't do very much for the time being," said Robin, smiling weakly. "So I'll think about our escape plan and time each stage of the operation. Be sure to get some warm clothes and boots. The other apprentices tell me it's going to get cold in a few days, and we can't afford to get sick."

"As for me, I'm going to bug Fafnir until she gives in," said Tara. "And we have to dream up a diversion to keep the Bloodgraves busy while we help my mom escape."

The afternoon aptitude tests were suspended because of the incident the day before and the absence of Lady Manticore. Tara suspected that the thunder and smoke in Magister's office may have been connected to that absence.

But the friends did get to see an initiation, and if they hadn't felt that they'd better get out of there really fast, it certainly convinced them.

A trumpet blast called all the Bloodgraves and their apprentices to the Initiation Hall, which was in the very heart of the Gray Fortress. A pair of giants guarded the entrance, which was also protected by a precipice so deep you couldn't see the bottom. Two whitish sheets hung above it, preventing any levitation.

Tara and her friends were anxiously wondering what would happen when suddenly something moved overhead—a greenish thing that glowed in the darkness. The something came closer, and to her horror Tara realized that it was an enormous spider! Well, not exactly a spider. It had eight legs and eight eyes, but its tail curved around like a scorpion's and a drop of poison hung from a nasty-looking stinger. What the spellbinders had mistaken for white sheets were in fact part of the spider's web.

"Yikes! A giant arachne!" murmured Cal. "I thought they only lived in gnome country."

Magister, who was leading the procession, bowed and said, "Lady Arachne, guardian of these high places, weave us a bridge over these spaces."

"To pass without danger to the other side, an answer to the riddle you must provide," answered the arachne in a surprisingly melodious voice. "In one word, one attempt, otherwise, your death you'll tempt. I will count time, while the riddle you unwind."

Magister bowed again. "I'm listening, Lady guardian."

"So, here it is," said the monstrous arachnid. "The first clue is what goes with peanut butter, and then put you and me in between. The answer is what others feel before my great superiority!"

"Ha!" Fabrice laughed. "That's obvious!"

The arachne finished, "To one hundred I will count, and then the riddle you must recount."

Magister obviously knew the answer.

"*Jelly* and *us* = *Jell* + *us* + *y* = Jealousy!"

The arachne bowed, folding her front legs, then scuttled up her thread.

"Bah, that's a pretty poor riddle," whispered Cal. "The peanut butter thing doesn't work. She should have said: 'The first clue is the first part of gelatine, the second one is you and me, the third is the letter after d.' Otherwise, it's really easy!"

"Well of course it's easy!" said an exasperated Sparrow, looking at the vaulted ceiling. "The guardian isn't about to sting her own boss! Just try to pass some other time, without Magister, and see how easy it is!"

While they were arguing, the enormous arachne was busy weaving a bridge across the abyss. Hanging by her thread, she first connected the two sides with four other threads, two for the ramp and two for the parapet. Then she wove the center at dizzying speed.

So the spellbinders wouldn't get caught on the sticky threads, she scattered the surface with bones. Big, flat bones that must have been part of one of her meals.

As they crossed the swaying bridge, Tara couldn't help shuddering, especially when she walked under the arachne's hairy stomach.

Then they reached the Initiation Hall. It was huge, like all the other rooms in the Gray Fortress. Floating in its center was a black granite altar and a black throne.

The room was lit by black candles whose flames burned with a red smoke. Seats covered with shiny black material were arranged around the room, facing the altar. Cal gasped when he noticed the sculptures that decorated them. The carved demons could have been the little brothers of the ones they had seen in Limbo.

A heavy, dead mood weighed on the room, and Tara found herself thinking that if the day ever came when the bad guys chose a pink-and-white decor, she would really be surprised.

There was a sudden movement. Four black snakes appeared on the table, hissing and slithering nervously.

"There weren't snakes, before," whispered Fabrice. "But when they tried to initiate Fafnir and it didn't work, it made Magister so angry that he added them."

"Why?" asked Sparrow, who was rigid with fear.

"You'll see," said Fabrice with a grimace. "And you'll understand why I've twice tried to run away."

The Bloodgraves and the apprentices around Tara and her friends were impatiently awaiting the future initiate. When he appeared, they saw it was the boy who had turned his opponent into a fish during their duel. He held his head high, but you could feel he was frightened.

At Magister's order, he levitated to the table, hesitating for a moment above the snakes. With a sharp nod of his mask, the Bloodgrave leader commanded him to lie down.

When he did, the four snakes initially made room for him, then all at once sank their fangs into his flesh, nailing him to the table.

The boy screamed as the venom flowed into his veins.

"You don't have any choice," said Magister softly. "Either the initiation succeeds or you die."

He levitated over to the black throne and sat down. Then he opened his gray robe, revealing a gleaming chest marked with a sickly red circle. Gray fumes rose from the circle and crept slowly toward the boy, penetrating his chest. The boy stiffened. But very quickly the pain gave way to relief. He didn't hurt anymore.

Magister closed his robe.

"Now free yourself!" he ordered.

The boy cast an anxious look at the snakes, then cried, "By Deliverus, rid me of these serpents, of my mind they're harmless figments." Like ghosts, the snakes faded away.

Feeling very proud, the boy got up and levitated over to the others, who surrounded and congratulated him.

Tara sensed that Magister was looking meaningfully at her, but she didn't give him the satisfaction of reacting. Deep down, though, she was very frightened. They had to get out of there—right away!

The Bloodgraves and their apprentices had prepared a big party for their new member after the monstrous initiation, so it was easy for the five friends to discreetly slip away. Then, like squirrels, they gathered the food, weapons, and packs they needed for the trip and hid them in their rooms.

The only remaining unknown in their delicate escape equation was Fafnir. Tara *had* to convince her.

While waiting for five o'clock to meet in the dining hall, Tara reviewed her strongest arguments. When she sat down in front of her, Fafnir gave her a hostile look.

"So, have you come to a decision?" Tara whispered.

"What choice do I have?" she said bitterly. "I'm in a bind, as you well know. I can't succeed without your help. Which means I owe you a favor. And a dwarf who owes a favor is a diminished dwarf, hobbled by the favor."

"You won't be hobbled long," said Tara quietly. "Help us escape and your debt will be paid."

"Yeah, and a fat lot of good it'll do me if we get caught! Seven of us . . . that's nuts!"

"'And then Angelica sent Kimi at me to get revenge.' Listen, I can't say whether we'll succeed or not, but we have to try. You have your reasons, we have ours. Let's join forces."

"Ehhh, I know I'm making a mistake," said Fafnir with a sigh, "but I really don't have a choice. Come to the left-hand tower storeroom tonight at two in the morning. That's when the giants usually nod off. That stupid Magister usually goes to bed at one in the morning. It should be quiet enough for us to work."

"What do you plan to do?" Tara was burning with curiosity.

"You'll see," said the dwarf, getting up. "But I warn you: if you or your friends are late, I'm not waiting. Got that?"

"Got it. See you later."

"Yeah, right."

The friends gathered to go over the final details, perfected the escape plan, then split up again.

Tara was waiting in her room when her mother contacted her. Selena was little more than a diffuse image, but Tara could hear her clearly.

"Mom? Are you okay?"

"Yes, darling, I'm fine. But I have very little time. I'm very frightened for you. You can't imagine how powerful Magister is. You wouldn't be able to resist him very long!"

"We're going to break out tonight, Mom. And you have to come with us."

"No."

Tara was about to outline their plan when she suddenly realized what her mother had said.

"No? What do you mean, no?"

"If you're able to escape, you have to come back with Chemnashaovirodaintrachivu. He's the only one who can break the spell I'm under. The spell that idiotic Bloodgrave put on me is very unusual. If I take one step outside the Fortress I will immediately turn onto a crystal statue, and shatter at the slightest sound. In fact, that's why I was able to develop this aptitude of projecting my essence by thought. But the spell is too powerful for me to overcome. You're my only hope."

Tara could feel tears rising and bravely tried to stop them.

"Are you saying you can't come with us? There must be some way!"

"If the situation weren't so serious, I would forbid you from even trying to escape. Unfortunately I have to let you take that chance. Tell me your plans, and I'll help as best I can. Hurry, darling, we have very little time."

"I have a map," Tara bravely began. "First we're going to head for the Swamps of Desolation. Fafnir the dwarf needs something there. Then I'll lend her Gallant so she can get home in time for her Exordium. Once she's there, she'll contact Master Chem and we'll come back here to free you."

"That's not going to work," said Selena, "We're very far from Hymlia. You have to find some way to bring Chem in less than six days. When you escape, Magister is going to hunt for you everywhere, but he won't evacuate the Fortress right away because he thinks it will take you at least ten days to reach civilization. You absolutely have to find a way to cut that time and contact Chemnashaovirodaintrachivu sooner. Once you're in touch, he'll tell you what to do. What are you doing for food and shelter?"

"Sparrow says that if we use magic we'll be detected by the Bloodgraves right away, so we've collected food, weapons, and blankets."

"Actually, you can use magic if you work very slowly and in a diffuse way," said Selena. "No point in burdening yourself. Just take a single sample of whatever you need. Once you're far from the fortress, concentrate your power and replicate the objects. In the surrounding magic fluid environment, no one will notice. Each morning, make whatever you don't need disappear. That way you'll travel farther and faster."

"Thanks, Mom, that's a very valuable tip. See, we need you!"

"I know, darling," said Selena, suddenly sounding very weary. "But in a moment I'm going to have to cast a forgetting spell on myself. If you manage to escape, the first person Magister will interrogate will be me, so I have to forget I ever saw you. I hope with all my heart that all goes well. I love you. Come back fast with the high wizard. Goodbye, darling!"

"Wait a second, Mom! Master Chem is sure to ask me questions when I see him. Do you know who the Bloodgrave master is? Can you describe him to me?"

Selena's tone was bitter. "That devil is completely paranoid, darling. In ten years I've never seen his face, and I don't have the slightest clue to his identity. Now I really have to leave you. Be careful. I love you!"

Tara was in such pain, she thought her heart was bleeding. But she understood why her mother didn't have any choice.

She checked the time: 1:30 already! At Robin's suggestion, who had designated himself the escape's master organizer, they had decided not to go to the storeroom all together, but singly, every ten minutes. That way, if one of them was caught or delayed, it wouldn't put the others at risk.

Tara took the fur-lined cape and boots she found in her closet— Cal had apparently paid a call—made sure she had her map and money, and quietly slipped out the room with Gallant. Silent as a shadow, he flew up ahead to warn her of any danger.

Everything was quiet. Fabrice had said that the fortress administrator and steward didn't exactly work themselves to death. At night, they only got up if a young spellbinder came to see them because he was sick or there was a problem. Otherwise they did what most adults did then: they snored.

Tara glided down the hallways, crossed the dining hall and the courtyard, and reached the storeroom. Its door was ajar. She hesitated for a moment, then pushed, praying that it wouldn't squeak. Fafnir must have thought of that and oiled the hinges, because the door swung open without a sound.

There was no one in the storeroom. Then, as Tara's eyes were adapting to the darkness, she heard a muffled sound from the basement. Tiptoeing along with Gallant at her heels, she headed in that direction.

At the bottom of a staircase was the place where wine and non-perishable food was stored. Someone had pushed one of the enormous lockers aside and dug a big hole in the wall.

Robin and Fabrice were already there, using wicker baskets to laboriously clear away a pile of dirt. Manitou saw Tara first and ran over to greet her.

Alerted by the dog, Fabrice looked up.

"Ah, there you are. Where's your mom?"

"She can't come. Magister put an evil spell on her. If she leaves the fortress she'll turn into a crystal statue and the slightest sound will break her—and kill her."

"Yikes! That's totally not cool. So what do we do?"

"We don't have any choice; we have to get out and come back with reinforcements. Anyway, let's start by getting out of this trap. Then we'll see what happens. What are you doing with those baskets?"

"I've been a prisoner for almost a year," a voice hoarse with fatigue interrupted them, and they started. "Dwarves don't like to be held prisoner. So what do they do when that happens? They dig tunnels!"

While they were talking, Fafnir had joined them. She was caked with dirt and carrying half a ton of rocks. Well, maybe not a half ton, but close.

"What a terrific idea!" whispered Tara. "But how did you hide the rubble?"

Fafnir gave a smile that was positively cunning.

"The giants love the taste of the local rocks. A few of them have even put on weight these last months. And they think I'm just doing it to be nice."

"What about the dirt?"

"I did what dwarves do when they dig tunnels. I hardened most of it and used it to strengthen the tunnel roof. The rest is in the basement at the back. I used it to build a new wall. Nobody noticed."

"Did you have to dig far?"

"This part of the fortress is the closest to the forest where they cut wood. So I only had to cover about fifty yards before reaching the outer wall. I just need to dig a few more inches, and we'll be out. I didn't want to do it sooner in case somebody took a walk in the forest and spotted the opening."

Tara was very impressed. In a few months, working all alone, Fafnir had managed to dig and clear away tons of rock and earth!

"So what do we do now?"

"We finish moving the dirt. Then as soon as your friends and your mother get here, we go."

"My mom isn't coming come with us," said Tara sadly. "So it's just Sparrow and Cal."

"Okay, but I've warned you," said Fafnir grimly. "If they're late, I'm not waiting for them, map or no map."

"I understand. They'll be here."

Still, Tara was worried. It was five minutes to two with no sign of Sparrow or Cal, though they had agreed to show up early so as not to risk missing the rendezvous.

She helped Fabrice move dirt while Robin, who was still in pain, rested a little. Two o'clock sounded and Fafnir reappeared.

"That's that!" she said with the satisfaction of a job well done. "One last push and we'll be free! Everybody ready?"

"Cal and Sparrow aren't here," answered Tara. "I don't get it."

"Too bad. We're leaving right away!"

"I'll send Gallant to get them. Maybe they've had a problem."

"That won't work. If they've been caught and you send your pegasus, they'll find us. I say we're leaving, now!"

Tara was opening her mouth just as Cal and Sparrow burst into the basement—with Angelica!

CHAPTER 16

THE SWAMPS OF DESOLATION

Sparrow looked as if she was about to have a fit.

"She was spying on us!" she hissed, pointing at Angelica. "She says she'll turn us in if we don't take her with us."

"Your carryings-on were so obvious, a blind man would've spotted them," said the tall girl contemptuously. "For your sake, I hope the Bloodgraves are less observant than I am."

"Well, we don't have any choice," said Tara resignedly. "We have to take her with us. Let's go."

Fafnir was about to protest but changed her mind when she caught Tara's look of fury. Instead, she lit a candle lantern and started down the tunnel.

"Follow me, and keep quiet," she whispered. "The chatrixes could hear and try to dig down to get us. So don't make a sound, or we're dead meat."

The tunnel looked as if it'd been drilled by a giant machine. The candlelight reflected off perfectly smooth walls. Being a dwarf, Fafnir moved quickly, whereas Fabrice, Robin, and Angelica were constantly bumping their heads. But they did it in silence, thoroughly frightened by Fafnir's warning.

In a few minutes they came to a wall of dirt and rock, and got to witness a demonstration of the dwarves' special talent. Fafnir put her hands on the barrier, and it seemed to melt, becoming soft and easy to dig. It took her only a few seconds to clear away the last rocks, and they found themselves in the open air beyond the outer wall.

Still in silence, she closed up the hole to hide it, then gestured for them to follow.

Unlike the forests Tara had explored on Earth, this one didn't have any trails. It was dark and dense, full of roots that kept tripping them and weird noises that kept them on edge. After an hour of laborious progress, Fafnir signaled for them to stop. Cautiously she held out the candle lantern, which she had carefully hidden under her shirt when they emerged from the tunnel. "Show me the map," she whispered. "We need to head toward the swamps now."

Tara brought out the map. She also told everybody about her mother's advice, but only after she had cast an Interpretus spell (over Fafnir's objection), so they could all understand each other. Cal, Sparrow, Tara, Robin, and Angelica were still under the Interpretus spell cast in Tingapore. But now that they were outside, the

Fortress's translation spell no longer worked on Fafnir, Fabrice, or Manitou. They could understand what the dwarf was saying, but until Tara cast the spell she couldn't understand them.

Cal was chagrined to realize they didn't need all the blankets and packs he had taken such pains to steal. They only needed to keep one of each. The same applied to the apples and hunks of bread, dried meat, and cheese that Sparrow had swiped from the kitchens. They did keep some things: potions and creams from the infirmary, and three swords and a bow and arrows. Robin had even found a beautiful, double-bladed axe for Fafnir. She immediately baptized it "Jewel" and happily swung it at every branch that dared get in her way.

Except for Angelica, who was complaining about her scratches and bruises, they all looked closely at the map. They weren't very far from the Fortress yet, and had a long way to go. But Fafnir predicted that the Bloodgraves would never imagine that they would head in the direction away from Hymlia.

"We should be in the clear soon," she said. "I figure we'll come out of the forest in about an hour. Then we'll have some mountains to cross, then a plain, and finally the swamps. Now that I have the map in my head we can go. I know the way."

Suddenly Blondin and Manitou started to growl, and Sheeba's thick fur stood straight up. The familiars were staring back they way they had come.

The travelers instinctively spread out in a half circle, covering each other. Robin handed out the swords and nocked an arrow to his bow. Angelica, who didn't understand what was happening, was just opening her mouth to speak when three enormous shadows bounded toward the group. The chatrixes had found them! Robin shot two arrows so quickly that his arms were a blur, and both hit their targets.

Angelica was knocked over by the third monster, but Sheeba ripped its throat out before it could bite her. An enormous Beast now towered over the tall brunette. She screamed before she realized that the Beast was picking up the body of the chatrix that had just attacked her.

"S-S-Sparrow? Is t-t-that you?"

"Well, what do you know!" said Sparrow mockingly. "I never thought I'd hear you stuttering too. Are you okay? Not hurt?"

"N-N-No. Your p-p-panther saved my life."

The Beast nodded, then called to the others: "Are you guys all right?"

The second dead chatrix lay on its side with arrows in its eye and heart. Fafnir had crushed the third one to death, but poor Manitou lay caught in its jaws.

Aghast, Tara came running. "Great-grandfather!"

With enormous effort, the dog freed itself from the chatrix's jaw. The black Lab's flank was covered with blood and drool, and he seemed in terrible pain.

"Ow, ow, ow!" sobbed Manitou. "Stupid dog! So *now* he lets me take over!"

"Great-grandfather, are you all right?"

"Don't worry, I'm fine. Just a little shaken up."

Then he turned to look at his side, saw how badly hurt he was, and fainted.

"I knew he wasn't a familiar," exclaimed Robin, "but still, hearing him speak comes as a shock."

"You think there are any more of those things?" asked Angelica anxiously, looking around her. "I would've done better to stay at the Fortress. We're all gonna die!"

"Feeling sorry about our little blackmail, are we?" Cal couldn't resist asking. "Not quite brave 'Miss Take Me with You or I'll Scream,' eh? Well, you'll have plenty more chances to scream, because now that you know where we're going, letting you go back to the Fortress is out of the question. Welcome to the real world!"

"Let it go, Cal!" said Tara. "Right now we have to take care of Manitou. You know more about chatrixes than I do, like how their venom affects other animals. Tell me how to care for my great-grandfather, and then we'll hit the road again. I don't know how those three managed to track us, but I'll bet there are more of them."

"Think we can risk that magic?" grumbled Fafnir. "Won't that get us caught?"

"No. Mom said that if we do it very slowly and in a diffuse way, we'll blend into the fluid all around us. We won't be detected."

Robin wasted no more time. Putting his hands on the Lab's lacerated side, he said, "By Healus may this wound be mended, and from further hurt your health defended!" As the healing spell took effect, the dog's wounds slowly closed, the bones mended, and the fur grew back. Manitou was soon himself again, except for one thing: he didn't wake up.

"Is he all right?" asked Tara. "Is it normal for him to still be unconscious?"

"Chatrix venom isn't necessarily deadly to another canid, but your great-grandfather should have come round," said Robin with a frown. "Listen, I think you should ask your pegasus to carry us ahead one by one. By shuttling us back and forth, we'll go a lot faster."

"You're a genius, you know that?" said Tara enthusiastically. "Gallant—of course! What an idiot I am! I didn't think of it. He's very strong. When we went flying at Travia he could carry me for hours without getting tired. I'm sure he can save us at least a day."

She turned to her familiar. "Do you understand, Gallant? Can you do it?" He mentally assured her that there was no problem, and she immediately restored him to his normal size.

"Take Robin and Manitou first," Tara suggested. "Fly into the mountains and then come back to get us. That's about half the distance we have to cover."

Robin tried to protest, arguing that he should stay behind to protect the others. But he gave in when Sparrow flexed her impressive muscles and displayed her claws and fangs. In terms of taking care of the others, she was a lot more powerful than he was.

Between her fear and the cold, Tara's teeth started chattering in spite of her fur cape and boots. Some muttered cursing nearby informed her that Cal, Fabrice, and Angelica were no better off. Only Fafnir and Sparrow didn't seem uncomfortable. The first because cold weather didn't bother her, the second because she hadn't shape-shifted back and was wearing her own personal fur coat.

Fabrice, who felt he had bumped his head a half million times, grumbled that OtherWorld woodcutters really weren't doing their job. How could they leave so many low branches on the trees?

At last they emerged from the forest and saw the plain stretching ahead of them and the foothills of mountains in the distance. Beyond the mountains lay a second plain and the Swamps of Desolation. After some time, they emerged from the forest. Now that they were out of the trees, they could walk all together instead of single file.

"Do think that those chatrixes were the only ones to track us?" asked Sparrow, nervously glancing back at the forest.

Cal shifted his pack, whose straps were cutting into his shoulders. "I think those three must have sensed our presence and dug down into the tunnel. If the rest of the pack had followed, there wouldn't be anything left of us but gnawed bones."

Angelica shuddered. "What if the others catch our scent and hunt us down? We wouldn't stand a chance! Let me go back to the Fortress, I'm begging you. I swear I won't say a word to anyone!"

"That's not the problem, Angelica," answered Tara dryly. "We can't accompany you, and if you're alone you'll be easy prey for chatrixes and any other wild animal. Best to stay with us."

"It's your fault." The tall girl's tone wasn't even aggressive, just a weary restatement of a reality she continued to endure. "It's because of you that I'm here!"

"Excuse me!" corrected Fafnir. "You should say it's *thanks* to her that you're here. I would have never taken you if she hadn't forced my hand, believe me."

"Because of her," Angelica insisted. "Normally I'd be in Omois now, chatting with people of refinement if that infernal Bloodgrave hadn't decided he absolutely had to add Tara Duncan to his personal collection!"

"Well you sure didn't stand any chance of being chosen yourself," muttered Cal.

"*What?*" she screeched. "I'm just as valuable as that little twit, and if the Bloodgrave master had realized it, he would've kidnapped me too."

"So what are you complaining about?" asked Fafnir.

Angelica opened her mouth . . . then closed it.

Cal burst out laughing.

They went on in silence. Angelica sulked, Fafnir pumped along on her short legs—which were plenty long enough, since Cal and Tara had trouble keeping up—and Sparrow spent her time sniffing in every direction like a sort of gigantic, very hairy wolf. She did a passable imitation of Tom Thumb's evil ogre: "*sniff!* . . . *sniff!* I smell fresh meat! I smell . . . I smell prey nearby."

It made Tara shudder.

They continued walking, trying to make good time. Tara had just begun to worry about Robin, Manitou, and Gallant when a shadow passed overhead. The handsome pegasus landed lightly near her and lowered his head to get Tara to scratch him between the ears.

As she petted him, he sent her images of Robin and Manitou comfortably settled in a cave. The dog was doing well, in spite of the chatrix poison. Robin thought that the spell that made him immortal—though in the body of a dog—was probably helping him fight it. The fact that he was still alive two hours after being bitten supported his theory.

"Fafnir, you'll be the next rider," Tara ordered. "I'm sure Robin will be standing guard. You can take over and tell him to get some sleep. Then when Cal arrives, you can go to sleep, and so on. We should each try to get at least four hours' sleep before we set out again."

"I don't need to sleep," the dwarf grumbled. "You think I'm some sort of sissy?"

Man! Is she ever touchy! thought Tara.

"Not at all," she answered diplomatically, "but you must have worked very hard to dig the rest of the tunnel. We don't know what we'll be facing in the swamps. Don't you think it would be smart if you got a little rest?"

"Well, maybe, yeah. I'll see when I get there. Let's go."

"Perfect. What about you?" she asked Gallant tenderly. "Not too tired?"

He mentally sent her images of a pegasus prancing around, and she smiled. He had a very personal way of telling her that all was well.

Gallant's brief euphoria lasted only until Fafnir climbed on his back, after telling the others which direction to take. Surprised by her weight, he staggered and grimaced. And his takeoff was distinctly less graceful than usual, especially since Fafnir gripped his mane like a drowning man clutching at a straw. Like all dwarves, she hated being up in the air. The pegasus urgently informed Tara that he wanted to keep his mane intact until the end of the trip.

"Fafnir, don't pull his mane out!" she yelled. "You don't need to hang on like that. He won't let you fall!"

"I'm not so sure about that," answered the dwarf. But she relaxed her iron grip a little, and Gallant sighed with relief. A moment later they had vanished into the night, and Tara got going again, lighting her way with the candle lantern that Fafnir had left her.

Gallant soon returned and continued ferrying them one after another. As the night imperceptibly began to lighten, Tara found herself alone with Sparrow, who said something that rattled her.

"I'm hungry!"

"Can't you wait? We'll be at the cave soon."

"Nah, I'm hungry now! Beast metabolism is faster, it burns more calories. I need protein."

"Well, all right. You want some bread? I think I have a little cheese too. The dried meat went with Cal."

"Bread? Cheese? Are you kidding? Protein means meat. I need meat!"

"Really? Well, there's not much I can do for you."

"Don't worry, I'll manage. See you later."

So Tara suddenly found herself alone in the middle of the prairie, and still in darkness. It was already six o'clock, but the sun had apparently decided to sleep in, which didn't make things easy. The thick clouds covering the sky probably had something to do with it. Tara hoped it wouldn't start raining on top of everything. Whistling bravely, and holding the candle lantern high so Sparrow wouldn't mistake her for something edible, she kept going.

Suddenly an enormous shadow appeared and held out a chunk of bloody meat under her nose.

"Want some?"

Well, one animal must've gotten up too early this morning.

"Yuck!" Tara exclaimed. "That's sweet of you, Sparrow, but I'm really not very hungry. And you know, I really like it better when the stuff I eat is cooked. Right now, I'm thinking croissants, butter, jam, and hot chocolate. But go ahead, enjoy yourself!"

Sparrow promptly wolfed the meat down in two bites. With a sigh of relief, she started licking herself clean, like a cat—a very big cat.

The sun finally decided it was time to get to work, and put in a timid appearance. The prairie changed, and Tara was startled to see that the grass wasn't green, as she'd expected, but blue. A few trees, outliers from the forest behind them, dotted the gentle rises. The grass was very thick and tall, and Tara was shaken to realize that any animal could have attacked them earlier. She guessed there could've been any number of predators in the grass, like lions, leopards, hyenas, and other beasts, exactly like on Earth. Where there were herbivores—like the one that ended up in Sparrow's stomach—there had to be carnivores. Tara decided to walk a little closer to her own personal carnivore, who was calmly striding along on her powerful legs.

Gallant finally appeared, and Tara was relieved to climb on his back.

"See you later!" she yelled to Sparrow. "I'll send Gallant back for you."

"Don't bother," answered Sparrow, waving a giant paw.

"What do you mean?" asked Tara, feeling suddenly very concerned. Was Sparrow planning to abandon them?

Her friend answered by suddenly speeding up, and galloping hell for leather. Caught by surprise, Gallant whinnied a challenge, and Sparrow roared her answer. Bounding along, she was able to go as fast as he was.

Very impressed, Tara figured they would save a lot of time, because Sparrow seemed able to keep up the pace. The pegasus wanted to go faster, but Tara prevented him.

"This isn't a game, for heaven's sake!" she yelled, feeling Gallant flex his powerful muscles. "I don't want you racing! Just stay even with her, and show her the way to go."

Gallant slowed down a little, and then speeded up again very gradually so she wouldn't notice. He was bucking a headwind, and the beast was gaining on him, to his fury. He dove to get out of the wind and started flying along next to her. Making such powerful leaps, Sparrow almost seemed to be flying by his side.

Suddenly Tara felt a kind of shudder, as if someone were spying on her. It froze her blood. The last time she had experienced that, a Bloodgrave was tracking her. She had Gallant dive to the ground. He had barely landed when she made him lie down under the only grove of trees in sight. She absolutely did not want to use her magic. Sparrow, who hadn't noticed anything, was already far ahead of them.

Tara and Gallant had just taken cover when she felt a quivering of the air. A wavering image of a Bloodgrave appeared in the sky, studying the blue prairie. He seemed to be scrutinizing the terrain with terrible acuity. She held her breath, and Gallant didn't move a feather. The Bloodgrave seemed to stay forever. Having noticed nothing, he finally disappeared. Gallant was about to stand up, but Tara stopped him.

"No," she whispered. "Wait."

It was a wise decision, because the image appeared again. Apparently seeing that nothing had changed, it disappeared again, this time for good.

Tara waited for several long minutes more, just to be on the safe side.

Suddenly she screamed. A pair of huge jaws with fangs had just appeared in front of her, ready to tear her to pieces.

"What's going on here?" asked Sparrow, who had come back to see.

"What's going on," answered Tara, spitting out the grass she'd practically swallowed, "is that the Bloodgraves are searching for us, and they very nearly spotted us!"

"Yikes! So what do we do?"

"We get the heck out of here. Gallant and I are going to fly very low, so please don't bump into us."

If Gallant was afraid, he didn't show it. And no sooner was Tara on his back than he resumed his race against Sparrow.

The pegasus and the beast reached the cave within two minutes of each other, with the pegasus in the lead, to his great joy. He was so tired that he only ate a few handfuls of oats and fell asleep right where he was. Sparrow, equally exhausted from her efforts, promptly followed suit.

Cal, Robin, Fabrice, and Fafnir were all asleep too. Angelica was crankily standing watch and vaguely keeping an eye on Manitou. The dog was dozing and groaning.

Tara collapsed on the fine sand of the cave floor. The shelter they had found was perfect. The small stream that had carved the cave furnished them with clear water. Robin had dug a pit and lit a fire, which warmed them without being visible from afar. And they were protected from the rain, which started falling just after Sparrow came in. The Bloodgraves wouldn't find them here.

Tara forced herself to eat a little bread and cheese, then closed her eyes. Feeling cold, she huddled against Gallant, who wrapped a wing around her. Enveloped in the pegasus's warmth, she fell into a deep sleep.

She felt she had only slept a few minutes when Robin came to shake her. The feeling was obviously shared by her companions, because she could hear a lot of grumbling. They ate in silence, barely awake. Outside, the rain fell with a discouraging steadiness and the day remained dark. Only the dwarf, who could see her goal approaching with every step, was in a good mood.

"Thanks to your pegasus we've saved almost a day and a half of walking," said Fafnir. "It's only a few more hours to the Swamps of Desolation. I suggest I go on ahead, because I can run for hours. Gallant is too tired to ferry us back and forth the way he did yesterday. If you leave right after me, you'll get there in about five hours, at your pace. That will leave me time to find the black roses and maybe even to extract the juice. Does that suit you?"

"It's fine with me," said Tara. "Go ahead, but be careful. And if something attacks you, for pity's sake don't hesitate to use magic so we can immediately come help you. Okay?"

The dwarf hefted her axe and flashed an evil grin. "Anybody who attacks me will have to deal with Jewel. So don't worry."

"Actually, I am worried. Promise me that if you're in trouble, you won't be stubborn. Call us. I'd rather get caught by the Bloodgraves than risk a friend's life."

Fafnir wrinkled her beautiful eyes. "I promise," she said huskily. "And you be careful too, my friend. See you later."

It didn't take her long to disappear.

"Ow! I'm sore all over!" said Cal, as he stretched.

"Me too," said Angelica, agreeing with Cal for once. Then she added casually, "You could leave me in the cave, you know. I'm in no danger here. I'm out of the cold, and if you leave me some food I can hold out until you come back with help."

"Listen Angelica, you don't know anything about chatrixes," said Robin seriously. "It's daylight, so we're in no danger for the time being. But I don't for a second think we're safe here. Unless a Bloodgrave comes along to hold them back, they'd swallow you in one bite. So don't kid yourself. You're coming with us."

Angelica glared at him in fury, then looked away.

Sparrow caught the tall girl's look and decided to keep a close eye on her.

In some ways, Sparrow was enjoying the situation. Her unexpected beast body was a joy. It was so strong and powerful, and especially so warm! She had seen her friends shivering through their few hours of sleep in spite of the fire, whereas she had slept like a log. But Tara grinned when she saw Sparrow stretch and then grumble when she hit her head on the low roof of the cave.

Suddenly a distinguished, if slightly shaky voice was heard: "Ow, I feel as if a herd of buffalo ran over me. Can somebody explain what happened?"

Tara turned and to her delight there was Manitou, bright-eyed and bushy-tailed. He was standing up, cautiously trying out each of his legs.

"Great-grandfather, you're awake! How do you feel?"

"I have pins and needles in my legs, and since I have four of them, I hurt everywhere," said the dog piteously. "Aside from that, I feel fine. It's strange, my last memory was of two jaws full of teeth, and then intense pain."

"You were bitten by a chatrix, and Robin patched you up," explained Cal. "You fought the poison all night long, and we're really happy to see that you won."

"Ah, so that's what it was! I remember now. The dog in my mind was so frightened of the chatrix that he turned the controls over to me for the first time in thirty years. I can still feel him down there, but he doesn't want to come out. Yippee! I'm free at last!"

At that, the black Lab started leaping for joy in every direction. Tara burst out laughing. It was so funny to see her great-grandfather playing the fool.

He padded over to Tara and looked at her with his big gentle Labrador eyes. "Well, I see you've got yourself in a peck of trouble! Reminds me of the time when you didn't know how to swim and you jumped into the deep end of the swimming pool!"

"So what happened?" asked Tara, who didn't remember the incident.

"Well, you soon discovered that it's hard to breathe underwater. Luckily this dog swims very well, so he went and fished you out."

"Hey, you guys must have tons of stories to tell each other!" exclaimed Cal.

"Yeah, but I hope they aren't all at my expense," said Tara.

They left the cave and headed for the plain leading to the Swamps of Desolation. The way was easy and the rain had stopped, so they made good time, even though they were still tired and their feet hurt. Tara's great-grandfather couldn't stop talking, as if he wanted to make up for his years of silence. She finally had to tell him to be quiet, because his stories were keeping her from being on the alert for Bloodgraves.

On a couple of occasions, Sparrow, Gallant, and Sheeba, who were ranging ahead to scout, warned them about herds of an animal like a musk ox, which they had to circle around. They were enormous beasts with long wooly coats. They were grazing peacefully on the blue grass, but you didn't want to get too close, in case they charged.

The group suspected there might be cattle in the area because they'd had the disagreeable pleasure of making new friends a short time before.

Blood flies were flying around when they spotted the young spellbinders. "Oooh! A swarm of humans!" squealed one with delight. "It's dinnertime, girls!"

They dove toward the fragile skin in tight formation, only to smash their stingers against the spell that Robin had wisely cast around his friends. Bitterly disappointed, they tried to get through, above, below, and around the shield, before flying off in discouragement toward more accommodating victims.

After three hours of walking, the group stopped for a quick lunch.

Robin very cautiously began to replicate the bread, cheese, and meat.

And Sparrow almost got them all killed.

In her beast shape, she had wandered off to see if she could find a bite to eat, and came nose to nose with a musk ox. She cautiously backed away so as not to bother the enormous animal . . . and bumped into her calf. The mother gave a terrible bellow and charged—followed by the entire herd.

Sparrow's friends were stunned to suddenly see the beast running toward them, followed by a half-dozen enormous animals weighing a ton and a half each and whose horns looked as if they had been carefully sharpened that very morning. Everyone ran like crazy. The lone stunted tree growing in the middle of the plain was very surprised to suddenly find so many people in its branches.

"Hey, where are your manners! Would you mind putting your feet somewhere else!"

Tara almost fell off her branch onto the ground. The tree was talking!

"Please forgive us for intruding," said Sparrow, "but we're being chased by a herd of—"

A thunderous rumble interrupted her as the herd roared past the tree. Only after the oxen were satisfied that the enemy was gone did they resume peacefully grazing.

"What's that to me?" asked the tree irritably. "Not only isn't there enough water around here, but now you're breaking my nicest branches."

An embarrassed Cal tried to put back the twig that he had snapped off, but without success. Whistling and trying to look casual, he discreetly let it fall to the ground.

"We're terribly sorry we hurt you," Sparrow continued cautiously, "but we're going to leave very soon."

"You got that right, because I'm dropping you right now."

"Wait, wait!" said Tara quickly, clinging desperately to a branch. "Let's make a deal."

"A deal? What kind of deal?"

"You let us stay in your branches until the herd moves away and in exchange, we . . . we'll give you water!"

"Water?" asked the tree suspiciously. "It rains enough for the grasslands around here, but not enough for me. I've been slowly dying of thirst for dozens of years. Where are you going to find water here? The nearest standing water is in the Swamps of Desolation."

"I think I may have a solution," said Robin. "Leave it to me."

The half-elf carefully wedged himself between two branches and went into a deep trance, sending his mind into the bowels of the earth. After a few minutes, he saw that a layer of granite lay over the aquifer, preventing water from rising to the tree's level. He slipped his mind into a fault and generated enough pressure to enlarge it. The water rose through the granite, an impermeable clay layer, and finally the topsoil, to emerge on the surface as a small, clear spring.

The tree's shout was so loud, it almost knocked them off its branches.

"Water! I feel water!"

"We're very happy for you and all, but please take it easy," said Manitou, who was feeling ill at ease. "Otherwise we'll be shish kebabs on those animals' horns."

Robin came out of his trance. "Just a few more minutes and it should be all set."

"Thank you! Thank you!" said the tree. "You saved my life. You can come climb my branches whenever you like. In fact, I want to give you something to thank you for finding water for me. A little gift."

A branch bent down toward Robin and dropped a small twig with a green bud into his hand.

"That's one of my twigs," said the tree. "All you have to do is point it at whatever you want to have grow, and say, 'By the tree that is alive, I want that plant to grow and thrive.' You'll see, it might be useful."

Perched in the branches, Robin wasn't quite able to bow, but he did his best.

"I'm very grateful to you," he said. "And now we're going to leave. The spring won't run dry, and it also won't be so strong as to rot your roots. We're the ones who are thankful to you."

"Go ahead. Goodbye!"

They very gingerly climbed down from the tree and tiptoed away. When they were a safe distance from the herd of oxen, Cal wheeled on Sparrow. "Were you out of your mind? Do you realize what you did?"

"I'm really sorry," said Sparrow, bowing her big head. "I was hunting and I bumped into this mommy cow who thought I was after her calf. She charged instantly!"

"I've worked hard enough this morning," Cal said, "so let's get a few things straight. From now on, no hunting. You stay with us and you eat what we have. Got that?"

"All right," agreed Sparrow, with a grumpy shrug.

"I approve," said Manitou, who hadn't much enjoyed the tree climbing. "And now I need some sustenance. What do we have to eat?"

"Same as yesterday," said Tara, pointing at the bag. "Bread, cheese, and dried meat."

"I would really like it, if from time to time during this adventure we could have meals worthy of the name," complained her great-grandfather in his distinguished voice. "Look at this stuff! It's pathetic! Where are the blinis, the caviar, the crème fraîche? Talk to me about a nice salmon in white butter with a gratin Dauphinois, a savory cassoulet with duck confit, and wonderful sausages. Talk to me about crystal glasses, fine silverware, and comfortable chairs. But not about bread and cheese, for pity's sake!"

The Lab sounded so pathetic, they burst out laughing.

For their lunch, Robin replicated what they had saved. It was enough for them, with one exception. After the beast had put away a third helping of dried meat, he asked her, "Do you plan to eat much more?"

Sparrow looked down at him. "I'm ten feet tall, Robin, with a stomach to match. You don't want me to hunt, which doesn't put me in a very good mood. So yes, I plan to eat more. A lot more!"

"All right, all right! Don't get mad. Just tell me how much you need and I'll take care of it. As long as I have the strength, that is."

"Replicate me the equivalent of half of one of those stupid oxen," Sparrow ordered mischievously. "That should do the trick."

He heaved a resigned sigh and started replicating the dried meat. When he had done a few pieces, Sparrow took pity on him. "That's enough," she growled. "I'm not hungry anymore . . . "

Robin flashed her a grateful smile, which vanished when she added: " . . . for the time being!"

They got underway again, and the plain gradually changed. The grass became sparser and the soil more spongy. Streams often cut across their path and several times Gallant had to carry them across wide expanses of stagnant water. Tara consulted the map often to be sure not to make a mistake, because the paths tended to all look alike.

They figured they weren't far from the island when a familiar voice suddenly yelled, "Stop!"

Manitou, who was ahead and about to put his paw on an odd-looking patch of earth, slammed into reverse—one advantage of having four legs.

"Don't come any closer, whatever you do!" yelled the dwarf. "It's quicksand!"

To their surprise, there was Fafnir, half sunk in the ground. To keep from going under completely she was clinging to a root with the energy of despair.

"What happened?" asked Fabrice.

"What happened is that I walked right into this stuff, and I'm sinking. Get me out of here!"

"Why didn't you use magic?" asked Cal politely, who was a bit mystified.

"It'll be a sad day when a dwarf has to rely on magic to get out of a tight spot. And I knew you weren't far behind me. So, have you stopped for tea or what? Do something!"

Manitou spoke up. "Sparrow, can you reach the tree right next to Fafnir?"

By stretching her body as far as possible, the beast was able to get a good grip on the tree with her claws, and she pulled the dwarf from her liquid tomb.

When Fafnir emerged from the quicksand they were horrified to see that her arms and legs were covered with dozens of blood-sucking leeches. The dwarf whipped out her knife, but the blade slipped harmlessly on their viscous bodies, and the leeches were so deep in her flesh she couldn't dig them out.

"Wait!" said Sparrow. "Don't try to pull them off. They have to let go by themselves."

"So what do I do?" cried the dwarf, who was in considerable pain.

"Don't move," said Sparrow. She quickly changed into human shape, then cried, "By Flamus heat these leeches all, 'til they give up and off they fall."

An intense red glow surrounded the dwarf and tongues of flame shot out, hitting the leeches. The instant they felt the heat, they let go and fell to the ground, revealing dozens of open wounds on Fafnir's body.

"Filthy leeches!" she yelled, as she trampled the huge slugs. "I could feel them sucking my blood, and there was nothing I could do about it!"

Fabrice gaped at the viscous bodies twisting on the ground. "Do you mean you'd rather be eaten alive than use magic? You really don't like magic, do you?"

"I don't even like the word," said the dwarf hoarsely. "All right, let's get going. Time's a-wasting. And thanks, Sparrow."

"Don't mention it. I'm sure that with a little more time you would've gotten out by yourself." Sparrow could see how much Fafnir hated having to be rescued. She knew the dwarves were individualists, but Fafnir gave a new dimension to the word "independent."

Over Fafnir's protests, she insisted on casting a Healus spell on the wounds to make sure they didn't get infected, and the bites faded quickly.

She then shape-shifted back into the beast and they set off again, following Fafnir, who now used her axe to probe the ground ahead of her.

Even moving cautiously, they soon came within sight of the Island of Black Roses. It was located in the very heart of the swamp, surrounded by bogs and quicksand. And it was sinister. Rarely had any of them seen such a desolate island. Aside from the skeletons of a few dead trees whose bare branches waved in the cold wind, the only growing things on the island were some black bushes along the shore. They had huge spines, as if to prevent anyone from approaching.

The friends shivered and unconsciously moved closer together.

"Here we are!" Fafnir happily announced, oblivious to the place's sinister aspect. "All we have to do is cross over to it. I seem to remember there are lots of snakes in this water, so it might be smart if we crossed on Gallant."

"Absolutely," agreed Tara, who didn't especially like snakes.

"I'm tired," moaned Angelica, sitting down on a fallen log. "I'd rather stay here. I'll wait for you."

Suddenly the fallen log came to life, and an enormous pair of jaws swung toward her.

"Aaah! A glurp!" she screamed. "Help!"

The glurp, a saurian whose long, thin head sported a mouth with thousands of teeth, would have swallowed the tall girl in a single bite. But Cal, who was the closest, yelled, "By Carbonus incinerate this vicious snake, its choice of victim was a bad mistake."

The same red ray that had wounded Tara's grandmother shot from his finger and hit the snake. It jerked as if it were being electrocuted and raced off to dive into the shallow water.

Angelica collapsed in tears. "I've had enough! I can't stand it anymore. I want to go home."

"There, there," said Cal kindly. "We'll be home soon enough. If you try not to sit down just anywhere, I promise we'll bring you home safe and sound."

The tall girl sniffed and didn't answer. Every minute and every second she cursed the day that Tara had shown up in her life. What in the world could she have done to deserve such a punishment?

"That was fantastic!" said Robin admiringly. "I didn't know you'd mastered the Carbonus."

"Actually, neither did I," Cal admitted. "I didn't even think; it just fired by itself. Do you think it could get us detected?"

"No," said Robin reassuringly. "According to Tara's mother, you have to generate a lot of energy for other spellbinders to feel it. So far nothing we've done has been especially dangerous."

"That's a relief," said Fabrice. "When I saw you cast the spell I really thought the bad guys would be here in two seconds."

"Well, there was a chance of that," said Cal, "but I had to save Angelica, didn't I?"

"I'm not saying you didn't," said Fabrice defensively, "just that I was scared."

"When you finish your little chat, maybe we can get going," grumbled Fafnir. "I have an Exordium in a few days, so let's move it!"

Gallant ferried them over the water and set them down on the island. But Cal almost lost Blondin in the crossing.

The fox was getting sick and tired of being up in the air all the time. He wriggled out of Cal's grasp for a moment and fell yelping into the water. No sooner had he hit the lake than the glurps dozing on the shore dove after him, jaws wide. Poor Blondin was screaming in terror when something grabbed him and yanked him out of the water just as the jaws closed on the hairs at the tip of his tail. Gallant's reflexes had saved the poor fox. When he saw him falling, the pegasus dove and snatched him in his teeth to deposit him on solid ground, terrified but safe.

Cal, whose heart was pounding, was so scared that he yelled at Blondin for a good ten minutes.

Sheeba took note and was careful not to move so much as a hair during her own crossing.

It didn't take Fafnir long to find her famous rose. The rosebushes had long black thorns and she had to wrap a blanket around her arm to keep her hand from being torn to shreds. Even so, she was surprised to see that the thorns seemed to cluster in greatest numbers right where she was trying to cut the flowers. The rosebush resisted her fiercely, but she ignored the pain and forced her way through.

As she started to cut the flowers, she sensed something like a dull moaning, and the rosebush trembled. She stopped in surprise, and the moaning stopped. She cut another rose and it revived. The sap from the rose on her hands was so dark it almost looked like blood. Fafnir remembered the story of the curse that struck those who picked the black roses in the Swamps of Desolation and hesitated, feeling a little worried. But then she resumed her work. After all, she wasn't about to let herself be stopped by fairy tales.

While Fafnir was cutting what she needed, Robin built a small fire. He scraped the bark from a tree, made a bowl, and started boiling water in it.

The dwarf handed him the roses mixed with her blood.

"Here you are," she said, pleased. "This should be enough for the brew. Bring it to a boil, then simmer it until the light brown juice becomes completely black."

Suddenly Manitou shouted: "Uh-oh, I think we have problems!"

"What now?" asked the dwarf in annoyance.

"That," said the dog, pointing a paw. A hundred Mud Eaters were silently emerging from their burrows on the shores of the lake.

CHAPTER 17

THE ATTACK

Fabrice gave a worried look at the long teeth and claws of their attackers, who had started yelping and gesturing when they saw them. "Do you think they're going to cross?" he asked.

"Nah, they're not that crazy," answered Fafnir. "And I'll bet you dollars to doughnuts those guys take their orders from our pal the Master of Bloodgraves."

"Darn it!" exclaimed Cal, his gray eyes narrowed. "This is a disaster!"

"Well, we're stuck on this island," Tara bravely pointed out, "but you aren't, Fafnir."

"What do you mean I'm not?"

"You can take off with Gallant. Because if we're recaptured, you'll be our only hope!"

"Even if I headed home right away, I'd never be able to send you help in time," said the dwarf. "Anyway, I'm not about to leave you alone now."

"Don't be a fool!" said Sparrow angrily, who of them all knew the dwarf people best. "If you aren't home in time for your Exordium, you'll be banished for life. Go on, get out of here!"

Fafnir's answer was laconic, but clear: "No."

Their discussion was interrupted by Manitou, who had started sniffing very energetically.

"Well, I'll be!" said the Labrador. "I smell . . . I smell something. It's faint, but the dog has a very sharp nose, and I smell . . . "

He walked over to an especially well-defended, black rosebush, with thorns nearly as long as daggers.

"There's something in there," he stated definitely.

Fafnir rolled her eyes. "So what?"

"I feel a kind of tingling at the end of my muzzle that's a sure sign of powerful magic. I'd like one of you to go take a look in there."

The dwarf chortled. "Master Manitou, it seems to me that of all of us, you'd be the best person to rummage around in there. I just cut myself to ribbons on those thorns. I'm not about to try again."

He sighed and wriggled under the rosebush. Oddly enough, where the bushes had furiously resisted Fafnir, they seemed to consider the Labrador just an animal, and he soon emerged with something in his mouth. The moment he came out, the bushes began to move and the thorny branches tried to seize him, but by then he was out of reach.

The travelers were all very curious to know what Manitou had found.

"Itsh a quartch rock," he managed.

"What?"

"I said it's a quartz rock," he repeated, after setting down a vaguely translucent stone. "It's odd, but I almost felt the rosebush was trying to keep me from taking it, like it was guarding it. The stone's not much to look at, with all those inclusions and cracks, but we might be able to use it."

"What do you mean, use it?" asked Fabrice, who was looking at the stone curiously.

Sparrow explained: "It's a piece of rock crystal, which is what we use for our telecrystals."

"Telecrystals?" asked Tara. "Oh, yeah, those OtherWorld mobile phones, right?"

"Correct," said Cal. "But right now, this is just a rough piece. To make it into a telecrystal, we'll have to magically polish it."

"Yuck!" spat the dwarf. "More magic? Well, leave me out, then. I'm off to drink my brew."

"You're not really going to do that, are you?" asked Cal, shocked. "Not now?"

"And why not now?"

"Because if you get banished by your people, you might need magic. Otherwise, how will you get by?"

The dwarf planted herself firmly in front of him.

"I don't think you get it, little human. I don't like magic. I hate magic. Magic has ruined my life, and there is no chance of my ever using it. So if I can get rid of it, I'm going to jump at the chance, banishment or no banishment. My talent for working metal has nothing to do with magic; it's the product of my skill and experience.

A good dwarf worker will always earn a decent living, banished or not. See you later."

Before Cal could say anything, Fafnir turned on her heel and left.

In the meantime, Manitou had set the piece of crystal on one of the blankets.

"Gather round everybody," he said. "You're going to have to polish the crystal without breaking it."

"How do we do that?" asked Angelica doubtfully.

"You'll use your magic force like a kind of vice to maintain the crystal's integrity. There are a lot of flaws in that stone, and the slightest slip-up could break it. Keep absolutely focused, because if it shatters, the return shockwave could hurt you. You have to succeed, otherwise we're lost. But if you manage to polish it, we'll be able to contact Travia and they'll come to help us."

Angelica immediately flopped down next to the stone. What? There was a way to get out of this hell and no one had told her? "What are you all waiting for?" she yelped. "Let's go! Come on, quick!"

Manitou said, "For some reason, I can't work magic in my present shape, but you can have the benefit of my advice. Robin, you'll start by polishing the stone very, very gently, so the Bloodgraves don't locate us. And show Tara each step of the polishing, so she understands exactly how it works; that way, she'll be able to use it more easily."

"I'll do as you say," said Robin, looking at the dog and smiling. "Forgive my candor, but I find it very hard to remember that you're a highly experienced spellbinder."

"If I were a truly experienced spellbinder I wouldn't have gotten myself trapped in the body of a dog," he grumbled. "But when it comes to crystal balls, I've polished hundreds of them in my life. So go ahead."

Robin took a deep breath and announced: "All right, I'm starting. While I'm polishing the stone, you must all concentrate on surrounding it with the magic in your minds. Above all, don't relax your focus; the crystal has to remain intact. I'm starting now. Tara, would you follow me, please?"

It was a magical moment. But when Tara melded her mind with Robin's, she got a big surprise: she didn't realize that she would be literally entering his mind. It was very different from what she'd expected. Especially since he made no effort to hide his thoughts. She was curious, and after a momentary hesitation, she snooped around a little and came across a thought that gave her pause. Oops! *He thinks I'm pretty!*

"I'm sorry, that thought got away from me," he said bashfully, while mentally blushing—quite an accomplishment, if you think about it. "Let's concentrate, please. I'm going to focus."

It wasn't easy, because Robin couldn't help thinking about lots of other things. About his friendship with Cal and Fabrice; his affection for Sparrow and his surprise at learning that she was a descendent of the beast; and his fear of being recaptured. He also thought about his father and his mother a lot. And then his thoughts circled back to Tara and how much he admired her courage, her deliciously analytical mind, her beautiful deep blue eyes . . .

Oh my! Tara thought with alarm on stumbling across that train of thought. *I have to concentrate on the crystal ball and especially not on what Robin thinks about me—even if I find it really sweet.*

Suddenly their task was very clear. She could feel Robin's magic take hold of the stone and very gently begin to shape it. He used his power like a scalpel. Very delicate cuts on the stone's edges chipped off tiny pieces that fell onto the blanket. Then he mentally filed the rough spots and polished the crystal. He was very careful. There were many cracks in the heart of the stone, and any clumsiness would cause it to break. Tara could also perceive the others' magic—Fabrice, Cal, and Sparrow's warmth along with Angelica's chill—surrounding the stone like a soft, strong hand to keep it from shattering.

Robin patiently demonstrated all the stages to Tara, who repeated them. When Robin went over an edge and polished it, he made it transparent. When Tara followed behind him, her magic made it luminous. And when they had finally finished—and heaved a big sigh of relief—the crystal ball glowed like a little lighthouse illuminating the night.

"Wow!" cried Sparrow ecstatically. "That's the most beautiful crystal I've ever seen! Incredible, how brightly it glows!"

But Robin was worried. "It's full of cracks, and the smallest bump could break it, in spite of all of our precautions. We should try to contact the wizard right away."

"Which of you is going to call Chem?" asked Manitou.

"I think there's no question that Tara's gift is the most powerful," said Robin thoughtfully. "What do you think?"

"Yes, that's a good choice."

"Is this gonna require a lot of energy?" asked Tara, who was stretching and grimacing. "Because I'm exhausted—just wasted."

"I thought you had the most powerful gift of all of us," sneered Angelica. "So show us what you can do, instead of complaining."

Tara ignored the tall girl and looked at Robin.

"I'm tired too," he said, working to loosen his tight shoulders. "We can rest for a few moments, but not too long. I'm also worried about the Mud Eaters. I don't know what they're up to, but I'll feel better after we've talked with Master Chem."

Tara nodded. Her magic might again escape her control if she was too tired. To avoid a catastrophe she had to relax before continuing. So she calmly stood up, took a piece of bread and cheese, and went to sit near Gallant, who was cropping the sparse grass.

"What the heck is she doing?" screeched Angelica. "I want to go home! Now!"

"Let the poor girl rest," ordered Manitou. "That exercise took a lot of effort from all of you. Get something to eat and take a break. We'll make contact later. Angelica, you have to understand that if we try now, and our first attempt fails because we're tired, we won't be able to try again for several hours. So we may as well give ourselves the best chance of success. Though I don't like having to wait any more than you do."

Remembering just in time that the black Labrador was an old spellbinder, Angelica restrained her urge to kick him.

A sudden din startled them. The Mud Eaters were screaming.

"Children! Come, danger, danger! Children, leave island, danger, danger! No sleep on island, come here, now! We not hurt children. Take back to great Master, nice Master, beautiful Master. Children come now!"

"Oh, brother," Fabrice said. "What do they want with us now?"

"They want us to surrender," said Fafnir, who was trying to get the vile taste of the black rose infusion out of her mouth by eating a few shriveled berries. "So they're trying to scare us. Pay no attention. That was a trick my great-great-grandfather stopped using ten centuries ago."

"But what if there really was a danger, or something evil on the island and night fell, what could we do?" asked Angelica frantically. "We don't even know what we're up against!"

"You know, you humans really worry a lot," mocked the dwarf. "What about this, what about that? Why don't you just take life as it comes? It's much simpler. Let yourself go, and appreciate what you're given."

Then she started spinning like a top, her arms outstretched and a big smile on her lips.

"Hey there," said Cal, looking at her carefully. "Just what exactly was in that infusion of yours?"

Unsteady on her feet, the dwarf shrugged, then tripped and wound up sitting on the ground. "Just something to make me understand that life is beautiful and I'm happy to be here with you under this splendid starry vault with thousands of luminous and mysterious suns. With beloved and courteous friends who were prepared to sacrifice their lives so I could escape. You know what? I love you!"

"She's completely drunk," whispered Manitou as he watched Fafnir struggling to her feet to recite more poetry to the stars.

"She said the brew would make her magic disappear," said Cal. "She didn't mention any side effects."

"Well, this is certainly a surprise!" the dog exclaimed. "Can you cut me a few of those black roses? I'd like to do some experiments when we get home—if the stupid dog leaves me in control, that is. Fafnir's reactions are very intriguing."

"I'll try and cut you a couple, but I'm not making any promises," said Fabrice, looking dubiously at the formidable thorns. "Do you think she'll be sick?"

"Oh, it takes more than a few plants to bring down a dwarf. They're the toughest beings I've ever seen. Don't worry. She'll have such a headache tomorrow: she might feel like some blacksmith is using her head for an anvil, but that's all."

Having finished her poetic offerings, Fafnir now launched into a dwarfish war song.

The valiant clan of the Fireforrrge
Went off to war for the one they adorrre:
The beautiful blacksmith Betaniiir
Taken by a dragoness far from heeere.

"Think she'll keep this up for long?" Cal screamed to Sparrow, plugging his ears.

For ransom she requires gold and jewwwels,
But for payment, she'll die a death most cruuuel.

"I don't know," Sparrow shouted back. "All I know is that there are many thousands of dwarf songs. She could actually sing for a year without stopping."

For the dwarfs are off to find a dragon to slaaay
They'll bleed her, and roast her, her body they'll flaaay.

"I'll have surrendered to the Mud Eaters long before that!" moaned Fabrice, who was desperately trying to protect himself against the incredible sounds rising from the dwarf's powerful throat.

Mercilessly, my brothers, off we go to warrr,
To hunt down the enemy we all abhorrr.

Terrified by the war songs, the Mud Eaters retreated, and within a few seconds had all run away from the shores. In the water, glurps and snakes fled to the far edges of the swamp. Even the black rose-bushes were quivering, pulling at their roots in an attempt to escape the vocal hurricane.

Hands on her ears, Tara laughed. "Well, it's effective, anyway!" she cried to Fabrice. "We can list it under 'Secret Weapons.'"

The dwarf paused and then cried: "And now for the chorus!"

Take the hammers and the laaances,
Sing the songs, and dance the daaances,
And victory will keep us waaarm,
For we the dwarves fear no haaarm!

"And now the next part!"

But when Betanir, courageously took the field,
She made that fiery dragon's yield.
With her hammer she struck with skiiill,
She cut her throat, she went for the kiiill.
The vile serpent was taken dowwwn
And Betanir was safe and souuund.
With priceless treasures she went off in gloryyyy
Trumpeting her triumph and telling her storyyy.
She shared the gold and silver with those of her claaan,
The price the dragon paid for the war she begaaaan.
Betanir became the queen of the dwaaarves
Their beloved queen forevermooore!

Fafnir signaled to them to sing, and resumed, rocking back and forth to the song's rhythm: "And now for the chorus!"

Take the hammers and the laaancees,

Sing the songs, and dance the daaances,
And victory will keep us waaarm,
For we dwarves fear no haaarm!

When Fafnir stopped, a great silence fell on the swamp. The dwarf staggered for a moment, grinning broadly, and suddenly collapsed in a heap. She was so dense that she hit the ground with a *boom!* and the island seemed to tremble under the shock.

"Yikes! She may have hurt herself," said Cal. "Give me a hand. We'll put her on a blanket."

Sparrow shape-shifted so she could help move the dwarf, and they stretched her out comfortably. They watched her with concern, but were soon reassured by her noisy snoring.

"All right, now that the concert is over, I think I better try to reach the wizard before something else happens," said Tara, laughing.

"Man, I didn't know dwarves sang like that," said Fabrice, whose ears were still ringing.

"It's best if you don't," said Sparrow. "When you hear their songs it usually means they're on the warpath and are attacking. So you understand why they don't have many fans on OtherWorld."

"Oh, I get it," he said. "First they flatten their opponents by singing, then just finish them off. Not a bad tactic!"

"Great-grandfather, do you know what I have to do?" Tara asked the dog, who was taking his paws off his ears.

"First of all, please call me Pops, or Grandpa, or Manitou. 'Great-grandfather' is a bit long, and it makes me feel old whenever I hear you say it. Second, stuff some cotton in my ears the next time Fafnir decides to launch another song cycle. And third, sit in front of the crystal ball, say the number you want to call, and think intensely of the person you want to communicate with. That's all there is to it. You can start talking as soon as their image appears."

"Uh-oh! The number!" Tara's face scrunched up in panic. "My mind's gone blank, I don't remember the number!"

Tara racked her brains, but it was for naught. She couldn't remember even a single digit! She felt like weeping. I mean really, what an idiot!

She started pacing, muttering, "004? No, that's not it . . . 005, 003, no . . . I can't believe that I don't remember . . . 008?"

"Maybe we could hypnotize her," suggested Fabrice as he watched his friend walk back and forth.

"No, with her gift that's too dangerous. She could kill us all just protecting herself."

"Yeah, well, we should probably avoid that. Maybe she could recite a list of numbers and finally remember the right ones. That's how I remember telephone numbers on Earth. Tara, did you use a mnemonic trick to memorize the number?"

"No, I just learned it by heart," she moaned, now in a complete panic. "But my mind's gone blank. And I left the piece of paper that Master Chem wrote it down on back in Travia."

At this point, Cal spoke up, "I didn't plan to tell you about this, but now I don't have any choice. Here's your paper!"

He pulled out a very wrinkled little piece of paper with the following in the dragon wizard's handwriting: 007 700 350 Chem-nashaovirodaintrachivu.

"Yes! That's it!" shrieked Tara. "But how come you have it? I don't understand."

"I'm the baby in a very big family," explained Cal with dignity. "And when I say the baby, I mean it. All my brothers and sisters are much bigger than me, and especially much stronger. If you're a baby, the only way to get by is to keep yourself very well informed. And the high wizard's unlisted number is a very valuable piece of information."

"You mean you stole it from Tara?" asked an astonished Sparrow.

"I didn't steal it: I borrowed it!"

"Who the heck cares?" yelled Angelica, standing up for Cal for the first time in her life—and, she hoped, the last. "Tara, dial the stinking number, and tell the wizard that I'm here and I want him to come get me!"

Repressing an urge to laugh, Tara flashed Cal a dazzling, grateful smile.

"You can steal whatever you like from me, anytime you like."

Tara sat down at the crystal ball but had some trouble concentrating. The ball glowed very brightly, and it seemed to have a life of its own. She could hear it singing in her mind, with unshakable good humor.

After a moment, Tara spoke:

"Is it . . . it normal for her to talk to me?"

"What?"

"Huh?"

"For her to what?"

"To talk to me. Or rather to sing in my mind. She says she loves me, that she had been held prisoner for hundreds of years in that black rosebush, that we freed her, and that she's very happy. Oh, and she also loves Robin very much, who made her so beautiful. She sings that she is part of this world's spirit, and that the spirit is happy to be with us, and so fully alive. Because it usually can't communicate with us, or only with great difficulty."

"Woof?" Manitou was so surprised, he barked. "Excuse me, I meant, *What?* You aren't telling me I found a living stone, are you?"

"Well, that's hard to say," said Cal, "because I've never heard of living stones."

"They're extremely rare. Even I've never seen one. Living stone veins are so deep underground that not even dwarves dig down that far. It's too hot and the pressure is too great. So this shouldn't have happened; I don't understand it. These stones are pure magical products. OtherWorld has a spirit of magic, and its manifestations are elementals of fire, water, earth, and wind, and also living trees. Living stones are another of its manifestations. Whoever possesses a living stone is forever connected with it, a little like with a familiar."

Manitou was interrupted by a whinny of protest.

"No, no, Gallant, don't be jealous," said Tara. "The living stone is saying that the person who brought her up from the depths of the island is evil. He tried to use the stone's power but she resisted, so he imprisoned her under the bushes to make her give in. But he didn't expect that an animal without any magic could deliver her. That's why the bushes allowed you to do it."

Manitou was still astonished.

"Listen Tara, your gift is already powerful. And this stone you've accidentally bonded with is a reservoir of natural magic. It's going to multiply your power enormously, so you have to be extremely careful. When you communicate with Master Chem, be sure to concentrate. If you just think about anything else, like swatting a mosquito that's about to bite you, could be enough to destroy the mosquito, the island we're on, the Swamps of Desolation, and maybe a chunk of the mountains a dozen miles away. Oh, and also be careful not to break the stone. That would kill it—or I assume it would, because I don't know much about living stones."

Trembling, Tara set the stone down with infinite care. *Couldn't things just be simple for once?* she wondered. *No such luck. I have to keep bumping into weird stuff on this nutty world. Life here can really be a drag at times.*

"So what do I do, then?"

"Put the stone in front of you and ask it to put you in contact with Master Chem. Theoretically, it ought to obey you."

"Theoretically? I hate it when you say that, Grandpa. All right let's go. Living stone, connect me with Master Chemnashaovirodaintrachivu number 007 700 350. Now!"

Nothing happened. The stone remained completely inert, and her song vanished from Tara's mind. Oops! Tara had forgotten to say the magic word.

"Er, please?"

For just a moment the ball's light shone unbearably brightly. Then an image appeared of an office, in shadow.

"I'd give my right paw to have a stone like that!" Manitou growled. "Why doesn't this sort of thing ever happen to me?"

"You can take my place any time you like, Grandpa."

They gathered round. Master Chem had apparently put his own crystal ball on his desk, because they could see papers and books all around it. His room was almost completely dark.

Without waiting for Tara's command, the living stone extended her power, and the crystal ball it was connected to began to glow as well. This allowed them to make out the enormous mass of the dragon sleeping near the table, and the pile of gold and jewels he was lying on. The high wizard had come back to Travia!

Cal smiled mischievously.

"Tell me, Master Manitou, would Chem be able to hear us if we asked the stone to enhance the range of his crystal ball?"

"Of course, why?"

"Because we can't wait for him to wake up by himself. We need him now, not ten hours from now."

Manitou shook his head. "You want to do a number on Chem, don't you? Don't try to look innocent. I could see you coming a hundred miles away. But you're right, for once, so go ahead."

"Master Chem, wake up!" Cal's voice thundered. *"It's me, Caliban! Wake up!"*

The sleeping dragon wizard shot straight up into the air, and when he landed it rocked the whole Castle.

"What? What?"

Awakened with a start, the dragon was completely confused. He stood up in a panic, scattered his papers every which way, stepped on his tail, lost his balance, flattened his armchair, and barely managed to steady himself against a ceiling beam.

"By my ancestors, what's going on?" he roared.

Suddenly Chem realized he was alone in his room and that his crystal ball was glowing strangely. When he walked over to it, he got a surprise.

"By my scales! Tara, Caliban, Gloria, Angelica, Fabrice, and Robin! Where are you calling from? Where are you? And why is my ball glowing like this?"

Manitou's head now appeared in the crystal ball.

"We know where the apprentices were taken!" he shouted. "The Bloodgraves kidnapped us and took us to their fortress, but we escaped. We're in Gandis, on the Island of Black Roses in the Swamps of Desolation. Your ball is glowing because we're communicating with you through a living stone that we just polished."

The dragon wizard's enormous jaw dropped for half a second, then he started erupting with questions. "Are you safe where you are right now? Is there a chance that the Bloodgraves can find you? Are you in any danger? *A what?*"

"There is every chance that the Bloodgraves can find us," said the dog, "and I have no idea if we're in danger or not. I wouldn't waste any time, if you ask me. And yes, we're communicating by way of a living stone. I'll tell you all about it later."

"Give me ten minutes to put together an assault force," said Chem. "Everybody here is on high alert. I'll leave my ball connected. I'll be right back."

"Wait!"

Tara's shout stopped the dragon in his tracks.

"You can't bring high wizards or ordinary spellbinders," she said quickly. "There are more than a hundred Bloodgraves in the Fortress and at least three hundred young spellbinders. They're the high wizards' children, and most have been infected by demonic magic."

This took Chem's breath away.

"What? Have the demons broken the pact?"

"It's much more subtle than that," answered Tara. "The demons are using Magister as their intermediary to infect humans. You dragons will have to not only fight the demons, but also the infected humans. The odds are stacked against you!"

The dragon shuddered.

"And I suppose we can't even accuse the demons because it's a Bloodgrave, and therefore a human, who's at the bottom of all this. It's fiendishly clever. The demons have turned our own allies against us. I'm going to immediately warn Chanvitramichatrinchivu, Mangourachivatrinchivu, Santramivinkratrinchiva, and the other dragons and dragonesses. I'll be right back!"

In spite of the urgency of the situation, Cal and Fabrice grinned at each other. Dragons sure liked complicated names!

Master Chem changed into human shape, and his magically amplified voice woke the entire Castle. The travelers were able to follow the operations by way of the living stone.

Chem moved incredibly quickly. In less than twenty minutes he had assembled a battalion of elves and their war pegasi spoiling for a fight, and almost as many dragons from every country on OtherWorld, who were just as eager to teach a lesson to whoever had dared kidnap their apprentice sorcerers. The old dragon refused help from the high wizards, to their great disappointment. But he couldn't turn down Master Dragosh, who gave him a simple choice: take him along to fight the Master of Bloodgraves, or he would resign and immediately apply for a position in Omois. Master Chem sighed and frowned, but had to say yes.

Then he took his crystal ball down to the Travia Castle courtyard.

"Here I am," he announced to Manitou through the ball. "We're ready. Are you far from the Bloodgraves' fortress?"

"Two days away," was the answer.

"Hmm, that's too close for you to risk creating a Transfer Portal. Okay, tell you what. I'll create the Portal at my end. It will appear here and on the island simultaneously. I'll then need a few minutes to generate enough magic power to get us through. I'm going to use the living stone to home in on your location and anchor the Portal. So pick it up, please."

"Er, I'm a dog, in case you've forgotten," said the black Lab. "I have paws, not hands. In this shape I can't do any magic."

"By Baldur's entrails, you're right! It slipped my mind. Ask Tara and her friends to pick up the living stone and hold it firmly while I target it to open the Portal."

"All right."

Manitou turned to find six young faces looking at him anxiously. The last time they'd seen a Portal, the boy who'd created it had died. They didn't especially care to follow his example.

"I know you're frightened," he said seriously, "but we don't have any choice. Without the high wizard's help, we have no chance of escaping the Master of Bloodgraves. If you follow my instructions carefully, everything should be fine."

Tara didn't much like that "should," but said nothing, concentrating instead on what lay ahead.

Suddenly a shout from Fafnir startled them.

"By my mother's hammer! They're attacking!"

Fafnir had her back to them and was holding her head in both hands, as if it might fly away. She was staring at the far shore.

"What the heck are you waiting for?" she yelled. "They're crossing over!"

The others rushed to join her, and she pointed at the vague dark shapes moving across the water. "Look! They've built rafts! Oh, how my head hurts! I don't understand. It isn't normal!"

"What isn't?" asked Fabrice who was beginning to panic. "That your head hurts?"

"No, the fact that they're attacking at night! Mud Eaters are day creatures, they're not nocturnal!"

In the distance, they could hear the Mud Eaters' litany: "Not stay on the island, danger! Danger! Take the children, bring the children back to nice Master, good Master, powerful Master!"

"I don't believe it!" said the astonished dwarf. "They're so afraid of some sort of danger to us on the island that they're daring to cross the water to capture and evacuate us." Then she got a grip on herself. "We have to set up our defenses."

Robin looked at the thorny rosebushes, then at the twig that the living tree gave them, and asked, "Tell me, Fafnir, are those black rosebushes thick?"

"Man, they're more than thick!" she said, showing her lacerated hand. "Why?"

"The tree said that with this branch, we can make anything grow that we want to. Care to give it a try?"

"There you go again! With you humans, it's always magic, magic, magic! As a dwarf, I probably shouldn't say this, but when all you have is a hammer everything looks like a nail."

Robin grinned, then pointed the twig toward the rosebushes, and said, "By the tree that is alive, I want that plant to grow and thrive."

A ray of green light shot from the twig to the black rosebushes, surrounding them in a bright greenish glow. The bushes trembled, then responded to Robin's will. They began to grow with breathtaking speed, sending out thorn-covered branches all around the island and enclosing it in a nearly impenetrable barrier.

Fabrice watched open-mouthed. What wouldn't his father give to have something like that? Nothing like it for tending his roses.

Manitou was practically hopping up and down with impatience.

"Look, that's all very well, but we can't deal with everything at once," he snapped. "The Portal is more important!"

"Wait, Grandpa," said Tara firmly. "Do you need everybody to hold the living stone?"

"No, three of you should be enough. Why?"

"Fine then," said Sparrow. "Go ahead and bring Master Chem and his dragons here. In my beast shape I'm tall enough to see over the bushes and I can see very well in the dark. Fafnir, Sheeba, and I will take care of everything."

Fafnir had a request for her: "Can you bring me some rocks?"

"Sure. I saw some sticking out of the mud over there. I'll get them right away!"

In a few moments, Sparrow had dug up some rocks that had been hidden by the rain and mud. They had oddly regular shapes, and she was stunned to realize that the entire island was cobbled with them! Well, that was a mystery she would clear up later, once they had gotten out of this mess.

She brought Fafnir a supply of the big, square stones. The dwarf hefted one and flashed a wicked grin. She looked over the bushes, calculated her trajectory, and heaved the stone into the darkness with the grace of a trained shot-putter. A moment later they heard a scream, the splash of tumbling bodies, and horrible biting and gulping noises.

"Ten at once," Sparrow counted soberly.

Manitou turned to the others:

"C'mon, let's deal with the Portal,"

Cal, Robin, Angelica, and Tara joined him in a circle. Somewhat apprehensively, Tara held the living stone in her hand.

"Chem is going to locate the Portal at the precise spot the living stone is placed," Manitou explained. "So put it in the center, and use your magic to prevent it from moving. Any questions?"

"I have one," said Angelica, who was trembling with fear. "What happens if Master Chem can't get through the Portal?"

"Do you hear the Mud Eaters?"

"Yes."

"If Chem doesn't make it, we'll have a long stay in the Eaters' burrows and then we'll be taken back to the Gray Fortress in chains."

Angelica swallowed hard and decided to concentrate.

Manitou looked into the living stone.

"Chem?"

"Yes, are you ready? What's the hang-up, for heaven's sake?"

"We're being attacked by the Mud Eaters. Open the Portal, we're all set."

"By Balthazar's horns, Baldur's entrails, and Grisol's rotten teeth!" cursed the high wizard. Then he quickly said, "By Transferus, Portal, open wide. Transfer me to the other side."

An enormous Portal opened before him, big enough to allow the elves mounted on their pegasi to pass through. Almost immediately, an identical Portal appeared in front of the young spellbinders, in the middle of their circle. It was right above the living stone, held motionless by their power.

Behind them, the sounds of battle suddenly intensified. The Mud Eaters had managed to set foot on the island. Protected by their thick fur and using their powerful claws, they were pushing their way through the rosebushes. That's when Sparrow, Sheeba, and Fafnir fell on them. Baring her threatening fangs, Sheeba forced them back. Fafnir heaved them into the water, swamping the other rafts. And Sparrow grabbed them two by two and banged their heads together, knocking them out. But despite the trio's fierce resistance, the Mud Eaters' pressure gradually forced them to retreat. Suddenly Fafnir tripped over a body she hadn't noticed and the struggling dwarf disappeared under a pile of Mud Eaters who started to tie her up.

Terrified, Tara suddenly lost control of her power. Her eyes turned completely blue and her magic merged with the living stone's. From the other side, she could hear the pegasi champing at the bit, waiting for the Portal to be ready to transfer them.

Tara was sure of what she was doing and had no intention of waiting. Without bothering to see if the Portal was fully activated, she mentally seized the dragons and elves waiting in Lancovit and instantly transferred them to the island.

In the next moment, Chem was stunned to realize that he, along with fifty elves on their pegasi, some fifty dragon wizards, Master Dragosh, and half the Travia Castle courtyard walls now found themselves on the Island of Black Roses, facing two hundred equally stunned Mud Eaters. Then the Portal slammed shut.

Master Chem didn't try to understand. Instead, he changed back into a dragon, and charged. The other dragons did the same, taking to the air while the elves and the vampyr leapt into action.

They attacked the Mud Eaters en masse, who couldn't understand what was happening to them. The dragons' wings blew them down and knocked them out, their fierce flames singed their fur, and their huge jaws terrorized them. The Eaters must have thought that hell itself had swallowed them up. Within seconds they were destroyed or driven into the water, to be dealt with by its inhabitants. The elves did the mopping up, but there wasn't much left to do. The Mud Eaters who weren't able to flee on rafts tried to swim, screaming when a glurp came close. There were many hungry glurps, so there was a lot of screaming.

In the darkness, nobody noticed the bushes stirring. Creepers with black, razor-sharp thorns moved toward the unconscious Mud Eaters. One of them came to, shaking his head as if dazed, and saw the tendrils reaching his companions. He let out a squeal of despair and tried to escape. But Robin had done good work, and rosebushes now covered almost the entire island. The Eater didn't stand a chance. The creepers tracked him, tripped him, and quickly enveloped him, stabbing his body with their thorns. Curiously, they were careful to leave the young spellbinders and the dog in peace.

An evil laugh that seemed to rise from a thousand voices then whispered in the darkness: "Free! I am free!" Tara was about to explore but the voice cautiously fell silent when the dragons returned, their fanged jaws open in wide smiles.

"They'll still be running tomorrow morning!" thundered a delighted Master Chem. "Come to my arms, children!"

Tara, who was talking with the living stone and was half hypnotized by the power of their symbiosis, didn't stir. With a shout of joy Robin hugged his father, T'andilus M'angil, who was heading the elf group. The others looked nervously at the dragon's sharp spines and scales.

Chem suddenly understood, and laughed.

"Oops, I'm sorry. I forgot. I'll change again."

Once he was back in human shape, Sparrow happily hugged him, half burying him in her fur. Cal and Robin, who were more reserved, greeted him with pleasure. Fafnir held him so tight, she almost broke his ribs. Sheeba gave him a welcoming roar.

"I'm so happy to see you all again," the old wizard shouted. "I have to admit, you really scared me! And how the devil did you manage to transfer all of us here before the Portal was fully activated?"

"We used the link that was already formed," said Tara in a strange, lilting voice. "Saving our three friends was very urgent, so we extended our power to your entire group. We apologize for the Castle courtyard. We didn't calculate that quite right."

"Bah!" said the wizard, puzzled by her tone. "They're just some old stones. We'll fix everything up when we get home."

Then he turned to Manitou and whispered, "What's the matter with her?"

"She's in communion with the living stone," said the dog. "I think she doesn't know how to break the symbiosis. And when she says 'we,' I imagine she's speaking for the stone and for herself."

The wizard heaved a worried sigh.

"Goodness gracious, a living stone? I thought I hadn't heard correctly earlier. I think I could break the link between the two of them, but her extraordinary power might be useful to us, so—"

"So what?" interrupted Manitou dryly.

"So if Magister hasn't been alerted by Tara's magical action, it would be stupid to recreate a Portal. We have to take everyone with us. The Mud Eaters could return and attack them again."

"Put the children on pegasi behind the elf warriors, and take them somewhere safe."

"No, that would deprive me of six fighters, and I need all the elves I've got to attack the Fortress."

"I completely disagree," said the dog. "You're going to put them in danger!"

"Manitou, this is war! Magister kidnapped those children and was willing to pervert them with demonic magic. I'm not going to use them to conquer the Fortress. I just want them to accompany us. They can stay a mile away, guarded by a couple of elves, and won't join in the fighting. Does that suit you?"

"Don't ask me, ask them!"

"What?"

"Stop thinking that the humans are only here for your little games, Chem. Ask them their opinion. And if they say no, it'll be no. Period."

The high wizard looked at him angrily, then shrugged.

"So be it . . . Tara!"

"Master?" replied the strange lilting voice.

"Your great-grandfather just reminded me that humans also have free will. What would you like to do? Come with us to the Bloodgrave Fortress or take cover somewhere while waiting for the fighting to be over?"

"Our mother is imprisoned in that Fortress, Master. We must come with you to free her."

"You see, Manitou," began the old wizard, "she—"

He suddenly interrupted himself.

"*Your mother?* But I thought she—"

"—was dead. So did we. But that's not the case. She is under a deadly spell that prevents her from leaving the Fortress. You are the only one who can release her from it. So of course we are going to come with you."

"Where Tara goes, we go," said Fabrice firmly, and the others concurred.

Master Dragosh came over to them.

"We're going to have a problem then," he said. "Who is going to transport the children?"

"I have an idea about that. But first I need the elves to go on ahead. Their pegasi can't fly as fast as we dragons can. And they should take Gallant with them."

He turned to Tara.

"Ask your familiar to go with the elves when they leave. Can you tell us where the Fortress is?"

"Yes, it's right here," she said, pulling out the map. By Detailus, show my location please, so I can travel at my ease."

The map obligingly opened up but couldn't help making a few remarks.

"Oh my, dragons!" said the chatty chart as it displayed the route they had just taken. "Scads of dragons! Kindly hold your breath, I'm extremely flammable. So you want to know the way to the Fortress? Well, it won't take you more than two hours as the crow flies— forgive me, the dragon."

"That's perfect," said Chem, raising an eyebrow. "May I borrow this map, Tara?"

"Of course, Master."

Chem turned to the Lancovit secret services chief, whose arm was still affectionately draped around his son Robin's shoulders.

"Master T'andilus?"

"Yes, High Wizard?"

"Here is a map of Gandis. The route is easy to follow. Leave now and be careful. It's essential that the Bloodgraves not notice your presence. Land nearby, but keep out of sight. Here, for example." He pointed to a spot on the map. "We'll join you there. Ah, just a second!"

"High Wizard?"

"I'm going to darken the coats of your pegasi." A startled Gallant neighed in protest, but the wizard ignored him. "They're much too visible the way they are."

He was right. When the pegasi had been turned black, they became shadows that melted into the night and disappeared in a great flight of feathers—led by an extremely grumpy Gallant.

The old wizard rubbed his hands.

"All right, it's our turn. Tara, have you ever shape-shifted before? I mean, ever taken some other form?"

"No, Master."

The strange lilting voice betrayed no surprise, and also no interest, as if Tara's emotions were submerged by something else.

"I want you to change into a dragon. I will ex—"

She gave him no time to finish his sentence.

"Very well, Master."

Tara began to swell and swell like a balloon. Chem stepped back in surprise. With a *pop!* a pair of wings sprouted from her shoulders, her skin turned to scales and her hands to claws. A spiny ridge rose on her back, her face lengthened, and crystal fangs sprouted in her jaws. Within moments, an enormous golden dragon with entirely blue eyes and a luminous crystal rock set in its forehead like a third eye had taken the girl's place.

"—plain," finished the wizard, thunderstruck. "Oh, I see you've already got the knack. That's good, very good. A little unnerving, but very impressive. Now, will you agree to carry your friends, so we can go faster? I will carry Angelica, Manitou, Master Dragosh, Robin, and Fabrice. You will have to take Cal, Fafnir, Sparrow, and Sheeba. My fellow dragons are too snobby to let anybody climb on their backs."

The other dragons hissed in annoyance and took off.

"Very well," Tara agreed. "Let our friends climb on our back. We are ready."

"Wait!" yelped Angelica. "What about me?"

The high wizard blinked.

"What's the matter, little Angelica?"

"The matter is that I want to go home. I don't want to wind up in the middle of the fight between spellbinders. Send me back!"

"No."

Tara's lilting voice had answered for the wizard.

"What do you mean, no?"

Angelica spun around, ready to slap her, until she realized that Tara was now fifty feet long—longer than a brontosaurus!

She turned imploringly to Master Dragosh.

"Don't you agree with me, Master?"

But the vampyr had already climbed onto the dragon's back.

"Angelica, the Master of Bloodgraves is extremely powerful," Tara said in her odd, lilting voice. "If we open another Transfer

Portal he might discover our presence, and we would lose the element of surprise. Climb onto Master Chem's back. As soon as we're finished with these monsters, you'll be able to go home."

"But . . ."

"If you keep arguing, we will leave you here with the Mud Eaters. Obey!"

Angelica turned to Master Chem, but he indicated there was nothing he could do. Shaking with rage, Angelica climbed onto his back, trampling the old dragon's scales. To give people more room, Chem changed his shape until he was as big as Tara.

They took off, and soon the island, the strange voice that had whispered in the darkness, and the black rosebushes were but a speck in the distance.

CHAPTER 18

AERIAL ACROBATICS

Tara was peacefully cruising along when the living stone released herself from their fantastic symbiosis, restoring Tara's consciousness to her. For a moment, she watched as the ground raced by . . . then suddenly realized she was six hundred feet above it! In a complete panic, she started pedaling in the air and stopped beating her wings—and immediately went into a steep dive.

"Heyyy!" yelled Cal. "Stop that! Pull up! *Pull up!*"

The ground was rushing up at them dangerously, and Tara suddenly understood that her wings were what kept them aloft. She desperately flapped them and barely avoided a collision with a huge tree . . . by flying underneath it. She leveled off with her muzzle skimming the branches rushing toward her but couldn't help clipping a top branch with her wing.

Knocked off balance, she lost some more altitude and pulled in her wings to pass beneath another giant tree. Then, by pushing off from an enormous trunk, she leaped upward through a providential opening in the dense forest, and with a desperate effort managed to climb back into the air.

"*You lunatic!*" screamed an enraged Fafnir. "What are you doing? Are you trying to kill us?"

"I'm . . . I'm flying!" cried Tara, flabbergasted. "I'm a *dragon* and I'm *flying!*"

"Good Lord, you've been a dragon for the last half hour, and it's only now that you're realizing it?" yelled Cal furiously. "I would have done better to climb aboard Master Chem. He's known he's been a dragon for hundreds of years."

"But how is it that I'm flying?" stammered Tara.

"By flapping your wings," cried Sparrow, who was being knocked around by her chaotic flight. "In fact, if you could flap them both together, it would be a lot better!"

"What's going on here?" cried Master Chem, who'd been watching Tara's aerial acrobatics with great surprise.

"What's going on is that I want to get down!" roared the terrified dwarf. "Get me down before she kills us all!"

The old dragon ignored her.

"Stop thrashing your legs around like that," he ordered Tara, who was doing more swimming in the air than flying, "and tell me what's going on with you."

"I don't know," answered Tara, trying to beat her wings smoothly. "We were on the Island of Black Roses waiting for you, the Mud Eaters attacked, and then after that there was this big void, like a black hole. Next thing I knew, I was hundreds of feet above the ground, I got dizzy, and I fell."

"Yeah, and we fell with her," Cal confirmed.

"I understand!" said Chem. "Your magic and the living stone's magic entered into a symbiosis, and it must have created a shock. You weren't aware of what you were doing. All right now, to fly smoothly, do what I'm doing: spread your wings wide, then bring them down as if you were bending your elbow inward. Our wings aren't like birds' wings; we have an extra joint. Don't fight the air; let it carry you. And look for updrafts; they'll help you soar."

Despite the semi-hysterical dwarf's thrashing around on her back, Tara very gradually managed to master flight, and then to enjoy it. She lost her balance once or twice, which didn't improve the humor of her passengers, but managed to fly more or less straight without running into anything.

They soon caught up with the elves and landed behind a hill that hid them from the Gray Fortress.

The landing was difficult. When Tara touched down, she forgot she was still moving fast, and tried to climb back up. But she no longer had enough speed, so she galloped furiously to keep from falling, tripped, lurched into the air, and wound up crashing nose first into the dirt, digging a thirty-foot-long trench in the ground.

Before they came in for a landing, Sparrow had a hunch that things wouldn't go well and cast a Fixus spell to help everyone stay on Tara's back. To look at them now, they couldn't believe they were still alive.

The dust had hardly begun to settle when Fafnir jumped down and, half weeping in spite of her dwarfish pride, fell to her knees to thank the dwarf gods for sparing her life, and swore never again to ever climb onto the back of anything that flew.

Cal, Sparrow, and Sheeba came staggering down after her.

The old dragon, by contrast, made an elegant landing.

"All right," he said, "now that we're all together, we have a Fortress to attack . . . No, Tara! Be careful! *Nooooooo!*"

Exhausted, Tara was yawning. She was surprised by Master Chem's shout and turned her head to him with her mouth still open, but it was too late.

A jet of flame shot from her throat and hit the dragon wizard, who yelled, scattering the elves and the pegasi and causing indescribable chaos.

The old wizard was hopping this way and that, trying to put out his burning dragon mane, while everyone else cautiously backed away from Tara. The elves rushed over to smother the flames with their capes before the smoke alerted the Gray Fortress Bloodgraves.

"Oh my!" cried Tara. "What happened to me?"

"When dragons yawn, they spit fire," yelled Master Chem. "When they have the hiccups too, for that matter."

"I'm terribly sorry," she stammered. "I didn't know that."

"Yeah, we noticed," said Cal. "All right, now that I've almost been flattened like a pancake and roasted like a chicken, I'd appreciate it if you would shape-shift back before we have another catastrophe."

"Absolutely," approved the old dragon, who explained to Tara how to restore her human body.

But without the help of the living stone, it wasn't that simple.

Using the power of her mind, Tara ordered her entire body to shrink, but only her wings obeyed, and she wound up with ridiculous little pigeon wings on the body of a dragon. Then she nearly fell over when one of her legs became human again, unable to support her several tons of weight. Her legs began to grow, but her tail shrank. She was able to regain her human head, but with a dragon's crest. Arms appeared and disappeared, her body shrank and became human—but with fifty-foot wings. These began to flap, raising a cloud of dust and lifting her many feet into the air before she was able to come back down, in a panic. The spectacle was so strange that even the elf T'andilus, the hardened head of the Lancovit secret services, forgot about his battle plan and gaped.

The dragons watching weren't openly laughing, but you could feel they were restraining themselves.

And Cal, Sparrow, Fabrice, and Fafnir looked extremely concerned.

Eventually, Tara managed to get rid of her giant wings and recovered her normal human body. After anxiously feeling herself all over for several minutes, she grinned at her friends, who were hugely relieved to have her whole again.

"Our battle plan is fairly simple," announced Master T'andilus, still shaking his head incredulously. "We can't attack the Gray Fortress until we know how it's defended. So I'm going to try to get in first and neutralize their defenses while you wait outside. At my signal, you'll all storm the Fortress. By making as little noise as possible we should be able to get to the heart of the complex before the Bloodgraves realize they're under attack. We'll approach under cover of the forest, following the path the young people took on their way out. Any questions?"

"Yeah, I have one," cried Cal, frowning. "We licensed thieves don't much like the unexpected. Why don't we use the bat instead?"

The startled vampyr turned to him as Master T'andilus asked, "What bat?"

"Master Dragosh can change shape," explained Cal, "but it's not like the dragons, it's more like part of his nature. He's in the habit of going out at night as a bat and flying around Travia Castle. I noticed that our spells didn't detect him, and neither did the anti-mosquito ones."

"I didn't realize I was being spied on," snapped Dragosh, glaring at Cal. "But the boy is right. I could try to slip into the Fortress in my bat shape. What would you like me to do?"

"Hm, I hadn't thought of that," said the old wizard. "Are you sure you want to take the chance?"

"I don't really have much choice," replied the vampyr stiffly.

"Very well," said Master T'andilus. "Basically, you have to get rid of the human sentinels and try to find the Spells Hall. Be especially careful because they could have wild demons defending it, who might be a little aggressive."

"Great!" said the vampyr with a grimace. "Putting what you just said in plain English, I'm supposed to blindly enter enemy territory without using magic, knock out anybody I run into, and find the defensive apparatus, while incidentally neutralizing any demons who might annihilate me."

Dragosh gave a hiss of annoyance. Then with a *poof!* he changed into a large black bat.

"Wait," said Master Chem. "Take my crystal ball and call Master T'andilus once you're inside. You have his number?"

The bat nodded, took the crystal ball in a hand, and waited attentively.

"While you're flying to the Fortress, we'll begin our advance," said the elf. "See you later!"

The vampyr nodded, then fluttered into the darkness.

Tara and Cal climbed onto Gallant, who was relieved to find his human companion in her more normal shape, and they flew off into the night. It only took them a few minutes to reach the edge of the forest. There, the dragons entrusted the young spellbinders to two elves, who would guard them.

"You'll stay here for the time being," explained Master Chem. "If we don't come back for you, it means that we have lost. In that case you'll have to flee and try to get to the nearest country, which is Hymlia. Warn OtherWorld that the demons have declared war on humans and dragons by infecting the Bloodgraves. The whole planet must fight this terrifying menace, otherwise all the free worlds will be lost!"

"We'll do it," Robin gravely agreed. "Fafnir will alert the dwarves, I'll warn my fellow elves, and the other peoples will all rise against this menace."

"Perfect," said the old wizard with a smile. "Tara, lend me your living stone so that I can communicate with everyone. Oh, and warn her that she will be changing owners temporarily. I don't want any bad surprises."

Tara addressed the living stone mentally. "You have to retransmit all communications to Master Chem. It's important, not to say vital!"

"*Why?*" asked the stone, which had trouble seizing the human concepts of "important" and "vital."

"Because there are many beings held against their will in the Fortress, and we need your help to free them."

"*You mean to free them the way you freed me from the black roses?*" asked the living stone. "*You want to polish them so that they become as beautiful as me? In that case, I agree. Even though I don't like being away from you, I will transmit the calls from the other crystal balls—who aren't particularly intelligent,*" she added smugly.

Tara smiled and handed the living stone to the old wizard.

"She agrees, Master Chem."

"Thank you," he said, cautiously taking the fragile crystal ball. "And don't too concerned. I have no intention of losing to those gray-shirted runts. We'll see each other soon."

"Master, please remember that my mother is imprisoned in the Fortress. You've got to find her and free her from the deadly spell."

"Don't worry. She'll be my main priority."

Exhausted and anxious, Tara let herself slump to the ground. Gallant lay down next to her and gave her arm a friendly rub with his nose. She stroked his velvety nostrils while worrying about the upcoming battle.

The minutes passed silently. They were all tired, even Sparrow, who was too agitated to sit still and was pacing, while listening intently. After half an hour of this, she quit and flopped down next to Tara.

"Ouch!" she said with a grimace. "I sure am sore!"

"Me too," said Fabrice. "And I want all this to be over and done with. When you come right down to it, life on Earth is really calm and peaceful. I'm not at all sure I want to stay on OtherWorld."

"If the Bloodgraves win, no one will be safe anywhere," Robin remarked soberly.

"So what are we waiting for?" cried Fafnir. "We aren't going to just sit here twiddling our thumbs while others do the fighting for us, are we?"

"But what do you want us to do?" asked Swallow, taken aback.

"This!" Bouncing up like a spring, she grabbed the two elf guards' heads and banged them together, knocking them out cold.

"What are you doing?" Manitou and Fabrice both asked in astonishment.

"I'm putting them to sleep," answered the dwarf, carefully hitching her axe on her back.

"We can see that," snapped Fabrice, "but why?"

"Because they probably would have stopped me from leaving. All right, I'm going to the Fortress. If any you would like a nice little fight, follow me. But hurry up, because those two elves aren't going to sleep forever. See you later!"

And the dwarf took off like an arrow through the forest, heading for the Gray Fortress.

Robin leaped to his feet, eyes bright with enthusiasm.

"She's right, they might need us! Let's go!"

"Are you sure?" Fabrice protested. "I feel we're the ones who need them, rather than the other way around. We're more likely to get in their way than anything else."

Sparrow agreed.

"I don't much like staying here either, but Fabrice is right. Master Chem will be furious if we disobey him."

"That's too bad," said Robin firmly. "At worst we'll get chewed out, at best maybe we can save somebody. In any case I can't stand staying here without knowing, so I'm going. If you want to follow me, it's now or never."

"I'm coming too," decided Sparrow, who promptly shape-shifted. "Anyway, nobody can do much to me in my beast shape."

"And I have to help save my mother from Magister," said Tara.

Angelica elected to stay behind, saying she wanted to protect the unconscious elves.

Protect them from what? Cal grumbled to himself. Squirrels? But he didn't press the point. They left her behind without regret.

While the young people were crossing the forest to join the elves and the dragons, Master Dragosh was cautiously flying down the halls of the Gray Fortress. He had gotten in without much trouble, through the open window of a Bloodgrave who liked fresh air at night. The bedroom door squeaked slightly when he opened it to go out—not easy with little bat hands—and he froze, rigid with fear. But the Bloodgrave only sleepily muttered, "No, Mom, not the frog. Not the frog!" Then he rolled over and went back to sleep. Heaving a sigh of relief, the vampyr slipped out into the dimly lit hall and took flight. Twice within a few minutes he was only saved by his very dark coloring. Two young spellbinders came out and walked to the toilets without seeing him, cautiously hanging above their heads. Once they were back in their rooms, the vampyr was able to continue his ghostly progression. As he passed a hall, he suddenly spotted something familiar: tapestries. The five tapestries of the Gray Fortress Transfer Portal.

"I'm in the Portal Room," he whispered into the crystal ball. "What should I do?"

"You need five tapestries for a transfer to work," said T'andilus. "Can you take one of them down and hide it? That way, nobody could use the Portal to escape."

Changing back into human shape, the vampyr unhooked the tapestry showing the unicorns. Then he changed again and flew up to hide it on top of the main beam, in the shadows by the ceiling. No one would think to look for it there.

"I've done it," he whispered into the crystal ball. "What now?"

"You have to find the Hall of Spells. There will probably be a guard inside."

The vampyr set out again and opened all the doors he encountered, closing them very, very carefully when he came across sleeping Bloodgraves. After a quarter of an hour of nerve-racking searching, he finally found the Hall of Spells. The Bloodgraves had posted only a single guard inside. Like a shadow, Dragosh slipped behind him, changed into human shape, and knocked him out. Ripping strips of the Bloodgrave's gray robe, he used them to tie, gag, and blindfold him.

Satisfied, he stood up. All right, he thought, now he had to figure out how to deactivate the evil spells.

"I'm there," he muttered into the crystal ball, "but the place is empty. There's nothing here."

"Defenses are usually materialized in objects," said T'andilus. "That's what you have to find, Master Vampyr."

The problem was, there wasn't anything special in the room. A table, a comfortable chair, tapestries and carpets, a few statues, and a sofa—that was it.

Wait a minute . . . there was something odd about those statues. Dragosh came closer, and held his breath. The three statues represented terrifying demons. The first featured a giant worm whose mouth was lined with mandibles and whose tentacles were ready to shoot out to seize prey. Stumps of arms emerged from the seething mass, with needle-sharp claws and horribly human eyes. The second was a two-headed wolf with a flayed torso from which half of a monstrous three-eyed baby burst with an array of long fangs dripping poison. The third had the head of a vicious moray eel and the body of an octopus. It was covered with wriggling larvae, who, when they split open, displayed thousands of tiny, bloody mouths with hooked beaks, eager to tear and rend.

When he realized what the statues were, Dragosh stumbled backward. The lost statues of Mu! Carved by the mad demon of Ragnarok! Everybody thought they had been destroyed when the ocean drowned the mythical continent of Mu, but the Master of Bloodgraves had obviously found them. Now the vampyr was sure that Magister had completely lost his mind. Controlling such demons called for the blackest and most dangerous magic. Make the slightest error in manipulation and you'd find yourself in the demons' stomachs!

"You won't believe this," he murmured to the crystal ball. "Take a look!"

The vampyr put the ball in front of the statues and watched as the elf and the dragon gasped in surprise.

"Those can't be . . . " murmured Chem.

"I'm afraid they are," Dragosh confirmed. "The lost statues, the demonic guardians of the Temple of Mu. And if these are defending the Fortress, then we have a very, very big problem!"

"We don't have any choice," said Master Chem. "You must deactivate those defenses. Find their system!"

This is going to cost me my life, Dragosh muttered to himself, stepping closer.

The statues were studded with jewels, and he noticed that they were blinking. Not very brightly, but definitely blinking, and in a regular pattern, from red to orange, and then from white to black. The vampyr grimaced. It was a code! If he had a couple of hours ahead of him he could figure it out, but here it was impossible. He needed help.

"I'm stuck," he whispered into the crystal ball. "There's a code to switch off the statues, and I don't know what it is."

"Let me see," whispered T'andilus.

"Take a look."

The elf carefully studied the blinking of the statues, then gave a sigh of relief.

"It's all right," he said. "I know that sequence. You have to first push on the black, then the white, then on the orange and the red at the same time. It's a pretty simple code."

"Good, I'll do that now," said the vampyr with a smile.

He was about to start with the first jewel when Master Chem interrupted him.

"Safir, wait! Don't touch anything! That's not normal!"

The vampyr jerked his hand back.

"What now? What's not normal?"

"If you were protecting your palace, would you use a code that was so easy to crack?"

The vampyr thought for a moment, and a cynical smile appeared on his lips.

"No, of course not. You think it's a trap?"

"I'm *positive* it's a trap! Look at the statues more carefully. See if there isn't something else."

The vampyr examined the demons with great care. Some details were so horrible that he instinctively looked away, before realizing that was exactly the desired reaction. He looked more closely . . . Yes! On each demon's back, in the midst of what looked like rotting, worm-eaten intestines, was a small, nearly invisible black stone. He described this to the old wizard.

"I think that's it," confirmed Master Chem. "Go ahead. If the demons come to life, get the heck out of there as fast as you can. Don't try to be a hero; you aren't powerful enough to stand up to them. But if nothing happens, we'll immediately attack the chatrixes and come join you. Go down and open the Fortress's main gate as soon as we secure the grounds."

"Wait!" broke in the elf, who was still chagrined that he hadn't anticipated the trap. "There are three demons, right?"

"Yes, three of them," answered Dragosh. "So what?"

"It might be smart to press all three statues' stones at the same time. If I were a Bloodgrave, I would have added this layer of protection, on the principle that a single spy wouldn't be able to break all three spells at once—unless he had three hands!"

"Very clever," said the vampyr with a grimace. "But not clever enough, since in my bat shape I have *four* hands! All right, I'm about to do it. Get ready!"

Dragosh shape-shifted. Fortunately, he was a large bat, and by stretching his wings he was able to reach all three stones at the same time. Holding his breath, he lightly touched the three stones. A groaning sound was heard, and the statues swayed. The vampyr backed away in fear, ready to fly off. But the statues stopped moving and stood still.

With a hand on his heart, Dragosh took a deep breath. He came close, examining the statues carefully, though this brought him uncomfortably close to the tentacles. Then he barely repressed a yell of victory that would have woken up the entire Fortress. The blinking of the stones had stopped.

He set the crystal ball in front of him.

"That's it," he whispered. "The demons won't be coming to life. You can go ahead."

The vampyr's signal triggered a frenzy of activity. While Dragosh was dealing with the statues, the elves had been picking a small purple flower in the forest, extracting an anesthetic sap, and dipping tiny darts in it. Now they had silently scaled the walls around the Fortress grounds. Their challenge was to knock the chatrixes out, but without using magic spells, because, like dwarves and giants, they're immune to offensive magic. And if just one chatrix howled and alerted the Bloodgraves, the elves were doomed.

The chatrixes caught their scent right away. With a dull yapping, their leader gathered them under the wall the elves were standing on, eager to attack the intruders on their territory. In his thirst for blood, their leader didn't bother howling. A serious mistake.

T'andilus smiled with satisfaction and lowered his arm.

At his signal, the elves puffed on their blowguns, and darts hit every one of the chatrixes. Yelping with surprise, the black monsters tried to bite their flanks where the darts had hit them. Then one started to sway, took a few shaky steps, and collapsed. The lead chatrix opened his mouth to howl a warning, but before he could, a long arrow slammed into his throat.

The other chatrixes were already unconscious. The elves dropped into the Fortress grounds and tied the monsters' paws and muzzles.

"Let's go," whispered Master Chem after climbing (with some difficulty) the outer wall.

Silent as shadows, the elves crossed the grounds. Ahead, the Gray Fortress main door swung open and Master Dragosh appeared, smiling broadly. He was in his human shape and with one hand was casually dragging the guard he had knocked out.

"The way is clear," Dragosh whispered. "Let's try to neutralize as many Bloodgraves as we can." He had already used Fabrice's indications to pinpoint their rooms, so missions were assigned and the mop-up begun.

The elves opened the doors, rushed in, and knocked out the rooms' occupants. Two dragons brought up the rear in case any Bloodgraves unexpectedly came to.

Everything went fine until they got upstairs.

The elves had neutralized their thirty-fifth Bloodgrave when a young woman who'd been having trouble sleeping rounded the hallway corner just as they were tiptoeing out of the rooms. In her terror, she had time to scream before being hit by the anesthesia darts and collapsing. That's when the battle began.

They had been caught napping, but the Bloodgraves were powerful wizards. They very quickly understood that the Fortress had been invaded and reacted by attacking the elves, who were easier targets than the dragons.

Blasts of demonic magic struck, burned, battered, and killed, and the elves defended themselves as best they could. They sheltered behind magic shields and fired spells and also arrows, an unexpected weapon that disconcerted the Bloodgraves.

Meanwhile, Tara and her friends had reached the outer wall of the Fortress grounds. They could hear the shouts as the fighting began. Sparrow and Robin climbed to the top of the wall and saw that it would be too dangerous to try to cross the grounds. The battle had quickly become a general melee. Dragons, elves, and Bloodgraves were firing spells in every direction, and explosions of magic were rocking the woods.

"Wow!" cried Cal. "You sure we ought to go in there?"

"Not through the grounds, anyway," said Sparrow, jumping back down from the wall. "We'd be toast in seconds."

"Well, we can always go underneath," remarked Fafnir. "Let's see what those gray-shirts have done to my tunnel."

They were disappointed to see that the opening of the tunnel had been blocked. But Fafnir waved them back and put her ear to the wall of stone and mud.

"It's all right," she said with satisfaction, wiping herself off. "They plugged the exit, probably to keep the chatrixes from escaping. But they haven't collapsed the whole tunnel."

She crouched down and pushed with her hands, using her strange power to liquefy the dirt and stones. In a moment she had cleared the entrance.

Tara miniaturized Gallant and they headed into the tunnel, going in the way they had come out two days earlier.

When they reached the storeroom everything was still, though they could hear spellbinders yelling outside through the open door. They were about to go out when Fafnir suddenly gestured to them not to move. Looking over the dwarf's shoulder, Tara saw something straight out of a nightmare. Flanked by Deria, the Bloodgraves master was striding angrily toward the Initiation Hall, towing behind him the hovering body of Tara's mother!

To clear the way, Magister shoved aside a Bloodgrave who was battling a dragon wizard. He blasted both of them with a jet of flame, then disappeared down the stairway leading to the Initiation Hall.

The seven looked apprehensively at the courtyard where the battle was raging.

"We don't have any choice," said an anguished Tara. "We have to get across the courtyard and find Mom, Deria, and Magister!"

"We'll split up into two groups," ordered Manitou. "Fafnir, Sparrow, and Fabrice, you come with me. We'll warn Master Chem that Magister is in the Initiation Hall. Meanwhile, Tara, Cal, and Robin, you follow Magister and keep an eye on him. But don't anyone intervene. And if a Bloodgrave attacks you, put your hands behind your back and sit down. That's a signal that you're not a combatant. Let yourself be captured. I don't want you risking your lives, understand?"

"Yes," answered Tara. "But why don't you take just Fafnir to protect you, and leave us Sparrow and Fabrice. We're going to need them."

Fafnir smiled broadly as she hefted her axe.

"No problem," she said. "I'm happy to guard the Lab, and if anybody touches a hair on his head, I'll turn them into dog food."

"Perfect. Let's go!"

Keeping their heads down, they made their way through the thick of the fighting. Bloodgraves, elves, and dragons were shooting spells, and rays—burning and freezing, blue, red, white, orange, and green—were crisscrossing everywhere. By some sort of miracle, after crawling, running, jumping, sliding, and dodging belligerents, they reached the other side of the courtyard more or less intact. Manitou's fur was singed from brushing too close to wizard fire.

Sparrow was shaking like a leaf after a dragon mistook her for an enemy and very nearly froze her. Cal was limping because he had missed his landing when he jumped away from two elves attacking a Bloodgrave. But Fafnir's eyes were glittering. She had managed to save a dragon and an elf by neatly knocking their adversaries out with the flat of her axe, and was eager to try again. This was her kind of fight!

Once in the corridor leading to the Initiation Hall, they split into two groups, as agreed.

When Tara's party reached the entrance to the Initiation Hall, the two giants guarding it drew their huge swords. Quickly, Robin said: "By Pocus you're paralyzed on the spot. You might want to move, but we'd rather you not." The turquoise mesh enveloped the giants, but it sizzled and frayed when it touched their skins, leaving them free to move.

With an evil smile, one of them thundered, "That doesn't work with us, kid. Don't try to go any further or we'll chop you to pieces."

Tara didn't give them time to taunt. Without bothering with a formula, she shouted "Melt!" and pointed at the ground.

The giants had no time to react. An enormous hole opened beneath their feet and their fall through four floors plus the basements was punctuated by a booming series of *ouch!, ow!,* and *aie!*

"Very efficient—and a neat trick to remember," commented Cal. "It would never have occurred to me. All right, let's go. We still have to get across that dangerous bridge."

The arachne was waiting for them. She had already removed the bridge she'd spun to allow Magister, Deria, and Tara's mother to cross, and she now hung on her silk thread, waving her mandibles with an awful creaking sound.

The kids now understood why Tara had wanted Fabrice and Sparrow along. In their little group, Fabrice was the one who loved riddles most, and Sparrow was the quickest to get them.

When they were a few steps from the precipice, the arachne descended and sang in her melodious voice: "To pass without danger to the other side, an answer to my riddle you must provide. It has two words, you get one try, and if you fail, you'll quickly die. I'll count each second while the riddle you reckon."

"Only one of us can answer her," whispered Sparrow. "And the riddle has two words."

"In that case, I'll give it a shot," said Fabrice bravely, who was bitterly regretting the day he ever took an interest in riddles.

He stepped up to the giant spider and cleared his throat: "I'm . . . I'm listening."

The monstrous arachnid spoke:

First half a degree in a chilly clime;
Second start of simian that likes to climb;
Third cut yourself a little slack;
Fourth share the ball, and don't hold back.
What happens to all of us in time
is fifth and last in my little rhyme.

"Hey, she didn't say what the whole thing was," cried Cal indignantly.

The arachne trembled and lowered herself a little on her thread.

"That's no big deal," hissed Fabrice through clenched teeth. "I'm not about to argue with a giant spider whose jaws are bigger than I am. Keep quiet, Cal!"

The arachne finished: "I will count to eighty-eight, then the answer you must relate."

"Why not to a hundred?" exclaimed Cal. "The last time, you said to a hundred!"

The arachne quivered in annoyance, lowered herself a little more with her mandibles right above Fabrice's head, and started to count. "One . . . "

"Cal, if you say another word the spider won't kill you, because I will," snapped Fabrice. "Okay, let's think. 'Half a degree' would be either *de-* or *gree*. Except for 'grease,' I can't think of many words that begin with 'gree,' so let's go with *de-*. The second clue is pretty easy. A simian is an ape or a monkey, and 'start' usually means the first syllable of word. 'Ape' only has one syllable, so the clue must be *mon-*. That gives us *de-* and *mon-*."

The arachne was already up to twenty and Tara was getting tense. But while his friends were trembling, Fabrice was so focused that he forgot about the danger.

"I'm stuck on the third clue," he said. "I know what cutting slack means, but is 'slack' the important word, or 'cut'? Or is it 'little'? I better focus on the last two clues. Maybe they'll help me fill in the third one. My guess is that to share a ball is to *toss* or *pass* it back and forth."

"I think I have an idea for the fifth clue," said Cal. "Two things happen to all of us eventually: we get old, and we die."

"Fabrice, is there any way to combine the fourth and fifth clues?" asked Tara. "Something like 'ball-die' or 'pass-die'?"

"I can't see it," he said. "Maybe there's another way of saying what we'll do in time. We die, we croak, we kick the bucket, we buy the farm, we eat it . . . Nah, none of those seems quite right."

The arachne was already up to sixty.

"Wait a minute," said Cal. "We're focusing on the wrong part. If you think about what we do in time, it's easy: we *age!*"

"That's right!" exclaimed Fabrice. "Which gives us ball-age . . . No, I know, *pass-age!* Of course: the word is *passage!*"

The arachne moved her venomous jaws. "Sixty-nine . . . seventy . . . "

"Okay, I've got to stay calm," said Fabrice, closing his eyes so as not to see the spider's jaws. "So far, we've got *de- mon-* something *passage*. Could the word be 'demonstration'? I'm still stuck on the third clue. What was it again? 'Cut yourself a little slack.' I just can't think of anything for 'slack.' Maybe we should focus on 'cut' instead. What is a cut? A slash, an incision . . . It's also a reduction in prices . . . A player who's dropped from a team is cut . . . I'm in trouble, gang. I'm getting tense and my brain is starting to freeze up!"

The arachne: "Eighty-three . . . "

"Relax, Fabrice," said Tara. "I'm sure you'll solve the riddle in the nick of time."

The arachne: "Eighty-six . . . "

"That's it!" yelled Fabrice.

"What is?" asked Cal.

"Tara said it: the word is *nick*, meaning a small cut! And it fits the clues perfectly! Why didn't I think of that?"

"I hope you're right, because I sure don't get it," said Cal.

The arachne spoke: "Eighty-eight! I've waited long enough for you. Give me your guess and hope it's true."

Fabrice turned to the spider, looked straight into her eight green eyes, and spoke: "Half a degree is *de*. The simian start is *mon*. The little cut is a *nick*. What we do with a ball is to *pass* it. And the thing we all do is *age*. Put them together, and you get *de + mon + nick + pass + age*. The answer to the riddle is *demonic passage!*"

The arachne didn't stir, and for a horrible moment they were sure they'd gotten it wrong. But then she backed up, muttering in disappointment, and said, "The riddle's solved in the right way, the bridge I'll spin without delay."

She retracted her poisonous fangs, ascended her thread, and started to weave a bridge between the two sides of the chasm. But suddenly a brilliant red ray flashed and severed the spider's thread, and she fell, howling with rage. She grabbed the threads she had already woven, but her weight snapped them and she tumbled into the abyss and hit the bottom with a sickening thud. Stunned, the friends looked toward the far side where the ray came from.

Standing there was Deria, defying them.

"You won't cross!" she yelled. "I just cast a spell on the abyss that prevents levitation. There's no point in trying. Go back the way you came before it's too late. I'm going to rejoin my master to tell him that the arachne is dead. Whatever you do, don't try to cross!"

There was terrible anguish in Deria's voice, as if she were trying to warn them about something. But for Tara, retreating wasn't an option. Magister had her mother, and Tara wasn't backing off if she had to face all the demons of hell.

Deria vanished into the darkness, and the five friends looked at each other.

"What do you want to do?" Cal asked Tara. "Try to cross, or wait for Master Chem?"

"What do you think?"

"Yeah, I shouldn't have even bothered asking," he muttered with resignation. "All right, step aside, everyone. Make way for a pro!"

The spider's fall had snapped the initial strands of her bridge, but they were still dangling on their side of the precipice. Cal grabbed one and cut off a decent length. Then he took two small pieces of metal from his pocket and assembled them into a neat little hook. This he tied to the thread, grumbling as the silk stuck to his fingers. He tested the tension by pulling on it: it was as strong as steel. He had created a perfect cable.

"I never go out without my tools," said Cal, grinning at the others' astonished looks. "The Bloodgraves didn't confiscate them because they must've thought they were useless pieces of junk— which was the idea."

Cal judged the height of the spider web hanging from the ceiling, then turned to Robin.

"I'm too short for this one," he said. "I don't think I'll manage to reach the web. You're an elf. Do you think you're strong enough to throw the hook up there?"

"I'm only a half-elf, but I think it's doable," Robin said with a grin.

He took the spider thread with the hook, swung it around his head a few times, and heaved it upward. The hook missed the web by about a foot. Robin tried several more times but with no better luck.

"Rats, I'm not tall enough," he groused. "I'm going to have to stand on someone's shoulders."

"All right, go ahead," said Fabrice resignedly, whose athletic build made him the perfect porter. "Climb onto my shoulders."

Robin stepped up, and skillfully balanced on Fabrice's shoulders, who tried hard to remain steady. Robin swung the hook again and threw it. This time it was high enough, and it snagged the web. He very cautiously tugged on it a few times, but it seemed to hold.

"I'll go first," he said, "and use being on Fabrice's shoulders to help give me momentum. I'm going at the count of three."

Gripping the thread, Robin leaped into space and soared across the abyss in a long, elegant curve.

"It's fine," he yelled. "Plenty of momentum to get across without any trouble. Climb on that little stone ledge next to you. That should help give you a head start."

That came as a relief to Fabrice, who feared he would be serving as everybody's springboard. He went second, followed by Sparrow and Tara, who both landed on their feet. Tara was afraid Deria would show up while they were crossing the abyss, but there was no sign of her.

"My turn now!" cried Cal, who was the last.

Robin sent the thread back and Cal grabbed it, but nobody realized that the hook had been gradually cutting into the spider web. That web was strong enough to hold the arachne's prey, but it wasn't designed for the repeated tugs of their swings across the gap. When Cal jumped, the hook cut through what little remained of the web, and it gave way just as he was above the middle of the precipice.

With a scream of terror, Cal vanished into the abyss.

CHAPTER 19

THOSE-WHO-GUARD

"Cal!" they all screamed.

"Quick," cried Tara, "we've got to go down and help him!"

Robin grabbed her arm as she leaned over the edge, desperately trying to see the bottom of the abyss. "Take it easy," he said. "We can't climb down, the walls are too smooth."

Sparrow yelled: "By Flamus, give me fire! Bright flame this instant I require!"

A large fire lit up the bottom of the chasm. By its light they could see the many bones littering it . . . and Cal's body, sprawled motionless on top of a huge boulder.

When she realized there was nothing to be done, Tara burst into tears. Her legs buckled and she slumped to the ground. Feeling shattered, Fabrice, Sparrow, and Robin surrounded her, trying to comfort each other.

"I should never have taken you with me," said Tara, sobbing. "I'm so sorry. It's my fault that he's dead."

"Don't say things like that," said Robin. "Cal knew the risks. He'd be furious if he saw you giving up now. And he'd be the first to say you have to save your mother, so his sacrifice wouldn't be in vain."

"But I can't," moaned Tara, overcome with guilt. "I can't buy my mother's life with Cal's. We have to stay here and wait for Master Chem. If we'd all stayed together, Cal would be alive now."

In spite of their arguments, Sparrow, Robin, and Fabrice weren't able to change Tara's mind. In fact, she was probably right. They decided not to continue until the dragons had caught up with them.

They were still weeping over their friend's death when a terrible yell brought them to their feet. For a moment they thought they were under attack and looked at the door to the Initiation Hall, but there was no one there. The sound was coming from behind them.

"By Baldur's steaming entrails and the putrid gullet of a snap-tooth, it stinks down here!"

Wild hope gripping their hearts, the friends looked down to where Sparrow's fire was sputtering out. There was Cal, sitting on his rock, trying to wipe something off that seemed to be covering his entire body.

"Cal!" yelled Fabrice. "Are you all right?"

"I'm fine," he said, sounding in a very foul mood, "except that I landed right on the belly of this disgusting spider and I'm covered with the juice of bugs and their body parts."

"Yuck! That's disgusting!" said Sparrow, who was gagging but wearing a huge smile.

"Disgusting maybe, but the arachne saved his life," said Robin. "What we thought was a rock was actually the spider's body. It must have cushioned his fall."

"Can you climb back up?" asked Tara, who was mad with joy.

"Yeah, I think so; there are plenty of holds. But I'll need a hand at the top because the cliff is pretty smooth up there."

Agile as a monkey, the young thief climbed the lower walls with impressive speed. Then Fabrice held Robin's legs as he leaned over the edge, grabbed Cal's hand, and hauled him up safe and sound.

Cal was dripping with putrid greenish muck, and cursing fluently. Sparrow and Tara would have rushed to hug him, but the reeking spider guts kept them at a distance, preserving his dignity. He quickly cast a Cleanus spell that left him clean and dry.

"Whew! That was a close call!" he said. "A few feet to either side, and it would've been goodbye Cal!"

"That's why we're going to wait for Master Chem," said Tara seriously, who was just starting to recover from her emotions. "I don't want to risk your lives for nothing."

"You've got to be kidding!" he exclaimed. "We aren't giving up so fast! Listen, all we have to do is go see what the Bloodgrave master is up to. We'll stay off to one side and not make a move until Master Chem gets here, okay?"

Tara didn't hesitate.

"Sounds good! Okay, follow me, and don't try anything on your own. I've had enough scares to last the next twenty years."

"Me too," added Sparrow, who was still shaken.

They tiptoed to the entrance to the Initiation Hall, only to find it totally, absolutely, and definitely empty.

"Hey! He isn't here!" whispered Fabrice.

"But the room only has one entrance," exclaimed Robin. "If there were others, there would be no point to the arachne."

"If there are other passages, Cal is elected to find them," said Tara. "But not to take them, understand?"

"Look, I just fell a hundred feet onto the stomach of a giant spider," he said, shuddering. "I'm not about to scare myself again, believe me. If I find a secret passage, I'll call you over and we'll discuss it."

The problem was, there wasn't any secret passage.

Despite their tapping, sniffing, and searching all through the hall, there was nothing there.

Then Tara noticed the slab of black granite still floating above their heads. She climbed the steps of the bleachers and carefully examined it. In the center of the slab there was a kind of glowing circle, a little lighter than the rest of the rock. She was intrigued, so she jumped from the bleachers onto the slab and touched the circle with a tentative finger. And vanished.

"Tara, what are you—?" cried Cal, as she disappeared. "Hey, quick! Tara's found the secret way out!"

Without thinking, he jumped onto the slab, touched the circle, and disappeared in turn.

"I'm going too!" yelled Robin. "Sparrow and Fabrice, stay here and protect each other, and tell Master Chem about the secret exit."

Before Sparrow and Fabrice had a chance to object, the half-elf had vanished.

When Robin landed he smoothly leapt to his feet in fighting posture, ready for action. But what he saw so astonished him that he froze.

The three spellbinders were surrounded by ocean.

Robin, Cal, and Tara were at the center of an enormous whirl-pool. Underfoot, slippery stones were covered with seaweed and algae. Stranded fish were flopping and dying in the puddles. High in the sky, a huge pale moon illuminated the landscape.

"Where . . . where are we?" stammered Cal.

"I'm not sure, but I think we're on Earth," said Tara, eyes narrowed in surprise. "That looks like our moon. And what's around us looks like a Greek temple, only underwater!"

Adorned with seaweed and coral, enormous white marble statues stared down at them from their pedestals. And a temple with many columns stood at the end of a great city square. Looking at the wall of water held back by the whirlpool, they could see fishes, octopi, and sharks swimming among the city ruins.

A voice behind them made them jump.

"Welcome to Atlantis! I've been waiting for this moment for a long time!"

They turned around.

There stood the Master of Bloodgraves.

Tara was already raising her hand to blast him when Magister stopped her.

"Wait! I don't want to fight you. You aren't likely to hurt me, and besides, magic doesn't work here. Those-Who-Guard don't allow it."

All around the group, Those-Who-Guard emerged from the water, armed with tridents. Their hands were webbed, their teeth sharp and pointed, and their skin a strange color somewhere between green and blue. Standing more than six feet tall, they were oddly handsome, with humanoid bodies covered with shining scales.

To Tara's great surprise, one of them, wearing a circle of gold on his head, suddenly bowed to her.

"*Salguvil, inglativ vlamblu, blugil,*" he gurgled.

Tara was about to say that she didn't understand when a kind of ringing sounded in her head. And suddenly it was clear! The meaning of the sentence exploded in her brain. He had just welcomed the *heir*!

"He recognizes you! I've succeeded!" cried Magister jubilantly.

"Succeeded at what?" asked Tara coldly. "Getting me to talk with a fish-man?"

"Much, much more than that, Your Imperial Majesty," he snickered. "He just recognized you as the heir of High Wizard Demiderus T'al Barmi. You've gotten through the First Circle!"

"All right, can somebody explain things to me?" interrupted Cal. "Because I'm all at sea here, so to speak."

With a wicked smile, Magister dropped his bombshell.

"Tara is the Imperial Spellbinder, heir to the throne of Omois and the direct descendant of Demiderus. Her father was Emperor Danviou T'al Barmi Ab Santa Ab Maru, the empress's brother!"

Cal opened his mouth and then closed it again, stunned. He wasn't alone. Robin and Tara were staring at Magister as if he had lost his mind.

"You and the Empress of Omois are the only people who can enter this temple, Tara. Those-Who-Guard are its first line of defense. Those-Who-Judge are its second. These defenses were put in place thousands of years ago. It was through this place—this rift—that the demons tried to invade Earth. When the dragons defeated them, they decided to sink Atlantis to keep anyone from opening the rift.

"Demons aren't very smart," continued Magister bitterly. "In seeking revenge, they tried to kill the descendents of the five high wizards, without realizing that they were imprisoning themselves forever. Only you and the empress are left, and she isn't available. So you're going to enter the temple and get me through the circle of Those-Who-Judge.

"And by the way, I sent Deria into another dimension to carry out a mission I assigned her. Your mother, on the other hand, is here in the temple. I've extended the deadly spell to cover her. She won't turn into crystal, but Those-Who-Judge must be aware of her presence by now, and are about to rip her to shreds. You only have a few minutes to save her."

"You monster!" cursed Tara, her jaw clenched. She reluctantly ordered Those-Who-Guard to release him. Magister brushed himself off, and with an ironic bow offered her the lead. Robin and Cal fell in behind him, ready to intervene.

Her heart pounding, Tara entered the temple. The stone was still slippery from the ocean water and they had to be careful not to fall. Walking silently between the carved columns, they reached the center of the building, where a gigantic statue awaited them. A forgotten, once all-powerful god brandished a lightning bolt in his left hand and a spear in his right.

Before him stood an altar.

On the altar lay Tara's mother.

Surrounded by Those-Who-Judge.

Those-Who-Guard had a definite physical presence, but Those-Who-Judge were immaterial spirits. Their hovering shapes turned eyeless faces to them. And those shapes had fangs and claws, which they could make perfectly tangible—and deadly.

Tara bowed and confidently declared, "I am Tara'tylanhnem T'al Barmi Ab Santa Ab Maru, the daughter of Danviou T'al Barmi Ab Santa Ab Maru, and a descendant of Demiterus T'al Barmi. My mother, Selena Duncan, has been brought here against her will by this human, Magister. I demand justice."

"You can demand all you like," said Magister coldly. "They don't judge actions. They are here only to prevent the demons from reopening the rift without one of the heirs' permission. Now we'll find out if your blood is pure enough to satisfy them!"

The spirits suddenly started whirling around Tara, who began to panic. Then, without warning, they dove and poured into her skull. She screamed and collapsed.

Cal and Robin were about to leap into action when Magister stopped them.

"Don't move, or we'll all die!" he yelled. "Let Those-Who-Judge act. They won't hurt her if they recognize her as the heir."

"And what if they don't?" screamed Robin, enraged.

"Then we can measure our life expectancy in seconds."

"You're a total nut job!" cried Cal. "I'm going to—"

No one would know what he would do, because Tara suddenly rose into the air, eyes wide open, glowing. Beneath her, the altar holding her mother's unconscious body opened, and Robin barely had time to catch her before she fell.

A gigantic black throne, hideously carved with demons and deformed animals, rose from the opening, taking its place under Tara exactly in the center of the room. Radiating intense heat, it quickly became red hot.

"The Throne of Silur," murmured a marveling Magister. "At last!"

The light from Tara's body hit the throne, which began to glow in turn. The head of a grotesque demon was carved on the top of the throne. A burning ray of red light shot from its revolting mouth into the eyes of the forgotten god looming massively over them.

With a terrible creaking, the statue raised its head. The ray now shone from its eyes to illuminate a drawing of a human in a spellbinder robe on the ceiling, and the temple roof split open in two halves.

The brilliant, cold moon appeared above them. Its beams fell on the throne, giving it a reddish halo. Tara's body stopped glowing, and she very slowly stepped down from the throne. She had remained conscious during the process.

Seeing that Magister was no longer paying her any attention, she rushed to her mother, whom Robin had stretched out behind a column.

"Is she all right?" she asked anxiously.

"Yes, she's just unconscious," he said. "What do we do now?"

"Those-Who-Judge explained the process to me," she said gravely. "Now that the temple is open, Magister will start his incantations to open the rift. By opening it, he will appropriate the throne's demonic powers, but at the same time he is opening a passage for the demons! He doesn't care, so long as he gets the power, but the demons will be unleashed on the Earth. It will be the Apocalypse. Under the demons' rule, humans will become cattle, serving only to feed them. Our species will disappear! I think I have found a way to prevent that, but you're going to have to protect me, because I will be completely defenseless. Do you think you can do that?"

"Do what you have to do," whispered Robin. "I'd give my life for you."

Tara blushed.

"I've already almost died twice today," said Cal, shrugging in resignation, "so once more or less makes no difference! Let's do it!"

Magister was standing under the throne. When the moonbeams struck the carved stone, they turned red. Reciting incantations, he seized the beams, made them material, and wove them like threads of cold light, creating a Portal that appeared on the wall.

Taking a deep breath, Tara went to stand behind her two friends, who had generated a powerful magic shield.

She concentrated, and a dazzling blue ray shot from her hands. Magister thought she was aiming at him and put up a shield as well. But the ray passed over his head and instead hit the Throne of Silur.

Tara had realized that she couldn't defeat Magister, so she was going after the object he most desired. The throne was burning with the demonic energy it contained, so she wasn't shooting not a ray of fire, but a ray of ice. When it hit the glowing throne, an enormous cloud of steam arose.

"Noooo!" yelled the infuriated Bloodgrave. "I'm going to stop you! 'By Destructus may these children die, and from these sacred precincts fly!'"

His destructive energy slammed into the shield Cal and Robin had conjured, but the two young spellbinders summoned all their strength and managed to resist it.

Meanwhile, Tara drew on the depths of her fear and her anger to amplify her power. Suddenly she could feel it flowing in her veins. Her eyes turned entirely blue and the icy ray reached its full force, enveloping the throne in a bluish glow. The stone groaned, torn by the vast temperature gap between its internal fire and the ray's intense cold.

Realizing that he didn't have time to kill the two young spellbinders, Magister returned to his incantations, racing to beat Tara and appropriate the demonic throne's power.

Bent to Magister's monstrous will, the moonbeams had almost finished weaving the passage. Demonic energy was escaping from Limbo in a flood of black light that washed over the throne and into his body, feeding his power. The opening had attracted the demons, and their shadows could now be seen: talons, claws, jaws, and fangs, ready to rip and tear.

In despair, Tara realized they were losing. But to her surprise, another blue-white ray suddenly flashed. Her mother had just joined forces with her!

When Selena regained consciousness, she didn't at first recognize the girl fighting to destroy the Throne of Silur. Then the forgetting spell she had cast on herself snapped, and she joined the fray.

In his fury, Magister recited a final incantation, and the first two demons, their bodies half dog, half octopus, managed to squeeze through the passage. Refusing to accept defeat, Tara yelled in turn and put all of her despair into the strength of her cry: "Freeze!"

The cold she was imagining was close to absolute zero. When it enveloped the throne, the black stone gave a final tortured groan and exploded. Chunks of black basalt shot in every direction, destroying the Portal and blasting the two demons. Only Cal and Robin's shield saved Tara and her mother from certain death. Magister took the full brunt of the explosion and was knocked to the ground.

The moonbeams started weakening. The light in the statue's eyes began to go out and the temple roof slowly closed.

"Nooooooo!" screamed Magister. "This will not be! By the silver moon of Etevelier, I order you to awaken!"

To their complete astonishment, the roof stopped moving, and the moon once again illuminated the eyes of the forgotten god.

"Who is it? Who dares awaken me?" rumbled the statue in a terrible voice.

"She did!" cried Magister, pointing at Tara, forgetting in his demented fury that he needed the girl. "She called on you! She wants to open the rift so the demons can invade the Earth! She must be destroyed!"

"Hey, that's not true!" protested Cal furiously. "He's the one who woke you up! We didn't do anything!"

But the forgotten god didn't listen. With a deafening screech, the statue tore itself from its pedestal and raised its spear to run Tara through.

Rigid with fear, she could only stare as death flew toward her. Suddenly Cal levitated and, quick as a cat, landed on the statue's shoulder. He tore off his spellbinder robe and used it to blindfold the god.

With moonbeams no longer reaching his empty eye sockets, the god stopped moving with his spear mere inches from Tara's heart. The temple roof began to close again.

Magister tried to destroy Cal's robe, but this time Selena was faster.

"No you don't!" she growled. "By Rigidus cause this man to perish, and his magic forever extinguish."

Selena's power wasn't enough to kill Magister, but it briefly paralyzed him. The temple roof closed shut with a loud crash. The throne was destroyed and the rift sealed again.

When Magister was able to get up, he reached for Tara, but They-Who-Judge intervened. Their immaterial bodies encircled him, claws and teeth glinting in the shadows. When he realized that they would no longer allow him to attack the heir, he howled with disappointment. Seizing a still-smoking piece of basalt, he slashed his arm and yelled:

"This isn't over, Tara! There's more than just the Throne of Silur! Keep looking over your shoulder, because I'll never be far behind!"

Then he drew a crimson circle of blood around himself, recited a spell, and vanished.

At that, the whirlpool magically holding the ocean back started to shrink, and millions of tons of water began closing in on them. Terrified, Tara realized that if they didn't get out of there very quickly, they would be crushed.

"What are we going to do?" screamed Cal, as the roaring whirlpool started to close in.

"Place the heir, place the heir on the altar, place the heir," chanted Those-Who-Judge.

They rushed to the altar and jumped onto it. The roar had now become deafening, a sign that the ocean was flooding into the temple. With a wall of water rushing toward them, Cal opened his mouth to cry out as Those-Who-Judge chanted a spell . . . and everything disappeared.

CHAPTER 20

ALL'S WELL THAT ENDS WELL, SORT OF

A moment later they found themselves in a puddle of sea water in the Initiation Hall, under the astonished eyes of Chem, T'andilus, Sparrow, Fabrice, Manitou, and Fafnir.

Sparrow ran to hug Tara before realizing that she was soaked.

"I was so afraid!" she exclaimed, then pulled back. "You're all wet. And why is Cal in his underwear?"

A very embarrassed Cal quickly pulled his robe on while glaring at Robin, who was unable to stifle an attack of nervous laughter.

"Yes," said Tara with a smile, "I'm wet and I'm exhausted. And I'll tell you all about Cal's underwear as soon as Master Chem has released Mom from Magister's deadly spell."

The old wizard, who had opened his mouth to ask for explanations, promptly closed it. Instead he walked around Selena, studying her carefully.

"Hmph! I see," he said, looking a little disdainful. "Very evil, and very complicated, but not impossible to counter. The formula involves a very ancient tongue . . . Hmmm . . . '*Illandus contrariant annihilus mortifera sanglarus poh!*'"

A kind of black mist rose from Selena's mouth and eyes and evaporated.

She screamed with joy.

"Free! I'm free at last! Free!"

She hugged everybody in sight. Robin, Fabrice, and Cal blinked in surprise, but Sparrow and Master Chem hugged her warmly. If Fafnir was surprised, she didn't show it.

Tara, Robin, and Cal learned that some of the Bloodgraves had vanished the moment Magister escaped. Master Chem had nearly gone crazy when he reached the bridge, saw the arachne's body at the bottom, and found only Sparrow and Fabrice in the Initiation Hall. Despite all their efforts, they weren't able to reactivate the passage to Atlantis and had been forced to wait for the group's return, their alarm growing as time passed.

Master Chem grimaced when he learned that Tara's group had destroyed the Throne of Silur. The demonic power objects were as important for the dragons as for the demons, which is why they hadn't been dismantled.

When he learned that Tara was the daughter of Danviou, the heir to the Empire of Omois, his eyes widened in surprise. So did Selena's, who had missed that part of the story. She now understood why Danviou had hidden his identity from her. He wanted to be sure that she loved him for himself and not for his title as heir to the Empire! Then she sighed and bowed her head. Something about that explanation didn't feel quite right. Her husband must have had some other reason to hide such an important "detail"!

Finally, Tara announced that Magister had apparently located other demonic objects and clearly planned to use her to access them. At that, she thought the old wizard was going to have a stroke.

"Certainly not!" he thundered. "Even if I have to stay with you twenty-six hours a day, that dog of a Bloodgrave—sorry, Manitou, I don't mean you—won't touch a hair on your head, on my word as a dragon!"

"Of course not," said Tara, who was none too keen at having the old wizard on her back all the time. "Now, let's get out of here. This place gives me the creeps."

When they reached the Gray Fortress courtyard, they found that the apprentice Bloodgraves—the former apprentice spell-binders—were in the elves' custody, and were being stripped of their enchantment.

As the young spellbinders were brought to them, the dragons treated them by driving out the demonic influence. The red circles on their chests disappeared one after another, and with them the demons' power. Tara couldn't help but laugh when she saw that some of the dragons unexpectedly found themselves turned into pigs, skunks, camels, or dogs. Clearly, some of the metaphors were still striking!

The nonspells were freed and sent home, overjoyed at finally escaping their enslavement to the sinister Bloodgrave master.

Having heard the high wizard's story, Master T'andilus decided to have the Gray Fortress searched from top to bottom. Master Dragosh joined him. What they found wasn't reassuring. In Magister's office they found plans. Plans for conquest and especially a list that the old wizard ripped from the elf's hands when he brought it to him.

"By my ancestors!" murmured Chem, deeply troubled, "He's found more of them."

"More of what?" asked Dragosh.

"Tara was right," he said. "This lunatic has managed to locate several of the demonic objects that we took from the demons. But the protections will only allow the heirs of the five high wizards to pass, which means that he will probably try to use Tara again. That's terrible!"

"You must neutralize Magister," murmured Dragosh. "You know what they did to my family. He must never be able to approach Tara again."

"I will protect her as best I can," Chem answered.

"Wouldn't it be best to . . . eliminate the problem?"

The old wizard looked up sharply from the list he was studying.

"Safir, I hope I didn't understand correctly what you just said!"

The vampyr refused to back off.

"If this girl's life is the only thing that stood between us and Limbo, I wouldn't hesitate," he hissed.

The old wizard stepped close to Dragosh, his eyes narrowed.

"This girl is the heir to an immense empire, my friend. She's not just a key giving access to the demonic universe. Remember that before you declare war on her."

Defeated, the vampyr bowed. But a cold glint remained in his eyes, and it didn't fool Master Chem. If Dragosh had to choose, he would do so without hesitation!

Tara, her mother, and her friends were still in the courtyard when the old dragon joined them, after carefully pocketing the list.

"We can return to the Royal Castle of Travia," he exclaimed joyously, "to celebrate both our victory and Tara's mother's return to the land of the living!"

"We've put the unicorn tapestry back in place, High Wizard," said T'andilus, who was in charge of operations. "The Portal is working again. You can return to the Castle whenever you like."

"Perfect! Good work," said Chem. "Keep an eye out for anything that looks suspicious, and send me your report. I don't care to hang around here any longer. Let's go!"

"Er, Master?"

"Yes, Tara, what is it?"

"Can you get someone to take Fafnir home? She drank an infusion of black roses that wiped out her magic powers, and her Exordium is coming right up."

"An infusion of black roses?"

The wizard was shocked.

"You must really hate magic to do something like that," he said to the dwarf.

"This stuff is all very well for you," Fafnir answered. "But an honest dwarf doesn't want anything to do with that funny business."

"Well, we're losing an excellent apprentice," said the wizard with a sigh, "but gaining a friend. Now that you've spent time living with us, I hope you'll get your fellow dwarves to see that they're wrong to reject magic outright. It can be very beneficial!"

"After what we've endured these last days because of your beneficial magic, I'm clear on this much: you can keep it!"

Chem couldn't help but smile.

"Well, goodbye then, Fafnir. Stay well, and may your hammer ring clear."

"Thanks, Master. May your anvil resound!"

The dwarf turned to her friends.

"That's it. I'm going."

"Thanks for everything you did for us, Fafnir" said Tara, hugging her tight. "You've been great. I hope we meet again!"

Fafnir grimaced a little, then hugged her back.

"Yeah, well, not too soon. I get the feeling you attract catastrophes like a magnet attracts filings. Anyway, good luck! May your hammer ring clear!"

"May your anvil resound," said Tara, who had picked up on the polite expression.

Fafnir waved goodbye to Robin, Cal, Fabrice, and Sparrow. She gave a curt nod to Angelica, whom the high wizard had sent for, and walked off with an elf toward the Portal Room.

"All right, it's our turn now," said Master Chem. "Let's go home."

Their return to Travia was not what you would call low key. It was the middle of the afternoon there, and everybody knew that the elves and dragons had launched an expedition to get their apprentices back. Those who had stayed behind were terribly worried, and when Master Chem and his group emerged from the Travia Portal Room, the whole palace, including the king and queen, was waiting for them.

Everyone was exhausted from the sleepless night and from the emotion of it all, so the high wizard suggested a nap before dinner.

Tara stepped back into her bedroom with a feeling close to veneration. As the guest of honor, her mother had been given a suite nearby.

When Tara woke up, she raced to her mother's suite and began to make up for ten years they had lost. They cried a little, and laughed a lot. The moment was . . . magical. Moved by their joy, the Castle adorned the walls with the most beautiful OtherWorld landscapes it could find.

When the two were somewhat recovered from the flood of feelings, they went down to join the others at a grand banquet presided over by the king and queen. They were the last people to enter the room. When they were seated, the high wizard spoke: "It is my great pleasure to announce that thanks to six brave young spellbinders and to Tara Duncan, we were able to find the Bloodgraves' lair and free our apprentices along with Tara's mother, who has been imprisoned for the last ten years."

A wave of applause cut him off.

"Thank you . . . thank you," he said, smiling. "Caliban, Robin, Tara, Gloria, Fabrice, and Angelica, along with Fafnir the Dwarf, succeeded in thwarting the kidnappers' plans!" (Angelica was very pleased to be included in the group even though she hadn't done much, and she gave Tara a nasty smile.)

This time, deafening cheers drowned out his speech.

"Thank you . . . thank you," he resumed modestly. "I didn't have much to do with it. They're the heroes. And now, let's eat!"

Tara and the others had to wait for their dinner, however. They were literally mobbed. Everybody wanted to know what had happened, and even though Cal moaned that he was starving, they had to tell them before they could touch their plates.

Just a few weeks before, nobody knew about Tara, or if they did, they were afraid of her. And now she was being celebrated like a true heroine.

Tara glowed with happiness. She was finally back with her mother and surrounded by her dearest friends. Cal was making everybody laugh with his comical descriptions. The high wizards had given their apprentices three weeks' vacation. Tara would be finally returning to Earth under the protection of two high wizards. These would certainly be the most wonderful moments of her life!

She had just finished her Soothsucker when she got a jolt. She had expected a fortune along the lines of, "A job well done, and you've had your fun." But that wasn't what appeared. Not at all.

Instead, she read: "Stay alert, if death you fear. The hunter is already drawing near."

Tara gulped, painfully aware of the grim accuracy of previous predictions. Then she shrugged with resignation. So the hunter was after her. All right, let him come.

She was ready too.

AN OTHERWORLD LEXICON

OtherWorld

OtherWorld is a planet where magic is very widespread. It has a surface about one and a half times that of Earth. OtherWorld orbits its twin suns in fourteen months; its days last twenty-six hours, and the year has 454 days. Two satellite moons, Madix and Tadix, orbit OtherWorld and create extreme tides on the equinoxes.

OtherWorld's mountains are much higher than those on Earth, and the ores found in them can be dangerous to mine because of explosions of magic. There is less water covering the planet than Earth. OtherWorld is 45 percent land and 55 percent water. Two of the seas are fresh water.

The magic that reigns on OtherWorld affects its fauna, flora, and climate. For this reason, seasons are very hard to predict. On OtherWorld you can get three feet of snow in the middle of summer. A so-called normal year has no fewer than seven seasons.

Many different races live on OtherWorld. The main ones are: humans, giants, trolls, vampyrs, gnomes, imps, elves, unicorns, chimera, tatris, and dragons.

Countries and Peoples of OtherWorld

Lancovit is the largest human kingdom. Its capital is Travia.

Lancovit is ruled by King Bear and his wife, Queen Titania. Its emblem is a white unicorn with a gold horn below a silver crescent moon.

Omois is the largest human empire. Its capital is Tingapore.

It is ruled by the Empress Lisbeth'tylanhnem Ab Barmi, Ab Santu T'al Maru and her half-brother, Emperor Sandor T'al Barmi Ab March Ab Brevis. Its emblem is the hundred-eyed purple peacock.

Hymlia is the land of dwarves. Its capital is Minat.

Hymlia is ruled by the Fireforge clan. Its emblem is an anvil and war hammer on an open mine entrance. Dwarves are extremely strong, often as wide as they are tall. They are OtherWorld's miners and blacksmiths and are excellent metalworkers and jewelers. They are known for having lousy personalities, hating magic, and liking long and complicated songs.

Gandis is the land of giants. Its capital is Geopole.

Gandis is run by the powerful Groar family. The Island of Black Roses and the Swamps of Desolation are in Gandis. Its emblem is a wall of spellblock stones below the OtherWorld sun.

Krankar is the land of trolls. Its capital is Kria.

Its emblem is a tree beneath a club. Trolls are enormous, hairy, and green. They have huge, flat teeth and are vegetarians. They have a bad reputation because they feed on trees and decimate forests, which horrifies the elves. They also tend to quickly become impatient, and to crush everything in their path.

Krasalvia is the land of vampyrs. Its capital is Urla.

Its emblem is an astrolabe under a star and the symbol for infinity (∞). Vampyrs are sages. They are patient and cultured, and spend most of their very long existence in meditation, devoting themselves to mathematics and astronomy. They search for the meaning of life.

They feed entirely on blood from the cattle they raise: brrraaas, mooouuus, horses, goats—imported from Earth—sheep, and so on. They can't drink the blood of some animals. In particular unicorn or human blood causes them to go insane, cuts their life expectancy in half, and makes them deathly allergic to sunlight. Their bite then becomes poisonous and allows them to enslave any humans they bite. Moreover, if their victims are contaminated by this corrupted blood they become vampyrs in turn, but corrupt and evil. Vampyrs who fall prey to this curse are ruthlessly hunted down by their fellows as well as by all the other peoples of OtherWorld.

Smallcountry is the land of gnomes, imps, fairies, and goblins.

Gnomes are short and stocky and wear their orange hair in a quiff. They feed on stones and are miners, like dwarves. The quiff is a very effective detector of dangerous gas. As long as it sticks straight up, all is well. But the moment it begins to slump, gnomes know there is dangerous gas in the mine, and they flee. For some reason, gnomes are also the only people who can communicate with Truth Tellers.

P'abo are the small, playful yellow imps of Smallcountry. They are the creators of the famous fortune-telling lollipops called Soothsuckers. They can project illusions and briefly make themselves invisible. They also love gold, which they keep in a hidden purse. If you find the purse, you can make the imp grant you two wishes in order to get its precious gold back. But it's risky to ask an imp for a wish because they are experts at misinterpretation, and the results can be unexpected.

Selenda is the country of elves. Its capital is Seborn.

Like spellbinders, elves have the gift of magic. They look generally human with a few differences: their ears are pointed and their very light eyes have a vertical pupil, like cats. Elves live in OtherWorld's forests and plains, and are renowned hunters. They also like fighting and all games that involve defeating an adversary, like wrestling. For that reason they are often used in police or surveillance forces, where their energy can be used judiciously. When elves start growing magic corn or barley, the peoples of OtherWorld get worried, because it means they will soon go to war. Since they won't have time to hunt in wartime, the elves start growing crops and raising cattle. Once the war is over, they return to their ancestral way of life.

Another peculiarity of elves: male elves carry the babies in a little pouch on their stomach, like marsupials, until the children are able to walk. Also, a female elf can't have more than five husbands.

Mentalir, the vast Eastern plain, is the land of unicorns and centaurs.

Unicorns are small horses with a single spiral horn that can be unscrewed, cloven hooves, and white coats. Some unicorns aren't very smart, but others are true sages, whose intellect can match that of dragons. This peculiarity makes it hard to classify them, either as people or animals.

Centaurs are animals that are half horse and either half man or half woman. There are two kinds of centaurs: ones where the upper body is human and the lower is horse, and ones where the upper body is horse and the lower is human. No one knows what magical manipulation produced centaurs. They are a complex people and don't mix with others except to obtain essential necessities, such as salt or salves. Centaurs are fierce and wild. They won't hesitate to shoot arrows at any stranger crossing their land.

In the plains, it is said that the shamans of the centaur tribes catch Pllops, the extremely poisonous blue and white frogs, and lick their backs to get visions of the future. The fact that the centaurs were practically exterminated by the elves during the great Starlings War suggests that the method is not very effective.

Limbo is the Demonic World, the domain of demons.

Limbo is divided into different worlds called circles. Demons are more or less powerful and more or less civilized, depending on the circle they occupy. The demons of Circles 1, 2, and 3 are wild and very dangerous. The demons of Circles 4, 5, and 6 are often called on by spellbinders within service exchange agreements. Spellbinders can get things they need from the demons, and vice versa. Circle 7 is the circle where the Demon King reigns.

The demons who live in Limbo feed on demonic energy provided by evil suns. If they leave Limbo to visit other worlds, they must feed on the flesh and minds of intelligent beings in order to survive. They were conquering the universe until the dragons appeared and defeated them in a memorable battle. Since then, the demons have been imprisoned in Limbo. They can only go to the other planets when specifically called by a spellbinder or by some other being with the gift of magic. Demons bitterly resent this restriction on their activities and are constantly searching for a way to free themselves.

Tatran is the land of the tatris. Its capital is Cityville.

The tatris are unusual in that they have two heads. They are very good at organization. They often have executive jobs or work in the highest levels of government, both because they like to and because of their physical peculiarity. They have no imagination and feel that only work is important. They are the favorite targets of the P'abo, the playful imps, who are unable to conceive of a people without any sense of humor. The imps have desperately been trying to make the tatris laugh for centuries. The P'abo have even created a prize for the first of them to accomplish that feat.

Dragons

The dragon planet is Dranvouglispenchir, not OtherWorld. Dragons are huge, very intelligent reptiles. They know magic and are able to take any shape, though most often human. In opposing the demons who were fighting them to rule the universe, the dragons had conquered all the known worlds until they collided with earthly spellbinders. After the battle they decided that it made more sense to make allies of the humans rather than enemies, particularly since they still had to fight the demons. So they abandoned their plan to dominate Earth. However, they refused to allow spellbinders to rule the Earth. Instead, they invited them to OtherWorld to train and educate them. After many years of suspicion, the earthly spellbinders finally accepted and came to live on OtherWorld.

OtherWorld Flora and Fauna

Arachnes: spiderlike animals that come from Smallcountry. The gnomes ride them, and their silk is famous for its strength. They have eight legs and eight eyes, and an unusual tail like a scorpion, with a poison stinger. Arachnes are very intelligent and love to challenge their future prey to solve riddles.

Blood flies: flies whose sting is extremely painful.

Brrraaas: huge cattle with very thick wool, which the giants make into clothing. Brrraaas are very aggressive and will charge anything that moves. As a result you often encounter brrraaas exhausted from chasing their own shadows. We say "Stubborn as a brrraaa."

Glurps: sauriens with a slim, green-and-brown head that live in lakes and swamps. They are extremely voracious. They can spend several hours underwater without breathing, waiting to catch an unsuspecting animal that has come to take a drink. They build nests in hiding places along the shore and store their prey in holes at the bottom of the lake.

Kalornas: beautiful forest flowers with pink and white petals. Their slightly sweet flavor makes them a delicacy for OtherWorld herbivores and omnivores. To avoid being eaten into extinction, kalornas have evolved three petals that work like eyes. These can detect the approach of a predator and allow the flowers to quickly hide underground. Unfortunately kalornas are also very curious. They often stick up their petals too soon and are promptly eaten. We say "As curious as a kalorna."

Kraken: a gigantic octopus with black tentacles. Because of its size it is found in OtherWorld's salt seas, but it can also live in fresh water. Krakens are a well-known danger to sailors.

Looky-looks: giant golden turkeys that constantly strut around and gobble and are very easy to hunt. We often say "Dumb as a looky-look" or "Vain as a looky-look."

Mooouuus: two-headed stags without antlers. When one head is eating, the other vigilantly watches for predators. To move, mooouuus travel sideways, like crabs.

Pegasi: winged horses whose intelligence is close to that of dogs. They don't have hooves but instead claws, in order to perch easily. They often build their nests at the top of steel giants, trees that can grow to 600 feet high and whose trunks can be 150 feet around.

Pllops: small, very poisonous blue and white frogs found on the Mentalir plains.

Sacats: large swarming, flying red and yellow insects. They are poisonous and very aggressive. They produce a honey that is much sought after on OtherWorld. Only dwarves can eat sacat larvae, which they consider a delicacy. Everyone else can wind up with a swarm of them in their stomach, as the shell of the larvae isn't dissolved by human or elfin digestive juices.

Snapteeth: animals originally from Krankar, the land of trolls. They look like fluffy, pink plush toys, and it's hard to tell their front from their back. Snapteeth are extremely dangerous. Their extensible mouth can triple in size, allowing them to swallow practically anything.

Spalenditals: a kind of giant scorpion from Smallcountry. When domesticated, they are ridden by the gnomes, who also work their very tough hide.

Gnomes love to eat birds and have practically wiped them out from their country. This has opened an ecological niche for insects and other animals. Since they no longer have any natural enemies, they have kept growing larger, with each generation more numerous than the preceding one. As a result, the gnomes' country is now overrun with giant scorpions, spiders, and millipedes.

Traducs: large animals raised by the centaurs for their meat and wool. They smell very bad, which protects them from all predators except Crrrèks. These are small, voracious wolves who are able to block their nostrils so they don't smell the traducs' stink. "You stink like a sick traduc" is a widespread OtherWorld insult.

Vrrirs: six-legged, gold-and-white felines, a favorite of the Empress of Omois. She has cast a spell on them so that they don't realize they are imprisoned in her palace. Instead of furniture and sofas, they see trees and comfortable stones. The courtiers are invisible to them, and when vrrirs are stroked, they think it is the wind blowing through their fur.

ABOUT THE AUTHOR

Sophie Audouin-Mamikonian is not only the most widely read fantasy writer in France, she's also the crown princess of Armenia. Sophie was inspired to start writing the *Tara Duncan* series after reading Shakespeare's play *A Midsummer Night's Dream* in 1987. Seventeen years later, in 2003, she published *Tara Duncan* in France and eventually in eighteen countries.

Born in southern France in 1961, Sophie was mainly raised by her grandparents, who spoiled her with candy and carefully chosen French classics: Alexandre Dumas and Victor Hugo along with Corneille and Molière. Possibly as a result, Sophie started writing stories at a very young age. Stuck in bed by a bout of appendicitis at age twelve, she picked up a pen and hasn't put it down since. Before earning her living as a writer, she earned a master's degree in diplomacy and strategy and worked in advertising with Jacques Séguéla at the Publicis agency in Paris.

Sophie is the niece of author and director Francis Veber, who wrote the screenplay for the movies *Dinner for Schmucks* and *Three Fugitives*. She is also the granddaughter of Pierre Gilles Veber, who wrote the script of the original 1952 film *Fanfan, la Tulipe*, which was remade in 2003 with Penelope Cruz.

Tara Duncan has been adapted for television by Moonscoop–Taffy Entertainment (*Casper, the Friendly Ghost; The Fantastic Four*) in co-production with the Walt Disney corporation. Sophie says that a musical comedy to be called *The Tara Duncan Show*, with magic and special effects, is being developed by TF1, France's premier television channel, with a budget of $12 million. When not writing, Sophie divides her time between her husband, her two daughters, and the medical organization Douleurs sans Frontières.

ABOUT THE TRANSLATOR

William Rodarmor is a journalist, editor, and French literary translator. In addition to *Tara Duncan*, his young adult translations include *The Book of Time* trilogy by Guillaume Prévost (Scholastic, 2007–09), *The Old Man Mad About Drawing* by François Place (Godine, 2003), *Catherine Certitude* by Patrick Modiano and Jean-Jacques Sempé (Godine, 2001), *Ultimate Game* by Christian Lehmann (Godine, 2000), and *The Last Giants* by François Place (Godine, 1993). His translation of *Tamata and the Alliance,* by famed sailor Bernard Moitessier, won the 1996 Lewis Galantière Award from the American Translators Association.

William has traveled all over the world but has a special fondness for France, about which he edited and translated two anthologies in Whereabouts Press's *A Traveler's Literary Companion* series: *French Feast* (2011) and *France* (2008). He is especially proud of two accomplishments: sailing solo from Tahiti to Hawaii in 1971 and winning the cartoon caption contest in *The New Yorker* in 2010. William lives in Berkeley, California, and often travels to New York City.

THANKS AND ACKNOWLEDGMENTS

It took seventeen years for my girl wizard Tara Duncan to see the light of day. I wrote *Tara Duncan et les Sortceliers* in 1987, the year my daughter Diane was born. That's the book you're reading as *Tara Duncan and the Spellbinders,* and the first in what is now a nine-volume series. But at the time, I couldn't get a single French publisher interested.

I waited, kept writing, and sometimes cried my eyes out. But my very sweet husband Philippe kept saying, "You have so much talent. You'll see; one of these days *Tara* is going to take off."

That day came thanks to a boy wizard with glasses and a scar on his forehead. Harry Potter's success had such an impact in France that when I sent out my manuscript for the nth time, three publishers suddenly wanted options on it.

Since then, the *Tara Duncan* books have been published in eighteen countries, adapted for television by Disney and Moonscoop, and sold some eight million copies. So the first person I want to thank is J. K. Rowling. After that I want to thank my wonderful and very patient husband Philippe, who is a kind of Superman, and my two daughters, Diane and Marine. They're my first readers, and they complain loudly when I don't write fast enough. Darlings, I love you.

Warm thanks are also due to my French publishers, to my New York agent Jennifer Lyons, an incredible warrior, and especially to Skyhorse publisher Tony Lyons, who was willing to publish a Frenchwoman with a crazy imagination, and to his editor Julie Matysik. And to Lori and Oscar Hijuelos, my Pulitzer Prize-winning, loyal, and great American friends who were the first to believe in Tara and pushed very hard to help me be published in America. To William Hickman, another great American friend, and Daniel Edmundson: *semper fidelis*, boys! Thanks too to my translator William Rodarmor. He has sweated bullets finding ways to render my sometimes unlikely wordplay, and we've shared a lot of laughs. William, you're the best.

Finally, I want to thank my American fans who have agitated for years to have *Tara Duncan* published in the Unites States. I feel I've been very lucky, and the wait has been well worth it.

Sophie Audouin-Mamikonian
Paris, March 2012